‖‖ ‖ ‖‖‖‖‖‖‖‖ ‖ ‖ ‖‖‖ ‖‖‖‖‖‖‖‖‖‖‖ ‖‖ ‖ ‖ ‖‖‖

✧ **W9-BLN-753**

The son of a wealthy and high-connected vintner, **Geoffrey Chaucer** (c. 1342–1400) received a classical education prior to becoming a page at the court of King Edward III. As soldier, statesman, public official, and court poet, he remained in contact with the most important people of his time. Chaucer was sent on several diplomatic missions to Italy, where he read and was deeply influenced by the works of Dante, Petrarch, and Boccaccio. The Italian influence is evident in his masterpiece, *The Canterbury Tales*, on which he worked intermittently for at least twenty years. Chaucer was buried in Westminster Abbey.

Donald R. Howard was the Olive H. Palmer Professor in the Humanities at Stanford University and the author of a number of noted books on medieval literature, including *The Three Temptations: Medieval Man in Search of the World* (1966), *The Idea of the Canterbury Tales* (1976), and *Writers and Pilgrims: Medieval Pilgrimage Narratives and Their Posterity* (1980).

Frank Grady is Professor of English at the University of Missouri–St. Louis, where he teaches medieval literature, literary theory, and film. He has published essays on both late medieval English literature and contemporary American popular culture, and he is currently editor of the annual of the New Chaucer Society, *Studies in the Age of Chaucer*.

Paul Strohm is Professor Emeritus at Columbia University and was formerly J. R. R. Tolkien Professor at the University of Oxford. He is the author of *Social Chaucer* (Harvard, 1989 and 1994) and other books on medieval literature, history, and society.

THE
CANTERBURY TALES

A SELECTION

Geoffrey Chaucer

With a Preface by Frank Grady,
an Introduction by Donald R. Howard,
and a New Afterword by Paul Strohm

Edited by Donald R. Howard
with the assistance of James Dean

SIGNET CLASSICS

SIGNET CLASSICS
Published by New American Library, a division of
Penguin Group (USA) Inc., 375 Hudson Street,
New York, New York 10014, USA
Penguin Group (Canada), 90 Eglinton Avenue East, Suite 700, Toronto,
Ontario M4P 2Y3, Canada (a division of Pearson Penguin Canada Inc.)
Penguin Books Ltd., 80 Strand, London WC2R 0RL, England
Penguin Ireland, 25 St. Stephen's Green, Dublin 2,
Ireland (a division of Penguin Books Ltd.)
Penguin Group (Australia), 250 Camberwell Road, Camberwell, Victoria 3124,
Australia (a division of Pearson Australia Group Pty. Ltd.)
Penguin Books India Pvt. Ltd., 11 Community Centre, Panchsheel Park,
New Delhi - 110 017, India
Penguin Group (NZ), 67 Apollo Drive, Rosedale, Auckland 0632,
New Zealand (a division of Pearson New Zealand Ltd.)
Penguin Books (South Africa) (Pty.) Ltd., 24 Sturdee Avenue,
Rosebank, Johannesburg 2196, South Africa

Penguin Books Ltd., Registered Offices:
80 Strand, London WC2R 0RL, England

Published by Signet Classics, an imprint of New American Library,
a division of Penguin Group (USA) Inc.

First Signet Classics Printing, October 1969
First Signet Classics Printing (Strohm Afterword), February 2013
10 9 8 7 6 5 4 3 2 1

Copyright © Donald R. Howard, 1969
Preface copyright © Frank Grady, 2005
Afterword copyright © Paul Strohm, 2013
All rights reserved. No part of this book may be reproduced, scanned, or distributed in
any printed or electronic form without permission. Please do not participate in or en-
courage piracy of copyrighted materials in violation of the author's rights. Purchase
only authorized editions.

 REGISTERED TRADEMARK—MARCA REGISTRADA

Printed in the United States of America

If you purchased this book without a cover you should be aware that this book is stolen
property. It was reported as "unsold and destroyed" to the publisher and neither the
author nor the publisher has received any payment for this "stripped book."

CONTENTS

PREFACE

A few years after I began teaching *The Canterbury Tales* at the college level, an article appeared in the *St. Louis Post-Dispatch* describing how officials at the high school in Eureka, Illinois—about 175 miles away—had suspended discussion of the *Tales* in a senior English class, in the face of complaints that the work was inappropriately racy and might not conform to community standards. I'd like to say that, outraged by this egregious mischaracterization, I rushed right out and set people straight in the bold, heroic manner long associated with Chaucer scholars. Actually, I left the task to the *Post*'s editors, who dryly remarked that, given the work had only been around for about six hundred years, it was easy to understand why the school board might need a little more time to study the issue, and then duly observed that daytime television regularly supplies us with more examples of human depravity than Chaucer ever dreamed of.

The episode did inspire me to do a little research—perhaps a more natural professorial reaction—and I confirmed that a similar episode had occurred less than a decade earlier, in Columbia County, Florida, and that over the last hundred years Chaucer has often kept company with other well-known subversives—Maya Angelou, Mark Twain, John Steinbeck, J. K. Rowling—on the list of authors most frequently challenged by high school curriculum hawks. In fact, for many years after the passage of the Comstock Law of 1873 (or to be more precise, the Act for the Suppression of Trade in, and Circulation of, Obscene Literature and Articles of Immoral Use), it was illegal to send a copy of *The Canterbury Tales* through the U.S. mail. And just recently, in a used bookstore in Michigan, I picked up an 1891 edition of the

General Prologue to the *Tales* that simply omitted line 691 (you'll have to look that one up; I think it's on page 30). So right away there's a good reason to read *The Canterbury Tales*—it's a banned book, or has been, and there's nothing better for one's mental and intellectual health than a steady diet of such dangerous reading.

For people who object to the alleged immorality of *The Canterbury Tales*—from the nineteenth-century crusader Anthony Comstock and his New York Society for the Suppression of Vice to present-day parents and school administrators—the notoriously difficult Chaucer is easy to understand because they find his meaning easy to fix. In fact, for them his work means only *one* thing, whether you call it lewdness or indecency or obscenity (if you're defending him, incidentally, you use the word "bawdy"—much quainter and tamer, and hardly threatening to community standards). There is, though, another, less preemptive way to look at Chaucer, a point of view nicely captured by one of my students in her end-of-semester course evaluation. In response to the question "Were there any features of the course not beneficial to your mastery of the literature?"—a sentence only an English teacher could love—she wrote, "It would be beneficial if Chaucer made any sense at all! I guess he makes sense, but I wish he would have an idea and stick to it and make it a lot easier on us."

In fact Chaucer goes out of his way to avoid making things easy for us, and this student was reacting to what, in the Introduction to this volume, Donald Howard calls with typical acuity (and rare inelegance) Chaucer's strategy of "accumulative discrediting": "No sooner do we get one point of view clearly in mind than we are given some reasons to doubt it." The General Prologue to the *Tales* provides many examples of this process in its portraits of the Canterbury pilgrims, typically four parts naïve admiration (even infatuation) and one part outrage, shaken into a cocktail so potent that it leads you to draw firm conclusions about the characters that, when you look back, turn out to be based on the flimsiest evidence, or no evidence at all. For example, the narrator says of the Merchant: "There wiste no wight that he was in dette," that is, literally, that "no one knew that he was in debt." Does that mean that he *wasn't* in debt—i.e., "certainly no one could say that *he* was in debt"—or that he really was in debt but successfully hid the fact by working diligently to give the impression of solvency ("So estatly was he of his governaunce"), uttering conventional business bromides ("His resouns he spak ful solempnely,/Souning alwey the encrees of his winning"), and dressing the part of a wealthy trader ("His bootes clasped fair and fetisly"), all the while living in fear of discovery and the evaporation of his credit rating? Is he Bill Gates, or Donald Trump, or Willy Loman?

Shakespeare scholars like to pretend that Shakespeare more or less invented this phenomenon (*Henry V*: stirring tribute to patriotic ideals or penetrating study of the degrading effects of war on even the noblest of heroes?), but really it's as old as poetry itself, and Chaucer is a practitioner without peer. And this approach to *The Canterbury Tales* provides among other things an indispensable context for the issue of Chaucerian lewdness (I mean, bawdiness). The farts and fornication of the Miller's Tale are not just juvenile indulgences or the irresistible outgrowths of some coarse and prurient (read: medieval) sensibility; rather, they are part of a carefully elaborated, brilliantly plotted plan—or rather, two plans. One is the plan of the tale, which is to distract jealous old John the Carpenter so that his coltish young wife, Alison, and their amorous boarder, Nicholas, can spend the night together "In bisiness of mirth and in solas," and the other is the plan of the *Tales*, according to which the love triangle of the Miller's Tale and the several comeuppances that make up its magnificently disastrous conclusion specifically recall the story that precedes it, the elevated and courtly Knight's Tale, in a way that retrospectively renders that tale's commanding Duke Theseus either faintly ridiculous, or faintly menacing, in his fussy efforts to co-opt that tale's every event to the service of his own reputation for aristocratic magnanimity, "as he were a god in trone." Hence another reason to read *The*

Canterbury Tales: not only the tales themselves but the relationships between the tales are dynamic and thought-provoking, and having one's thoughts provoked is generally a good thing, too.

But who are these Knights and Millers and Merchants, and why are they telling tales of any sort? What exactly is *The Canterbury Tales* about?

The Canterbury Tales is a collection of stories told by a group of medieval English pilgrims traveling from greater London to Canterbury Cathedral, about sixty miles southeast. In the General Prologue, the narrator of the collection—a stand-in for the poet Chaucer—introduces us to the twenty-nine other pilgrims, varied in occupation and status, and to the Host of the Tabard Inn, where they coincidentally meet one April evening in the late fourteenth century. After an evening of convivial eating and drinking, the Host proposes a tale-telling contest that will help pass the time on the long ride, and volunteers to come along as organizer and judge. (Note to those of you who will have to write essays about the *Tales*: do *not* confuse the narrator of the poem with the Host; they are two very different characters.) His offer is quickly and unanimously accepted—pretty much the last time this merry company will agree on anything—and the next morning they set out, with the Knight telling the first tale. There are twenty-four tales in all (eleven in this edition)—only a fraction of the contest, according to the Host's original plan—and they come down to us in somewhat fragmentary form, arranged in what we in fact call *fragments*, tales or groups of tales that are linked together by prologues and epilogues and other pilgrim banter. In the medieval manuscript copies that survive—fifty-five more or less complete ones, eighty-two or eighty-three in all—the First Fragment, unsurprisingly, always comes first, comprising the General Prologue, the Knight's Tale, the Miller's Prologue and Tale, the Reeve's Prologue and Tale, and the Cook's Prologue and Tale (the last being unfinished). After that, the order of the tales can vary considerably from manuscript to manuscript, Chaucer never having provided a definitive final sequence before his death.

A couple of important observations follow from this brief description. First, it's worth bearing in mind that while the Prologue suggests that the tales exist for the sake of the pilgrimage—they're allegedly meant to relieve the tedium of the long ride to Canterbury—in fact the pilgrimage exists for the sake of the tales, as a structuring frame that helps Chaucer to organize his poem and to experiment with different literary styles and modes. Thus, when the Miller obstreperously insists on telling a tale to "quite" the Knight's opening number (the word literally means "match" or "repay," but quickly acquires an explicitly aggressive edge), what is on one level a clash of genres—courtly romance versus comic fabliau—gets refigured as a clash of personalities, and as Professor Howard writes, "The order of the tales thus comes to be directed by inner forces of social conflict and interplay of character, by disagreement and aggression." At least, that *seems* to be the case, and the more we subscribe to this dramatic view, the more fully we collaborate with Chaucer's effort to disguise an aesthetic contrivance as a roadside drama. Indeed, this may be the most effective aspect of his fiction making, since it has spawned a virtual industry of "dramatic criticism" of *The Canterbury Tales* devoted to understanding the interplay of themes and topics as reflective of the relationships among the pilgrims, whose fully rounded, psychologically complete personalities are seen as determining—rather than deriving from—the content of their tales. (On the other hand, it may be the case that the rest of us don't really have personalities either—just a raft of stories that we tell about ourselves, to ourselves and others, in which case we would have to give Chaucer an entirely different kind of credit.)

Another factor that contributes to the dramatic illusion of the *Tales* is the way in which they are doubly, sometimes triply, *voiced*—not so much narrated as narrativized, as the process of telling a story typically becomes part of the story itself. "Chaucer the pilgrim"—as we traditionally refer to the narrator—makes this point repeatedly, when he apologizes for possibly getting things out of order or for repeating some of the more disreputable (remember: bawdy!) tales, which

might fail to conform to the principles of "moralitee and ho-
linesse," but the pilgrims adopt this style too, to sometimes
dizzying effect. The Wife of Bath, for example, can be found
at one point in her Prologue (which is of course being re-
counted to us by the narrator) quoting herself quoting her
husband quoting St. Paul—immediately after which she
brings us up short by claiming that "all was false." One well-
known effect of this voicing is the enormous difficulty of
pinning down exactly where Chaucer himself stands on a
given issue, since every utterance in *The Canterbury Tales* is
always already someone else's—a narrator's, a pilgrim's, a
character's. The ironic distance caused by such slipperiness
makes it hard to know exactly where to rest. Professor How-
ard, for example, wants to take the very end of the Pardoner's
Tale, when the Knight effects a reconciliation between the
mocking Host and the furious Pardoner, as an affirmative
moment and an example of Chaucer's "profoundly comic
and forgiving spirit," but when we apply the principle of "ac-
cumulative discrediting" to this scene, we realize that the kiss
of reconciliation that the Knight elicits (or coerces?) sits only
twenty lines away from the Host's original insulting remark
about kissing the Pardoner's dirty breeches, and within hail-
ing distance of a similarly misdirected kiss at the end of the
Miller's Tale. Such echoes might just as well lead us to con-
clude that Chaucer's own view, at least at this moment, is
more skeptical than forgiving.

One could argue that such skepticism ought to have a par-
ticular appeal to twenty-first-century readers, who hate to be
fooled, though they don't mind being surprised. And there
are some surprising things about Chaucer, from our post-
modern perspective. It's customary (almost required, in
fact—Professor Howard does it on page xxix) when introduc-
ing *The Canterbury Tales* to quote the seventeenth-century
English poet John Dryden, who in the course of declaring
Chaucer the "Father of English Poetry," said of the *Tales* that
"here is God's Plenty"—a remark generally taken to indicate
that, in the engaging variety of the pilgrims and their stories,
Chaucer provides us with the broadest possible picture of

fourteenth-century English life and lore. But of course that's part of the effect of the tales too, rather than some kind of objective truth about them; though his diverse cast gives the impression of being fully representative, Chaucer's pilgrim group is actually heavily weighted toward the urban and bourgeois classes—the likeliest milieu, perhaps, for the son of a well-to-do wine merchant with courtly connections, but one that has little to say about the 92 percent of the population still working the land (represented on the pilgrimage by a single peasant plowman, whose tale apparently doesn't make the cut). It's also worth noting that Dryden makes his remark in the course of introducing his own translation of a portion of the *Tales*, updated for the readers of his era (yes, even in 1700 people found it difficult to read Middle English) and including only "such Tales of Chaucer as savour nothing of Immodesty." The flip side of the "God's Plenty" remark, then, if it's true, is that *The Canterbury Tales* should contain matter to annoy and distress, as well as please and entertain, just about everyone not possessed of the boundless love of a St. Francis or the hopeful simplicity of a Forrest Gump.

And this turns out to be the case. Witness the selection of tales that make up this very volume (compiled, significantly, in the late 1960s): among the missing are the more pious tales of the Man of Law, the Clerk, and the Second Nun, the gory little moralized anecdotes of the Physician and the Manciple, and two tales that, in their virtual plotlessness, would certainly have starved our modern appetite for narrative—the plodding Tale of Melibee (told, in fact, by Chaucer the pilgrim), a trackless desert of proverbial quotations, and the almost unreadable Parson's Tale, a translated treatise on the Seven Deadly Sins, whose urgent schematicization of evil has largely lost its appeal for us, despite our generally being what the Pardoner would call "envoluped in sinne." (What remains are the Retractions, at the very end of the *Tales*—a surprise I won't spoil for you right now—and the Prioress' pious and anti-Semitic miracle of the Virgin.) These tales are Chaucer's too, though they point to a religiously sentimental and sententious Chaucer who hardly seems to correspond to the gentle ironist of, say, the Nun's Priest's Tale.

At the same time *The Canterbury Tales* is rich with an anticlericalism—satirical criticism, express or implied, of the representatives of the medieval church—that almost always seems to catch modern readers by surprise. While we may think of the Middle Ages as a time of dissent, usually followed by a burning at the stake (a comparatively rare event, claims a recent Vatican report), it's difficult for us to think of it as a time with a *tradition* of dissent, however cynical we might be about our own contemporary institutions (corrupt politicians, avaricious CEOs, unscrupulous developers, chemically enhanced athletes, egotistical entertainers). But Chaucer's portraits of the religious folk in the General Prologue show that he was thoroughly acquainted with the various conventions of medieval ecclesiastical satire, and even the wholly positive portrait of the Parson is constructed by means of implied contrasts with his evil twin, who abandons his parishioners and runs off to London to do chantry work. The tales of the Friar and Summoner, not included here, are the best and most typical examples; ruthless competitors in the crowded marketplace for souls, each tells a tale specifically designed to humiliate the other, personally and professionally (which is what "quiting" had come to mean by then).

Another customary move for us preface writers is to refer to the sixteenth-century Scottish poet Gavin Douglas, who said of his "master" Chaucer that he was "evir (God wait) all womanis frend" ("Ever, God knows, all women's champion"). And it's true that Chaucer has long had a reputation for being especially sympathetic toward his female characters, for being unusually progressive—downright unmedieval—in his representation of the relationship between the sexes. On the other hand, you don't need to possess very well-developed feminist instincts to find it odd that Emelye—the beautiful Amazon princess in the Knight's Tale who inspires such devotion in her two suitors that they are transformed from loyal blood brothers to bloody (if still chivalrous) enemies—has only one thirty-seven-line speech (and one wordless shriek) in a tale over 2200 lines long; or that in the veritable orgy of *gentilesse* that concludes the Franklin's Tale, the one character prohibited from demonstrating generosity of spirit is the long-suffering wife Dorigen; or that the Wife of Bath, long renowned as a proto-feminist paragon, concludes her tour-de-force Prologue married (her fifth time) to the physically and psychologically abusive (if evidently irresistibly sexy) scholar Jankyn, treating him "as kinde/As any wife from Denmark unto Inde," after which she goes on to tell a tale about how to redeem a rapist.

Of course, that's not really Chaucer speaking—that's the Knight, or the Franklin, or the Wife, each of them clearly hobbled by a devotion to some constraining ideology, while the poet hovers serenely just above them, ironically detached from (though not entirely unsympathetic to) their blinkered attempts to figure out the world through the stories they tell. At least, that's what he wants you to think. "Now, for the poet, he never affirms, and therefore never lieth," wrote Sir Philip Sidney, and though he probably wasn't thinking of his predecessor Chaucer (whom he elsewhere praises as a kind of inspired primitive), it's nevertheless an apt remark to end with. His pilgrims busily affirm things left and right, while his narrator modestly claims to be nothing but a simple reporter: "I mot reherse/Hir tales alle, be they bet or werse,/Or elles falsen some of my mattere." Believe him at your own risk.

—Frank Grady

INTRODUCTION

It is a habit of modern criticism to praise writers for their originality, and Chaucer is often so praised. Dryden called him "the father of English literature"—for he was, if anyone, the initiator of an English literary tradition, and was the inventor of the English rhyming decasyllabic couplet. From the historical studies of the nineteenth and twentieth centuries we know now that Chaucer's style reflects many of the conventions of medieval poetry and rhetoric, and that his tales are based on folk tales or on narratives borrowed from Boccaccio, Petrarch, Nicholas Trivet, and so on. When we think about this "background," with its enormous element of convention and stereotype, it becomes harder to see what is original in him. Perhaps very little. Originality was not the virtue for medieval poets that it is for us; where we may scorn what is "derivative" in an author, the medievals would have praised his taste in choosing well. Nor did they romanticize their poets as moderns do. They were uninterested in a poet's "development" and did not seek out in his work clues to his personality or his private life. Moreover, writers themselves did not see the act of composition in quite the romantic way a modern writer might. Poets were called "makers" and were viewed more often as craftsmen than as creators or artists. In his earlier works, Chaucer often presents himself humorously as a bookish scholar and naïve pedant hovering over "old books" and citing "authorities"—a mere scribe copying and adapting with myopic diligence. What is missing in this image of the poet, and what we must therefore remove from our minds, is the printing press; for it was only that technological improvement—a century after Chaucer's time—which let writers imagine themselves initiating an un-

predictable process of reproduction and addressing a "pub-
lic" of unseen readers.

In these respects Chaucer was somewhat ahead of his
time. More than other English writers of his age he saw him-
self as an originator and creator, expecting a reputation and
a measure of fame; in this he was more like his Italian con-
temporary Petrarch, whom he names with honor in the
Clerk's Prologue. It has never been fashionable to call Chau-
cer a humanist, and it is true that he was untouched by many
of the fads which characterized the incipient humanism of
Italy in the fourteenth century. Yet he knew about Petrarch
and Boccaccio and knew some of their works. Like them, he
was interested in the ancient world and in ancient writers.
Like them, he was concerned about the accurate preservation
of texts (but especially those of his own works): in one of his
short poems he scolds his scribe for making mistakes, and at
the end of *Troilus and Criseyde* begs copyists to take care.
Like them, too, he showed an interest in fame. In his earlier
House of Fame, though it depicts fame as mere unpredictable
noise not bestowed justly, he evinces this interest; at the end
of the *Troilus,* though he modestly hopes that his work will
be "subject to all poesy," he wishes it a place in literary tradi-
tion; in the Prologue to *The Legend of Good Women* and
again in the Man of Law's Prologue, he puts into the mouths
of characters lists of his own works; and he gives a similar
list in his "Retraction," though disclaiming all such as "sounen
into sin."

He was perhaps also ahead of his time in the way he en-
visaged his audience. Medieval writers sometimes used the
phrase "readers and hearers"—by which they meant, proba-
bly, that their work would more often than not be read aloud.
Chaucer himself evidently read his works to the court of
Richard II—there is a manuscript drawing of him doing so,
executed a few years after his death. Much has been made of
the notion that he wrote his poems for oral delivery and thus
conceived of them as performances before a court audience.
Nevertheless, Chaucer seems to have imagined readers un-
known to himself poring over his works. At the close of the

Troilus he worries about the "diversity of our tongue"—that is, about whether speakers of other dialects would understand him and copy him correctly. And before the Miller's Tale he warns those who might be offended by its coarseness to "turn over the leaf and choose another tale." In this last he seems to have in mind the more characteristically modern reader—a solitary person with book in hand. But literacy was not in the least common, the possession of books was rare, and a "reading public" in the modern sense scarcely existed at all. Chaucer himself says he owned sixty books (an enormous private library for those days) and read in bed (a luxurious use of expensive candles); when he envisages other readers like himself, solitary men who own their own books, he has in mind something new and still unusual.

All of this is the Chaucer we know from his works—Chaucer the writer and man of letters. What kind of private person he was is entirely a matter of guesswork. The intimate sense of his personality which we get from his writings—the "Chaucerian" irony and wit, the close observation of detail, his tolerant interest in people—is possibly our best and worthiest knowledge of the man himself. Bits and scraps of documents give us some facts about his whereabouts and employment as a civil servant, although none of them state that this Geoffrey Chaucer was the poet. But it is safe to assume that poet and civil servant were the same. Had there been two men of the same name at court, it would have occasioned comment; and there is one passage (*The House of Fame,* lines 652–60) where he describes finishing his "rekenynges" and coming home only to sit at another book, like a hermit, until bleary-eyed. We can build up a picture of a young man from an upper-middle-class home, sent to a noble house and then abroad to be trained in the niceties of high-born conduct, for a time possibly a student at the Inns of Court, where he would have had training in law and finance. (There is a report from the sixteenth century that the old records of the Inner Temple showed he was fined two shillings for beating a Franciscan friar in Fleet Street.) He was employed by the Crown on various ambassadorial missions to France, Spain, Flanders, and

Italy, and held various civil service posts—Clerk of the Customs, Clerk of the King's Works—to which he was appointed by the King. He was especially under the patronage of John of Gaunt. His marriage to Philippa Roet was apparently arranged through these alliances in a businesslike manner; he had two sons and possibly two daughters. He jokingly refers to himself in his early poems as an outsider to love; but he probably means by this—if he means anything serious—that his social position, that of an "esquire," made the aristocratic conventions of love inappropriate for him. It is true that as an important functionary and as court poet he mixed freely with titled aristocrats of the greatest importance; but it is also true that he was not fully their equal. His ironic detachment and self-humor probably spring in part from this relationship with an aristocratic audience.

When Chaucer writes "I" in *The Canterbury Tales,* we have therefore a complex self-projection. Our first glimpse of him, in the second sentence of the General Prologue, is of a pilgrim: he has joined a group of twenty-nine other pilgrims at the Tabard Inn in Southwark and has spoken to all of them. Thus he is an observer, just one of a group—accurate, interested, reporting in close detail what he has seen and learned. As he proceeds in this role, we get an idea of his character, and it is that of an exceedingly naïve fellow. He thinks the pilgrims are all perfectly wonderful people and describes each with enormous enthusiasm, admiring them, in bourgeois fashion, for their appearance and their success—even when that success is in duplicity or thievery.

This unduly accepting observer is telling about the beginning of a pilgrimage from which he has now returned. No doubt he learned much more in a week or so than he would have seen at first glance in the inn. Like any returned traveler he must have picked up some gossip along with the facts and made some guesses or surmises. But as we get further into his descriptions of his fellow pilgrims, we realize that he is reporting many more details than the average observer would normally see or guess. He knows how the Friar goes about his daily rounds, what he keeps concealed in his hood, how he hears confessions. He knows how the Prioress behaved in her convent and how the Summoner abused his office. He even knows what the Monk *thinks* (it seems unlikely that the Monk would have told all this) and hints broadly that the Monk's "outriding" and hunting was in fact a hunt for women. In short, though we started with a pilgrim-observer returned from his travels and reporting what he remembers, we end up with an almost omniscient observer and reporter who knows their thoughts and secrets.

Obviously behind this observer stands the poet himself, who can imagine and write down what he pleases. Indeed the first voice we hear, in the opening sentence of the General Prologue, is the poet's. The familiar lines, "Whan that April with his showres soote/The drought of March hath perced to the roote," are not "realistic observation," though often so described, but rely on learning and poetic convention. We are not told that the flowers have blossomed, but that "the showers of April have penetrated March's dryness, bathing the veins in such liquid as engenders flowers." We are not told that the winds blew, but that "Zephyr with his sweet breath has breathed into the sprouts." We are given astronomical measurements for the position of the sun and are taught that birds sleep at night with their eyes open as Nature directs them. The pilgrimage itself is introduced with a generalization. What we are getting here is *authority*; the poet's voice is steeped in tradition, learning, science—all of it preserved in books. When he turns to the pilgrims, we get (so he says) *experience*, for the pilgrim-observer claims to be telling us what he saw and heard. Authority plus experience—that is really the "method" of the General Prologue. To the medieval mind "authority" was a superior basis for knowledge. But it is hard not to feel that Chaucer shared somewhat the Wife of Bath's opinion:

> Experience, though noon auctoritee
> Were in this world, is right enough for me . . .
> (Wife of Bath's Prologue, 1–2)

The pilgrim-observer, who gives us experience, is naïve, wide-eyed, and uncritical. It is as if the poet has put on a mask—the mask of the fool. Imagine Chaucer reading the work aloud to a sophisticated upper-class audience and you catch this irony. Take the Monk. "There was this very fine Monk (he says), an outrider, who loved venery—a manly man, capable of being an abbot; he had many wonderful horses in his stable, and when he rode you could hear his bridle jingle in a whistling wind, as loud and clear as a chapel bell. Where he was in charge, the rule of St. Maur or St. Benedict, because old and rather strict—why, this monk let old things go by and held with the *new* world . . ." As the details mount up we get a most clear picture. The Monk is permitted to ride outside the monastery in order to take care of its business; but he derives far too much pleasure from this. He loves hunting (the sport of aristocrats), keeps fine horses, is handsomely dressed, even wearing a gold pin in the suspicious shape of a love knot. "Venerie" (hunting) is likely a pun on "venereal" (having to do with Venus); "hunting" often suggested sexual escapades; the hare was and still is a symbol of lechery (he goes, moreover, "pricking" after hares). The pilgrim continues to be enthusiastic—he agrees wholeheartedly: "I said his opinion was good. Why should *he* study? Why should *he* work with his hands, as St. Augustine commanded? How shall the world be served?" The poet of course knows that the Monk was violating his vows and was very far from admirable. We understand this without being told. As we continue to read the General Prologue, we come more and more to see evil in the pilgrims—the worst, the Summoner and Pardoner, are saved for the end. And because the pilgrim-observer remains uniformly enthusiastic and accepting, the irony becomes greater.

But Chaucer is not using this ironic device to *condemn* their abuses. From a Christian point of view, all men are sinners; the Christian, as St. Augustine had said, must "love the man but hate his sin." To condemn other men for their shortcomings would itself be a sin of pride. From this point of view, the pilgrim-observer is a kind of holy fool, and his generous, affable acceptance of everyone is a figure of Christian charity. But this charity is fragmented from the other side of Christian behavior—wisdom and knowledge, including self-knowledge—and is exaggerated in its simplicity. Certainly Chaucer is not recommending naïveté. He lets us see the abuses; and like him, we recognize them for abuses and must disapprove of them. The attitude, characteristic of the Christian Middle Ages, can be formulated like this: men themselves are God's creatures and therefore fundamentally good; the institutions they are connected with—monasticism, knighthood, labor, the professions and businesses—are only good or bad insofar as men use them well or ill. Thus, St. Francis' *ideal* was good; the way Friar Huberd of *The Canterbury Tales* practices that ideal is bad. Evil in men is the result of the Fall; with all men, as with Adam, it is the product of wrong choices; but it is parasitic and does not alter the fact of their goodness as creatures. When we see evil in others, we are not supposed to click our tongues like puritans; we should love them as God's creatures and worry about our own sins first. Chaucer indeed ends *The Canterbury Tales* with the Parson's Tale (omitted in the present volume)—a sermon on penitence. And to this he adds his own act of penance.

In the General Prologue the pilgrims are described roughly in groups as they might have fallen together in the inn or on the road. The Knight, his son the Squire, and their Yeoman ride together. The clergy fall into a group: two nuns, a priest, a monk, and a friar. The Sergeant of the Law and the Franklin, members of the upper bourgeoisie, are described one after the other. And various guildsmen and tradesmen fall into proximity, including Shipman, Doctor, and Wife of Bath. This is all realistic enough and reflects the makeup of fourteenth-century English society. But inserted among the rest are three *ideal* portraits, those of the Knight, the Parson, and the Plowman. These three are exactly what they should be in the light of medieval social ideals—the Knight a high-minded adventurer serving just causes, the Parson a humble parish priest who practices what he preaches, the Plowman a dutiful worker who "lives in peace and perfect charity." The three ideal portraits represent the medieval conception of the Three Estates—nobles, clergy, and commons. (Perhaps the Clerk is also an idealized figure representing a newer milieu sequestered from society, the universities. But, like the Squire, he is not yet fully a part of adult life and may stand apart in this way.)

Against this ideal is set the harsh reality. To the medieval mind things were arranged in hierarchies, and man's goal was perfection. On the other hand perfection was not absolutely attainable because of original sin and humanity in fact disposed itself into degrees of *im*perfection. While Chaucer thought of the class structure in ideal terms, the better part of the pilgrims come from the middle class, as Chaucer himself did, and this realistically describes conditions of fourteenth-century life; yet there is no idealized portrait of a middle-class pilgrim. The ideal, then, was rigid, hierarchical, and typically disposed into three parts; the reality was turbulent and many-faceted. As the result of the plague—the Black Death which swept England four times during Chaucer's lifetime— England was depopulated by at least a third. The result was a considerable social upheaval, a new demand for laborers, and therefore a new independence among the laboring classes. Chaucer begins his description of the pilgrims with the Knight, and begins the tales with the Knight's Tale. Both choices are appropriate—the man of highest rank *should* come first. But in the General Prologue this proper order by rank quickly falls apart; and in the tales the Host's good intentions are foiled when the drunken Miller butts in to "quite" the Knight's tale. Chaucer clearly intended to let the actualities of fourteenth-century life burst forth in this way; he even apologizes for doing so in the General Prologue:

> Also I pray you to foryive it me
> Al have I not set folk in hir degree
> Here in this tale as that they sholde stonde:
> My wit is short, ye may well understonde. (743–46)

There is, then, an intentional quality of haphazardness and randomness in the prologue and among the tales. For some time readers of the poem therefore considered the General Prologue a "portrait gallery" and the tales themselves a collection or anthology. In recent years critics have come to see in both a degree of arrangement and order, and hence a degree of unity. The General Prologue begins with the Knight, groups the pilgrims roughly by their livelihood, and ends with the most awesomely depraved of the pilgrims, the Summoner and Pardoner. The tales begin with the Knight, fall in some cases into dramatic units or juxtapositions, and end with the Parson's sermon. In spite of this evident planning, however, the randomness of the pilgrimage is pressed upon the reader in a gamelike way: quite literally the pilgrimage is a game—"I shall begin the game," declares the Knight before his tale, and after it the Host cries, "the game is well begunne." It starts as a game of chance: at the end of the General Prologue the Host has them draw straws to see who will begin:

> Anon to drawen every wight began,
> And shortly for to tellen as it was,
> Were it by aventure, or sort, or cas,
> The sooth is this: the cut fill to the Knight.
> (842–45)

The real truth, as every reader can see, is that it was very far from "aventure," "sort," or "cas" (the three terms are as good as synonymous): behind the lucky accident, short of some sleight of hand by the Host, is the directing hand of Chaucer and the providential rightness of things. The game of chance seems to have hidden rules. But no sooner are these rules set up than they fall back into randomness: the Host calls next on the Monk, he being probably next in rank, but the Miller drunkenly intervenes. After him comes the Reeve, for reeves (farm managers) are natural enemies of millers; and besides, the two are exact opposites in temperament. The order of tales thus comes to be directed by inner forces of social conflict and interplay of character, by disagreement and aggression.

This tension between rule and chance reflects the medieval attitude toward the universe itself. God's Providence governed the universe, and all things worked according to a divine plan. But such a necessity in the nature of things could not be known to man's beclouded reason; neither did it limit man's free will to make moral choices. From man's point of view the universe therefore *seemed* haphazard; chance ("Fortune") seemed to govern the course of human affairs, and all earthly things seemed transitory, mutable, and untrustworthy. But behind this phenomenon of flux was the directing hand of Providence: hence, in the total order of things, every outcome was just and right. Life itself was a journey or pilgrimage in which men seemed to meander uncertainly toward the just certainties of the Last Things—death, judgment, heaven, and hell.

"Pilgrimage" was a perfect metaphor for human life conceived in this way, and Chaucer was aware of this when he chose a pilgrimage as the setting for the tales. Pilgrimages were often condemned by churchmen because of the self-indulgent holiday conduct of pilgrims; the Wife of Bath herself is a great joiner of pilgrimages, and knew, we find out, much about "wandering by the way." *The Way* was the controlling principle of pilgrimages, for they had a planned route and an ostensibly religious purpose. Egeus in the Knight's Tale articulates the pilgrimage metaphor when he says,

> This world nis but a thurghfare full of wo,
> And we been pilgrims passing to and fro:
> Deeth is an end of every worldly sore. (1989–91)

And at the end, the Parson introduces his sermon with these words:

> —And Jesu for His grace wit me sende
> To shewe you the way, in this viage,
> Of thilke parfit glorious pilgrimage
> That highte Jerusalem Celestial. (48–51)

Indeed the text of the Parson's sermon, from *Jeremiah* 6, deals with penitence as a means of choosing the Way, the right road in life:

> Standeth upon the ways, and seeth and axeth of old paths
> (that is to sayn, of old sentences) which is the good way,
> and walketh in that way, and ye shall find refreshing for
> your souls.

While the pilgrimage to Canterbury must be understood thus as a metaphor, it is nonetheless real. Like the medieval pilgrimages themselves, it has both a quotidian and a spiritual dimension. From the simplest quotidian point of view it describes thirty pilgrims who meet at the Tabard and ride to Canterbury telling tales as they go; and seen this way the General Prologue is indeed a portrait gallery, and the tales a collection. The pilgrims are, by the Host's plan, each to tell two tales going and two returning, but they do not all tell even one, and there is no return voyage. Since Chaucer did not finish the work, it is almost always assumed that if he had there would have been one hundred twenty tales, half told on the way back to London. But is the work meant to be viewed with that much realism? In real life, the journey to the shrine of St. Thomas à Becket at Canterbury was a very popular pilgrimage. The pilgrims did really tell tales—a "Canterbury tale" came to mean a tall tale or lie. Thus a gamelike falseness and unreality are suggested even by the realistic setting and straightforward title of the work. We are, moreover, meant to suspend our disbelief in important particulars: we know that the pilgrims did not tell their tales in rhyming couplets or stanzaic forms, and that no one could *hear* a tale told to a group of thirty while riding horseback through open country. The pilgrims themselves suspend *their* disbelief and enter upon an elaborate game in which an innkeeper assumes leadership over a group composed in good part of his betters; he has them hold up their hands in agreement (line 783) before he has told them his plan! In short, the world we enter upon is very far from the real world of the everyday. It is a world of game, of carefree assent, a topsy-turvy world where social rank is set aside, where drawn straws turn out miraculously right "by aventure, or sort, or cas"—a holiday atmosphere surging with discord and tension, its goal the Martyr's shrine.

This unreality points to the spiritual dimension of the pilgrimage. At the outset we are with Chaucer the pilgrim at the Tabard; when he tells us that he will describe each pilgrim, we feel as if he must be describing them as he first saw them in the inn. But in fact he describes them as he saw them on the road—we get precise details about their horses, how they rode, who rode with whom. Beyond that, we get details of their private lives (the Franklin has a "table dormant" at home, loves to serve food and drink to his guests; the Prioress keeps little dogs in her abbey, feeds them with roasted meat, milk, wastel bread) and even details of their private thoughts (the Pardoner liked best to sing the offertory because just after that he would preach his sermon to win silver). Time is suspended in this whole account. We have first a single point of time (the night before the pilgrimage), then inner psychological time (what Chaucer remembers from the whole journey), then a timeless and ubiquitous omniscience in which Chaucer projects himself into their thoughts and feelings at other times and in other places. In the same way our normal sense of place is turned aside. We are at the Tabard, then on the road, then back at the Tabard planning the game; and during this sweeping view we are taken into the Prioress' convent, the Monk's "celle," the Reeve's sly little world of livestock, garners, bins, and auditors. We are in that realm where thought and imagination permit us to project ourselves into the experience of others—in the author's mind and, with him, in the minds of the pilgrims. As we empathize with Chaucer, we join him in empathizing with them; and in this empathic realm time and place become malleable, existing only as they have or give meaning.

When *The Canterbury Tales* is seen in this way, its completeness is a relative matter. Chaucer the returned pilgrim could go on reciting the four tales each pilgrim told going and coming until he had told one hundred twenty tales, but the conception and design would stay the same. We are meant to see how life is a pilgrimage, and we see this by seeing into the author's consciousness. It is the nature of consciousness and of memory that we *could* see more; yet we could see the central conception without some of the tales we have. Memory is almost inexhaustible, and the completeness of memories relies on the structuring of details rather than on the accumulation of them. The one-way motion of the pilgrimage from London to Canterbury, which is what the text gives us, carries out the metaphor of life as a pilgrimage. If the return trip had been represented by more tales, this would not have altered the central conception unless the General Prologue were altered as well. It is hard not to imagine that such a return journey would have seemed anticlimactic, and it is entirely possible that Chaucer never meant to portray it. Not, of course, that we shouldn't be infinitely grateful if there were more; but what we have, as Dryden perceived, is God's plenty.

Moreover, the return journey does not go unacknowledged, for we see that the author has returned, like Dante, to recount his experience. What he tells is of a movement from tavern to cathedral, from home to shrine, from fellowship and chitchat to penance and retraction. Because the General Prologue prepares us in this way for the tales and their tellers as well as for the unidirectional shape of the pilgrimage, it must be regarded as one of the great pieces of thematic writing. Like the great opening "overture" of Proust's *A la Recherche du Temps Perdu* it encapsulates and sets the nature and governing principles of a work which would be indeterminately shorter or longer, less or more detailed, without being the less whole. It is perhaps for this reason that J. V. Cunningham understood about the General Prologue that it takes its character from the medieval dream-vision. In it a structure of memories and received ideas takes shape and, like consciousness itself, renders up the design of the whole in vivid associations of feeling and perception.

*   *   *

The tales themselves can be read with pleasure separately and at random; but the General Prologue accustoms us to the conditions which make them parts of a design. Each tale is told by a character we already know. These characters are in relationship with each other—are members of a single society who ally and clash. In addition, the tales are being re-counted by Chaucer himself, like an actor re-creating the roles of the storytellers and playing all the parts.

This conception of a series of dramatic monologues which itself tells a story was probably Chaucer's most original stroke. Each tale, as it reflects the personality of its teller, tells its own revealing story about the pilgrim himself and thus contributes to the description of the pilgrimage. Chaucer has often been praised as a dramatic genius, and that he was. The dialogue in the tales has the qualities of good drama, for the personages talk like individuals and reveal their characters in the way they talk. The same is true of the pilgrims themselves. The Clerk's discourse is idealistic and ironic; the Wife's ebullient and nos-talgic; the Miller's hardy, buoyant, and salacious; the Reeve's acerb, self-pitying, and awesomely sly. If the essence of drama is conflict, the pilgrimage is a wonderfully dramatic situation, for many of the pilgrims fall quite spontaneously into dis-agreement. The Friar and Summoner eye each other askance and tell outspoken tales against each other—since both have their hands in the pockets of ordinary layfolk, they are com-petitors. There is no love lost between the Miller and Reeve. The Friar ruffles at the Wife's theological notions. And a whole group of tales makes up a discussion of marriage.

Beyond this dramatic excitement, the fully elaborated story of the pilgrimage reveals Chaucer's own mentality and, though very subtly, his opinions. This aspect of *The Canter-bury Tales* has most engaged the attention of critics in recent years. It is the hardest problem because Chaucer's presence in the work is its most ambiguous element. Very possibly he did not want to seem too outspoken, but caution is not the reason he *gives;* and indeed in important matters—religion, politics, domestic harmony—his ideas were not at all radical. What he *says* is that he will tell the facts accurately. They are

more daring and surprising than opinions, and it is for them
that he makes a good-natured apology:

> But first I pray you of your curteisye
> That ye n'arette it not my villainye
> Though that I plainly speke in this mattere
> To telle you hir wordes and hir cheere,
> Ne though I speke hir wordes proprely.
> For this ye knowen also well as I:
> Whoso shall tell a tale after a man,
> He moot reherce as neigh as ever he can
> Everich a word, if it be in his charge—
> Al speke he never so rudelich and large—
> Or elles he moot tell his tale untrewe,
> Or feine thing, or finde wordes newe;
> He may not spare although he were his brother.
> He moot as well say oo word as another.
> Christ spak himself full brod in holy writ,
> And well ye wot no villainy is it.
> Eek Plato saith, whoso can him rede,
> The wordes mot be cosin to the deede. (725–42)

His use of "low" stories told by rude fellows is evidently
what could have given offense to the gentlefolk of his audi-
ence. And before the Miller's contribution, which Chaucer
calls a "churl's tale," he states his position:

> And therefore every gentil wight, I praye,
> Deemeth not, for God's love, that I saye
> Of yvel entent, but for I mot reherse
> Hir tales alle, be they bet or werse,
> Or elles falsen some of my mattere.
> And therefore, whoso list it not y-heere
> Turn over the leef and chese another tale.
> For he shall find enoughe, greet and smalle,
> Of storial thing that toucheth gentilesse
> And eek moralitee and holinesse.
> Blameth not me if that ye chese amiss. (63–73)

In spite of this pose of objectivity, or perhaps because of it, Chaucer's own views show through the tales. Principally they do so by a process of accumulative *discrediting*. No sooner do we get one point of view clearly in mind than we are given some reasons to doubt it. The result is a tentative, questioning spirit for which Chaucer is normally reckoned tolerant and ironic. This does not mean he was without values, for he lets the profoundest values of his civilization assert themselves in the most spontaneous and convincing way. One of those values, however, was that placed upon the tentative and inquiring mind; irony itself involves disinterestedness, openness, and skepticism. Such a frame of mind is not thought "medieval" by some, but I believe it was. The Church taught that revealed truth was absolute, but this did not mean that all Christians knew an absolute truth: man's reason was clouded by ignorance, truth was not known absolutely except to God, and many kinds of knowledge were "forbidden" and unattainable to man. On the other hand, Christians believed that "whatsoever things were written aforetime were written for our learning" (*Romans* 15:4). People had begun to believe in Chaucer's day that experience might be added to the canons of authority and logic as a way of knowing truth. The universities, for which Chaucer shows an affectionate regard, had evolved a pedagogical method which relied largely on argument and disputation; their sense of truth was far more discursive than we imagine it. Moreover, the growing power of the middle-class professionals—men like the Sergeant of Law, the Franklin, and of course Chaucer himself—must have made manifest in fourteenth-century society a spirit of compromise, mutual concession, caution, and pragmatism. Whatever its sources and expressions, *The Canterbury Tales* evinces a conception of the variousness of worldly truth; we are reminded throughout that there is much to be said on all sides and, at the end, that we are imperfect seekers of the perfect Way.

Chaucer's method of stating-and-discrediting thus sets up a kind of serial dialogue, which works at different levels and by different devices; and we shall see this most clearly if we pluck apart the strands for examination.

(1) Within individual tales, each reputedly told by a pilgrim, Chaucer sometimes lets his own voice discredit the tale. This is most notable in the Knight's Tale: we are kept in mind of Chaucer's presence behind the Knight's recital of his story. In reducing Boccaccio's epic, the *Teseida,* to a much shorter romance, Chaucer omitted vast stretches of the narrative. In summarizing or passing over these (the rhetorical device called *occupatio*), he comments on the unwieldiness of the story. At one point, for instance, occurs the line "But of that story list me not to write" (343). This is often treated as a mistake on Chaucer's part—obviously the Knight is not "writing," so the line seems a leftover from an early version before it was assigned to the Knight and included in *The Canterbury Tales.* If this were the only such line, the explanation would be valid; but there are others. For instance, telling of Palamon's imprisonment, Chaucer says,

> Who coude ryme in English proprely
> His martyrdom? Forsooth, it am not I.
> Therefore I pass as lightly as I may:
> It fill that in the seventh yeer, of May
> The thridde night, as olde bookes sayn
> (That all this story tellen more plain) . . . (601–6)

Indeed, throughout the Knight's Tale there is an undertone of ironic self-humor, sometimes in the form of exaggeration—as where the two heroes fight ankle deep in their own blood ("And in this wise I let hem fighting dwelle," the poet adds)—and sometimes in comic relief of a highly anticlimactic sort. An example of this last occurs indeed at the climactic moment, the death of Arcite:

> Dusked his eyen two and failed breeth—
> But on his lady yet cast he his eye.
> His laste word was: *"Mercy, Emelye!"*
> His spirit chaunged house and wente ther
> As *I* came never, I can not tellen wher;
> Therefore I stint—I nam no divinistre:

Of soules find I not in this registre,
Ne me ne list thilke opinions to telle
Of hem, though that they writen where they dwelle.
Arcite is cold, ther Mars his soule gie.
Now wol I speken forth of Emelye.
    Shright Emely . . . (1948–59)

It must be understood that this element in the tale does not
keep us from taking it seriously, does not discredit the Knight
personally, and does not turn the tale into a parody. But it
introduces an undertone of skepticism toward the story and
so toward the tradition of romance and the body of aristo-
cratic convention with which it was intertwined.

(2) What we already know about a pilgrim sometimes dis-
credits his tale. The Miller is an excellent example. He
openly pokes fun at the Knight's tale, declaring outright that
he will "quite" (match, or repay) it. Not twenty lines into his
story he repeats a line out of the Knight's Tale—"Alone,
withouten any compaigny"—which the Knight had used in a
serious context (as the Miller, of course, does not). His story,
like the Knight's, is about two suitors after a young woman
who is in the custody of an older man. But where the Knight's
tale was of princes and high love in ancient Athens, the Mill-
er's is about ordinary people and earthy love in present-day
Oxford. One lover is a young student at the university, out for
a lush time; the other, Absolon, is a clerk in minor orders, the
sexton or janitor in the local parish, an affected bumpkin who
has somehow picked up the clichés of courtly love. The
"lady" is a skittish wench, age eighteen, described with very
appropriate animal imagery borne out in her later conduct.
And she is married to an old carpenter, uxorious, jealous, and
dumb. In this atmosphere the conventions and language of
courtly love, being utterly out of place, become artificial and
ludicrous; and the situation is resolved in a Rabelaisian spirit
complete with farts and hot pokers.

The buoyant quality of the tale gives us a very different
view of medieval love conventions. But if the Miller discred-
its those conventions, his looseness of tongue, his drunken-

ness, and his churl's mentality, hilarious as they are, discredit him. We cannot say that this is what Chaucer thinks about high love, only that this is what the Miller thinks. Chaucer leaves it at that.

(3) Some tales discredit the tale preceding them. Just as the Miller's Tale "quites" the Knight's Tale, the tale following—the Reeve's—"quites" the Miller's. We know we are not meant to take the Miller's Tale as the last word, nor the Reeve's Tale either. What we get from the Reeve is another low-class point of view. The moment the Miller says he will tell a legend and life about a carpenter, the Reeve bristles paranoically: "Stint thy clappe!"— shut your mouth, he says, it's a sin and a folly to injure or defame anyone. When it is the Reeve's turn, he begins with a sly, self-pitying utterance about how old he is, intended to enlist the sympathy of the audience and disclaim any evil intent. He quickly gives himself the lie—he will "quite" the Miller right in his own churl's terms: "I pray to God his necke mot tobreke—" He is in fact burning up with a bitter anger and is bent on revenge. His last words are "Thus have I quit the Miller in my tale."

The Reeve's story is again a tale of two clerks, and there are an eligible female and an older man as well. But now the clerks are from Cambridge, not Oxford; they speak a comic north-country dialect; and the rival older man is, needless to say, a miller. In the darkest bedroom in literary history one of the clerks climbs into bed with the miller's daughter while the other tricks his wife into climbing into bed with *him*. The wife, a haughty woman who considers herself socially superior because she is a priest's bastard child, doesn't know she is in the wrong bed (the Reeve cannot resist commenting that she hadn't had such a good time in years). During it all the drunken husband snores away. At last the clerks are found out and there ensues a battle; the wife hits her husband over the head by mistake, and the clerks escape. It is as funny a tale as the Miller's, but it has a less buoyant quality: it reflects the sly, acerb spirit of the Reeve himself. To the Miller, the "nice manners" of the Knight's Tale seemed merely artificial and ridiculous, and he represented them in the absurdly effete Absolon. But the Reeve's view is different. The initial "nice manners" of the clerks and of the miller and his wife just barely manage to hide the ill will and guile of the miller and the suspicion of the clerks. To the Reeve, "nice manners" are suspect; beneath them he sees what is uppermost in his own character—a sly meanness, a habit of distrust and guile. His is no more a final view of love or manners than the Miller's had been; but it is another view, a counterpart to the Miller's. The next tale, the Cook's, might very well have presented still another low-class view tending to discredit the others; but alas Chaucer did not finish it.

(4) From these three tales we can see a further device for presenting various views which partially discredit one another: tales are arranged in groups. There are three groups of this kind. One, which we have already discussed, is the sequence Knight-Miller-Reeve. A second, less certainly intentional, includes Shipman, Prioress, Sir Thopas, Melibee, Monk, and Nun's Priest. A third is the so-called "marriage group."

Since the Melibee and the Monk's Tale are omitted in the present volume, we may as well omit any detailed discussion of the group which includes them. Besides, the grouping of these tales is greatly in debate. Perhaps, as one critic suggests, they are about storytelling itself and represent by turns the principles of "mirth" and "doctrine." The Shipman's Tale, intended as one of mirth, is consciously immoral; in it all that was sacred in medieval society—marriage, monastic vows, "brotherhood" among friends—is violated. The Prioress' Tale, intended as one of doctrine, is *un*consciously immoral; she tells a story of a supposed "ritual murder" by Jews—the ancient slander recently described in Malamud's *The Fixer*. Her unthinking, harsh anti-Semitism is an ironic contrast to the genteel manners and delicate sensibility ascribed to her in the General Prologue, and that contrast is profoundly sobering. Sir Thopas, told by Chaucer himself in his role of naif, is a parody of a metrical romance and makes fun of the traditional literary knight-errant. But Chaucer then turns from mirth to doctrine and tells a serious tale in prose, the

Melibee—a treatise, as it actually is, of high-minded advice about proper conduct for aristocrats. Then follows the Monk's tiresome recital of "tragedies."

The Nun's Priest's Tale, the last in this series, is remarkable—witty, satirical, profoundly intelligent. A mock-epic, its form satirizes the stylized conventions of medieval rhetoric. Its content satirizes the conventions of aristocratic conduct: its principal characters, a rooster and hen, talk to each other in the clichés of courtly love. It satirizes, too, almost every intellectual fashion of the later Middle Ages—the arguments about the meaning of dreams, the question of predestination versus free will, medieval medicine and astrology, antifeminist doctrines, the citing of "authorities," the idea of Fortune. Even the Peasants' Revolt is brought in. Its technique is to build up pomposities to the point where they may be taken seriously, then pinprick them by reminding us that the pompous interlocutors are barnyard fowls. In the end, a sly fox captures the rooster by getting him to close his eyes and sing; but the rooster escapes by getting the fox to open his mouth and shout triumphantly at his pursuers. So the moral is simple: one should keep his eyes open and keep his mouth shut. Probably no advice could better be applied to the heady tales which have gone before. The Monk's Tale was surely pompous (the Monk himself was even described as a rooster in his prologue); the Melibee could be seen as pompous for its sententiousness, as could the Prioress' Tale for its naïve smugness. The spirit of the Nun's Priest, by contrast, perfectly involves that unpompous and ironic tentativeness which we call "Chaucerian." The Nun's Priest concludes by quoting St. Paul (Chaucer himself in his Retraction will quote the same text):

> But ye that holden this tale a follye
> As of a fox, or of a cock and hen,
> Taketh the moralitee, good men.
> For Saint Paul saith that all that written is
> To our doctrine it is y-writ, ywis:
> Taketh the fruit and let the chaff be stille. (618–23)

The "marriage group" has a clearer thematic unity. Since Kittredge first described this sequence, critics have argued over its validity and differed about which tales should be included. Basically, the notion is this: the Wife of Bath initiates a discussion of marriage, arguing two points—that marriage is a desirable form of moral perfection, and that marriage can be happy only when the wife has the "maistrye," the upper hand. Her own prologue, with its account of her five husbands, illustrates the point admirably; and her tale is a grand wish-fulfillment of her yearning to be young again and to dominate her men. There are many ambiguities in her lusty and outspoken view which make her prologue and tale (in Root's phrase) a great human document. Among them is the fact that her fifth husband, the youngest and poorest of the lot, pleased her most, though he was the one who nearly gained power over her, and her tale ends with the lady obeying the husband with a surprising submissiveness.

The other tales (after an interruption, omitted here, by the Summoner and Friar) present radically different views. The Clerk, a young man studying at Oxford, is an idealist. He tells a noble tale of a wife, Griselda, who patiently submits to her husband's sadistic testing of her; it is too long to include in this volume, but the ending has been printed to show the heavy irony with which the Clerk admits that his ideals are never followed in these times. It is followed by the tale of the Merchant, an older man who has just had an unhappy brief marriage to a young woman. He tells the story of January, the foolish and self-willed old knight who after a lifetime of bachelorhood marries and is promptly cuckolded by a young toothsome lass, logically named May. The Merchant's view is one of total disillusionment and cynicism: the spiritual (and physical) blindness of old January reflects the Merchant's own self-contempt, and the moral of his tale is that happiness in marriage occurs only when the husband can let himself be utterly deceived.

So far then, after the Wife's proclamation, we have an idealistic view and a cynical one. According to Kittredge the debate was resolved by the Franklin, who shows the spirit of compromise characteristic of his class. At the beginning of his tale he outlines a kind of marriage based on mutual concession: the husband is to be "servant in love but lord in marriage"—i.e., he will have the position of superiority but in fact submit to the lady's will; she in turn will be a "humble, true wife"; and in this way they will attain happiness in marriage. There is something here to satisfy all the points of view so far represented. The remainder of the tale is elaborately bound up with the idea of keeping bargains and having "gentilesse." Kittredge believed, and probably most people agree, that this compromise was meant to be the last word on the subject and reflects Chaucer's own opinion. On this score I am skeptical: there is something faintly ludicrous about the Franklin's literal-minded characters and the fantastical situation they get involved in. This seems somewhat to discredit the neat finality of the Franklin's proposal; and indeed the Franklin's own character—he is ostentatious about his wealth and dreadfully keen on "gentilesse"—makes him an unlikely mouthpiece for serious views. His idea of marriage is different from the old conventional one of the aristocrats or from the ironic one we would expect of Chaucer. And the husband in his tale does in fact give stern orders to the wife when things get difficult. On the other hand, the value he puts upon mutual concession in marriage was to become the middle-class ideal, and still is. If Chaucer did not agree with it, he at least saw it coming.

If the Franklin's Tale is not meant to be a final word on marriage, Chaucer may have intended the Second Nun's Tale (here omitted) to serve that function. It is a statement of the Church's highest ideal of marriage, a chaste marriage in which neither partner has dominance but both submit themselves humbly to the will of God. How seriously Chaucer might have admired this ideal is open to question. It is a nun's conception of marriage, certainly, and its simple piety seems naïve: the husband rushes meekly off on the first night of his honeymoon to get baptized! On the other hand, the Second Nun, like the Nun's Priest, is a faceless figure about whom there is nothing to be discredited. Moreover, this kind of pietistic legend was popular in the Middle Ages and taken seriously. Such stories provided medieval men with ideals against which to measure their conduct. The unreality of the story does not render it absurd but puts it among those works which describe a potentially perfect life in an imperfect world.

(5) If Chaucer has any device for making affirmative statements, not discredited in any way, it is that of putting some tales in a position of finality. We have seen that the Nun's Priest's Tale stands in a final position and represents the disinterested, ironic view which one thinks of as characteristically Chaucerian. And we have seen that the marriage group ends with a tale—either the Franklin's or the Second Nun's—which suggests a final assertion. But the best example is the Parson's Tale, a long prose treatise on penitence which comes at the end of the whole work. It is told by the ideal Parson whose character has no flaw to discredit it, and the tale itself has in it no ironic or ludicrous qualities. This, clearly, is intended as sound "doctrine."

What I have been trying to describe is a principle of unity or wholeness in *The Canterbury Tales*. The work is complete in design but not in execution—the General Prologue provides us with a central conception of the whole, and the tales themselves show principles of grouping and ironic contrast which make them less a string of separate stories and more a structure or design. Part of our difficulty in seeing this design of the whole springs from our own preconceptions about wholeness. To us the unity of a work ought to be "organic"—every part and element should have a function which contributes to one total response. Our own aesthetic predilections are most easily seen, perhaps, in architecture: a modern building is thought good if it seems of a piece, a single conception which can be grasped and felt from any vantage point. Details in such a design must be functional and "integral," not decorative or extraneous. In the same way, our rhetoric is one of "logical" development, topic sentences, transitions, and beginning-middle-end organization. With respect to literature, "organic unity" has been a major conception of criticism since the nineteenth century, and such an idea is reflected in book-trade jargon which seeks "development" and admires what "jells." We prefer a work with "an idea" and tend to scorn what seems "unnecessary" or "unmotivated." But it was not so in the Middle Ages.

The medievals admired detail, digression, and effulgence quite as much as they admired order. They liked details or images to have more than one possible meaning; they were not bothered but delighted by decorative detail which drew attention to itself; and they did not feel that details should be "consistent." On the contrary, they painted realistic and sometimes even lewd drawings in the margins of psalters and prayer books, covered their cathedrals with exquisite carvings often grotesque and earthy, and read romances whose intricate plots led the reader into mazes of happenstance. Their sense of order and structure involved hierarchy and multiplicity in a way that ours does not. They would not have understood what we mean by a "story line," an "artistic whole," even "a work" or "a book." Their rhetoric was one of development by expansion, dilation, set descriptions, "apostrophes," and digressions. The kind of style they liked—it is sometimes called "gothic"—is not unfamiliar to us, for we continue to admire the gothic cathedrals for their effulgence of design and minutiae of detail as well as for their overall structure. And if we could manage to revive in ourselves something like the gothic sensibility, it would help us understand *The Canterbury Tales* as it was meant to be understood.

The medievals would not have seen a contradiction in the earthy content of some tales and the idealistic affirmations of others. To them it would have seemed natural and proper to end a work with a religious utterance; they would not have felt that it "cancelled out" anything. There is probably a parallel in Chaucer's Retraction. It is almost certainly authentic and would have been conventional. That Chaucer in "revoking" his secular works expected them to be destroyed or unread is out of the question; but he probably did mean that he wished, looking back, to be remembered and held accountable for those works which contained "moralitee and devocioun." Even so, he reminds us that the Bible says, "All that is written is written for our doctrine." Probably from this viewpoint the medieval reader would have looked back upon the "enditings of worldly vanitees" with an understanding of their real, if limited, value. "Mirth" and "solace" would always give way before "doctrine" and "sentence"—in the end.

The best but most complicated example of our trouble in relating parts to the whole is the Pardoner's Tale. Of all the tales, it is the one hardest to find a place for. Evidently it was, at the time of Chaucer's death, in a manuscript fragment along with the Physician's Tale (which precedes it); but this fragment stands in no relation to any other, and can go in three possible places. (To us this seems regrettable and makes the work unfinished; to the medievals it would have seemed a more relative matter, for they were accustomed to unfinished works—their cathedrals and their manuscripts being notable examples.)

The Pardoner's Prologue and Tale are a sermon. He gives a demonstration of how he preaches in order to dupe the "lewed" people and win silver from them. Arch-hypocrite, perverter of religion, preyer upon piety and simplicity—all these abuses may justly be heaped upon him. There is something monstrous and diabolical in his cynical antisermon; yet it is a magnificent performance—one can hardly fail to be delighted by his intelligence, his articulateness, and his outrageous guile. He lures and challenges us, almost mocks us, with his cleverness: he is at once charming and abhorrent, comic and terrifying. The Host addresses him derisively "thou bel amy"; the "gentils" cry out that he must tell no ribaldry. From the General Prologue we have learned of his immorality; but we have also learned something far more revealing—what was, or so he must have hoped, his secret. He is a eunuch. The entire physical description suggests this in detail. Strange and frightening he might seem to anyone, with his beardless face, his stringy flaxen hair, his piping voice. To the medievals eunuchry seemed a kind of abomination, and they used it to symbolize the deprival of God's grace. Hence the Pardoner's physical deformity is a symbol and counterpart of his moral depravity. And his concealed anguish and guilt is a deeper and more spiritual secret, revealed only at the end of his tale.

In short, he is a grotesque figure—gargoylelike, misshapen, hideously comic. Yet he is here in *The Canterbury Tales,* and his prologue and tale are among the best. He tells the pilgrims, "For though myself be a full vicious man,/A moral tale yet I you telle can." And this he does, preaching convincingly against avarice—his purpose, of course, to get fat offerings. His prologue is itself a confession—or anticonfession, for in it he boasts of his evil. His tale is, like his own story, one of divine retribution. He is the portrait of a man wallowing with uneasy and anguished braggadocio in his own depravity. But among perverters of the Way, he is an artist, an evil genius.

When his sermon is over, a puzzling incident occurs. "And lo, sirs, thus I preeche," he ends, and adds what seems a heartfelt blessing: "may Jesus Christ grant you His pardon, for that is best, I will not deceive you." At once, perhaps embarrassed by this outpouring of generous feeling, he turns about and tries to inveigle them into buying his pardons anyway! It is a master fraud's effort to administer a wondrous coup de grâce—to confront, challenge, and swindle them all in a last glorious mockery. And, in this effort, he looks about and lights on the Host as an ally:

> For he is most envoluped in sinne.
> Come forth, sir Host, and offer first anon,
> And thou shalt kiss the relics everichon,
> Ye, for a grote—unbuckle anon thy purs.
> (614–17)

But the Host, offended, hurls at him an enormous and gross insult—"I wish I had your balls in my hand, I'd cut them off." Needless to say he has hit the Pardoner's most vulnerable point, and the Pardoner lapses into angry silence. The Host avows that he will not "play" with an angry man. Then the

Knight comes forth—the pilgrims are now laughing—and bids them embrace and be merry again. They do so, and the incident is allowed to lapse into the greater design of *The Canterbury Tales*. "Anon they kist, and riden forth hir waye."

Gross and outrageous as the Pardoner is, he seems in the end deflated, mysterious, and sad. Here Chaucer's urbane tolerance and his Christian charity meet. He condemns neither the Host for his cruelty nor the Pardoner for his depravity. We do not see the real feeling of either which lurks beneath the surface of their peacemaking. They become pilgrims again, seekers of the Way, on which the Parson in a true sermon is soon to counsel them. We are brought off at a distance, from which they are no longer "round" or realistic characters, but figures in a design. It is the most intense moment on the pilgrimage, and the final note of forgiveness, which is profoundly touching, matches the final penitential closing of *The Canterbury Tales* itself. Pardoners sell forgiveness, which is best. Yet the tale tricks every reader into the momentary sin of failing to pardon; a critic with such deep human understanding as Kittredge could conclude that the Pardoner was the "one lost soul" on the pilgrimage. But, as Chaucer makes us see, this is for God to decide. The two angry pilgrims embrace in a token of forgiveness *and riden forth hir waye.* In that moment, if at any single point in the work, we catch the profoundly comic and forgiving spirit of Geoffrey Chaucer.

—Donald R. Howard

A NOTE ON THIS EDITION

The text, though eclectic, is indebted especially to *The Text of the Canterbury Tales,* eds. J. M. Manly and Edith Rickert (8 vols., Chicago, 1940), a work of inestimable value to all editors. Paragraphing and punctuation are my own.

The spelling is normalized, and made modern as far as is consistent with Middle English pronunciation. I have attempted, as much as common sense allows, to adopt uniform spellings for Middle English words rather than keep the helter-skelter variants of Middle English manuscripts. From such variants I have chosen that spelling most like standard modern spelling (e.g., *had* for "hadde," *find* for "fynd," *hert* for "herte"). Where Middle English had alternate pronunciations in Chaucer's dialect, I have often selected the pronunciation whose spelling approximates modern spelling (e.g., *saw,* not "sawgh"); but I have tried to preserve dialect doublets where Chaucer used them to good advantage. I have tried to introduce no spellings which are exclusively modern (thus *heer* rather than "hair," *greet* rather than "great," *throt* rather than "throat"); and to alter no spellings which could affect pronunciation (thus *wol* rather than "will," *namore* rather than "no more," *suster* rather than "sister").

The final *-e* is retained only under these conditions: (1) when it is pronounced (see pp. xlvii–xlix); (2) when the more nearly modern spelling ends in *-e* (as in *mine* or *have;* or in *there,* spelled in the modern way except when it means "where"); (3) when its omission might cause confusion with similar words or other pronunciations (thus *binethe,* because it looks more like modern "beneath," whereas *bineth* suggests a verb form); and (4) when it helps suggest the length of the preceding vowel (e.g., *speke,* not "spek" lest it suggest the pronunciation "speck").

Since perfect consistency is not possible, there remain in this text enough spelling variants to introduce the student to the mysteries of Middle English orthography. For example, words like *ordre* are so spelled when they seem to elide with the following word. Many old spellings are kept to preserve a rhyme or a prosodic effect. And of course variants like *land/lond, widow/widwe,* or *were/weren* themselves reflect variants in the speech of Chaucer's London.

I am much indebted to the principles and sentiments of E. T. Donaldson, *Chaucer's Poetry* (New York, 1958), pp. iii–vi, though I have gone further in simplifying spelling. My purpose was not to preserve the appearance of Middle English on the page, nor to enforce a needless consistency, but by eliminating as best I could any nonfunctional old spellings to make a Middle English text which the student or general reader can read with ease and pronounce with accuracy.

—D.R.H.

ON PRONOUNCING CHAUCER

Pronouncing Chaucer's English as he pronounced it preserves rhythm and rhymes and brings out the richness of sound which distinguishes his verse. Mispronounced with modern sounds, Chaucer's poetry loses much of its prosodical energy and variousness. Although we cannot know certainly what English sounded like in fourteenth-century London, we can make a reasonable reconstruction from such evidence as rhymes or puns, and from the overall history of English pronunciation. The spelling in the present text is normalized or standardized as an aid to reading and pronouncing. The following rules of thumb will help.

1. *Pronounce all consonants.* Spelling was not standardized in Chaucer's time but roughly phonetic: people wrote what they expected to hear. Thus *knight* was pronounced with a *k* at the beginning, and with *gh* pronounced like German *ch*. *Folk* had an *l* pronounced, and *write* a *w*. Note also that *ch* was always pronounced as in *church;* and *r* was trilled or flapped, as it is today in parts of Britain. In words of French origin, there are two exceptions: initial *h* (as in *honour*) was not pronounced, and *gn* (as in *sign*) was pronounced *n*.

2. *Pronounce final -e at the end of a line, and elsewhere as rhythm requires.* Chaucer probably did not pronounce final -*e* in everyday speech, but he used it for poetical purposes. At the end of a line it is always pronounced. It has the reduced sound "uh" (as we pronounce the *e* in "mechanic" or "waited"). There are other syllabic *e*'s, not final, which may be pronounced—e.g., bath*e*d, cropp*e*s, Eng*e*lond.

As an aid to learning how syllabic *e*'s work in the scan-

sion of Chaucer's verse, the *e*'s which should be pronounced
(but are not pronounced in modern English) have been
marked in the General Prologue in the following manner:

> In all the orders four is none that kan
> So much of daliaunce and fair langage̲.
> He hadde̲ made full many a marriage̲
> Of yonge̲ women at his owne̲ cost;
> Unto his ordre he was a noble post.
> Full well beloved and familiar was he
> With frankelains over all in his contree . . .

The careful reader can easily develop an "ear" for Chaucer's
verse with this much assistance; more would be a crutch.
Besides, such marking cannot be authoritative—there are too
many variables. For one thing scholars disagree about the scan-
sion; there is even a small minority who claim the verse scans
without any pronounced *e*'s, and among the vast majority
who agree that some *e*'s must be pronounced no two would
agree on every line. It is not always certain where Chaucer
meant to *write* a final *-e* since scribes who copied the manu-
scripts often added them indiscriminately. And not all those
he *did* write have to be pronounced. The opening line is a
good example:

> Whan that April with his showres soote

The manuscripts favor the spelling "Aprille,"* and a possible
pronunciation of the word puts the accent on the second syl-
lable. Hence the line may read *Whán thăt Ápríl wíth* . . . or
Whán thăt Áprílle wíth . . . (It may even read *Whán thăt
Ápríllĕ wíth* . . . , for it is perfectly possible to have two short
syllables in a metrical foot; here the *-e* would normally be
dropped, but coming before the caesura it might have been
pronounced in a very reduced way or as a plus-juncture.) For

---

* See Robert O. Evans, "Whan that Aprill(e)?," *Notes and Queries*, n.s. IV
(1957), 234–37.

that matter we cannot be absolutely certain if Chaucer said *Whán thăt* or *Whăn thát*. There are other variables as well. Some words may be pronounced in more than one way even in a single dialect (as was possibly the case with April/ Aprill<u>e</u>). Moreover, English has now, and likely had then, four degrees of stress, so that the "weak and strong" stresses of the verse support a more elaborate and variable stress according to the meaning of sentences and the emphasis a performer wants to give them. (Thus above there are maximum stresses on "April," "showres," and "soote.")* Such interpretative emphasis sometimes affects a final *-e;* for example, one can say *Yét hăd hé bŭt lítĕl góld ĭn cóffrĕ* (GP 298) or *Yĕt háddĕ hé . . .* The difference depends on whether you emphasize "yet" or "had," but if you emphasize "had," you need a weak syllable after it. Again, there is nothing to prohibit *two* weak syllables (*Yét háddĕ hé . . .*).

3. *Chaucer has six diphthongs.* A diphthong is two vowel sounds pronounced together as a continuing glide (not two letters in the spelling of a sound)—e.g., the "i" in modern *prize* is a diphthong ("ah-ee"), but "ea" in *meat* is not. In Modern English only some diphthongs are spelled with two letters; in Middle English nearly all were:

---

* See M. Halle and S. J. Keyser, "Chaucer and the Study of Prosody," *College English,* XXVIII (1966), 187–219.

Spelling	Middle English Example	Pronounced as in Modern English
ei, ey, ai, ay	vein, pain, may	"pie"; or better yet, a sound halfway between "pie" and "pay": the vowel of "pat" plus the vowel of "be"
au, aw	cause, draw	"how"
ew	few, lewed, shew, beautee	the vowel of "bet" plus the vowel of "full." The sound occurs mainly in these four words.
ew, u	new, trew, knew, cure	the vowel of "be" plus the vowel of "Luke." (Thus *cure* was pronounced as it is in Modern English.)
oi, oy	boy	"boy"
ou, ow	thought, know	the vowel of "ought" plus the vowel of "full"

(Note: the spelling "ou" or "ow" was not always a diphthong, but sometimes a vowel pronounced like Modern English *root;* thus Middle English *house* would have been pronounced like "hoos.")

The ending -ion (-ioun) was always pronounced in two syllables.

4. *Pronounce vowels with their "continental" values, as in German or French.*
Vowels might be long or short. The distinction refers to the length of time they were held while pronounced, plus the quality of the sound (see chart below). Roughly, vowels were long in stressed syllables unless immediately followed by two or more consonants in the same word.*

* Exceptions: all vowels before *ld* are long, as are *i* and *o* before *mb*, and *i* and *u* before *nd*.

The spellings "e" and "o" each represent two vowel pronunciations, called "open" and "close" (referring to the relative position of the lips while articulating them). The following rules will decide which is which in most cases, though there are exceptions:

Rule of thumb for close and open e: go by the modern spelling. Words spelled with double *e* ("ee") in Modern English (or sometimes "ie" as in "thief") had close *e* in Middle English and were pronounced as in modern "bait"; other long *e*'s were open, and were pronounced as in modern "bed."

Rule of thumb for close and open o: go by the modern pronunciation. Words pronounced in Modern English like *hope, so,* etc. had open *o* in Middle English, and were pronounced as in modern "law"; other long *o*'s were close, and were pronounced as in modern "low."

The Middle English examples in the following table are from the opening lines of the General Prologue. The student would be well advised to memorize the famous lines as a means of practicing.

LONG VOWELS

Sound	Middle English Example	Pronounced as in Modern English
ā	bathed	"father"
close ē	sweet	"bait"
open ē	heeth	"bed"
ī	ins*pired*	"beet"
close ō	roote	"low"
open ō	open	"law"
ū	shoures	"Luke"
[ü	vertu; pronounced as in French *tu;* used for this vowel in words of French origin.]	

SHORT VOWELS

Sound	Middle English Example	Pronounced as in Modern English
ă	whan, hath	"part"
ĕ	yong<u>e</u>	"even"
	hem	"bet"
ĭ	his	"bit"
ŏ	londes, of	"bottle"*
ŭ	sunne	"full"

---

* As pronounced in England and New England, i.e., rounded toward the sound in "bought," not as in American "*bah*ttle."

CHRONOLOGY

1343 (?) Born in London, son of John and Agnes Chaucer; had at least one sister, Catherine. Father and grandfather, wine merchants, both held public office, as Chaucer himself was to do.
Schooling possibly at St. Paul's Cathedral School, London. By the time he reached maturity, he knew Latin, French, and Italian.

1357 Served as a page in the household of Lionel, Earl of Ulster (the King's son), and Elizabeth, Countess of Ulster; this would have been a phase of his education.

1359–60 In France with the English army, was taken prisoner near Reims and released on ransom, to which the King contributed. Returned to England in May, then back to France during peace negotiations, serving as courier.

1361–66 Whereabouts unknown. He may have been for a time with Lionel in Ireland. He may also have been a student at the Inns of Court, where he would have received training in law and finance appropriate to his subsequent career as a public servant.

? Married Philippa Roet. They had a son Thomas and a younger son, Lewis. There are records of an Elizabeth and an Agnes "Chaucy" in the circle of John of Gaunt, possibly daughters of the poet.

1366 In Spain, probably on diplomatic mission.

1367 In the service of King Edward III; enrolled among the Esquires of the Royal Household. Beginning about this time and for the remainder of his life, Chaucer was in contact with the important people of his age, both on the continent and at home, among them the chief poets of his day.

1368   Abroad in the King's service.

1369   In France, in military service, probably with John of Gaunt on a campaign in Picardy. Throughout this period of his life Chaucer was under the protection of John of Gaunt. Gaunt's wife, the Duchess Blanche, died in this year; Chaucer's *Book of the Duchess* is an elegy to her.

1370   Abroad in the King's service.

During these early years Chaucer wrote some of his shorter works, such as the *ABC* and lyrics based on French models. Probably translated part of the *Romaunt of the Rose*.

1372–73   In Italy, to negotiate with Genoa about the use of an English port for commerce; visited Florence; undoubtedly bought some Italian books, among them Dante's *Divine Comedy*. From this period can be dated the influence of Italian literature on Chaucer. *The House of Fame* begun about this time, unfinished; *Anelida;* two tales later to show up in *Canterbury Tales* likely begun now—the legend of St. Cecilia (Second Nun's Tale) and the "tragedies" of the Monk's Tale.

1374   Took up residence in London at Aldgate (May). Appointed Controller of Customs and Subsidy of wools, skins, and hides in Port of London (June). Enjoyed great financial prosperity.

1376   On mission of secret service to the King.

1377   In Flanders on secret mission for the King; in France, in connection with negotiations for peace. Coronation of Richard II (June 22). The new King confirmed Chaucer's office as Controller of Customs.

In France, evidently to negotiate a marriage between King Richard and the daughter of the King of France.

1378   In Italy (Lombardy) to secure help in the war
        with France. Probably from this trip he became
        acquainted with the work of Petrarch and Boc-
        caccio.

1380   Released by one Cecily Chaumpaigne from legal
        action *"de raptu meo"*; it is not known whether
        raptu here means "rape" or "abduction" nor is it
        known what, if anything, Chaucer had to do with
        the case.

1380–86 *Parliament of Fowls* written; *Palamon* (the ante-
        cedent of the Knight's Tale); translation of Bo-
        ethius. Was writing various poems and ballads and
        working on *Troilus and Criseyde.* Began *Legend
        of Good Women* possibly at request of the new
        Queen, continued working on it for some years in
        a desultory way before abandoning it.

1382   Appointed Controller of the Petty Customs on
        wines and other merchandise.

1385   Received permission to have a deputy in the
        wool custom; appointed Justice of the Peace in
        Kent and took up at least partial residence there,
        probably at Greenwich.

1386–87 *Troilus and Criseyde* completed.

1386–89 Ended service in the Customs and left the house
        in Aldgate; the reason is unknown (the hostility
        of Gloucester toward the King's appointees has
        been suggested). Fell into debt.

1386   Appointed Knight of the Shire; sat in Parliament
        only the one year, was not reappointed. The of-
        fice was evidently secured by the King's influ-
        ence, but Gloucester and his adherents now
        began to gain control over the young King.

1387 (?) Death of his wife.
        In Calais on official mission, its purpose unknown.
        During this period he was working on the Gen-
        eral Prologue and the earlier Canterbury Tales.
        The idea of writing "some comedye" is men-
        tioned at the end of *Troilus and Criseyde.*

1389–91   Richard II came of age; appointed Chaucer Clerk of the King's Works, an important office. He was in charge of royal palaces, chapels, parks, etc. Resigned commission in 1391, his reason unknown. Had many workmen under him on various projects, handled large amounts of money. The government owed him a considerable sum when he turned in his accounts. In September 1390, was twice robbed and once assaulted by the same band of robbers, public funds being involved.

1391   Appointed Deputy Forester of the royal forest of North Petherton; his son Thomas was later appointed to the same post.

1391–92   *Treatise on the Astrolabe.*

1393–1400 Worked on *The Canterbury Tales* plus a few minor poems, e.g., "Envoy to Bukton" (ca. 1396), "Complaint to his Purse" (its envoy written in 1399, addressed to new King Henry IV). It is very difficult to determine the order in which *The Canterbury Tales* was written. Those written earlier were doubtless revised. Chaucer worked on a number of poems at once, leaving many unfinished. There is evidence that he changed his mind several times about which pilgrim should tell which tale; and the order of the tales was never definitively settled.

1399   Coronation of Henry IV. Chaucer's annuities renewed, additional annuity of forty marks granted. Took long-term lease on house in garden of Westminster Abbey. Was engaged in "arduous and urgent matters" in the King's service.

1400   Died October 25; buried in "poet's corner," Westminster Abbey.

SELECTED
CANTERBURY TALES

THE GENERAL PROLOGUE

Whan that April with his showres soote°
The drought of March hath perced to the roote
And bathed every vein in swich licour,°
Of which vertu° engendred is the flowr;
Whan Zephyrus,° eek,° with his sweete breeth   5
Inspired° hath in every holt and heeth°
The tender croppes,° and the yonge sunne
Hath in the Ram his halve course y-runne,°
And smalle fowles° maken melodye
That sleepen all the night with open ye   10
(So pricketh hem Nature in hir corages°),
Than longen folk to goon on pilgrimages,
And palmers for to seeken straunge strondes°
To ferne halwes,° kouth° in sundry londes:
And specially, from every shires ende   15
Of Engelond, to Canterbury they wende,
The holy blissful martyr° for to seeke

---

1 **his showres soote** its sweet showers   3 **swich licour** such moisture
4 **Of which vertu** by whose power   5 **Zephyrus** the west wind, prev-
alent in spring according to tradition   5 **eek** also   6 **Inspired** breathed
into   6 **holt and heeth** wood and heath (i.e., land with trees and land
without trees)   7 **croppes** twigs   7–8 **yonge sunne . . . y-runne** the
sun at the beginning of its yearly course, past Aries ("the Ram"), the
first sign of the Zodiac. "Half course" evidently means the second half,
which falls in April   9 **fowles** birds   11 **corages** hearts. So Nature
urges them in their hearts to make melody   13 **palmers . . . strondes**
experienced pilgrims (long) to seek out foreign shores   14 **To ferne
halwes** to distant shrines   14 **kouth** known   17 **blissful martyr**
blessed martyr, St. Thomas à Becket, murdered at Canterbury in 1170.
As a saint he would be in eternal "bliss." His shrine was the object of
the most popular pilgrimage

That hem hath holpen whan that they were sek<u>e</u>.°
    Befell that in that seson on a day,
20 In Southwerk at the Tabard° as I lay,
Redy to wenden° on my pilgrima<u>ge</u>
To Canterbury, with full° devout cora<u>ge</u>,
At night was come into that hostelry<u>e</u>
Well nine and twenty° in a compaigny<u>e</u>
25 Of sundry folk, by aventure° y-fall<u>e</u>
In fellowship, and pilgrims were they all<u>e</u>
That toward Canterbury wolden° rid<u>e</u>.
The chambres and the stables weren wid<u>e</u>,°
And well we weren esed att<u>e</u> best<u>e</u>.°
30 And shortly, whan the sunne was to rest<u>e</u>,
So had I spoken with hem everichon°
That I was of hir fellowship anon,°
And mad<u>e</u> forward° erly for to ris<u>e</u>
To take our way, there as I you devis<u>e</u>.°
35   But natheless,° while I have time and spac<u>e</u>,
Ere that I ferther in this tal<u>e</u> pac<u>e</u>,°
Me thinketh it accordant to resoun
To tell<u>e</u> you all the condicioun°
Of ech of hem, so as it seem<u>ed</u> me,
40 And which they weren, and of what degree,°
And eek in what array that they were inn<u>e</u>;

---

18 **seke** sick   20 **Tabard** an inn in London just south of the Thames. It actually existed. A tabard (short coat) would have been depicted on the sign outside. The building burned down in 1676; there is a small pub on the site today called by the same name   21 **wenden** go   22 **full** very   24 **Well nine and twenty** as many as twenty-nine. There would have been thirty pilgrims including Chaucer himself, but not including the Host, who tells no story (see line 814). By actual count this makes twenty-nine, but the group is joined by the Canon's Yeoman   25 **aventure** chance   27 **wolden** would, i.e., intended to   28 **wide** capacious   29 **well . . . beste** we were well entertained in the best way   31 **with . . . everichon** with every one of them   32 **anon** right away   33 **And . . . forward** and (we) made an agreement   34 **there . . . devise** as I shall describe for you   35 **natheless** nevertheless   36 **pace** pass   38 **condicioun** position in society   40 **And . . . degree** and which was which, and of what social rank

And at a knight, than, wol° I first beginne:
   A KNIGHT there was—and that a worthy man—
That fro the time that he first began
To riden out,° he loved chivalrye,   45
Trouth and honour, freedom and curteisye.°
Full worthy was he in his lordes werre,°
And thereto had he ridden, no man ferre,°
As well in Christendom as in hethenesse,°
And ever honoured for his worthinesse.   50
At Alisandre° he was whan it was wonne;
Full ofte time he had the bord bigonne°
Aboven alle naciouns in Pruce;°
In Lettow° had he reised,° and in Ruce°—
No Christen man so oft of his degree.   55
In Gernade° at the seege eek had he be
Of Algezir, and riden in Belmarye.°
At Lyeis° was he and at Satalye°
Whan they were won, and in the Greete See
At many a noble armee had he be.°   60
At mortal battails had he been fifteene,

---

42 **wol** will   45 **riden out** go on knightly expeditions, i.e., to wars, crusades, etc.   45–46 **chivalrye ... curteisye** chivalry (the Knight's unwritten code of conduct): truth (loyalty to one's obligations), honor (a sense of honorable dealings), courtesy ("courtliness," observance of social forms). The phrases sum up qualities ideally expected of knights 47 **werre** war   48 **ferre** farther   49 **hethenesse** lands governed by heathens   51 **Alisandre** Alexandria; it was won in 1365. This and the other campaigns mentioned had taken place within the past forty-five years. All were religious campaigns against the infidels. It is unlikely that Chaucer had an actual knight in mind: the passage seems rather to present an idealized portrait of a high-minded adventurer   52 **the bord bigonne** sat at the head of a table, in the place of honor, presumably with the Teutonic Knights during a campaign against the pagans in Prussia   53 **Pruce** Prussia   54 **Lettow** Lithuania   54 **reised** fought   54 **Ruce** Russia   56 **Gernade** Grenada. The campaign in 1344 resulted in the capture of the city Algeciras from the Moors of Spain   57 **Belmarye** in north Africa near modern Morocco   58 **Lyeis** near Antioch, won from the Turks in 1367   58 **Satalye** Adalia 59–60 **Greete ... he be** he had been on many an armed expedition ("armada") in the Mediterranean

And foughten for our faith at Tramissene
In listes thries,° and ay slain his fo.
This ilke° worthy Knight had been also
65 Sometime with the lord of Palatye
Again another hethen in Turkye.°
And evermore he had a sovereign pris;°
And though that he were worthy, he was wis,°
And of his port° as meek as is a maide.
70 He never yet no villainy ne saide
In all his life unto no manner wight.°
He was a veray, parfit gentil° knight.
    But for to tellen you of his array,
His horse were goode but *he* was not gay.°
75 Of fustian he wered a gipoun°
All bismotered with his habergeoun,°
For he was late y-come from his viage,
And wente for to doon his pilgrimage.
    With him there was his son, a yong SQUIER,°
80 A lover and a lusty° bacheler
With lockes crull° as they were laid in presse.°

63 **listes thries** three times in single hand-to-hand combats (as a cham-
pion representing his side). This may have been an old-fashioned and
romantic practice by Chaucer's time   64 **ilke** same   66 **another he-
then in Turkye** the exact battle is not known. The line may suggest an
alliance of Christians with one heathen ruler against another; but prob-
ably "another" means other than the army encountered at Tramissene
67 **sovereign pris** distinctive excellence and renown   68 **though . . .
wis** though he was valiant, he was prudent   69 **port** bearing   70–
71 **He . . . wight** a very emphatic statement with its four negatives: "he
never before said anything rude in his whole life to any person of any
kind"   72 **veray, parfit gentil** true, perfect. "Gentle" has a broad
meaning—the quality of a gentleman   74 **His . . . gay** his horses were
good, but he himself was not fancily dressed   75 **gipoun** tunic worn
under the coat of mail; "fustian" was cotton and linen   76 **haber-
geoun** coat of mail. It has stained (bismotered) the tunic underneath
79 **squier** squire—a "bachelor"—i.e., a young noble aspiring to
knighthood. Squires were trained in a noble household not necessarily
their father's. They learned all the arts pertinent to aristocracy, from
the conventions of "courtly" love to the art of carving meat; but war-
fare was their principal concern   80 **lusty** vigorous   81 **crull**
curly   81 **as . . . presse** as if they had been put in a hair-curler

Of twenty yeer of age he was, I guesse.
Of his stature he was of even° lengthe,
And wonderly deliver,° and of greet strengthe.
And he hadde been sometime in chivachye°   85
In Flandres, in Artois, and Picardye,
And born him well, as of so litel space,°
In hope to standen in his lady° grace.
    Embrouded° was he, as it were a meede,°
All full of freshe flowres, white and rede;   90
Singing he was, or floiting,° all the day—
He was as fresh as is the month of May.
Short was his gown, with sleeves long and wide.
Well coud he sit on horse and faire° ride.
He coude songes make, and well endite,°   95
Joust, and eek daunce, and well purtray° and write.
So hot he loved that by nightertale°
He slept namore than doth a nightingale.°
Curteis he was, lowly,° and servicable,
And carf biforn his fader at the table.   100
    A YEMAN° had he and servants namo°
At that time, for him liste ride so°—

83 **even** medium, average   84 **deliver** agile   85 **chivachye** expedition
of cavalry. The places named in the next line suggest a so-called crusade
of 1383, not entirely a reputable one because of plundering. This does not
reflect on the Squire's character, but may suggest that knightly exploits
were not what they used to be. The campaign was recent; the place was
close to home and Flanders was somewhat of a joke, being a nation of
burgers. In short, he had as yet little experience of great exploits
87 **as . . . space** considering how short a period of time was involved
88 **lady** lady's   89 **Embrouded** embroidered   89 **as . . . meede** like a
meadow. There is a suggestion that he is dressed in an unusually sumptu-
ous way   91 **floiting** playing the flute, or perhaps whistling   94 **faire**
beautifully, well   95 **coude . . . endite** could write melodies and com-
pose words to them   96 **purtray** paint, draw   97 **nightertale** nighttime
98 **nightingale** nightingales sing all night during the mating season,
hence are traditionally associated with lovers   99 **lowly** modest
101 **Yeman** yeoman, a servant to the knight and his son. He is above the
rank of an ordinary servant and acts (see line 117) as a forester or game-
keeper, perhaps having a small plot of land for his own   101 **namo** no
more   102 **for . . . so** for it pleased him to ride in this way. *Liste* is an
impersonal verb

And he was clad in cote and hood of greene.
A sheef of pecock arrwes, bright and keene,°
105 Under is belt he bare full thriftily.°
Well coud he dress his tackle° yemanly:
His arrwes drouped not with fetheres lowe,
And in his hand he bare a mighty bowe.
A not-heed° had he with a brown visage.
110 Of woodecraft well koud° he all the usage.
Upon his arm he bare a gay bracer,°
And by his side a swerd and a buckler,
And on that other side a gay daggere,
Harneised° well and sharp as point of spere.
115 A Christophre° on his brest of silver sheene.
An horn he bare, the baudrik° was of greene.
A forster° was he soothly, as I guesse.
　　There was also a nun, a PRIORESSE,
That of hir smiling was full simple and coy.°
120 Hir greetest ooth was but by Seinte Loy;°
And she was cleped Madame Eglentine.
Full well she song the service divine,
Entuned in hir nose full seemely.
And French she spak full fair and fetisly,°
125 After the scole of Stratford-atte-Bowe—
For French of Paris was to hir unknowe.
At mete° well y-taught was she withalle:
She let no morsel from hir lippes falle,

104 **keene** sharp   105 **thriftily** carefully, properly   106 **dress his tackle** take care of his arrows; the feathers are trim, which gives them a clear flight   109 **not-heed** close-cut hair   110 **koud** knew   111 **bracer** leather guard for the forearm to protect it from the bowstring   114 **Harneised** fastened to a handle   115 **Christophre** medal of St. Christopher   116 **baudrik** baldric, a belt over one shoulder to hold his hunting-horn   117 **forster** forester   119 **coy** modest   120 **Seinte Loy** St. Elegius, called Eloy in French. St. Loy had once refused to swear, so an oath by him was in effect no oath at all. He was also a fashionable saint in elegant circles of the time. Note that the Prioress's own name is very elegant (Eglentine means "sweetbriar"), as are her table manners   124 **fetisly** fastidiously—but she speaks with an English accent. The English upper class knew French   127 **mete** meals. The following lines give a notion of medieval table manners

Ne wet hir fingers in hir sauce deepe;
Well coud she carry a morsel, and well keepe°   *130*
That no drop ne fill upon hir brest.
In curteisy was set full muchel hir lest.°
Hir overlippe wiped she so clene
That in hir cup there was no ferthing° seene
Of grece, whan she drunken had hir draughte.   *135*
Full seemely after hir mete she raughte.°
And sikerly° she was of greet disport,°
And full plesaunt, and amiable of port;°
And pained hir to countrefete cheere
Of court,° and to been estatlich of mannere,°   *140*
And to been holden digne° of reverence.
    But, for to speken of hir conscience,°
She was so charitable and so pitous
She wolde weep if that she saw a mous
Caught in a trap, if it were deed or bledde.   *145*
Of smalle houndes° had she that she fedde
With rosted flesh, or milk and wastel breed;°
But sore wept she if one of hem were deed,
Or if men smote it with a yerde smerte.°
And all was conscience and tender herte.   *150*
    Full seemely hir wimple pinched was,°

---

130 **keepe** see to it   132 **In . . . lest** her pleasure was very much set on
courtly conduct   134 **ferthing** tiny spot   136 **after hir mete she
raughte** she reached for her food   137 **sikerly** certainly   137 **disport**
affability   138 **amiable of port** pleasant in her conduct   139–
40 **pained . . . court** took pains to emulate the manners of the court
140 **estatlich of mannere** dignified in her behavior   141 **digne** worthy
142 **conscience** sensitivity   146 **Of smalle houndes** some little dogs.
"Of" is sometimes used in this partitive way   147 **wastel breed** a fine
bread; her dogs get nothing but the best   149 **with a yerde smerte** with
a stick sharply   151 **Full . . . was** her wimple (white headpiece, going
down about the face and neck) was pleated very attractively. There is
some question whether this was strictly according to the rules. She wears
it off her forehead, has colored beads, keeps dogs, and owns a curious
gold medal, all of which suggests a little tendency toward self-
indulgence. Lowes said she showed "the delightfully imperfect submer-
gence of the woman in the nun"

Hir nose tretis,° hir eyen grey as glass,
Hir mouth full small, and thereto soft and red.
But sikerly she had a fair foreheed—
155 It was almost a spanne° brood, I trowe;
For hardily,° she was not undergrowe.
Full fetis° was hir cloke, as I was war.
Of small coral about hir arm she bar
A pair of bedes, gauded all with greene,°
160 And thereon heng a brooch of gold full sheene,
On which there was first written a crowned *A*,
And after, *Amor vincit omnia.*°
Another NUNNE with hir hadde she
That was hir chapeleyne, and preestes three.°
165   A MONK there was, a fair for the maistrye°—
An outrider, that loved venerye;°
A manly man, to been an abbot able.
Full many a daintee° horse had he in stable,
And whan he rode men might his bridle heere

152 **tretis** graceful—a cliché for ladies' noses. The gray eyes, small mouth, and wide forehead were also standard equipment for beautiful women in medieval romances   155 **spanne** distance from thumb to little finger when the hand is outstretched   156 **hardily** certainly   157 **fetis** neat. Cf. line 124   159 **bedes ... greene** she wears a rosary made of small bits of coral; the larger beads are green   162 **Amor vincit omnia** "Love conquers all." Whether this meant celestial love or earthly love was probably no clearer to the Prioress than to us. At any rate, courtly love was aristocratic. The "crowned A" is likely a royal emblem but otherwise mysterious; one conjecture is that the brooch was a medallion struck for the coronation of Queen Anne (1382)   164 **chapeleyne ... three** the "chapeleyne" is an assistant accompanying her—the "second nun," who tells the legend of St. Cecilia. One priest is the "Nun's Priest" (or perhaps "Nuns' Priest") who tells the tale of Chanticleer. The extra two priests would put the number of pilgrims up to thirty-one (see line 24); however, "preestes three" could mean the Nun's Priest plus the Monk and Friar, whose descriptions follow   165 **fair for the maistrye** a fine one, excellent above all others   166 **outrider ... venerye** one whose duty was to ride about tending the property of the abbey; that he loved "venerye" (hunting) suggests an abuse, for hunting by monks was condemned. Hunting was an aristocratic sport, and the Monk's love of horses and fine clothes is altogether questionable. There is also a sexual suggestion, for "hunting" may hint at hunting women, as "venerye" may suggest Venus   168 **daintee** splendid, valuable

Ginglen in a whistling wind as clere   170
And eek as loud as doth the chapel belle.
Ther as° this lord was keeper of the celle,°
The rule of Saint Maure or of Saint Beneit,°
By cause that it was old and somedeel strait°—
This ilke Monk let olde thinges pace   175
And held after the newe world the space.°
He yaf not of that text a pulled hen°
That saith that hunters been not holy men,
Ne that a monk, whan he is reccheless,°
Is likned til a fish that is waterless   180
(This is to sayn, a monk out of his cloister);
But thilke° text held he not worth an oystre.
And I said his opinion was good:°
What° shold he study and make himselven wood°
Upon a book in cloistre alway to poure,   185
Or swinken° with his handes and laboure,
As Austin bit?° How shall the world be served?
Let Austin have his swink to him reserved!
Therefore he was a prickasour° aright.
Greyhounds he had as swift as fowl in flight.   190
Of pricking and of hunting for the hare°
Was all his lust,° for no cost wold he spare.

172 **Ther as** where   172 **keeper of the celle** prior of a smaller mon-
astery subordinate to a great abbey   173 **The rule ... Beneit** St.
Benedict, and St. Maur (his disciple), had written the oldest monastic
rules. The line suggests that the monk is a Benedictine   174 **somedeel
strait** somewhat strict   175–76 **let ... space** let old things (like the
rule of St. Benedict) pass, and took up with the new world in the
meantime   177 **pulled hen** "he didn't give a plucked hen for that text
which says . . ." Cf. line 182. A plucked hen would be of little value to
him, compared with a fat swan (line 206)   179 **reccheless** careless (of
his duties)   182 **thilke** that   183 **I . . . good** here the reader begins to
see that Chaucer's role as a wide-eyed, enthusiastic observer is ironic.
Obviously Chaucer did not approve of these abuses   184 **What** why
184 **wood** mad   186 **swinken** work   187 **As Austin bit** as St. Au-
gustine commands   189 **prickasour** hard rider; but doubtless it is a
pun   191 **pricking . . . hare** pricking was tracking a rabbit by his
prints ("pricks"); since rabbits were symbols of lechery and hunting
was open to double meaning, there is doubtless a pun here as well
192 **lust** pleasure

I saw his sleeves y-purfiled at the hand
With gris,° and that the finest of a land;
195 And for to festne° his hood under his chin
He had of gold wrought a full curious pin—
A love-knot in the greeter end there was.
His heed was bald, that shone as any glass,
And eek his face, as he had been anoint.
200 He was a lord full fat and in good point:°
His eyen steep,° and rolling in his heed,
That stem_ed as a furnais of a leed,°
His boot_es souple, his horse in greet estat—
Now certainly he was a fair prelat.
205 He was not pale as a forpin_ed° ghost;
A fat swan loved he best of any rost.
His palfrey° was as brown as is a berry_e.

     A FRERE° there was, a wanton and a merry_e,
A limitour,° a full solempn_e° man.
210 In all the orders four is none than kan°
So much of daliaunce° and fair langag_e.
He hadd_e made full many a marriag_e
Of yong_e women at his own_e cost;°
Unto his ordre he was a noble post.
215 Full well beloved and familier was he

193–94 **y-purfiled . . . with gris** edged with expensive fur
195 **festne** fasten 200 **in good point** in good shape 201 **steep**
sparkling 202 **stemed . . . leed** sparkled like a fire under a cooking-
pot 205 **forpined** pined away, wasted 207 **palfrey** riding horse
208 **Frere** friar. There were four mendicant orders—the Dominicans
("Blackfriars"), Franciscans ("Greyfriars"), Carmelites ("Whitefri-
ars"), and Augustinian friars ("Austin" friars, who also wore black).
Unlike monks, who remained in cloisters, the friars went among the
people, begging for their sustenance; all surplus was given to the poor
and sick. The noble idea—that of St. Francis—easily lent itself to
abuse, and by Chaucer's time friars were widely criticized 209 **limi-
tour** friar with the assigned right to beg in a particular district ("limit")
209 **solempne** impressive 210 **kan** knows 211 **daliaunce** chitchat,
usually flirtatious 212–13 **made . . . cost** arranged many a marriage
of young women free of charge; the line implies that he seduced them
first

With frankelains° over all in his contree,
And with worthy women of the town.
For he had power of confessioun
As said himself, more than a curat,
For of his ordre he was licenciat.°   220
Full sweetly herde he confessioun
And plesant was his absolucioun;
He was an esy man to yive penaunce
There as he wist to have a good pitaunce.°
For unto a povre ordre for to yive   225
Is signe that a man is well y-shrive:°
For if he yaf, he dorste make avaunt,°
He wiste that a man was repentaunt;
For many a man so hard is of his herte
He may not weep although him sore smerte: 230
Therefore, instede of weeping and prayeres,
Men mote° yive silver to the povre freres.
    His tippet was ay farsed° full of knives
And pinnes, for to yiven faire wives.
And certainly he had a murry note:°   235
Well coud he sing and playen on a rote;°
Of yeddings he bare outrely the pris.°
His necke white was as the flowr-de-lis.
Thereto he strong was as a champioun.
He knew the taverns well in every town,   240
And every hostiler and tappestere,°

216 **frankelains** wealthy landowners   220 **licenciat** his power of hearing confessions; this license given to friars put them in conflict with parish priests (curates) because it deprived the latter of some revenue. It is true that friars had power to absolve certain serious sins which a parish priest would normally refer to the bishop   224 **There as ... pitaunce** where he knew he would get a good donation; hence he is nice to people when they confess, doesn't scold them, and gives easy penances   226 **y-shrive** confessed   227 **dorste make avaunt** dared to state   232 **mote** should   233 **tippet was ay farsed** hood was always stuffed   235 **murry note** fine singing voice   236 **rote** stringed instrument played by plucking   237 **Of yeddings ... pris** for popular songs he won the prize hands down   241 **hostiler and tappestere** innkeeper and barmaid

Bet than a lazar or a beggestere.°
For unto swich a worthy man as he
Accorded not, as by his facultee,°
245 To have with sike lazars acquaintaunce:
It is not honest, it may not avaunce,°
For to deelen with no swich poraille,°
But all with rich, and sellers of vitaille!
And over all there as profit shold arise—
250 Curteis he was, and lowly of servise.°
    There was no man nowhere so vertuous;
He was the beste begger in his hous.
For though a widow hadde not a shoe,
So plesant was his *In principio*°
255 Yet wold he have a ferthing ere he wente.
His purchase was well better than his rente.°
And rage he coud as it were right a whelpe!°
In love-days° there coud he muchel helpe,
For there he was not like a cloisterer,
260 With a thredbare cope,° as is a poor scholer,
But he was like a maister° or a pope.
Of double worsted was his semicope,
That rounded as a bell out of the presse.
Somewhat he lipsed for his wantounesse°
265 To make his English sweet upon his tonge.
And in his harping, whan that he had songe,
His eyen twinkled in his heed aright

---

242 **Bet ... beggestere** better than a leper or a beggar-woman
244 **as by his facultee** for a man of his position   246 **It ... avaunce**
it isn't respectable, it won't get you anywhere   247 **poraille** poor
people, "rabble"   249–50 **And ... servise** and in all places where
profit would arise.... Note that the last phrase is used of the Squire
(line 99)   254 **In principio** first words of the Gospel according to St.
John, a great favorite of friars when entering a house   256 **His ...
rente** (?) what he got in these questionable ways was much better than
what he got legitimately   257 **And ... whelp** and he could live it up
just like a puppy   258 **love-days** days for settling disputes out of
court; friars often acted as arbiters   260 **cope** cloak   261 **maister** the
master's degree had enormous prestige then   264 **lipsed ... wantou-
nesse** lisped as a fetching mannerism. Lisping, like a white neck (line
238), was thought to suggest lechery

As doon the sterres in the frosty night.
This worthy limitour was cleped Huberd.

   A MARCHANT was there with a forked beerd,°   270
In motlee,° and hy° on horse he sat;
Upon his heed a Flandrish bever hat,°
His bootes clasped fair and fetisly.
His resons° he spak full solempnely,°
Souning alway the encrees of his winning.°   275
He wold the see were kept for any thing°
Bitwixe Middleburgh and Orewelle.
Well coud he in eschaunge sheeldes selle.°
This worthy man full well his wit bisette;°
There wiste no wight that he was in dette,°   280
So estatly was he of his governaunce°
With his bargains and with his chevisaunce.°
Forsooth he was a worthy man withalle.
But, sooth to sayn, I noot° how men him calle.

   A CLERK° there was of Oxenford also   285
That unto logic hadde long y-go.°

---

270 **forked beerd** the "forked" beard was a fashionable shape for the
bourgeoisie. Chaucer himself wore one   271 **motlee** cloth woven in a
pattern, perhaps a special one denoting the guild of merchants he be-
longed to   271 **hy** high, in a high saddle   272 **Flandrish bever hat**
Flemish hat of beaver fur   274 **resons** views   274 **solempnely** im-
pressively, pompously   275 **Souning . . . winning** always touching
upon the increase in his profits   276 **He . . . thing** he wanted the sea
to be kept safe at all costs. . . . The route was between the Netherlands
and Suffolk; the cargo would have been wool; and the danger was from
pirates   278 **Well . . . selle** he well knew how to sell Crowns in the
money exchanges. "Shields" were gold coins; the merchant made
profit on differences in the rate of exchange. The practice was illegal
279 **his wit bisette** used his head   280 **There . . . dette** no one knew
that he was in debt. (Or, perhaps, "No one knew how much he was in
debt")   281 **estatly . . . governaunce** dignified (i.e., discreet) in do-
ing business   282 **chevisaunce** money-lending   284 **noot** ne wot, i.e.,
don't know   285 **clerk** the clerk is a student at Oxford and thus prepar-
ing for the priesthood; "clerk" has the general sense of "churchman" and
(here) the specific sense of "scholar"   286 **unto logic . . . y-go** had long
since proceeded to the study of logic. Logic was among the last subjects
in the curriculum; later we find he has also studied at Padua—in short
he is comparable to a graduate student or post-doctoral fellow

As leene was his horse as is a rake,
And he was not right fat, I undertake,
But looked hollwe, and thereto sobrely.°
290 Full thredbare was his overest courtepy°—
For he had geten him yet no benefice,
Ne was so worldly for to have office;°
For him was lever have° at his beddes heed
Twenty bookes,° clad in black or red,
295 Of Aristotle and his philosophye,
Than robes rich, or fithel, or gay sautrye.°
But all be that he was a philosophre°
Yet hadde he but litel gold in coffre;
But all that he might of his freendes hente,°
300 On bookes and on lerning he it spente,
And bisily gan for the soules praye
Of hem that yaf him wherewith to scholeye.°
Of study° took he most cure and most heede,
Not oo word spak he more than was neede,
305 And that was said in form and reverence,°
And short and quick,° and full of heigh sentence;°
Souning in moral vertu was his speeche;°
And gladly wold he lern and gladly teeche.

289 **looked . . . sobrely** looked undernourished and, in addition,
grave 290 **overest courtepy** outer short cloak 292 **office** em-
ployment outside the church; "benefice" would be a post in the
church. The line implies that he will indeed become a priest
293 **him . . . have** "it was preferable to him to have" 294 **Twenty
bookes** a huge number, which would have cost roughly the price of
a small house in the city. He does not necessarily have the books,
but would like them 296 **fithel . . . sautrye** fiddle, or handsome
psaltery (also a stringed instrument) 297 **philosophre** a pun, the
word also meant alchemist (alchemy attempted to make gold of
base metals) 299 **hente** get 302 **scholeye** pursue his studies
303 **study** thinking 305 **in form and reverence** with propriety
and modesty 306 **short and quick** concise and to the point
306 **heigh sentence** deep significance 307 **Souning . . . speeche**
what he said reflected moral strength

A SERGEANT OF THE LAWE,° war° and wis,
That often hadde been at the Parvis° 310
There was also, full rich of excellence.
Discreet he was, and of greet reverence—
He seemed swich, his wordes weren so wise.
Justice he was full often in assise
By patent and by plein commissioun.° 315
For his science° and for his heigh renown
Of fees and robes° had he many oon.
So greet a purchasour was nowhere noon;
All was fee simple to him in effect—
His purchasinge might not been infect.° 320
Nowhere so bisy a man as he there nas;
And yet he seemed bisier than he was.
In termes had he caas and doomes alle°
That from the time of King William were falle.
Thereto he coud endite and make a thing,° 325
There coud no wight pinchen at° his writing;
And every statute koud he plein by rote.°

---

309 **Sergeant of the lawe** a very high office. About twenty were appointed
by the King, and from their number were selected the chief baron of the
Exchequer, the judges of the King's court, and the circuit judges. The
portrait is sometimes thought to be a personal satire of Thomas Pynchbek,
Justice of Common Pleas from 1391 to 1396   309 **war** wary,
cautious   310 **Parvis** a porch of St. Paul's Cathedral at which lawyers
met for consultation   314–15 **Justice ... commissioun** the Justices in
Assise were circuit judges who presided in county courts. *By patent* refers
to the "letters patent" from the King making an appointment, and *plein
commissioun* was a statement of full (plein) jurisdiction   316 **science**
knowledge   317 **robes** robes, often very rich ones, were a form of pay-
ment; the King often granted robes to public servants   319–20 **fee sim-
ple ... infect** he purchased land for himself in "fee simple"—i.e., having
outright ownership which would descend to all his heirs male or female;
with his legal knowledge his purchasing could not be invalidated (*infect*)
323 **In ... alle** he could reel off all the cases and decisions ... (but
"terms" may refer to annual law books which he owned)   325 **Thereto ...
thing** moreover, he could draft and draw up a legal document
326 **pinchen at** find a loophole in. The line may be a sly reference to
Thomas Pynchbek   327 **koud ... rote** he knew entirely by memory

He rode but homely in a medlee° cote,
Girt with a ceint° of silk, with barres° smalle.
330 Of his array tell I no lenger tale.
       A FRANKELAIN° was in his compaignye.
White was his beerd as is the dayesye;
Of his complexion he was sanguin.°
Well loved he by the morrwe° a sop in win.°
335 To liven in delit was ever his wone,°
For he was Epicurus' owne sone,
That held opinion that plein delit
Was veray felicitee parfit.°
An householder and that a greet was he—
340 Saint Julian° he was in his contree.
His breed, his ale, was always after oon°—
A better envined° man was never noon.
Withoute bake mete° was never his hous,
Of fish and flesh, and that so plentevous°
345 It snowed in his house of mete° and drinke—
Of alle daintees that men coude thinke.
After the sundry sesons of the yeer
So chaunged he his mete° and his supper.
Full many a fat partrich had he in muwe,°
350 And many a breem, and many a luce in stuwe;°

328 **medlee** woolen cloth, dyed first and then woven in a pattern. His
would have been striped in brown and green   329 **ceint** cincture, sash
329 **barres** metal bars to keep the sash from bunching up   331 **Franke-
lain** Franklins were landowners, the ancestors of "country squires."
Their social position was high   333 **sanguin** in medieval medical
theory a sanguine complexion, resulting from the dominance of blood
over the three other bodily humors, made for a bold, outgoing character
334 **by ... morrwe** in the morning   334 **sop in win** (Fr. *soupe*) a
cake in wine sauce—a delicacy   335 **wone** habit   336–38 **For ...
parfit** Epicurus was thought, wrongly, to have believed in a life of
pleasure   340 **St. Julian** patron saint of hospitality   341 **after oon**
of the same high quality   342 **envined** possessing a wine cellar
343 **bake mete** meat baked in pies—another delicacy   344 **plente-
vous** plentiful   345 **mete** here, "food"   348 **mete** here, "dinner."
Changing diet by seasons was considered posh   349 **muwe** cage
350 **breem ... stuwe** carp and pike in a private fish pond

Woe was his cook but if° his sauce were
Poignant and sharp, and redy all his gere.°
His table dormant in his hall° alway
Stood redy covered all the longe day.
   At sessions there was he lord and sire.°   355
Full ofte time he was knight of the shire.°
An anlaas, and a gipser° all of silk
Heng at his girdle, white as morne milk.
A shireve° had he been, and a contour.°
Was nowhere swich a worthy vavasour.°   360
   An HABERDASHER and a CARPENTER,
A WEBBE, a DYER, and a TAPICER°—
And they were clothed all in oo liveree°
Of a solempne and a greet fraternitee.
Full fresh and new hir gere apiked° was;   365
Hir knives were chaped° not with brass
But all with silver; wrought full clene and well
Hir girdles and hir pouches everydeel.
Well seemed ech of hem a fair burgeis
To sitten in a yeldhall on a dais.°   370
Everich, for the wisdom that he kan,
Was shaply for to been an alderman.°
For catel hadde they enough and rente,°

---

351 **but if** unless   352 **gere** equipment, such as knives   353 **table dormant** a dining table set up in the main room (hall). Also posh; tables were usually removable   355 **sessions . . . sire** he presided over sessions of the Justices of the Peace   356 **knight of the shire** member of Parliament   357 **anlaas, and a gipser** dagger and pouch 359 **shireve** shirereeve, i.e., sheriff: the King's administrator in a county   359 **contour** (?) auditor; part of a sheriff's duties was to collect taxes and account for them   360 **vavasour** minor nobleman, or any man of substance   361–62 **Haberdasher . . . tapicer** the "Five Gildsmen" are of different trades—haberdasher, a dealer in small goods; webbe, a weaver; tapicer, a rug-maker   363 **oo liveree** one livery: the costume presumably of a parish trade guild   365 **apiked** fixed up   366 **chaped** ornamented   369–70 **burgeis . . . dais** a burgess good enough to preside (as an alderman) in a guildhall   372 **alderman** a burgess had to own a certain amount of property to be an alderman, i.e., head of a guild and member of a town council   373 **catel . . . and rente** property and income

And eek hir wives wold it well assente,
375 And elles certain were they to blame:
It is full fair to been y-cleped "Madame,"
And goon to vigilies all bifore,°
And have a mantel royalich y-bore!

A COOK they hadde with hem for the nones,
380 To boil the chickens with the marybones,°
And powdre-marchant tart, and galingale.°
Well coud he know a draught of London ale.
He coude rost, and seeth,° and broil, and frye,
Maken mortreux,° and well bake a pie.°
385 But greet harm was it, as it thoughte me,
That on his shin a mormal° hadde he.
For blankmanger,° that made he with the beste.

A SHIPMAN° was there, woning fer by weste°—
For aught I wot, he was of Dertemouthe.
390 He rode upon a rouncy as he kouthe,°
In a gown of falding° to the knee.
A dagger hanging on a laas had he
About his neck, under his arm adown.
The hot summer had made his hew all brown.
395 And certainly he was a good fellawe!
Full many a draught° of wine had he drawe
Fro Bourdeux-ward, while that the chapman sleep.°

---

377 **vigilies . . . bifore** religious ceremonies on the eve of a holy
day; marching at the head of a procession was an honor, and
their wives are great social climbers   380 **marybones** marrow
bones   381 **powdre-marchant tart, galingale** spices   383 **seeth**
boil   384 **mortreux** a hash or stew   384 **pie** meat pie
386 **mormal** an open sore—unappetizing, but its unsanitary as-
pects could have been overlooked   387 **blankmanger** a main
dish of capon   388 **Shipman** owner and captain of a ship
388 **woning . . . weste** who lived far in the west (Dartmouth was
a major port)   390 **rode . . . kouthe** rode on a small horse as
best he coud   391 **falding** wool   396 **draught** a quantity
drawn from the cask, probably for drinking   397 **while . . .
sleep** while the merchant slept. The merchant sometimes trav-
eled with the cargo; his sleeping could afford a chance for theft,
or at least a drink, from the cargo of wine

Of nice conscience took he no keep.
If that he fought and had the higher hand,
By water he sent hem home to every land.°   400
   But of his craft—to recken well his tides,
His stremes and his daungers him bisides,
His herberwe° and his moon, his lodemenage°—
There nas none swich from Hulle to Cartage.
Hardy he was and wise to undertake.°   405
With many a tempest had his beerd been shake.
He knew alle the havens as they were
Fro Gotland to the Cape of Finistere,
And every crike in Brittain and in Spaine.
His barge y-cleped was the Maudelaine.   410
   With us there was a DOCTOR OF PHYSIC;°
In all this world ne was there none him lik
To speke of physic and of surgerye.
For he was grounded in astronomye;°
He kept° his pacient a full greet deel   415
In houres by his magic naturel;°
Well coud he fortunen the ascendent
Of his images° for his pacient.
He knew the cause of every maladye,
Were it of hot or cold, or moist or drye,°   420
And where engendred and of what humour.
He was a veray parfit practisour.
The cause y-know,° and of his harm the roote,

---

400 i.e., he threw his prisoners overboard   403 **herberwe** harbor
403 **lodemenage** navigation   405 **to undertake** in his ventures and
risks   411 **physic** medicine   414 **astronomye** astrology was part of
medieval medicine   415 **kept** watched—waiting for the propitious
astrological time for treatment   416 **magic naturel** astrology and re-
lated sciences   417–18 **fortunen . . . images** making projections of
constellations, signs of the zodiac, etc. ("images") which had favorable
influences; used in treatment (See Curry, *Chaucer and the Medieval
Sciences*, Chapt. I)   420 **hot . . . drye** the basic qualities, found in
pairs in the four elements and the four bodily humors, as well as in
planets and diseases. The balance of bodily humors was a major prin-
ciple of medical practice   423 **y-know** known

Anon he yaf the sike man his boote.°
425   Full redy had he his apothecaries
To send him drugges and his letuaries,°
For ech of hem made other for to winne;°
Hir frendship nas not newe to beginne.
    Well knew he the old Esculapius,°
430 And Deiscorides and eek Rufus,
Old Ipocras, Hali, and Galien,
Serapion, Razis, and Avicen,
Averrois, Damascien, and Constantin,
Bernard, and Gatesden, and Gilbertin.
435 Of his diete mesurable was he,
For it was of no superfluitee
But of greet norishing and digestible.
His study was but litel on the Bible.
    In sanguine and in pers° he clad was all,
440 Lined with taffata and with sendal.°
And yet he was but esy of dispence.°
He kepte that he won in pestilence;°
For gold in physic is a cordial°—
Therefore he loved gold in special.
445   A good WIFE was there OF biside BATHE,°
But she was somedeel deef, and that was scathe.°
Of cloth-making she hadde swich an haunt,°

---

424 **boote** cure 426 **letuaries** medicinal syrups 427 **ech . . . winne**
then, as now, doctors and pharmacists were sometimes in collusion for
mutual profit 429 **Esculapius** this and the list following were the
great medical authorities of the ancient world and the Middle Ages; the
last three were Englishmen of the mid-fourteenth century 439 **sagu-
ine, pers** bright red, blue-gray 440 **taffata, sendal** kinds of silk
441 **esy of dispence** cautious in spending 442 **pestilence** plague
(The Black Plague hit England in 1348, 1362, 1369, and 1376)
443 **cordial** medicinal stimulant; powdered gold was actually used as
a medicine. It was also sometimes added to prescriptions in small
amounts to raise their price 445 **biside Bathe** a suburb of Bath, prob-
ably St. Michael's. Chaucer may have passed through the town often.
Some hold that the portrait is based on a living model because of its
minute particularity 446 **scathe** too bad. The reason for her deafness
is explained in her prologue 447 **haunt** skill

She passed hem of Ypres and of Gaunt.°
In all the parish wife ne was there noon
That to the offring before hir shold goon°— 450
And if there did, certain so wroth° was she
That she was out of alle charitee.
Hir coverchiefs full fine were of ground°—
I dorste swere they weyeden ten pound
That on a Sunday weren upon hir heed! 455
Hir hosen weren of fine scarlet red,
Full strait y-teyd,° and shoes full moist and newe.
Bold was hir face, and fair, and red of hewe.
She was a worthy woman all hir live.
Husbands at chirche door° she hadde five, 460
Withouten° other compaigny in youthe
—But thereof needeth not to speke as nouthe.°
    And thries had she been at Jerusalem.
She hadde passed many a straunge streem—
At Rome she hadde been, and at Bologne, 465
In Galice at Saint Jame, and at Cologne.°
She koude° much of wandring by the waye:
Gat-toothed° was she, soothly for to saye.
Upon an ambler° esily she sat,
Y-wimpled well, and on hir heed an hat 470
As brood as is a buckeler or a targe,°
A foot-mantel° about hir hippes large,

---

448 **Ypres, Gaunt** Ypres and Ghent were centers of the Flemish wool
trade   450 **offring . . . goon** a mark of prestige   451 **wroth** annoyed
453 **Hir coverchiefs . . . ground** her kerchiefs were of a very fine tex-
ture. They were worn over wire frames   457 **strait y-teyd** tightly tied
460 **chirche door** the marriage ceremony was performed on the
church porch, after which the couple went to the altar for mass
461 **Withouten** not to mention   462 **as nouthe** right now   463–
66 **Jerusalem . . . Cologne** the great pilgrimages of the later Middle
Ages   467 **koude** knew. The line has an obvious double meaning
468 **Gat-toothed** having a space between the two front teeth; it was
thought a sign of a bold, lascivious character   469 **ambler** horse in-
tended for "ambling," as opposed to a palfrey for faster riding, a
courser for warfare, etc.   471 **buckeler, targe** kinds of shields
472 **foot-mantel** outer skirt

And on hir feet a pair of spures sharpe.
In fellowship well coud she laugh and carpe.°
475 Of remedies of love she knew parchaunce,
For she koud of that art the olde daunce.°
    A good man was there of religioun,
And was a povre PERSON° of a town—
But rich he was of holy thought and werk.
480 He was also a lerned man, a clerk,
That Christes gospel trewly wolde preche.
His parishens° devoutly wold he teche.
Benign he was, and wonder diligent,
And in adversitee full pacient,
485 And swich he was y-preved ofte sithes.
Full loth were him to cursen for his tithes,°
But rather wold he yiven, out of doute,
Unto his povre parishens aboute
Of his offring and eek of his substaunce;°
490 He coud in litel thing have suffisaunce.
Wide was his parish, and houses fer asunder,
But he ne lafte nought° for rain ne thunder,
In sickness nor in meschief, to visite
The ferrest° in his parish, much and lite,
495 Upon his feet, and in his hand a staff.
    This noble ensample to his sheep he yaf:
That first he wrought, and afterward he taughte.
Out of the Gospel he tho° wordes caughte.
And this figure he added eek thereto:
500 That "if gold ruste, what shold iren do?"
For if a preest be foul, on whom we truste,
No wonder is a lewed° man to ruste!

---

474 **carpe** joke   476 **olde daunce** all the wheeling and dealing of
love; a distinctly sexual reference, like "remedies of love," which sug-
gests Ovid's *Remedia Amoris*   478 **person** parson, parish priest
482 **parishens** parishioners, congregation   486 **Full . . . tithes** it was
very disagreeable to him to excommunicate anyone for nonpayment of
tithes   489 **Of . . . substaunce** what he got from voluntary contribu-
tions and from the income of his benefice   492 **ne lafte nought** did
not fail   494 **ferrest** farthest   498 **tho** those   502 **lewed** simple

And shame it is, if a preest take keep—
A shitten° shepherd and a clene sheep!
Well ought a preest ensample for to yive   505
By his clenness how that his sheep shold live.
　He sette not his benefice to hire,
And let his sheep encumbred in the mire,
And ran to London unto Sainte Poules,
To seeken him a chauntery for soules,   510
Or with a bretherheed to been withholde;°
But dwelt at home and kepte well his folde,
So that the wolf ne made it not miscarrye.
He was a shepherd, and not a mercenarye.
And though he holy were and vertuous,   515
He was to sinful men not despitous,°
Ne of his speeche daungerous ne digne;°
But in his teeching discreet and benigne,
To drawen folk to heven by fairnesse,
By good ensample—this was his bisinesse.   520
But it were any person° obstinat,
What so he were, of heigh or low estat,
Him wold he snibben° sharply for the nones.
A better preest I trow there nowhere none is!
He waited after no pomp and reverence,   525
Ne maked him a spiced conscience,°
But Christes lore and his apostles' twelve
He taught—but first he followed it himselve.
　With him there was a PLOWMAN,° was his brother,
That had y-lad of dung full many a fother.°   530
A trewe swinker° and a good was he,

504 **shitten** dirty   507–11 **He ... withholde** a common practice of
the day, much criticized: priests sublet their landholding and made
further money praying for the soul of a rich patron in an endowed
chantry, or being retained (*withholde*) by a guild as their caplain
516 **despitous** contemptuous   517 **daungerous ne digne** withdrawn
or unapproachable   521 **it were any person** if any person were
523 **snibben** reprimand   526 **spiced conscience** touchy awareness
529 **Plowman** the plowman was a stock figure for the good simple
laborer—*Piers Plowman* is the locus classicus   530 **fother** cartload
531 **trewe swinker** honest worker

Living in pees and parfit charitee.
God loved he best with all his hoole herte
At alle times, though him gamed or smerte,°
535 And than his neighebor right as himselve.
He wolde thresh, and thereto dike and delve,°
For Christes sake, for every povre wight,
Withouten hire, if it lay in his might.
His tithes payde he full fair and well,
540 Both of his propre swink and his catel.°
In a tabard he rode upon a mere.°
    There was also a Reeve and a Millere,
A Somnour and a Pardoner also,
A Manciple and myself; there were namo.
545   The MILLER was a stout carl° for the nones.
Full big he was of brawn and eek of bones:
That proved well, for overall there he cam
At wrastling he wold have alway the ram.°
He was short-shouldred, brood—a thicke knarre.°
550 There was no door that he nold heve off harre,°
Or breke it at a renning with his heed.
His beerd as any sow or fox was red,
And thereto brood, as though it were a spade.
Upon the cop° right of his nose he hadde
555 A wert,° and thereon stood a tuft of heeres,
Red as the bristles of a sowes eres.
His nosethirles° blacke were and wide.
A swerd and buckeler bare he by his side.

534 **though ... smerte** whether in joy or trouble   536 **dike and delve** dig ditches and dig in general   540 **propre ... catel** i.e., on his own work and on his possessions   541 **mere** mare, ridden by poor folk   545 **stout carl** thick-set fellow. This and the other details about him are based on the medieval science of physiognomy, a phase of medicine and astrology; they denote a shameless, noisy, lecherous character   547–48 **overall ... ram** wherever he showed up, he would always win the first prize (traditionally a ram) in wrestling matches   549 **knarre** knotty—"a thick, muscular fellow"   550 **heve off harre** pull off its hinges   554 **cop** tip (or, perhaps, bridge)   555 **wert** wart—probably a mole   557 **nosethirles** nostrils

His mouth as greet was as a greet furnais.
He was a jangler and a goliardais°—   560
And that was most of sin and harlotries.°
Well coud he stelen corn and tollen thries°—
And yet he had a thumb of gold,° pardee.
A white cote and a blue hood wered he.
A baggepipe° well coud he blow and soune,   565
And therewithal he brought us out of towne.

　　A gentil MANCIPLE was there of a temple,°
Of which achatours° mighte take exemple
For to be wise in buying of vitaille:
For whether that he paid or took by taille,°   570
Algate he waited so in his achat°
That he was ay biforn° and in good stat!
Now is not that of God a full fair grace
That swich a lewed mannes wit shall pace
The wisdom of an heep of lerned men?   575
Of maistres had he mo than thries ten
That weren of law expert and curious!°—
Of which there were a dozein in that hous
Worthy to been stewards of rent and lond
Of any lord that is in Engelond,   580
To make him live by his propre good
In honour dettless, but if he were wood,°

560 **a jangler and a goliardais** a loudmouth and a big joker   561 **har-
lotries** ribaldry   562 **stelen . . . thries** steal wheat and take three times
his toll (the portion of the grain which was his due payment)   563 **thumb
of gold** the proverb "an honest miller has a thumb of gold" suggests there
are no honest millers. The thumb might turn yellow from sampling grain;
but otherwise might be used to weight down a scale while "tolling"
565 **baggepipe** medieval bagpipes, usually having but one pipe, were
notably phallic; Robertson, *Preface to Chaucer*, provides illustrations
567 **manciple . . . temple** purchasing agent or steward for one of the
Inns of Court (law schools)   568 **achatours** buyers   570 **by taille** on
credit   571 **Algate . . . achat** anyway, he was so careful about a
purchase   572 **ay biforn** always ahead of the game   577 **curious** skill-
ful, the students at the Inns of Court were often young nobles who might
use legal training in looking after their inheritance   581–82 **live . . .
wood** live on his income, honorably debtless, unless he were crazy

Or live as scarsly° as him list desire,
And able for to helpen all a shire
585   In any case that mighte fall or happe—
And yet this Manciple set hir aller cappe!°
      The REEVE° was a slender, cholerik° man.
His beerd was shave as neigh as ever he can;
His heer was by his eres full round y-shorn;
590   His top was docked like a preest biforn.°
Full longe were his legges and full lene,
Y-like a staff—there was no calf y-seene.
Well coud he keep a gerner° and a binne—
There was noon auditour coud on him winne!°
595   Well wist he by the drought and by the rain
The yeelding of his seed and of his grain.
His lordes sheep, his neet,° his dayerye,
His swine, his horse, his stoor, and his pultrye
Was holly in this Reeves governinge,
600   And by his covenant yaf the reckeninge.
Sin that his lord was twenty yeer of age,
There coud no man bring him in arrerage.°
There nas bailiff, ne hierd, ne other hine,
That he ne knew his sleight and his covine;°
605   They were adrad of him as of the deeth.°
His woning° was full fair upon an heeth;
With greene trees shadwed was his place.
He coud better than his lord purchace;
Full rich he was astored prively.
610   His lord well coud he plesen subtilly,

583 **scarsly** frugally   586 **set . . . cappe** made suckers of them all
587 **Reeve** the manager of a farm, chosen from among the serfs
587 **cholerik** the dominance of choler among his humors would sug-
gest a sly, irritable character   590 **docked . . . biforn** snipped short in
front like a priest; short hair suggested servility   593 **gerner** store-
house for grain   594 **winne** get one up on him. He probably kept rec-
ords by memory; then once a year an auditor would draw up written
records. A bit of cheating is suggested   597 **neet** cattle   602 **arre-
rage** arrears   603–04 **There . . . covine** there wasn't a bailiff, herds-
man, or other worker that he didn't know their tricks and cheats
605 **the deeth** i.e., the plague   606 **woning** dwelling

To yive and lene him of his owne good,
And have a thank, and yet a cote and hood.°
    In youth he hadde lerned a good mister:°
He was a well good wright, a carpenter.
    This Reeve sat upon a full good stot°   *615*
That was all pomely° grey and highte Scot.
A long surcote of pers upon he hadde,
And by his side he bare a rusty blade.
Of Northfolk was this Reeve of which I telle,
Beside a town men clepen Baldeswelle.   *620*
Tucked° he was as is a frere aboute,
And ever he rode the hindrest of our route.°
    A SOMNOUR° was there with us in that place
That had a fire-red cherubinnes face—
For saucefleem° he was, with eyen narrwe;   *625*
As hot he was and lecherous as a sparrwe,
With scaled° browes black and piled° beerd.
Of his visage children were aferd.
There nas quicksilver, litarge, ne brimstoon,
Boras, ceruce, ne oil of tartre noon,   *630*
Ne oinement that wolde clense and bite,
That him might helpen of the whelkes° white,
Nor of the knobbes° sitting on his cheekes.
Well loved he garlek, oinons, and eek leekes,°

611–12 **To . . . hood** i.e., he gave or lent things to his lord which he
had stolen from him—and the lord would thank him or give him a gift!
613 **mister** trade   615 **stot** farmhorse   616 **pomely** dappled
621 **tucked** his coat tucked up   622 **hindrest . . . route** last of the
company; he is keeping his eye on everyone   623 **Somnour** the sum-
moner is a minor police officer for the Archdeacon's court, which had
authority over matrimonial matters and moral conduct. His job is to
serve summons for any such offense. Summoners were given to graft
and bribery   625 **saucefleem** infected, inflamed. He suffers from *al-
opicia* (perhaps acne, but medieval medical authorities associated it
with leprosy); hence his fire-red face—like cherubim, which were
conventionally depicted in rosy colors   627 **scaled** scabby
627 **piled** scraggly   632 **whelkes** pimples   633 **knobbes** boils, sores
634 **garlek . . . leekes** apart from the smell, and the contribution they
would make to his skin disease, garlic, onions, and leeks would have
been known to the learned as symbols of moral depravity

635 And for to drinke strong wine red as blood.
     Than wold he speke and cry as he were wood.
     And whan that he well drunken had the win,
     Than wold he speke no word but Latin—
     A fewe termes had he, two or three,
640 That he had lerned out of some decree;
     No wonder is—he herd it all the day,
     And eek ye knowen well how that a jay
     Can clepen "Watte"° as well as can the Pope:
     But whoso coud in other thing him grope,°
645 Than had he spent all his philosophye:
     Ay *Questio quid juris*° wold he crye.
       He was a gentil harlot° and a kinde.
     A better fellaw sholde men not finde.
     He wolde suffer, for a quart of win,
650 A good fellaw to have his concubin
     A twelfmonth, and excuse him atte fulle;
     Full prively a finch eek coud *he* pulle.°
     And if he fond owhere° a good fellawe,
     He wolde teechen him to have noon awe
655 In swich case of the Ercedekenes curs,°
     But if a mannes soul were in his purs°—
     For in his purse he shold y-punished be.
     "Purse is the Ercedekenes hell," said he.
     But well I wot he lied right in deede:
660 Of cursing ought ech guilty man him drede,
     For curse wol slee right as assoiling° savith—
     And also ware him of a *significavit*.°

---

643 **"Watte"** jays were then taught to say "Walter" as parrots are now taught to say "Polly"   644 **grope** challenge   646 **Questio quid juris** "The question is, what part of the law (applies) . . ." Probably the usual opening phrase of a legal discussion; the summoner picks up this but of course understands nothing that follows!   647 **gentil harlot** nice guy   652 **finch . . . pulle** "pulling a finch" meant seducing a woman   653 **owhere** anywhere   655 **Ercedekenes curs** Archdeacon's power to excommunicate   656 **But . . . purs** unless a man's soul were in his purse   661 **assoiling** absolution   662 **significavit** writ of arrest issued on a Bishop's order—in effect, "and also don't get arrested"

In daunger° had he at his owne guise
The yonge girles of the diocise,
And knew hir counseil, and was all hir reed.°   665
A garland had he set upon his heed
As greet as it were for an ale-stake.°
A buckeler had he made him of a cake.
   With him there rode a gentil PARDONER°
Of Rouncival, his freend and his compeer,°   670
That straight was comen fro the court of Rome.
Full loud he song, "Come hider, love, to me."
This Somnour bare to him a stiff burdoun°—
Was never trump of half so greet a soun.
   This Pardoner had heer as yellow as wex,   675
But smooth it heng as doth a strike of flex:°
By ounces° heng his lockes that he hadde,
And therewith he his shouldres overspradde,
But thin it lay, by colpons oon and oon.°
But hood for jolitee° wered he noon,   680
For it was trussed up in his wallét:°

---

663 **In daunger** under his thumb   665 **knew . . . reed** knew their se-
crets and was their advisor   667 **ale-stake** sign on a tavern, often
with a garland hung from it   669 **Pardoner** pardoners were in minor
orders, or sometimes hired laymen, who sold indulgences from town
to town. They were notorious for their abuses and were strictly regu-
lated by prohibitions against false relics, preaching without permis-
sion, wearing clerical garb they were not entitled to wear, entering
taverns, etc. Some "pardoners" were out-and-out frauds; others,
though legitimate, kept more than their share of the proceeds, which
were to be used for such causes as crusades or hospitals. Some par-
doners forged small written indulgences bearing a fake papal seal.
There was a hospital called Our Lady of Rouncivalle, near Charing
Cross; and pardoners from it were commonly satirized. But offering
alms after a true confession and receiving an indulgence in return was
itself legitimate, though it lent itself to abuses   670 **compeer** com-
panion. The pardoner travels with the summoner: Pardoners needed
permission from the Archdeacon to enter a diocese   673 **stiff bur-
doun** strong bass accompaniment   676 **strike of flex** bunch of flax
677 **ounces** strands   679 **by colpons oon and oon** in strips, one by
one   680 **for jolitee** to be a sport   681 **trussed . . . wallét** folded up
in his saddlebag

Him thought he rode all of the newe jet°—
Dischevelee save his cap he rode all bare.°
Swich glaring eyen had he as an hare.
685   A vernicle° had he sowed upon his cappe;
His wallét biforn him in his lappe,
Bretful of pardon, comen from Rome all hot.
A voice he had as small as hath a goot.
No beerd had he, ne never sholde have—
690   As smooth it was as it were late y-shave.
I trow he were a gelding or a mare.°
But of his craft, fro Berwik into Ware
Ne was there swich another pardoner!
For in his male he had a pillwebeer°
695   Which that he said was Oure Lady° veil;
He said he had a gobbet° of the sail
That Sainte Peter had whan that he wente
Upon the see, till Jesu Christ him hente;
He had a crois of latoun,° full of stones;
700   And in a glass° he hadde pigges bones.
But with thise "relikes," whan that he fond
A povre person° dwelling upon lond,
Upon a day he gat him more moneye
Than that the person gat in monthes twaye!
705   And thus with feined flattery and japes
He made the person and the peple his apes.°
But trewely to tellen atte laste,

682 **newe jet** latest fashion   683 **Dischevelee . . . bare** with hair flying
he rode all bareheaded, except for his cap   685 **vernicle** a small replica
of St. Veronica's handkerchief, which she gave to Christ on Calvary to
wipe His face with. It bore an imprint of the face; the original was
preserved in Rome   691 **gelding or a mare** castrated horse or female
horse. The line suggests that the Pardoner is either a castrated eunuch
or a *eunuchus ex nativitate*, i.e., one born without sexual glands (anor-
chism). Curry shows that other details—a small voice, no beard, etc.—
would have suggested this   694 **male . . . pillwebeer** in his pouch he
had a pillowcase   695 **Lady** Lady's   696 **gobbet** piece   699 **crois of
latoun** cross of brass   700 **glass** glass case   702 **person** parson
706 **apes** he made monkeys of them

He was in chirch a noble ecclesiaste:°
Well coud he rede a lesson or a storye,
But alderbest he song an offertorye,   710
For well he wiste, whan that song was songe,
He moste preech and well affile° his tonge
To winne silver, as he full well coude—
Therefore he song the murrierly and loude.

*   *   *

Now have I told you soothly in a clause°   715
Th'estate,° th'array, the numbre, and eek the cause
Why that assembled was this compaignye
In Southwerk at this gentil hostelrye
That hight the Tabard, faste by the Belle.°
But now is time to you for to telle   720
How that we baren us that ilke night
Whan we were in that hostelry alight.
And after wol I tell of our viage,°
And all the remnant of our pilgrimage.
But first I pray you of your curteisye   725
That ye n'arette it not my villainye°
Though that I plainly speke in this mattere
To telle you hir wordes and hir cheere,°
Ne though I speke hir words proprely.°
For this ye knowen also well as I: 730
Whoso shall tell a tale after a man,
He moot reherce° as neigh as ever he can
Everich a word, if it be in his charge°—
Al speke he never so rudelich and large°—
Or elles he moot tell his tale untrewe,   735

---

708 **ecclesiaste** preacher   712 **affile** sharpen   715 **clause** few words
716 **estate** rank   719 **faste by the Belle** close to the Bell (another inn
in Southwark)   723 **viage** trip   726 **That . . . villainye** that you
won't chalk it up to my bad manners   728 **cheere** conduct   729 **pro-
prely** accurately   732 **moot reherce** must report   733 **charge** ability
734 **large** openly

Or feine thing, or finde wordes newe;°
He may not spare although he were his brother.
He moot as well say oo word as another.
Christ spak himself full brod in holy writ,
740　And well ye wot no villainy is it.
Eek Plato saith, whoso can him rede,
The wordes mot be cosin to the deede.
　　Also I pray you to foryive it me
Al have I not set folk in hir degree°
745　Here in this tale as that they sholde stonde:
My wit is short, ye may well understonde.

　　　　　　　*　　　*　　　*

　　Greet cheere made our Host us everichoon,
And to the supper set he us anon.
He served us with vitaille at the beste.
750　Strong was the wine, and well to drink us leste.
　　A seemly man our HOSTE° was withalle
For to been a marshall in an halle.°
A large man he was, with eyen steepe;
A fairer burgeis was there none in Chepe—
755　Bold of his speech, and wise, and well y-taught;
And of manhood him lackede right naught.
Eek thereto he was right a mirry man,
And after supper playen° he began,
And spak of mirth amonges other thinges—
760　Whan that we had made our reckeninges°—
And saide thus: "Now, lordings, trewely,
Ye been to me right welcome, hertely!

---

736 **Or . . . newe** or be making something up, or putting words in
someone's mouth　744 **degree** order of social rank　751 **Hoste** his
name is given as Harry Bailly in the Cook's Prologue (line 34).
There was an actual innkeeper in Southwark of that name during the 1380's.
He held various political offices　752 **marshall . . . halle** overseer of
service in a palace　758 **playen** to fool around　760 **made our reck-
eninges** paid our bills

For by my trouth, if that I shall not lie,
I saw not this yeer so mirry a compaignye
At ones in this herberwe° as is now!   765
Fain wold I doon you mirthe, wist I how.
And of a mirth I am right now bethought,
To doon you ese,° and it shall coste nought:
Ye goon to Canterbury—God you speede:
The blissful martyr quite you your meede!°   770
And well I wot as ye goon by the waye
Ye shapen you to talen° and to playe;
For trewely, comfort ne mirth is noon
To ride by the way dumb as a stoon.
And therefore wol I maken you disport   775
As I said erst, and doon you some comfort:
And if you liketh all, by one assent,
For to standen at my judgement,
And for to werken as I shall you saye,
Tomorrwe whan ye riden by the waye—   780
Now by my fader soule that is deed,
But ye be mirry I wol yive you mine heed.
Hold up your hands withouten more speeche."°
Our conseil was not longe for to seeche—
Us thought it was not worth to make it wis,°   785
And graunted him withouten more avis,
And bade him say his voirdit° as him leste.
"Lordings," quod he, "now herkneth for the beste—
But taketh it not, I pray you, in disdain:
This is the point, to speken short and plain,   790
That ech of you, to shorte with our waye°
In this viage, shall telle tales twaye—
To Canterbury-ward, I mene it so,

---

765 **herberwe** inn   768 **doon you ese** amuse you   770 **quite you
your meede** grant you your reward   772 **talen** tell tales   783 **Hold
up your hands** like a politician, he gets them to make a gesture of
agreement before he has said anything   785 **Us . . . wis** it seemed to
us not worthwhile to quibble   787 **voirdit** verdict   791 **shorte with
our waye** with which to shorten our journey

And homeward he shall tellen other two,
795 Of aventures that whilom have bifalle.
And which of you that bereth him best of alle—
That is to sayn, that telleth in this cas
Tales of best sentence and most solas°—
Shall have a supper at our aller cost,°
800 Here in this place, sitting by this post,
Whan that we come again fro Canterbury.
And for to make you the more murry
I wol myself goodly with you ride,
Right at mine owne cost, and be your guide.
805 And whoso wol my judgement withsaye°
Shall pay all that we spende by the waye.
And if ye vouchesauf that it be so,
Tell me anon, withouten wordes mo,
And I wol erly shape me° therefore."
810   This thing was graunted and our othes swore
With full glad hert, and prayden him also
That he wold vouchesauf for to do so,
And that he wolde been our governour,
And of our tales judge and reportour;°
815 And set a supper at a certain pris,
And we wol ruled been at his devis,
In heigh and low.°And thus by one assent
We been accorded to his judgement.
And thereupon the wine was fet° anon;
820 We dronken and to reste went echon
Withouten any lenger tarryinge.
    Amorrwe whan that day began to springe
Up rose our Host and was our aller cock,°

---

798 **sentence ... solas** moral significance and pleasure. These were
the two effects of storytelling in the medieval view   799 **at our aller
cost** at the cost of us all   805 **withsaye** deny   809 **shape me** get my-
self ready   814 **reportour** reporter of their merits   817 **In ... low** in
all respects   819 **fet** fetched. It was a custom to have a drink of wine
before going to bed   823 **was ... cock** acted as a rooster for us all
(i.e., woke us)

And gadred us togidre in a flock;
And forth we riden, a litel more than pas,° 825
Unto the watering° of Saint Thomas.
And there our Host began his horse arreste,
And saide, "Lordings, herkneth if you leste!
Ye wot your forward and it you recorde:°
If evensong and morrwesong accorde, 830
Let see now who shall tell the firste tale.
As ever mote I drinke wine or ale,
Whoso be rebel to my judgement
Shall pay for all that by the way is spent.
Now draweth cut° ere that we ferrer twinne:° 835
He which that hath the shortest shall beginne.
Sir Knight," quod he, "my maister and my lord,
Now draweth cut, for that is mine accord.
Cometh neer," quod he, "my lady Prioresse,
And ye, sir Clerk, let be your shamefastnesse— 840
Ne studieth° not. Lay hand to, every man!"
    Anon to drawen every wight began,
And shortly for to tellen as it was,
Were it by aventure, or sort, or cas,°
The sooth is this: the cut fill to the Knight.° 845
Of which full blithe and glad was every wight,
And tell he most his tale, as was resoun,
By forward and by composicioun,°
As ye han herd. What needeth wordes mo?
And whan this good man say that it was so, 850
As he that wise was and obedient
To keep his forward by his free assent,
He saide, "Sin I shall begin the game,

---

825 **pas** a short walk   826 **watering** brook. It was two miles on the
road to Canterbury   829 **Ye . . . recorde** you know your agreement
and you remember it   835 **draweth cut** draw straws   835 **twinne**
depart   841 **studieth** think, muse   844 **aventure, or sort, or cas** by
chance, or luck, or circumstance; essentially they are synonyms
845 **to the Knight** this is no surprise; it would be normal for the one
of highest rank to begin   848 **composicioun** agreement

What, welcome be the cut, a' Goddes name!
855 Now let us ride, and herkneth what I saye."
And with that word we riden forth our waye,
And he began with right a mirry cheere
His tale anon, and said as ye may heere.

THE KNIGHT'S TALE

PART ONE

Whilom,° as olde stories tellen us,
There was a duke that highte Theseus:
Of Athens he was lord and governour,
And in his time swich a conquerour
That greeter was there none under the sunne.   5
Full many a riche contree had he wonne:
What with his wisdom and his chivalrye,
He conquered all the regne of Femenye,°
That whilom was y-cleped° Scythia,
And weddede the queen Ipolyta,   10
And brought hir home with him in his contree,
With muchel glory and greet solempnitee,°
And eek hir yonge suster° Emelye.
And thus with victory and with melodye
Let I this noble duke to Athens ride,   15
And all his host in armes him beside.
   And certes, if it nere too long to heere,°
I wold have told you fully the mannere
How wonnen was the regne of Femenye
By Theseus and by his chivalrye,   20

---

1 **Whilom** once upon a time   8 **Femenye** the country of the Amazons, whose inhabitants were all women   9 **y-cleped** called   12 **solempnitee** ceremony   13 **suster** sister   17 **if . . . heere** if it weren't too long to listen to. The rhetorical device used here, called *occupatio*, permits a writer to summarize a great deal of material by stating what he will not deal with. The Knight's Tale is an adaptation of Boccaccio's *Teseida*, and is much shorter than its original; many omitted passages are treated as this one is

And of the greet bataille for the nones°
Betwixen Athenes and Amazones,
And how asseged was Ipolyta,
The faire hardy queen of Scythia,
25 And of the feest that was at hir weddinge,
And of the tempest at hir home-cominge.
But all that thing I mot as now forbere.
I have, God wot, a large feeld to ere,°
And waike° been the oxen in my plough;
30 The remnant of the tale is long enough.
I wol not letten° eek none of this route;°
Let every fellaw tell his tale aboute,°
And let see now who shall the supper winne.
And ther I left I wol ayain beginne.
35   This duke of whom I make mencioun,
Whan he was comen almost to the town
In all his wele and in his moste pride,
He was ware as he cast his eye aside
Where that there kneeled in the highe waye
40 A compaigny of ladies, twaye and twaye,
Ech after other, clad in clothes blacke.
But swich a cry and swich a woe they make
That in this world nis creature livinge
That herde swich another waymentinge;°
45 And of this cry they nolde never stenten°
Till they the reines of his bridle henten.°
    "What folk been ye that at mine home-cominge
Perturben so my feeste with cryinge?"
Quod Theseus. "Have ye so greet envye
50 Of mine honour, that thus complain and crye?
Or who hath you misboden° or offended?
And telleth me if it may been amended
And why that ye been clothed thus in black?"

---

21 **for the nones** in particular 28 **ere** plow 29 **waike** weak
31 **letten** hinder 31 **route** company 32 **aboute** in his turn
44 **waymentinge** lamenting 45 **stenten** stop 46 **henten** grasped
51 **misboden** harmed

The eldest lady of hem alle spak,
Whan she had swouned with a deedly cheere,°   55
That it was routhe° for to seen and heere.
     She saide, "Lord to whom Fortune hath yiven
Victory, and as a conquerour to liven,
Nought greveth us your glory and your honour,
But we biseeken mercy and succour: 60
Have mercy on our woe and our distresse!
Some drop of pitee, thurgh thy gentilesse,
Upon us wretched women let thou falle!
For certes, lord, there is none of us alle
That she ne hath been a duchess or a queene.   65
Now be we caitives,° as it is well seene,
Thanked be Fortune and hir false wheel,°
That none estate assureth to be well.
Now certes, lord, to abiden° your presence,
Here in this temple of the goddess Clemence   70
We have been waiting all this fortenight.
Now help us, lord, sith it is in thy might!
I, wretche, which that weep and waile thus,
Was whilom wife to King Cappaneus
That starf° at Thebes—cursed be that day!   75
And alle we that been in this array°
And maken all this lamentacioun,
We losten all our husbands at that town,
While that the seege thereaboute lay.
And yet now the old Creon, wailaway,   80
That lord is now of Thebes the citee,
Fulfilled of° ire and of iniquitee—
He, for despit and for his tyrannye,
To do the dede bodies villainye

---

55 **cheere** appearance   56 **routhe** pity   66 **caitives** captives, or
wretches   67 **Fortune . . . wheel** the wheel of Fortune was the prin-
ciple of chance in the universe; it showed that earthly things are transi-
tory and that there is no certain justice in this wicked world. The theme
occurs often in the Knight's Tale   69 **abiden** wait for   75 **starf** died
76 **array** condition   82 **Fulfilled of** filled with

85 Of all our lordes whiche that been slawe,°
    Hath all the bodies on an heep y-drawe,
    And wol not suffren hem by noon assent
    Neither to been y-buried nor y-brent,°
    But maketh houndes ete hem in despit!"
90 And with that word, withouten more respit,
    They fillen gruf° and criden pitously,
    "Have on us wretched women some mercy,
    And let our sorrwe sinken in thine herte!"
       This gentil duke down from his courser° sterte
95 With herte pitous whan he herd hem speke.
    Him thoughte° that his herte wolde breke
    Whan he saw hem so pitous and so mat,°
    That whilom weren of so greet estat.
    And in his armes he hem all up hente,
100 And hem comforteth in full good entente,
    And swore his ooth, as he was trewe knight,
    He wolde doon so ferforthly° his might
    Upon the tyrant Creon hem to wreke,°
    That all the peple of Greece sholde speke
105 How Creon was of Theseus y-served,
    As he that had his deeth full well deserved.
    And right anon withouten more abood°
    His banner he desplayeth and forth rood
    To Thebesward, and all his host beside.
110 No neer° Athenes wold he go° ne ride,
    Ne take his ese fully half a day,
    But onward on his way that night he lay,
    And sent anon Ipolyta the queene,
    And Emely hir yonge suster sheene,°
115 Unto the town of Athenes to dwelle,
    And forth he rit:° there is namore to telle.

---

85 **slawe** slain 88 **y-brent** burnt 91 **gruf** facedown 94 **courser**
war horse 96 **Him thoughte** it seemed to him (the verb is impersonal)
97 **mat** distracted 102 **so ferforthly** as much as he could 103 **hem
to wreke** to avenge them 107 **abood** delay 110 **neer** nearer
110 **go** walk 114 **sheene** fair 116 **rit** rides

The red statue of Mars with spere and targe°
So shineth in his white banner large
That all the feeldes glittren up and down.
And by his banner born is his penoun°   120
Of gold full rich, in which there was y-bete
The Minotaur, which that he wan° in Crete.
Thus rit this duke, thus rit this conquerour,
And in his host of chivalry the flowr,
Till that he came to Thebes and alighte   125
Fair in a feeld ther as he thought to fighte.
    But shortly for to speken of this thing,
With Creon which that was of Thebes king
He faught, and slow° him manly as a knight
In plain° battail, and put the folk to flight.   130
And by assaut he wan the citee after,
And rent adown both wall and spar° and rafter,
And to the ladies he restored again
The bones of hir freendes that were slain,
To doon obsequies as was tho the guise.°   135
But it were all too long for to devise
The greete clamour and the waymentinge
That the ladies made at the brenninge
Of the bodies, and the greet honour
That Theseus, the noble conquerour,   140
Doth to the ladies whan they from him wente;
But shortly for to tell is mine entente.
    Whan that this worthy duke, this Theseus,
Hath Creon slain and wonne Thebes thus,
Still in that feeld he took all night his reste,   145
And did with all the contree as him leste.
    To ransack in the taas° of bodies dede,
Hem for to strep of harneis and of weede,°
The pilours° diden bisiness and cure°

---

117 **targe**   shield   120 **penoun**   penant   122 **wan**   conquered
129 **slow** slew   130 **plain** open   132 **spar** beam   135 **guise** custom
147 **taas** pile   148 **strep . . . weede** strip of armor and clothes
149 **pilours** pillagers   149 **cure** care

150 After the battail and disconfiture.
And so bifell that in the taas they founde,
Thurgh-girt° with many a grevous bloody wounde,
Two yonge knightes, ligging by and by,°
Both in one armes° wrought full richely;
155 Of whiche two, Arcita hight that oon,
And that other knight hight Palamon.
Not fully quick° ne fully deed they were;
But by hir cote-armures° and by hir gere°
The heraudes knew hem best in special
160 As they that weren of the blood royal
Of Thebes, and of sustren two y-born.
Out of the taas the pilours han hem torn
And han hem carried soft unto the tente
Of Theseus, and he full soon hem sente
165 To Athenes to dwellen in prisoun
Perpetuelly; he nolde no raunsoun.°
And whan this worthy duke hath thus y-doon,
He took his host and home he rit anoon,
With laurer crowned as a conquerour.
170 And there he liveth in joy and in honour
Term of his life. What needeth wordes mo?
And in a tower, in aguish and in wo,
Dwellen this Palamon and eek Arcite
For evermore; there may no gold hem quite.°
175   This passeth yeer by yeer and day by day,
Till it fill ones in a morrwe of May
That Emely, that fairer was to seene
Than is the lily upon his stalke greene,
And fresher than the May with flowres newe
180 (For with the rose colour strof hir hewe—

---

152 **Thurgh-girt** pierced through   153 **ligging by and by** lying near
each other   154 **in one armes** dressed alike and having the same coat
of arms (since they are of the same family)   157 **quick** alive
158 **cote-armures** cloth surcoats worn over armor, on which was em-
broidered a coat of arms   158 **gere** equipment   166 **nolde no raun-
soun** did not want a ransom   174 **quite** ransom

I noot which was the fairer of hem two)
Ere it were day, as was hir wone° to do,
She was arisen and all redy dight,°
For May wol have no sluggardye anight.
The seson pricketh every gentil herte,   185
And maketh it out of his sleep to sterte,
And saith, "Arise and do thine observaunce."
This maketh Emely have remembraunce
To doon honour to May and for to rise.
Y-clothed was she fresh for to devise: 190
Hir yellow heer was broided in a tresse
Behind hir back a yerde long, I guesse,
And in the garden at the sun upriste°
She walketh up and down, and as hir liste
She gadreth flowres party° white and rede   195
To make a subtil° gerland for hir heede,
And as an angel hevenishly she song.
   The greete tower that was so thick and strong,
Which of the castel was the chief dungeoun,
Ther as the knightes weren in prisoun   200
(Of which I tolde you and tellen shall)
Was even joinant° to the garden wall
Ther as this Emely had hir playinge.
Bright was the sun and cleer that morrweninge,
And Palamon, this woeful prisoner,   205
As was his wone by leve of his jailer,
Was risen and romed in a chambre on heigh,
In which he all the noble citee seigh,°
And eek the garden, full of braunches greene,
Ther as the freshe Emely the sheene   210
Was in hir walk and romed up and down.
This sorrweful prisoner, This Palamoun,
Goth in the chambre roming to and fro,
And to himself complaining of his wo.

---

182 **wone** habit   183 **dight** dressed   193 **at the sun upriste** at the
sun's   rising   195 **party**   particolored   196 **subtil**   ingenious
202 **even joinant** directly adjacent   208 **seigh** saw

215 That he was born full oft he said alas!
     And so bifell, by aventure or cas,
     That thurgh a window thick of many a barre
     Of iren greet and square as any sparre,
     He caste his eye upon Emelya
220 And therewithal he bleint° and cride "A!"
     As though he stongen were unto the herte.°
     And with that cry Arcite anon up sterte
     And saide, "Cosin mine, what aileth thee
     That art so pale and deedly on to see?
225 Why cridestou?° Who hath thee done offence?
     For Goddes love, take all in pacience
     Our prison, for it may noon other be.
     Fortune hath yiven us this adversitee.
     Some wicke aspect or disposicioun
230 Of Saturn,° by some constellacioun,
     Hath yiven us this, although we had it sworn.°
     So stood the heven whan that we were born.
     We mot endure it; this is the short and plain."
          This Palamon answered and said again,
235 "Cosin, forsooth, of this opinioun
     Thou hast a vain imaginacioun.°
     This prison caused me not for to crye,
     But I was hurt right now thurghout mine eye
     Into mine hert, that wol my bane° be.

---

220 **bleint** blanched, turned white   221 **stongen . . . herte** the
"wound" of love, which enters through the eye and afflicts the heart, is
traditional. Paleness, sighing, and weeping are among its symptoms.
Cf. lines 238, 257–58   225 **cridestou** didst thou cry   230 **Saturn** an
evil planet. Arcite blames the stars, working along with Fortune, for
their plight. A "wicke aspect" (evil arrangement of heavenly bodies),
or a "disposicioun" of one planet within the "constellation" of planets,
has affected them from birth. Astrology was legitimately a science,
which helped to explain the element of chance in human life; it is not
inconsistent with the principle of Fortune's wheel   231 **although . . .
sworn** although we had sworn to the contrary. The point is that man
has no power in the face of destinal forces save to accept them patiently
236 **vain imaginacioun** empty fantasy   239 **bane** death

The fairness of that lady that I see   240
Yond in the garden romen to and fro
Is cause of all my crying and my wo.
I noot wher° she be woman or goddesse,
But Venus is it soothly, as I guesse."
And therewithal on knees down he fill   245
And saide, "Venus, if it be thy will
You in this garden thus to transfigure
Before me, sorrowful, wretched creature,
Out of this prison help that we may scape.
And if so be my destinee be shape   250
By eterne word to dien in prisoun,
Of our linage have some compassioun,
That is so low y-brought by tyrannye."

    And with that word Arcite gan espye
Whereas this lady romed to and fro,   255
And with that sight hir beautee hurt him so
That if that Palamon was wounded sore,
Arcite is hurt as much as he or more.
And with a sigh he saide pitously,
"The freshe beautee sleth me suddenly   260
Of hir that rometh in the yonder place,
And but I have hir mercy and hir grace,
That I may seen hir at the leste waye,°
I nam but deed:° there nis namore to saye."

    This Palamon, whan he tho wordes herde,   265
Despitously he looked and answerde,
"Whether saistou this° in ernest or in play?"

    "Nay," quod Arcite, "in ernest, by my fay.°
God help me so, me list full yvele playe."°

    This Palamon gan knit his browes twaye;   270
"It were to thee," quod he, "no greet honour

---

243 **I noot wher** I know not whether. . . . The confusion of women
with goddesses is a commonplace of love poetry 263 **I . . . waye** I
may at least see her 264 **I nam but deed** I am no better than dead
267 **Whether saistou this** do you say this 268 **fay** faith 269 **me . . .
playe** it pleases me very little to fool around

For to be false, ne for to be traitour
To me, that am thy cosin, and thy brother,°
Y-sworn full deep, and ech of us til other,
275 That never, for to dien in the paine,
Till that the deeth departe shall us twaine,
Neither of us in love to hinder other,
Ne in noon other cas,° my leve brother;
But that thou sholdest trewely forthren me
280 In every cas, as I shall forthre thee.
This was thine ooth, and mine also, certain.
I wot right well thou darst it not withsayn.°
Thus artou of my conseil° out of doute,
And now thou woldest falsely been aboute°
285 To love my lady whom I love and serve,
And ever shall till that mine herte sterve.°
Now certes, false Arcite, thou shalt not so.
I loved hir first, and tolde thee my wo
As to my conseil and my brother sworn
290 To forthre me, as I have told biforn.
For which thou art y-bounden as a knight
To helpe me, if it lay in thy might,
Or elles artou false, I dare well sayn."
     This Arcite full proudly spak again:
295 "Thou shalt," quod he, "be rather false than I;
And thou art false, I tell thee outrely°—
For *par amour*° I loved hir first ere thou.
What wiltou sayn? Thou woost not yet now

---

273 **brother** "sworn brotherhood" was an oath of loyalty between
friends, sometimes made by commingling blood (hence the term
"blood brothers"). It was a very sacred relationship: cf. line 275—"even
though we die by torture." From this relationship, more than from their
family tie (as cousins), springs their conflict of love versus honor
278 **cas** circumstance   282 **withsayn** deny   283 **of my conseil** in on
my secret   284 **been aboute** make ready   286 **sterve** perish, die
296 **outrely** straight out; cf. "utterly"   297 **par amour** in the way of
love. Arcite's argument is that Palamon thought she was a goddess and
was therefore just having an attack of religion ("affeccion of
holinesse"—line 300)

Wheither she be a woman or goddesse:
Thine is affeccion of holinesse,   *300*
And mine is love as to a creature,
For which I tolde thee mine aventure,
As to my cosin and my brother sworn.
I pose that thou lovedest hir biforn:°
Wostou not well the olde clerkes sawe,   *305*
That 'Who shall yive a lover any lawe?'
Love is a greeter lawe, by my pan,°
Than may be yive to any erthly man;
And therefore positif law and swich decree
Is broke alday for love in ech degree.   *310*
A man mot needes love, maugree his heed:
He may not fleen it though he shold be deed,
Al be she maide, widwe, or elles wif.
And eek it is not likely all thy lif
To standen in hir grace. Namore shall I,   *315*
For well thou wost thyselven, verraily
That thou and I be dampned to prisoun
Perpetuelly; us gaineth no raunsoun.
We strive as did the houndes for the boon:—
They fought all day, and yet hir part was noon;   *320*
There came a kite, while that they were so wrothe
That bare away the bone bitwix hem bothe.
And therefore, at the kinges court, my brother,
Ech man for himself—there is none other.°
Love if thee list, for I love and ay shall—   *325*
And soothly, leve brother, this is all:
Here in this prison mote we endure,
And everich of us take his aventure."°
    Greet was the strife and long bitwix hem twaye,

---

304 **I . . . biforn** "Suppose *you* loved her first." Arcite raises a hypo-
thetical point: "Wouldn't *you* agree love has no law?"—a self-
defeating argument if ever there was one; note his previous appeal to
legality (lines 297ff.)   307 **pan** skull   324 **none other** no other way.
"At the King's court each man for himself" is a proverb   328 **aven-
ture** chance

330 If that I hadde leiser for to saye.
    But to th'effect: it happed on a day,
    To tell it you as shortly as I may,
    A worthy duke that hight Perotheus,
    That fellaw was unto duke Theseus
335 Sin thilke day that they were children lite,°
    Was come to Athens his fellaw to visite,
    And for to play, as he was wont to do;
    For in this world he loved no man so,
    And he loved him as tendrely again.°
340 So well they loved, as olde bookes sayn,
    That whan that one was deed, soothly to telle,
    His fellaw went and sought him down in helle—
    But of that story list me not to write.°
    Duke Perotheus loved well Arcite,
345 And had him know at Thebes yeer by yeer,
    And finally at request and prayere
    Of Perotheus, withouten any raunsoun,
    Duke Theseus him let out of prisoun
    Freely to goon where that him list overall,
350 In swich a guise as I you tellen shall.
    This was the forward,° plainly for t'endite,
    Bitwixen Theseus and him Arcite:
    That if so were that Arcite were y-founde
    Ever in his life, by day or night or stounde,°
355 In any countree of this Theseus,
    And he were caught, it was accorded thus:
    That with a swerd he sholde lese his heed.

335 **lite** little   339 **he . . . again** i.e., Theseus loved him in return
343 **list . . . to write** "It doesn't please me to write." One would expect
the Knight to say "tell," so the line is sometimes considered a slip on
Chaucer's part, or a vestige from an earlier version not intended for
The Canterbury Tales. But of course everyone knows that while the
Knight is supposedly telling the tale Chaucer is really writing it: who
could tell a rhymed tale on horseback riding through open country?
Here and elsewhere perhaps Chaucer ironically permits his own voice
to seep through   351 **forward** agreement   354 **or stounde** or at any
time

There was noon other remedy ne reed,
But taketh his leve,° and homeward he him spedde.
Let him be ware: his necke lith to wedde.°   360
    How greet a sorrwe suffreth now Arcite!
The deeth he feeleth thurgh his herte smite.
He weepeth, waileth, crieth pitously;
To sleen himself he waiteth prively.
He said, "Alas the day that I was born!   365
Now is my prison worse than biforn—
Now is me shape eternally to dwelle
Not in purgatory, but in helle!
Alas that ever knew I Perotheus,
For elles had I dwelled with Theseus,   370
Y-fettered in his prison evermo!
Than had I been in bliss and not in wo.
Only the sight of hir whom that I serve,
Though that I never hir grace may deserve,
Wold have suffised right enough for me.   375
O dere cosin Palamon," quod he,
"Thine is the victory of this aventure:
Full blissfully in prison maistou dure°—
In prison?—certes, nay, but in Paradis!
Well hath Fortune y-turned thee the dis,°   380
That hast the sight of hir—and I th'absence.
For possible is, sin thou hast hir presence,
And art a knight, a worthy and an able,
That by some cas, sin Fortune is chaungeable,
Thou maist to thy desire some time attaine.   385
But I, that am exiled, and barreine°
Of alle grace, and in so greet despair
That there nis erthe, water, fire, ne air,°

358–59 **noon . . . leve** no other remedy or counsel but to take his leave
(*lit.* "but takes his leave." Such ellipses in grammar are not unusual)
360 **to wedde** under a bond or pledge   378 **dure** remain   380 **dis**
dice   386 **barreine** barren   388 **erthe . . . air** these were the four
elements of which all things were composed—in short, nothing can
help him

Ne creature that of hem maked is,
390 That may me help or doon confort in this—
Well ought I sterve in wanhope° and distresse.
Farewell my life, my lust, and my gladnesse!
Alas, why plainen folk so in commune
On purveyance of God,° or of Fortune,
395 That yiveth hem full oft in many a guise
Well better than they can hemself devise?
Some man desireth for to have richesse,
That cause is of his murdre or greet sicknesse;
And some man wold out of his prison fain,
400 That in his house is of his meinee° slain.
Infinite harmes been in this mattere:
We wot not what thing that we prayen here—
We faren as he that drunk is as a mous.°
A drunke man wot well he hath an hous,
405 But he noot which the righte way is thider,
And to a drunke man the way is slider.°
And certes in this world so faren we:
We seeken fast after felicitee,
But we goon wrong full often, trewely.
410 Thus may we sayen all, and namelich I,
That wende° and had a greet opinioun
That if I mighte scapen fro prisoun,
Than had I been in joy and parfit hele,°
Ther now I am exiled fro my wele!°
415 Sin that I may not seen you, Emelye,
I nam but deed! There nis no remedye!"
    Upon that other side Palamon,
Whan that he wist Arcite was agon,
Swich sorrwe he maketh that the greete towr

---

391 **sterve in wanhope** die in despair   393–94 **why plainen . . . God**
Why do people commonly complain about God's providence?   400 **of
his meinee** by the people of his own household   403 **drunk . . . as a
mous** proverbial; compare "drunk as a skunk" or "drunk as a coot"
406 **slider** slithery   411 **wende** imagined   413 **hele** well-being
414 **wele** good circumstances

Resouneth of his yowling and clamour.   *420*
The pure fettres of his shinnes greete
Were of his bitter salte teres wete.
"Alas," quod he, "Arcita, cosin min,
Of all our strife, God wot, the fruit is thin!
Thou walkest now in Thebes at thy large,°   *425*
And of my woe thou yivest litel charge.°
Thou maist, sin thou hast wisdom and manhede,
Assemblen all the folk of our kinrede,
And made a wer° so sharp on this citee
That by some aventure or some tretee   *430*
Thou maist have hir to lady and to wif,
For whom that I most needes lese my lif.
For as by way of possibilitee,
Sith thou art at thy large, of prison free,
And art a lord, greet is thine avantage,   *435*
More than is mine, that sterve here in a cage.
For I mot weep and waile while I live
With all the woe that prison may me yive,
And eek with pain that love me yiveth also,
That doubleth all my torment and my wo!"   *440*
Therewith the fire of jalousy up sterte
Within his brest, and hent° him by the herte
So woodly° that he like was to biholde°
The boxtree or the ashen deed and colde.
Than said he: "O cruel goddes that governe   *445*
This world with binding of your word eterne,
And writen in the table of adamaunt
Your parlement and your eterne graunt,
What is mankinde more unto you holde
Than is the sheep that rowketh° in the folde?   *450*
For slain is man right as another beest,
And dwelleth eek in prison and arrest,
And hath sickness and greet adversitee,

---

425 **at thy large** at large   426 **charge** care   429 **wer** war   442 **hent**
grasped   443 **woodly** madly   443 **he . . . biholde** to look at him he
was like . . . (i.e., he was pale and white)   450 **rowketh** crouches

And ofte times guiltless, pardee.
455 What governance is in this prescience
That guilteless tormenteth innocence?°
And yet encresseth this all my penaunce,
That man is bounden to his observaunce,°
For goddes sake, to letten of his wille,°
460 Ther as a beest may all his lust fulfille.
And whan a beest is deed he hath no paine,
But man after his deeth mot weep and plaine,
Though in this world he have care and wo;
Withouten doute, it may stonden so.°
465 The answer of this let I to divines,°
But well I wot that in this world greet pine is.
Alas, I see a serpent° or a theef,
That many a trewe man hath done mischeef,
Gone at his large and where him list may turne.°
470 But I mot been in prison thurgh Saturne,
And eek thurgh Juno, jalous and eek wood,
That hath destroyed well nigh all the blood
Of Thebes, with his waste walles wide!°
And Venus sleth me on that other side
475 For jalousy and fere of him Arcite!"
     Now wol I stint of Palamon a lite,
And let him in his prison stille dwelle,
And of Arcita forth I wol you telle:
     The summer passeth and the nightes longe
480 Encreesen double wise the paines stronge
Both of the lover and the prisoner—
I noot which hath the woefuller mister:°
For shortly for to sayn, this Palamoun

455–56 **What . . . innocence** What kind of governance is there in
this foreknowledge which torments innocence but has no guilt in
doing so?   458 **to his observaunce** as a matter of obligation
459 **to letten of his wille** to restrain his own desires   464 **it may
stonden so** it is how things are   465 **let I to divines** I leave to
theologians   467 **serpent** scoundrel   469 **Gone . . . turne** has
gone at large and can go where he likes   473 **waste walles wide**
wide walls partly destroyed   482 **mister** situation

Perpetuelly is dampned to prisoun,
In chaines and in fettres to been deed;   485
And Arcite is exiled upon his heed
For evermo as out of that contree,
Ne nevermo he shall his lady see.
    You lovers ax I now this questioun:°
Who hath the worse, Arcite or Palamoun?   490
That one may seen his lady day by day,
But in prison mot he dwell alway;
That other where him list may ride or go,
But seen his lady shall he nevermo.
Now deemeth as you liste, ye that can,   495
For I wol telle forth as I began.

PART TWO

Whan that Arcite to Thebes comen was,
Full oft a day he swelt° and said "Alas"—
For seen his lady shall he nevermo.
And shortly to concluden all his wo,   500
So muchel sorrwe had never creature
That is or shall while that the world may dure!
His sleep, his mete, his drink is him biraft,
That lene he wex and dry as is a shaft;
His eyen hollow and grisly to biholde,   505
His hewe fallow,° and pale as ashen colde;
And solitary he was and ever alone,
And wailing all the night, making his mone.
And if he herde song or instrument,
Than wold he weep, he mighte not be stent.°   510
So feeble eek were his spirits and so lowe,
And chaunged so that no man coude knowe
His speeche nor his voice, though men it herde;

---

489 **questioun** the Knight poses a typical *"demande d'amour"*: sto-
ries were often interrupted or concluded with such questions, which
were then debated. Cf. the end of the Franklin's Tale.   498 **swelt**
weakened   506 **fallow** jaundiced   510 **stent** stopped

And in his gere° for all the world he ferde°
515 Not only like the lover's maladye
Of Hereos,° but rather like manie,
Engendred of humour malencholic,
Biforn his owne celle fantastic.°
And shortly, turned was all up-so-down
520 Both habit and eek disposicioun
Of him, this woeful lover daun Arcite.
    What shold I all day of his woe endite?
Whan he endured had a yeer or two
This cruel torment and this pain and wo
525 At Thebes in his contree, as I saide,
Upon a night in sleep as he him laide
Him thought how that the winged god Mercurye
Biforn him stood, and bade him to be murrye.
His sleepy yerde° I hand he bare uprighte;
530 An hat he wered upon his heres brighte—
Arrayed was this god, as he took keep,°
As he was whan that Argus took his sleep,
And said him thus: "To Athens shaltou wende.°
There is thee shapen° of thy woe an ende."
535   And with that word Arcite woke and sterte:
"Now trewely, how sore that me smerte,"
Quod he, "to Athens right now wol I fare!
Ne for the drede of deeth shall I not spare
To see my lady that I love and serve.
540 In hir presence I recche not to sterve."°

514 **gere** changeableness   514 **ferde** fared, behaved   516 **lover's
malady of Hereos** i.e., of Eros—a temporary madness induced by
love, described in medieval medical treatises. The symptoms were
sleeplessness, depression, paleness, loss of appetite, hysteria. See
Modern Philology, XI, 491   516–18 **manie . . . fantastic** "mania,"
brought about by the humor of melancholy in the front part of the brain
(the "cell fantastic"). The front cell of the brain was thought to harbor
fantasy, the middle one reason, and the back one memory   529 **yerde**
Mercury's wand, capable of inducing sleep   531 **as he took keep** as
Arcite noticed   533 **wende** go   534 **There . . . shapen** there is pre-
pared for you   540 **I recche not to sterve** I don't care if I die

And with that word he caught a greet mirrour,
And saw that chaunged was all his colour,
And saw his visage all in another kinde;
And right anon it ran him in his minde
That sith his face was so disfigured   545
Of malady the which he had endured,
He mighte well, if that he bare him lowe,°
Live in Athens evermore unknowe,
And seen his lady well nigh day by day.
And right anon he chaunged his array,   550
And clad him as a poore laborer,
And all alone, save only a squier
That knew his privetee and all his cas°—
Which was disguised poorly° as he was—
To Athens is he gone the nexte° way.   555
And to the court he went upon a day,
And at the gate he proffreth his servise,
To drudge and draw what so men wol devise.
And shortly of this matter for to sayn,
He fill in office with a chamberlain,°   560
The which that dwelling was with Emelye;
For he was wise, and coude soon espye
Of every servant which that serveth here.
Well coud he hewen° wood and water bere,
For he was yong and mighty for the nones,   565
And thereto he was strong and big of bones,
To doon what any wight can him devise.
A yeer or two he was in this servise,
Page of the chambre of Emely the brighte—
And "Philostrate" he saide that he highte.   570

  But half so well-beloved a man as he
Ne was there never in court of his degree!°
He was so gentil of condicioun

---

547 **bare him lowe** acted low-class   553 **privetee ... cas** his secret
and all his circumstance   554 **poorly** as a poor man   555 **nexte**
nearest   560 **fill ... chamberlain** got into the service of a steward
564 **hewen** chop   572 **degree** social class

That thurghout all the court was his renown.
575 They saiden that it were a charitee
That Theseus wold enhauncen his degree,
And putten him in worshipful servise,
Ther as he might his vertu° exercise.
And thus within a while his name is spronge,
580 Both of his deedes and his goode tonge,
That Theseus hath taken him so neer,
That of his chambre he made him a squier,
And gaf him gold to maintene his degree.
And eek men brought him out of his contree,
585 Fro yeer to yeer, full prively his rente°—
But honestly and slyly he it spente
That no man wondred how that he it hadde.
And three yeer in this wise his life he ladde,
And bare him so in pees and eek in werre,°
590 There was no man that Theseus hath derre.°
    And in this blisse let° I now Arcite,
And speke I wol of Palamon a lite:
    In derkness and horrible and strong prisoun
This seven yeer hath seten Palamoun,
595 Forpined,° what for woe and for distresse!
Who feeleth double sore and hevinesse
But Palamon, that love distraineth so
That wood out of his wit he goth for wo?
And eek thereto he is a prisoner—
600 Perpetuelly, not only for a yeer.
Who coude ryme in English proprely
His martyrdom? Forsooth, it am not I.
Therefore I pass as lightly as I may:°

---

578 **vertu** good character and ability—hence he should have a more
honored occupation (worshipful servise) 585 **rente** income
589 **werre** war   590 **hath derre** liked better (dearer)   591 **let** leave
595 **Forpined** pined or wasted away   601–03 **Who . . . may** again,
an echo of Chaucer's own voice; the Knight is certainly not "ryming."
Notice line 606: Chaucer is here struggling to condense an unwieldy
narrative

It fill that in the seventh yeer, of May
The thridde° night, as olde bookes sayn   605
(That all this story tellen more plain),
Were it by aventure or destinee—
As whan a thing is shapen it shall be°—
That soon after the midnight, Palamoun,
By helping of a freend, brak his prisoun,   610
And fleeth the citee, fast as he may go,
For he had yive his jailer drinke so
Of a claree, made of a certain win
With nercotics and opie of Thebes fin,°
That all that night, though that men wold him shake,   615
The jailer sleep, he mighte not awake;
And thus he fleeth as fast as ever he may.
The night was short and faste by the day,
That needes cost° he most himselven hide.
And til a grove faste there beside   620
With dredful° foot than stalketh Palamoun—
For shortly, this was his opinioun,
That in that grove he wold him hide all day,
And in the night than wold he take his way
To Thebesward, his freendes for to praye   625
On Theseus to help him to werreye.°
And shortly, outher he wold lese his lif,
Or winnen Emely unto his wif—
This is th'effect and his entente plain.
    Now wol I turn to Arcite again,   630
That litel wist how neigh that was his care,°
Till that Fortune had brought him in the snare:

604–05 **May . . . thridde** May 3 was thought an unlucky day
608 **As . . . be** the phrase explains "destinee": when a thing is deter-
mined, it will happen. "Aventure" is chance   612–14 **drinke . . . fin**
drink some claree (wine mixed with honey and spices), made of a
special wine with narcotics in it and the fine opium of Thebes. Such
drugs were used to cure love-melancholy; hence Palamon's possession
of them, perhaps   619 **needes cost** by necessity   621 **dredful** timid
626 **werreye** make war   631 **That . . . care** who little knew how near
trouble was

The bisy larke, messager of day,
Salueth in hir song the morrwe grey,
635 And firy Phebus riseth up so brighte
That all the orient laugheth of the lighte,
And with his streemes dryeth in the greves°
The silver droppes hanging on the leves.
And Arcita, that in the court royal
640 With Theseus is squier principal,
Is risen and looketh on the murrye day;
And for to doon his observaunce to May,
Remembring on the point° of his desir,
He on a courser startling° as the fir
645 Is riden into the feeldes him to playe,
Out of the court were it a mile or twaye;
And to the grove of which that I you tolde
By aventure his way he gan to holde,
To maken him a garland of the greves,
650 Were it of woodebind or hawthorn leves;
And loud he song ayain the sunne sheene,
"May, with all thy flowres and thy greene,
Welcome be thou, faire freshe May,
In hope that I some greene gete may!"°
655 And from his courser with a lusty herte
Into the grove full hastily he sterte,
And in a path he rometh up and down
Thereas by aventure this Palamoun
Was in a bush, that no man might him see—
660 For sore afered of his deeth was he.
No thing ne knew he that it was Arcite;
God wot he wold have trowed° it full lite.
But sooth is said, gon sithen many yeeres,°
That "feeld hath eyen and the wood hath eres":
665 It is full fair a man to bere him evene,°

637 **greves** foliage 643 **point** object 644 **startling** leaping
654 **some ... may** may get something green. His song may be a wish
for love 662 **trowed** believed 663 **gon ... yeeres** since many years
ago 665 **It ... evene** it is very good for a man to conduct himself
with restraint

For alday meeten men at unset stevene.°
Full litel wot Arcite of his fellawe
That was so neigh to herknen all his sawe,°
For in the bush he sitteth now full stille.

    Whan that Arcite had romed all his fille, 670
And songen all the roundel lustily,
Into a study he fill suddenly,
As doon thise lovers in hir quainte geres°—
Now in the crop, now down in the breres,°
Now up, now down, as bucket in a welle. 675
Right as the Friday, soothly for to telle,
Now it shineth, now it raineth faste,
Right so can gery Venus° overcaste
The hertes of hir folk; right as hir day
Is gereful, right so chaungeth she array— 680
Seld is the Friday all the wike y-like.°
Whan that Arcite had song, he gan to sike,°
And set him down withouten any more:
"Alas," quod he, "that day that I was bore!
How longe, Juno, thurgh thy crueltee 685
Woltou werreyen° Thebes the citee?
Alas, y-brought is to confusioun
The blood royal of Cadme and Amphioun—
Of Cadmus, which that was the firste man
That Thebes bilt or° first the town began, 690
And of the citee first was crowned king.
Of his linage am I and his offspring,
By veray line,° as of the stock royal.
And now I am so caitiff° and so thrall,
That he that is my mortal enemy, 695

666 **For ... stevene** for men constantly meet each other at unexpected
times   668 **so ... sawe** so close as to hear all he said   673 **quainte
geres** strange moods   674 **crop ... breres** now in the treetop, now
down in the briars   678 **gery Venus** changeable Venus. Friday is Ve-
nus's day and was said to have different weather from the rest of the
week   681 **all ... y-like** like the rest of the week   682 **sike** sigh
686 **werreyen** make war upon   690 **or** ere, before   693 **veray line**
direct descent   694 **caitiff** wretched

I serve him as his squier povrely!°
And yet doth Juno me well more shame,
For I dare not biknow° mine owen name,
But there as I was wont to hight Arcite,
700 Now hight I Philostrate, not worth a mite!
Alas, thou felle Mars! Alas, Juno!
Thus hath your ire our linage all fordo,
Save only me and wretched Palamoun,
That Theseus martyreth in prisoun!
705 And over all this, to sleen me outrely,
Love hath his firy dart so brenningly
Y-sticked thurgh my trewe careful herte,
That shapen was my deeth erst than my sherte!°
Ye sleen me with your eyen, Emelye!
710 Ye been the cause wherefore that I die!
Of all the remnant of mine other care
Ne set I nought the mountance of a tare,°
So that I coud doon ought to your plesaunce!"
And with that word he fill down in a traunce
715 A longe time. And after he up sterte.
    This Palamon, that thought that thurgh his herte
He felt a cold swerd suddenliche glide,
For ire he quoke, no longer wold he bide.°
And whan that he had herd Arcite's tale,
720 As he were wood, with face deed and pale,
He stert him up out of the bushes thicke
And said, "Arcite, false traitour wicke,
Now artou hent, that lovest my lady so,
For whom that I have all this pain and wo—
725 And art my blood, and to my conseil sworn,
As I full oft have told thee herebiforn,
And hast bijaped° here duke Theseus,
And falsely chaunged hast thy name thus.

---

696 **povrely** in a humble capacity 698 **biknow** reveal
708 **shapen . . . sherte** my death was predestined before my shirt, i.e.,
before my first garment was made. A commonplace 712 **moun-
tance . . . tare** value of a weed 718 **bide** wait 727 **bijaped** duped

I wol be deed or elles thou shalt die!
Thou shalt not love my lady Emelye,   *730*
But I wol love hir only and namo!
For I am Palamon, thy mortal fo,
And though that I no wepne have in this place,
But out of prison am astert° by grace,
I drede not that outher thou shalt die,   *735*
Or thou ne shalt not loven Emelye.
Chees which thou wolt, or thou shalt not asterte."
    This Arcite with full despitous herte,
Whan he him knew and had his tale herd,
As fierce as leon pulled out his swerd,   *740*
And saide thus: "By God that sit above,
Nere it that thou art sick and wood for love,
And eek that thou no wepne hast in this place,
Thou sholdest never out of this grove pace,
That thou ne sholdest dien of my hond!   *745*
For I defy the suretee and the bond
Which that thou saist that I have made to thee.
What, veray fool, think well that love is free,
And I wol love hir, maugree° all thy might!
But for as much thou art a worthy knight,   *750*
And wilnest to darrein° hir by battaile,
Have here my trouth, tomorrwe I wol not faile,
Withouten witing of any other wight,
That here I wol be founden as a knight,
And bringen harneis° right enough for thee—   *755*
And chees the best, and leeve the worst for me.
And mete and drinke this night wol I bringe
Enough for thee, and clothes for thy beddinge.
And if so be that thou my lady winne
And slee me in this wood ther I am inne,   *760*
Thou maist well have thy lady as for me."°
This Palamon answered, "I graunt it thee."

---

734 **astert** escaped   749 **maugree** in spite of   751 **wilnest to dar-
rein** wish to decide (your claim to) her   755 **harneis** armor   761 **as
for me** as far as I am concerned

And thus they been departed till amorrwe,
Whan ech of hem had laid his faith to borrwe.°
765   O Cupid, out of alle charitee!
O regne,° that wold no fellaw° have with thee!
Full sooth is said that love ne lordshipe
Wol not, his thankes, have no fellawshipe;°
Well finden that Arcite and Palamoun!
770   Arcite is riden anon unto the town,
And on the morrwe ere it were dayes light,
Full prively two harneis hath he dight,
Both suffisant and meete to darreine
The battaile in the feeld bitwix hem twaine;
775 And on his horse, alone as he was born,
He carrieth all this harneis him biforn;
And in the grove at time and place y-set
This Arcite and this Palamon been met.
    To chaungen gan the colour in hir face,°
780 Right as the hunters in the regne of Trace,
That standeth at the gappe° with a spere,
Whan hunted is the leon or the bere,
And hereth him come rushing in the greves,
And breketh bothe boughes and the leves,
785 And thinketh, "Here cometh my mortal enemy!
Withoute fail he moot be deed or I,
For outher I mot sleen him at the gappe,
Or he mot slee me if that me mishappe."
So ferden they in chaunging of hir hewe.
790   As fer as everich of hem other knewe,
There nas no "Good day" ne no saluinge,
But straight, withouten word or rehersinge,
Everich of hem help for to armen other,
As freendly as he were his owne brother.
795 And after that with sharpe speres stronge

---

764 **to borrwe** as a pledge   766 **regne** rule   766 **fellaw** companion
768 **his . . . fellawshipe** willingly have any companionship   779 **face**
faces   781 **gappe** the space between hunters and game

They foinen ech at other° wonder longe—
Thou mightest weene that this Palamoun
In his fighting were a wood leoun,
And as a cruel tiger was Arcite:
As wilde bores gonnen they to smite,   800
That frothen white as foom, for ire wood—
Up to the ankle fought they in hir blood.
And in this wise I let hem fighting dwelle,°
And forth I wol of Theseus you telle.

The destinee, ministre general,   805
That executeth in the world overall
The purveyance° that God hath seen biforn,
So strong it is that, though the world had sworn
The contrary of a thing by ye or nay,
Yet sometime it shall fallen on a day   810
That° falleth not eft° within a thousand yeer.
For certainly, our appetites heer,
Be it of wer, or pees, or hate, or love,
All is this ruled by the sight above.
This mene I now by mighty Theseus,   815
That for to hunten is so desirous,
And namely at the greete hert in May,
That in his bed there daweth him° no day
That he nis clad and redy for to ride
With hunt and horn and houndes him beside;   820
For in his hunting hath he swich delit
That it is all his joy and appetit
To been himself the greete hertes bane;°
For after Mars he serveth now Diane.°

Cleer was the day, as I have told ere this,   825
And Theseus, with alle joy and bliss,
With his Ipolyta the faire queene,

---

796 **foinen . . . other** thrust out at each other   803 **dwelle** continue
807 **purveyance** foreknowledge   811 **That** what   811 **eft** again
818 **daweth him** dawns for him   823 **bane** death   824 **Diane** god-
dess of hunting

And Emelye clothed all in greene,
On hunting been they riden royally,
830 And to the grove that stood full faste by,
In which there was an hert, as men him tolde,
Duke Theseus the straighte way hath holde,
And to this land he rideth him full right.
For thider was the hert wont have his flight,
835 And over a brook, and so forth on his waye.
This Duke wol han a course° at him or twaye,
With houndes swich as that him list commande.
And whan this Duke was come unto the lande,
Under the sun° he looketh, and anon
840 He was ware of Arcite and Palamon,
That foughten breme° as it were boles° two!
The brighte swerdes wenten to and fro
So hidously that with the leste strook
It seemed as it wolde fell an ook!
845 But what they were no thing he ne wot.
This Duke his courser with the spores smot,
And at a stert he was bitwix hem two,
And pulled out a swerd, and cried, "Ho!
Namore, up° pain of lesing of your heed!
850 By mighty Mars, he shall anon be deed
That smiteth any stroke that I may seen!
But telleth me what mister° men ye been,
That been so hardy for to fighten heer,
Withouten judge or other officer,
855 As it were in a listes royally?"
    This Palamon answerde hastily
And saide, "Sir, what needeth wordes mo?
We have the deeth deserved bothe two.
Two woeful wretches been we, two caitives,
860 That been encumbred of° our owne lives;

---

836 **course** charge, run   839 **Under the sun** in a low sun (?); or, per-
haps, shielding his eyes   841 **breme** furiously   841 **boles** bulls
849 **up** on   852 **mister** kind of   860 **encumbred of** burdened by,
tired of

And as thou art a rightful lord and judge,
Ne yive us neither mercy ne refuge;
But slee me first, for sainte charitee,
But slee my fellaw eek as well as me;
Or slee him first, for though thou knowest it lite,   865
This is thy mortal foe, this is Arcite,
That fro thy land is banished on his heed,°
For which he hath deserved to be deed;
For this is he that came unto thy gate,
And saide that he highte Philostrate.   870
Thus hath he japed thee full many a yeer,
And thou hast maked him thy chief squier;
And this is he that loveth Emelye.
For sith the day is come that I shall die,
I make plainly my confessioun   875
That I am thilke woeful Palamoun,
That hath thy prison broken wickedly.
I am thy mortal foe, and it am I
That loveth so hot Emely the brighte,
That I wol die present in hir sighte;   880
Wherefore I axe deeth and my juwise.°
But slee my fellaw in the same wise,
For both have we deserved to be slain."
    This worthy Duke answered anon again
And said, "This is a short conclusioun.   885
Your owne mouth by your confessioun
Hath dampned you, and I wol it recorde:
It needeth not to pine you with the corde°—
Ye shull be deed, by mighty Mars the rede!"°
    The queen anon for veray womanheede   890
Gan for to weep, and so did Emelye,
And all the ladies in the compaignye.
Greet pitee was it, as it thought hem alle,
That ever swich a chaunce sholde falle;
For gentilmen they were of greet estat,   895

867 **on his heed** on pain of losing his head   881 **juwise** sentence
888 **pine . . . corde** torture   889 **rede** red is associated with Mars

And nothing but for love was this debat;
And saw hir bloody woundes wide and sore,
And alle criden, bothe lass and more,
"Have mercy, lord, upon us women alle!"
900 And on hir bare knees adown they falle,
And wold have kist his feet ther as he stood;
Till at the last aslacked was his mood°—
For pitee renneth soon in gentil herte°—
And though he first for ire quoke and sterte,
905 He hath considered shortly, in a clause,
The trespass of hem both, and eek the cause;
And although that his ire hir guilt accused,
Yet in his reson he hem both excused,
As thus: He thoughte well that every man
910 Wol help himself in love if that he can,
And eek deliver himself out of prisoun.
And eek his herte had compassioun
Of women, for they wepten ever in oon.
And in his gentil hert he thought anon,
915 And soft unto himself he saide, "Fy
Upon a lord that wol have no mercy,
But be a leon both in word and deede
To hem that been in repentance and drede,
As well as to a proud despitous man
920 That wol maintene that he first began.°
That lord hath litel of discrecioun
That in swich case kan no divisioun,°
But weyeth pride and humbless after oon."°
And shortly, whan his ire is thus agoon,
925 He gan to looken up with eyen lighte,
And spak thise same wordes all on highte:°
"The God of Love, ah, *benedicite!*

---

902 **aslacked . . . mood** his anger was assuaged   903 **For . . . herte**
the line is a great favorite of Chaucer's   920 **maintene . . . began**
keep up what he first started (i.e., stubbornly)   922 **kan no divisioun**
sees no distinction   923 **weyeth . . . oon** weighs pride and humility
equally   926 **on highte** aloud

How mighty and how greet a lord is he!
Agains his might there gaineth none obstacles.
He may be cleped a god for his miracles!   930
For he can maken at his owen guise°
Of everich hert as that him list devise.
Lo, here this Arcite and this Palamoun,
That quitly° weren out of my prisoun,
And might have lived in Thebes royally,   935
And witen° I am hir mortal enemy,
And that hir deeth lith in my might also—
And yet hath Love, maugree hir eyen two,
Brought hem hider bothe for to die.
Now looketh, is not that an heigh follye?   940
   Who may been a fool, but if he love?
Behold, for Goddes sake that sit above,
See how they bleed! Be they not well arrayed?
Thus hath hir lord the God of Love y-payed
Hir wages and hir fees for hir servise.   945
And yet they weenen for to be full wise,
That serven Love, for aught that may bifalle.
But this is yet the beste game° of alle,
That she for whom they have this jolitee
Can hem therefore as muche thank as me!°   950
She wot namore of all this hote fare,
By God, than wot a cockoo of an hare.°
But all mot been assayed,° hot and cold—
A man mot been a fool, or yong or old.
I wot it by myself full yore agoon,   955
For in my time a servant° was I oon.
And therefore, sin I know of Love's paine,
And wot how sore it can a man distraine,°
As he that hath been caught oft in his las,°

931 **at ... guise** at will 934 **quitly** freely 936 **witen** know
948 **game** joke   950 **Can ... me** is as much obliged to them for it as
to me   952 **than ... hare** than a cuckoo knows about a hare. (Some
editors give the reading "or an hare.") 953 **assayed** tried out
956 **servant** i.e., of Love   958 **distraine** afflict   959 **las** snare

960 I you foryive all holly this trespass,
     At request of the queen that kneeleth here,
     And eek of Emely my suster dere;
     And ye shall both anon unto me swere
     That never mo ye shall my contree dere,°
965 Ne make wer upon me, night nor day,
     But been my freendes in all that ye may.
     I you foryive this trespass everydeel."
         And they him sworen his axing° fair and well,
     And him of lordship and of mercy prayde;
970 And he hem graunteth grace, and thus he saide:
         "To speke of royal linage and richesse,
     Though that she were a queen or a princesse,
     Ech of you both is worthy, douteless,
     To wedden whan time is. But, natheless—
975 I speke as for my suster Emelye
     For whom ye have this strife and jalousye—
     Ye wot yourself she may not wedden two
     At ones, though ye fighten evermo.
     That one of you, al be him loth or lief,°
980 He mot go pipen in an ivy leef°—
     This is to sayn, she may not now have bothe,
     Al be ye never so jalous ne so wrothe.
     And forthy I you put in this degree,°
     That ech of you shall have his destinee
985 As him is shape, and herkneth in what wise—
     Lo, here your end of that I shall devise:
         My will is this, for plat° conclusioun,
     Withouten any replicacioun°—
     If that you liketh, take it for the beste:
990 That everich of you shall goon where him leste,
     Freely, withouten raunson or daunger,
     And this day fifty wikes, fer ne neer,°
     Everich of you shall bring an hundred knightes,

964 **dere** harm   968 **axing** what he asked   979 **al . . . lief** whether it
be disagreeable or agreeable to him   980 **pipen . . . leef** whistle (for
consolation) using an ivy leaf as a reed   983 **degree** state   987 **plat**
plain, flat   988 **replicacioun** protest   992 **fer ne neer** more or less

Armed for listes up° at alle rightes,°
All redy to darrein hir by battaile.   995
And this bihote° I you withouten faile,
Upon my trouth and as I am a knight,
That whether of you bothe that hath might—
This is to sayn, that whether he or thou
May with his hundred as I spak of now   1000
Sleen his contrary, or out of listes drive—
Than shall I yive Emely to wive
To whom that Fortune yiveth so fair a grace.
The listes shall I maken in his place,
And God so wisly on my soule rewe,°   1005
As I shall even judge been and trewe.
Ye shall none other ende with me maken,
That one of you ne shall be deed or taken.
And if you thinketh this is well y-said,
Say your avis,° and holdeth you apaid.°   1010
This is your end and your conclusioun."
   Who looketh lightly now but Palamoun?
Who springeth up for joye but Arcite?
Who coude tell or who coud it endite
The joye that is maked in the place,   1015
Whan Theseus hath done so fair a grace?
But down on knees went every manner wight,
And thanken him with all hir hert and might,
And namely the Thebans ofte sithe.°
And thus with good hope and with herte blithe   1020
They take hir leeve, and homeward gonne they ride
To Thebes, with his olde walles wide.

PART THREE

I trow men wolde deem it necligence
If I foryet to tellen the dispence°
Of Theseus, that goth so bisily   1025

---

994 **Armed . . . up** cf. "dressed up"   994 **at alle rightes** in all respects
996 **bihote** promise   1005 **rewe** pity   1010 **avis** opinion   1010 **apaid**
satisfied   1019 **ofte sithe** many times   1024 **dispence** expenditure

To maken up the listes royally,
That swich a noble theatre° as it was
I dare well sayen in this world there nas.
The circuit a mile was aboute,
1030 Walled of stone and ditched all withoute.
Round was the shape in manner of compass,
Full of degrees, the height of sixty pas,°
That whan a man was set on oo degree°
He letted not his fellow for to see.°
1035   Eestward there stood a gate of marble whit,
Westward right swich another in th'opposit;
And shortly to concluden, swich a place
Was none in erth as in so litel space.°
For in the land there was no crafty man
1040 That geometry or ars-metrik kan,°
Ne purtrayour, ne kerver of images,
That Theseus ne yaf him mete and wages,
The theatre for to maken and devise.
And for to doon his rite and sacrifise,
1045 He eestward hath, upon the gate above,
In worship of Venus, goddess of love,
Doon make an auter° and an oratorye.
And on the gate westward, in memorye
Of Mars, he maked hath right swich another,
1050 That coste largely of gold a fother.°
And northward in a touret on the wall,
Of alabastre white and red coral,
An oratory riche for to see,
In worship of Diane of chastitee,
1055 Hath Theseus doon wrought° in noble wise.

1027 **theatre** arena   1032 **Full . . . pas** constructed fully in steps,
sixty yards high   1033 **on oo degree** on one step   1034 **letted . . .
see** did not keep someone else from seeing   1038 **as . . . space** of com-
parable size   1040 **ars-metrik kan** knows arithmetic   1047 **auter**
altar   1050 **fother** cartload   1055 **doon wrought** had made. The
kind of symbolical scenes which follow occur often in medieval
literature

But yet had I forgeten to devise
The noble kerving and the portraitures,
The shape, the countenance, and the figures,
That weren in thise oratories three.

*   *   *

First, in the temple of Venus maistou see,   *1060*
Wrought on the wall, full pitous to beholde,
The broken sleepes and the sikes° colde,
The sacred teres and the waymentinge,
The firy strokes of the desiringe
That Love's servants in this life enduren,   *1065*
The othes that hir covenants assuren,
Plesance and Hope, Desire, Foolhardinesse,
Beautee and Youthe, Bawdery, Richesse,
Charmes and Force, Lesinges,° Flatterye,
Dispence, Bisiness, and Jalousye,   *1070*
That wered of yellow goldes° a garland,
And a cockoo sitting on hir hand;
Feestes, instruments, caroles, daunces,
Lust and array,° and all the circumstances
Of love, which that I° reckened and recken shall,   *1075*
By order weren painted on the wall,
And mo than I can make of mencioun.
For soothly all the Mount of Citheroun,°
Ther Venus hath hir principal dwellinge,
Was shewed on the wall in portrayinge,   *1080*
With all the garden and the lustinesse.
Not was foryeten the porter Idelnesse,
Ne Narcissus the fair of yore agoon,
Ne yet the folly of king Salomon,

1062 **sikes** sighs   1069 **Lesinges** lies   1071 **goldes** marigolds. Yellow is the color of jealousy; the cuckoo in the next line is associated with cuckoldry   1074 **Lust and array** pleasure and dress   1075 **I** conventional in descriptions; the knight speaks as if he had been there   1078 **Citheroun** Cythera, where Venus rose from the sea

1085 Ne yet the greete strength of Ercules,
  Th'enchantments of Medea and Circes,
  Ne of Turnus with the hardy fierce corage,
  The riche Cresus, caitiff in servage.
  Thus may ye seen that wisdom ne richesse,
1090 Beautee ne sleighte,° strengthe, hardinesse,
  Ne may with Venus holde champartye,°
  For as hir list, the world than may she gie.°
  Lo, all thise folk so caught were in hir las°
  Till they for woe full ofte said alas.
1095 Suffiseth here ensamples one or two,
  And though I coude recken a thousand mo.
   The statue of Venus, glorious for to see,
  Was naked, fleting° in the large see,
  And fro the navel down all covered was
1100 With wawes° green and bright as any glass.
  A citole° in hir right hand hadde she,
  And on hir heed, full seemly for to see,
  A rose garland fresh and well smellinge,
  Above hir heed hir douves° flickeringe.
1105 Biforn hir stood hir sone Cupido;
  Upon hir shouldres winges had he two,
  And blind he was, as it is ofte seene;
  A bow he bare, and arrwes bright and keene.

*   *   *

  Why shold I not as well eek tell you all
1110 The portraiture that was upon the wall
  Within the temple of mighty Mars the rede?
  All painted was the wall in length and brede
  Like to the estres° of the grisly place
  That hight the greete temple of Mars in Trace,

1090 **sleighte** trickery 1091 **champartye** rivalry 1092 **gie** govern
1093 **las** snare 1098 **fleting** floating 1100 **wawes** waves 1101 **ci-
tole** stringed instrument 1104 **douves** doves were thought to be
"maxime in coitu fervidae" 1113 **estres** interior parts

In thilke colde frosty regioun   *1115*
Ther as Mars hath his sovereign mansioun.
   First on the wall was painted a forest,
In which there dwelleth neither man ne beest,
With knotty, knarry, barrein trees olde,
Of stubbes sharp and hidous to beholde,   *1120*
In which there ran a rumble in a swough,°
As though a storm shold bresten every bough.
And downward on an hill under a bente°
There stood the temple of Mars armipotente,°
Wrought all of burned steel, of which th'entree   *1125*
Was long and strait and ghastly for to see,
And thereout came a rage and swich a veze°
That it made all the gate for to reze.°
The northern light in at the doores shoon,
For window on the wall ne was there noon   *1130*
Thurgh which men mighten any light discerne.
The door was all of adamant eterne,
Y-clenched overthwart and endelong°
With iren tough; and for to make it strong
Every piler the temple to sustene   *1135*
Was tonne-greet,° of iren bright and sheene.
There saw I first the derk imagininge
Of Felony, and all the compassinge,°
The cruel Ire, red as any gleede,°
The pike-purs, and eek the pale Drede,   *1140*
The smiler with the knife under the cloke,
The shepne° brenning with the blacke smoke,
The treson of the murdring in the bed,
The open Wer with woundes all bibled,°
Contek° with bloody knife and sharp menace;   *1145*

1121 **in a swough** in the form of a great wind   1123 **bente** hillside
1124 **armipotente** powerful in arms   1127 **veze** blast (of wind)
1128 **reze** shake   1133 **overthwart and endelong** crosswise and
lengthwise   1136 **tonne-greet** as thick as a tun (barrel)   1138 **com-
passinge** scheming   1139 **gleede** live coal   1142 **shepne** stable
1144 **bibled** covered with blood   1145 **Contek** strife

All full of chirking° was that sorry place!
The sleer° of himself yet saw I ther—
His herte blood hath bathed all his heer;
The nail y-driven in the shode° anight;
1150 The colde Deeth with mouth gaping upright.
Amiddes of the temple sat Meschaunce,
With disconfort and sorry countenaunce.
Yet saw I Woodness,° laughing in his rage;
Armed Complaint, Outhees,° and fierce Outrage;
1155 The caroine° in the bush with thort y-corve,°
A thousand slain and nought of qualm y-storve,°
The tyrant with the prey by force y-raft,
The town destroyed—there was nothing laft.
Yet saw I brent the shippes hoppesteres,°
1160 The hunte° strangled with the wilde beres,
The sow freten° the child right in the cradel,
The cook y-scalded for all his longe ladel.
Nought was forgetten by the infortune of Marte
The carter overridden with his carte—
1165 Under the wheel full low he lay adown.
There were also of Martes divisioun°
The barbour and the butcher and the smith
That forgeth sharpe swerdes on his stith.°
And all above depainted in a towr
1170 Saw I Conquest, sitting in greet honour,
With the sharpe swerd over his heed
Hanging by a subtil twines threed.
Depainted was the slaughtre of Julius,
Of grete Nero, and of Antonius—
1175 Al be that thilke time they were unborn,

1146 **chirking** creaking or scraping sound   1147 **sleer** slayer
1149 **shode** skull   1153 **Woodness** madness   1154 **Outhees** outcry
1155 **caroine** corpse   1155 **y-corve** cut   1156 **of qualm y-storve**
killed by pestilence (which would have come under the influence of
Saturn)   1159 **shippes hoppesteres** dancing ships   1160 **hunte**
hunter   1161 **freten** finished devouring   1166 **of ... divisioun** in
Mars' jurisdiction   1168 **stith** anvil

Yet was hir deeth depainted therebiforn,
By menacing of Mars, right by figure!°
So was it showed in that portraiture,
As is depainted in the sters above
Who shall be slain, or elles deed for love.   1180
Suffiseth one ensample in stories olde:
I may not recken hem alle, though I wolde.
   The statue of Mars upon a carte stood
Armed, and looked grim as he were wood.
And over his heed there shinen two figures   1185
Of sterres, that been cleped in scriptures
That one Puella, that other Rubeus.°
This god of armes was arrayed thus:
A wolf there stood before him at his feet,
With eyen red, and of a man he eet—   1190
With subtil pencil depainted was this storye
In redouting° of Mars and of his glorye.

        *   *   *

   Now to the temple of Diane the chaste
As shortly as I can I wol me haste,
To telle you all the descripsioun.   1195
Depainted been the walles up and down
Of hunting and of shamefast° chastitee.
There saw I how woeful Calistopee,°
Whan that Diane agreved was with here,
Was turned fro a woman til a bere,   1200
And after was she made the Lode-Sterre—
Thus was it painted, I can say you no ferre.°

1177 **menacing ... figure** the threat of Mars figured in the stars
1187 **Puella ... Rubeus** these were figures in geomancy, the art of
interpreting dots hurriedly made on paper. Both are devoted to Mars
1192 **redouting** reverence 1197 **shamefast** modest 1198 **Calis-
topee** Callisto. Jove lay with her, and Diana was angry because she
was no longer a virgin. Juno changed her into a bear, and Jove put her
in the heavens (as Ursa Major). The connection of mythology and as-
trology seemed natural to the medievals 1202 **ferre** farther

Hir son is eek a ster, as men may see.
There saw I Dane° y-turned til° a tree—
1205 I mene not the goddesse Diane,
But Penneus' daughter, which that highte Dane.
There saw I Atheon° an hert y-maked,
For vengeance that he saw Diane all naked—
I saw how that his houndes have him caught
1210 And freten° him, for that they knew him nought.
Yet painted was a litel further moor
How Athalante° hunted the wilde boor,
And Meleagre, and many another mo,
For which Diane wrought him care and wo.
1215 There saw I many another wonder storye,
The which me list not drawen to memorye.
    This goddess on an hert° full hye seet,
With smalle houndes all about hir feet,
And underneth hir feet she had a moone—
1220 Waxing it was, and sholde wanie soone.
In gaudee° green hir statue clothed was,
With bow in hand and arrwes in a cas;
Hir eyen caste she full low adown
Ther Pluto hath his derke regioun.
1225 A woman travailing° was hir biforn,
But for hir child so longe was unborn,
Full pitously Lucina° gan she calle,
And saide, "Help, for thou maist best of alle."
Well coud he painte lifly that it wroughte;
1230 With many a florin he the hewes boughte.

*   *   *

Now been thise listes made, and Theseus,
That at his greete cost arrayed thus

1204 **Dane** Daphne   1204 **til** into   1207 **Atheon** Actaeon   1210 **freten** devoured   1212 **Athalante** Atalanta   1217 **hert** harts were associated with chastity   1221 **gaudee** yellowish   1225 **travailing** in labor   1227 **Lucina** goddess of childbirth

The temples and the theatre everydeel,
Whan it was done him liked wonder well.
But stinte I wol of Theseus a lite,   1235
And speke of Palamon and of Arcite.
    The day approcheth of hir returninge,
That everich shold an hundred knightes bringe
The battaile to darrein, as I you tolde.
And til Athens, hir covenant for to holde,   1240
Hath everich of hem brought an hundred knightes,
Well armed for the wer at alle rightes;
And sikerly there trowed many a man
That never sithen that the world bigan,
As for to speke of knighthood of hir hand,   1245
As fer as God hath maked see and land,
Nas of so few so noble a compaignye.
For every wight that loved chivalrye,
And wold, his thankes, han a passant name,°
Hath prayed that he might been of that game—   1250
And well was him° that thereto chosen was;
For if there fill tomorrwe swich a cas,
Ye knowen well that every lusty knight
That loveth paramours° and hath his might,
Were it in Engelond or elleswhere,   1255
They wold, hir thankes, wilnen to be there.
To fighten for a lady, *ben'dic'te*
It were a lusty sighte for to see!
    And right so ferden they with Palamon.
With him there wenten knightes many oon;   1260
Some wol been armed in an habergeoun,°
And in a brestplate and in a light gipoun;°
And some wol have a paire plates° large;
And some wol have a Pruce° sheeld or a targe;°

1249 **wold . . . name** would willingly have an outstanding reputation
1251 **well was him** (there was) happiness for him   1254 **paramours**
with knightly devotion   1261 **habergeoun** coat of mail   1262 **gi-
poun** tunic   1263 **paire plates** set of plate-armor   1264 **Pruce**
Prussian   1264 **targe** round shield

1265 Some wol been armed on his legges well,
     And have an ax, and some a mace of steel—
     There nis no newe guise that it nas old.°
     Armed were they as I have you told,
     Everich after his opinioun.
1270   There maistou seen coming with Palamon
     Lygurge° himself, the grete king of Trace.
     Black was his beerd and manly was his face;
     The cercles of his eyen in his heed,
     They gloweden bitwixen yellow and red,
1275 And like a griffon looked he aboute,
     With kempe heres° on his browes stoute.
     His limes greet, his brawnes hard and stronge,
     His shouldres brod, his armes round and longe,
     And as the guise was in his contree,
1280 Full hye upon a chaar° of gold stood he,
     With foure white boles in the trais.°
     Insted of cote-armure° over his harneis,
     With nailes yellow and bright as any gold
     He had a beres skin, col-black for old.°
1285 His longe heer was kembed behind his back—
     As any raven's fether it shone for black.
     A wreth of gold, arm-greet,° of huge wighte,°
     Upon his heed, set full of stones brighte,
     Of fine rubies and of diamaunts;
1290 About his chaar there wente white alaunts,°
     Twenty and mo, as greet as any steer,

1267 **nis ... old** is no new (Fourteenth-century) fashion that was not
found among the ancients. The line implies that there is nothing new
under the sun   1271 **Lygurge** Lycurgus is described, according to Curry
(*Chaucer and the Medieval Sciences*) as a "Saturnalian" type, i.e., under
the influence of Saturn in astrology. Saturn has favored Palamon. The
figure of Emetrius, described below in Arcite's throng, is a Martian type.
Chaucer thus employs the medieval science of astrology to give consis-
tency to the armies   1276 **kempe heres** shaggy hairs   1280 **chaar**
chariot   1281 **boles in the trais** bulls in the traces (i.e., attached to his
chariot)   1282 **cote-armure** tunic worn over armor   1284 **for old**
black because of age; the bearskin has gilded claws   1287 **arm-greet**
thick as an arm   1287 **wighte** weight   1290 **alaunts** hunting dogs

To hunten at the leon or the deer,
And followed him with mosel° fast y-bounde,
Collared of gold, and tourettes filed rounde.°
An hundred lordes had he in his route, 1295
Armed full well, with hertes stern and stoute.

    With Arcita, in stories as men finde,
The greet Emetrius, the king of Inde,
Upon a steede bay trapped in steel,
Covered in cloth of gold, diapred° well, 1300
Came riding like the god of armes, Mars.
His cote-armure was of cloth of Tars,°
Couched with perles white and round and greete;
His saddle was of brend° gold new y-bete.
A mantlet upon his shoulder hanginge, 1305
Bretful of rubies red as fire sparklinge;
His crispe heer like ringes was y-runne,°
And that was yellow and glittred as the sunne;
His nose was heigh, his eyen bright citrin,°
His beerd was well begunne for to springe; 1310
A fewe fraknes° in his face y-spreind,°
Bitwizen yellow and somdeel black y-meind;°
And as a leon he his looking caste.
Of five and twenty yeer his age I caste;
His beerd was well begunne for to springe; 1315
His voice was a trumpe thunderinge;
Upon his heed he wered of laurer greene
A garland fresh and lusty for to seene;
Upon his hand he bare for his deduit°
An egle tame, as any lily whit. 1320
An hundred lordes had he with him there,
All armed, save hir heedes, in all hir gere,

1293 **mosel** muzzle   1294 **tourettes filed rounde** rings for attaching
a leash, filed into roundness (?)   1300 **diapred** patterned, decorated
1302 **cloth of Tars** silk   1304 **brend** refined   1307 **crispe .. y-
runne** curly hair flowed in rings   1309 **citrin** yellow (probably hazel
or light brown), consistent with his Martian characteristics
1311 **fraknes** freckles; also Martian   1311 **y-spreind** scattered
1312 **y-meind** mixed   1319 **deduit** amusement

Full richely in alle manner thinges;
For trusteth well that dukes, erles, kinges,
1325 Were gadred in this noble compaignye,
For love and for encrees of chivalrye.
About this king there ran on every part
Full many a tame leon and leopart.
        And in this wise thise lordes all and some
1330 Been on the Sunday to the citee come
Aboute prime,° and in the town alight.
This Theseus, this Duke, this worthy knight,
Whan he had brought hem into his citee,
And inned hem, everich at his degree,°
1335 He feesteth hem and doth so greet labour
To esen hem and doon hem all honour,
That yet men weenen that no mannes wit,
Of noon estate, ne coud amenden it.
The minstralcy, the service at the feeste,
1340 The grete yiftes to the mest° and leste,
The rich array of Theseus' palais,
Ne who sat first or last upon the dais,
What ladies fairest been and best dauncinge,
Or which of hem can dauncen best and singe,
1345 Ne who most feelingly speketh of love,
What hawkes sitten on the perch above,
What houndes liggen on the floor adown—
Of all this make I now no mencioun,
But all th'effect; that thinketh me the beste.
1350 Now cometh the point,° and herkneth if you leste:

*   *   *

The Sunday night, ere day bigan to springe,
Whan Palamon the larke herde singe—

1331 **prime** nine a.m.   1334 **inned . . . degree** lodged them, each one
by his rank   1340 **mest** most (in rank)   1350 **the point** very much
the point indeed: note how in their prayers which follow each prays for
what he really wants, in accordance with his character

Although it nere not day by houres two
Yet song the lark; and Palamon right tho,
With holy hert and with an heigh corage,   *1355*
He rose to wenden on his pilgrimage,
Unto the blissful Cytherea benigne—
I mene Venus honourable and digne.
And in hir hour° he walketh forth a pas
Unto the listes ther hir temple was,   *1360*
And down he kneeleth, and with humble cheere
And herte sore, he said as ye shall heere:
    "Fairest of fair, O lady mine Venus,
Daughter of Jove and spouse to Vulcanus,
Thou gladder° of the Mount of Citheron: *1365*
For thilke love thou haddest to Adon,°
Have pitee of my bitter teres smerte,
And take mine humble prayer at thine herte!
Alas, I ne have no langage to telle
Th'effect ne the torments of mine helle.   *1370*
Mine herte may mine harmes not biwraye°;
I am so confus that I can not saye
But mercy, lady bright, that knowest welle
My thought, and seest what harmes that I feele.
Consider all this, and rew upon my sore,   *1375*
As wisly as I shall for evermore,
Emforth° my might, thy trewe servant be,
And holden wer° alway with chastitee.
That make I mine avow, so ye me helpe.
I keepe nought of armes for to yelpe,°   *1380*
Ne I n'axe not tomorrwe to have victorye,
Ne renown in this cas, ne vaine glorye

1359 **hir hour** each day is named for a planet, and each successive
hour belongs to a planet—beginning with the one for which the day is
named and proceeding in rotation with this sequence: Sun, Venus,
Mercury, Moon, Saturn, Jupiter, Mars. Thus on "Sunday night" the
twenty-third hour comes around to Venus; this is when Palamon prays
to his goddess 1365 **gladder** gladdener 1366 **Adon** Adonis
1371 **biwraye** show   1377 **Emforth** according to   1378 **holden wer**
be at odds   1380 **yelpe** boast

Of pris of armes blowen up and down:
But I wold have fully possessioun
1385 Of Emely, and die in thy servise.
Find thou the manner how and in what wise—
I recche not but it may better be
To have victory of hem, or they of me,
So that I have my lady in mine armes!
1390 For though so be that Mars is god of armes,
Your vertu is so greet in heven above
That, if you list, I shall well have my love.
Thy temple wol I worship evermo,
And on thine auter, wher° I ride or go,°
1395 I wol doon sacrifice and fires bete.°
And if ye wol not so, my lady sweete,
Than pray I thee tomorrwe with a spere
That Arcita me thurgh the herte bere;
Than rekke I not, whan I have lost my lif,
1400 Though that Arcita win hir to his wif.
This is th'effect and end of my prayere:
Yif me my love, thou blissful lady dere!"

     Whan the orison was done of Palamon,
His sacrifice he did, and that anoon,
1405 Full pitously, with alle circumstaunces°—
Al° tell I not as now his observaunces.
But at the last the statue of Venus shook,
And made a signe whereby that he took
That his prayer accepted was that day;
1410 For though the signe shewed a delay,
Yet wist he well that graunted was his boone,
And with glad hert he went him home full soone.

                    *   *   *

     The third hour inequal° that Palamon
Began to Venus' temple for to goon,

1394 **wher** whether 1394 **go** walk 1395 **bete** light 1405 **circum-
staunces** ceremonies 1406 **Al** although 1413 **hour inequal** daylight
hour (one-twelfth the time between sunrise and sunset despite the length
of the day). The sunrise hour of Monday (Moon's day) is Diana's

Up rose the sun, and up rose Emelye—   *1415*
And to the temple of Diane gan hie.
Hir maidens that she thider with hir ladde,
Full redily with hem the fire they hadde,
Th'encens, the clothes, and the remnant all°
That to the sacrifice longen° shall—   *1420*
The hornes full of meeth,° as was the guise.
There lacked nought to doon hir sacrifise.
Smoking the temple, full of clothes faire,
This Emely with herte debonaire
Hir body wesh with water of a welle.   *1425*
(But how she did hir rite I dare not telle,
But it be any thing in general—
And yet it were a game° to heeren all.
To him that meneth well it were no charge;
But it is good a man be at his large.°)   *1430*
Hir brighte heer was kembed untressed all;
A corown of a green ook cerial°
Upon hir heed was set, full fair and meete.
Two fires on the auter gan she bete,
And did hir thinges as men may beholde   *1435*
In Stace of Thebes° and thise bookes olde.
Whan kindled was the fire, with pitous cheere
Unto Diane she spak as ye may heere:
    "O chaste goddess of the woodes greene,
To whom both heven and erth and see is seene;   *1440*
Queen of the regne of Pluto, derk and lowe,
Goddess of maidens, that mine hert hast knowe
Full many a yeer, and wost what I desire,
As keep me fro thy vengeance and thine ire,
That Atheon aboughte cruelly: *1445*

1419 **Th'encens . . . all** the incense, the cloth hangings, and all the rest
1420 **longen** belong   1421 **meeth** mead   1428 **game** joy   1429–
30 **no charge . . . large** no matter, but it is good for a man to be free
1432 **ook cerial** a kind of oak; the crown is of its leaves   1436 **Stace
of Thebes** Statius' *Thebaid*

Chaste goddess, well wostou that I
Desire to been a maiden° all my lif,
Ne never wol I be no love ne wif,
I am, thou wost, yet of thy compaignye,
1450 A maid, and love hunting and venerye,
And for to walken in the woodes wilde,
And not to been a wife and be with childe.
Not wol I knowe compaigny of man.
Now help me, lady, sith ye may and can,
1455 For tho three formes° that thou hast in thee.
And Palamon, that hath swich love to me,
And eek Arcite, that loveth me so sore,
This grace I praye thee withoute more,
As sende love and pees bitwix hem two,
1460 And fro me turn away hir hertes so
That all hir hote love and hir desir,
And all hir bisy torment and hir fir,
Be queint° or turned in another place.
And if so be thou wolt not do me grace,
1465 Or if my destinee be shapen so
That I shall needes have one of hem two,
As send me him that most desireth me.
Behold, goddess of clene chastitee,
The bitter teers that on my cheekes falle!
1470 Sin thou art maid and keeper of us alle,
My maidenhood thou keep and well conserve,
And while I live, a maid I wol thee serve."
    The fires bren upon the auter clere,
While Emely was thus in hir prayere,
1475 But suddenly she saw a sighte quainte:°
For right anon one of the fires queinte,°
And quicked again, and after that anon
The other fire was queint and all agon,
And as it queint it made a whistelinge,

1447 **maiden** virgin   1455 **three formes** the Moon (in heaven), Diana (on earth), Proserpina (in hell)   1463 **queint** quenched
1475 **quainte** strange   1476 **queinte** was quenched

As doon thise wete bronds in hir brenninge,   1480
And at the brondes' end out ran anon
As it were bloody droppes many oon.
For which so sore aghast was Emelye
That she was well nigh mad, and gan to crye—
For she ne wiste what it signified;   1485
But only for the fere° thus hath she cried,
And weep that it was pitee for to heere.
And therewithal Diane gan appere,
With bow in hand, right as an hunteresse,
And saide, "Daughter, stint thine hevinesse.   1490
Among the goddes hye it is affermed,
And by eterne word written and confermed,
Thou shalt be wedded unto one of tho
That han for thee so muche care and wo—
But unto which of hem I may not telle.   1495
Farewell, for I ne may no lenger dwelle.
The fires which that on mine auter brenne
Shull thee declaren ere that thou go henne
Thine aventure of love as in this caas."
And with that word the arrwes in the caas°   1500
Of the goddess clatteren fast and ringe,
And forth she went, and made a vanishinge.
For which this Emely astoned was,
And saide, "What amounteth this, alas?
I putte me in thy proteccioun,   1505
Diane, and in thy disposicioun!"
And home she goth anon the nexte° waye;
This is th'effect—there is namore to saye.

*   *   *

The nexte hour of Mars follwinge this,
Arcite unto the temple walked is   1510
Of fierce Mars, to doon his sacrifise,
With all the rites of his payen° wise.

1486 **for the fere** out of fear   1500 **caas** quiver   1507 **nexte** nearest
1512 **payen** pagan

With pitous hert and high devocioun,
Right thus to Mars he said his orisoun:
1515   "O stronge god, that in the regnes colde
Of Trace honoured art and lord y-holde,
And hast in every regne and every land
Or armes all the bridle in thine hand,
And hem fortunest° as thee list devise:
1520   Accept of me my pitous sacrifise!
If so be that my youthe may deserve,
And that my might be worthy for to serve
Thy godheed, that I may be one of thine,
Than pray I thee to rew upon my pine,
1525   For thilke pain and thilke hote fir
In which thou whilom brendest for desir
Whan that thou usedest° the beautee
Of faire, yonge, freshe Venus free,
And haddest hir in armes at thy wille—
1530   Although thee ones on a time misfille,°
Whan Vulcanus had caught thee in his las,
And foond thee ligging° by his wife, alas!
For thilke sorrwe that was in thine herte,
Have routh° as well upon my paines smerte!
1535   I am yong and unkonning, as thou woost,
And as I trow, with love offended most
That ever was any lives creature.°
For she that doth me all this woe endure
Ne reccheth never wher I sink or flete;°
1540   And well I wot ere she me mercy hete,°
I mot with strengthe win hir in the place°—
And well I wot withouten help or grace
Of thee ne may my strengthe not availe.
Than help me, lord, tomorrwe in my battaile,

1519 **fortunest** give them (good or bad) fortunes   1527 **usedest**
exploited   1530 **misfille** it went wrong   1532 **ligging** lying
1534 **routh** pity   1537 **lives creature** living creature   1539 **wher . . .
flete** whether I sink or float   1540 **ere . . . hete** before she promises
me mercy   1541 **place** lists

For thilke fire that whilom brente thee,   1545
As well as thilke fire now brenneth me,
And do that I tomorrwe have victorye.
Mine be the travaille, and thine be the glorye!
Thy sovereign temple wol I most honouren
Of any place, and always most labouren   1550
In thy plesance and in thy craftes stronge.
And in thy temple I wol my banner honge,
And all the armes of my compaignye,
And evermo until the day I die
Eterne fire I wol before thee finde.°   1555
And eek to this avow I wol me binde:
My beerd, mine heer, that hangeth long adown,
That never yet ne felt offensioun
Of rasour ne of shere, I wol thee yive;
And been thy trewe servant while I live.   1560
Now lord, have routh upon my sorrwes sore!
Yif me the victory—I axe namore."
    The prayer stint of Arcita the stronge,
The ringes on the temple door that honge
And eek the doores clattereden full faste,   1565
Of which Arcita somewhat him aghaste.
The fires brenden upon the auter brighte
That it gan all the temple for to lighte.
A sweete smell anon the ground up yaf.
And Arcita anon his hand up haf,°   1570
And more encens into the fire he caste,
With other rites mo, and at the laste
The statue of Mars began his hauberk ringe,
And with that soun he herd a murmuringe,
Full low and dim, and saide thus: "Victorye!"   1575
For which he yaf to Mars honour and glorye.
And thus with joy and hope well to fare
Arcite anon unto his inn is fare,
As fain° as fowl is of the brighte sunne.

*   *   *

1555 **finde** provide for   1570 **haf** raised   1579 **fain** glad

1580   And right anon swich strife there is begunne
         For thilke graunting in the heven above
         Bitwixe Venus, the goddess of love,
         And Mars, the sterne god armipotente,
         That Jupiter was bisy it to stente°—
1585 Till that the pale Saturnus the colde,
         That knew so many of aventures olde,
         Foond in his old experience an art
         That he full soon hath plesed every part.°
         As sooth is said, eld hath greet avantage:
1590 In eld is bothe wisdom and usage;
         Men may the old atrenne and not atrede.°
         Saturn anon, to stinten strife and drede,
         Al be it that it is again his kinde,°
         Of all this strife he can remedy finde.
1595   "My dere daughter Venus," quod Saturne,
         "My course,° that hath so wide for to turne,
         Hath more power than woot any man.
         Mine is the drenching° in the see so wan;°
         Mine is the prison in the derke cote;°
1600 Mine is the strangling and hanging by the throte,
         The murmur and the cherles' rebelling,
         The groining° and the privee empoisoning.
         I do vengeance and plain correccioun
         While I dwell in the sign of the leoun.
1605 Mine is the ruin of the hye halles,
         The falling of the towers and of the walles
         Upon the miner or the carpenter.
         I slow Sampson, shaking the piller;
         And mine be the maladies colde,
1610 The derke tresons, and the castes° olde;
         My looking° is the fader of pestilence.

1584 **was ... stente** had trouble stopping it   1588 **part** side, party
1591 **Men ... atrede** one can outrun the old, but not outwit them
1593 **kinde** nature   1596 **course** i.e., as a planet   1598 **drenching**
drowning. These disasters were normally ascribed to Saturn
1598 **wan** dark   1599 **cote** dungeon   1602 **groining** groaning
1610 **castes** deceits   1611 **looking** gaze

Now weep namore, I shall doon diligence
That Palamon, that is thine owen knight,
Shall have his lady as thou hast him hight.
Though Mars shall help his knight, yet natheless,   *1615*
Bitwixe you there moot be some time pees,
Al be ye not of oo complexioun°—
That causeth alday swich divisioun.
I am thine aiel,° redy at thy wille.
Weep now namore; I wol thy lust° fulfille."   *1620*
   Now wol I stinten of the gods above,
Of Mars and of Venus, goddess of love,
And telle you as plainly as I can
The greet effect for which that I began.

PART FOUR

   Greet was the feest in Athenes that day,   *1625*
And eek the lusty seson of that May
Made every wight to been in swich plesaunce
That all that Monday jousten they and daunce,
And spenden it in Venus' high servise.
But by the cause that they sholde rise   *1630*
Erly for to seen the greete fight,
Unto hir reste wenten they at night.
And on the morrwe whan the day gan springe,
Of horse and harneis noise and clatteringe
There was in hostelries all aboute;   *1635*
And to the palais rode there many a route°
Of lordes upon steedes and palfreys.
There maistou seen devising° of harneis,
So uncouth° and so rich, and wrought so well
Of goldsmithry, of brouding,° and of steel;   *1640*
The sheeldes brighte, testers, and trappures,°

1617 **oo complexioun** one temperament   1619 **aiel** forefather
1620 **lust** desire   1636 **route** band   1638 **devising** preparing
1639 **uncouth** wondrous   1640 **brouding** ornamentation   1641 **testers, and trappures** headpieces, and horse-coverings

Gold-hewen helmes, hauberks, cote-armures,
Lordes in parements° on hir courseres,
Knightes of retenue and eek squieres
1645 Nailing the speres° and helmes bockelinge;
Gigging° of sheeldes, with lainers lacinge°—
There as need was they were no thing idel;
The fomy steedes on the golden bridel
Gnawing; and fast the armurers also
1650 With file and hammer pricking° to and fro;
Yemen on foot and communes many oon,
With shorte staves, thick as they may goon;
Pipes, trumpes, nakers,° clariouns,
That in the battaile blowen bloody souns;
1655 The palais full of peple up and down—
Here three, there ten, holding hir questioun,
Divining of° thise Theban knightes two.
Some saiden thus, some said it shall be so;
Some helden with him with the blacke beerd,
1660 Some with the bald, some with the thicke-herd.°
Some said he looked grim, and he wold fighte°—
"He hath a sparth° of twenty pound of wighte."
Thus was the halle full of divininge
Long after that the sunne gan to springe.
1665   The greete Theseus, that of his sleep awaked
With minstralcy and noise that was maked,
Held yet the chambres of his palais riche,
Till that the Theban knightes, both y-liche°
Honoured, weren into the palais fet.°
1670 Duke Theseus is at a window set,
Arrayed right as he were a god in trone;
The peple presseth thiderward full soone,

1643 **parements** rich clothing   1645 **Nailing the speres** fastening the
points onto shafts   1646 **Gigging** fastening straps   1646 **lainers lac-
inge** lacing (them) with thongs   1650 **pricking** spurring their horses
1653 **nakers** horns (?); the word more often means drums   1657 **Di-
vining of** speculating about   1660 **herd** haired   1661 **he . . . fighte**
they are pointing at different warriors   1662 **sparth** battle-axe
1668 **y-liche** alike, equally   1669 **fet** brought

Him for to seen and doon heigh reverence,
And eek to herkne his hest° and his sentence.
An heraud on a scaffold made an "O!"   *1675*
Till all the noise of peple was y-do.°
And whan he saw the peple of noise all stille,
Thus shewed he the mighty dukes wille:
"The lord hath of his high discrecioun
Considered that it were destruccioun   *1680*
To gentil blood to fighten in the guise
Of mortal battaile now in this emprise;°
Wherefore, to shapen that they shall not die,
He wol his firste purpose modifye:
No man, therefore, up° pain of loss of lif,   *1685*
No manner shot,° ne pole-ax, ne short knif,
Into the listes send or thider bringe.
Ne short-swerd for to stoke° with point bitinge,
No man ne draw ne bere it by his side.
Ne no man shall unto his fellaw ride   *1690*
But oo course with sharp y-grounde spere—
Foine, if him list, on foot, himself to were.°
And he that is at meschief° shall be take,
And not slain, but be brought unto the stake
That shall been ordained on either side;   *1695*
But thider he shall by force,° and there abide.
And if so falle the chieftain be take,
On either side, or elles sleen his make,°
No lenger shall the tourneyinge laste.
God speede you: go forth and lay on faste.   *1700*
With long swerd and with maces fighteth your fille.
Go now your way. This is the lordes wille."
    The voice of peple touchede the hevene,
So loude cride they with merry stevene,°

1674 **hest** command 1676 **y-do** done, finished 1682 **emprise**
undertaking 1685 **up** upon 1686 **shot** arrows 1688 **stoke** stab
1692 **Foine . . . were** let him parry, if he likes, on foot, to defend
himself 1693 **at meschief** in trouble 1696 **thider . . . force** he shall
go thither of necessity 1698 **sleen his make** slay his opponent
1704 **stevene** voice

1705 "God save swich a lord that is so good:
       He wilneth no destruccion of blood!"
          Up goon the trumpes and the melodye,
       And to the listes rit° the compaignye,
       By ordinance, thurghout the citee large,
1710 Hanged with cloth of gold and not with sarge.°
       Full like a lord this noble Duke gan ride,
       Thise two Thebans upon either side.
       And after rode the Queen and Emelye,
       And after that another compaignye
1715 Of one and other after hir degree.
       And thus they passen thurghout the citee,
       And to the listes come they bitime—
       It was not of the day yet fully prime.
          Whan set was Theseus full rich and hye,
1720 Ipolyta the queen and Emelye,
       And other ladies in degrees aboute,
       Unto the setes presseth all the route,
       And westward thurgh the gates under Marte
       Arcite and eek the hundred of his parte,
1725 With banner red, is entred right anon.
       And in that selve° moment Palamon
       Is under Venus eestward in the place,
       With banner white and hardy cheer and face.
       In all the world, to seeken up and down,
1730 So even withouten variacioun
       There nere swiche compaignies twaye;
       For there was none so wise that coude saye
       That any had of other avantage,
       Of worthiness, ne of estate ne age,
1735 So even were they chosen for to guesse;
       And in two renges° faire they hem dresse.
          Whan that hir names rad° were everichon,
       That in hir numbre guile was there non,
       Tho were the gates shet and cried was loude:

1708 **rit** rides   1710 **sarge** serge   1726 **selve** self-same   1736 **renges**
ranks   1737 **rad** read

"Do now your devoir,° yonge knightes proude!"   *1740*
   The heraudes left hir pricking up and down.
Now ringen trumpes loud and clarioun.
There is namore to sayn, but west and eest
In goon the speres full sadly in th'arest,°
In goth the sharpe spur into the side—   *1745*
There seen men who can joust and who can ride:
There shiveren shaftes upon sheeldes thicke—
He° feeleth thurgh the herte-spoon° the pricke.
Up springen speres twenty foot on highte;
Out goon the swerdes as the silver brighte;   *1750*
The helmes they to-hewen and to-shrede;
Out brest the blood with sterne° streemes rede.
With mighty maces the bones they to-breste;
He thurgh the thickest of the throng gan threste;
There stumblen steedes strong, and down goth all!°   *1755*
He rolleth under foot as doth a ball;
He foineth on his feet with his trunchoun;°
And he him hurtleth with his horse adown;
He thurgh the body is hurt and sithen y-take,
Maugree his heed, and brought unto the stake—   *1760*
As forward° was, right there he most abide;
Another lad° is on that other side.
   And some time doth hem Theseus to reste,°
Hem to refresh and drinken if hem leste.
Full oft aday have thise Thebans two   *1765*

1740 **devoir** duty   1744 **sadly in th'arest** firmly into their rests (a
device on the armor for holding the spear aimed)   1748 **He** one (cf.
line 1661). "He" is used in this impersonal way throughout the passage
1748 **herte-spoon** the hollow just below the breastbone   1752 **sterne**
dreadful   1741–55 **The heraudes . . . all!** in this passage Chaucer
imitates the clash of arms by lapsing into alliterative verse. Without
dropping the rhyme, of course, or the blank verse either, he simulates the
old native English poetry, chiefly heroic in its tradition, which relied
upon the repetition of a single initial sound three or more times in a line.
This goes on until the climactic line "and down goth all!"   1757 **foi-
neth . . . trunchoun** parries with the shaft of his spear   1761 **forward**
agreement   1762 **lad** lead (to the stake)   1763 **doth . . . reste** Theseus
causes them to rest

Togidre y-met and wrought his fellaw wo:
Unhorsed hath ech other of hem tweye.
There is no tigre in Vale of Galgopheye,°
Whan that hir whelp is stole whan it is lite,
1770 So cruel on the hunt as is Arcite,
For jalous hert, upon this Palamoun.
Ne in Belmarye° there nis no fell leoun,
That hunted is or for his hunger wood,
Ne of his prey desireth so the blood,
1775 As Palamon to sleen his foe Arcite.
The jalous strokes on hir helmes bite—
Out renneth blood on both hir sides rede.
     Some time an end there is of every deede:
For ere the sun unto the reste wente,
1780 The stronge king Emetrius gan hente
This Palamon as he fought with Arcite,
And made his swerd deep in his flesh to bite,
And by the force of twenty is he take,
Unyolden, and y-drawen to the stake.
1785 And in the rescous° of this Palamoun,
The stronge king Lygurge is born adown,
And King Emetrius, for all his strengthe,
Is born out of his saddle a swerdes lengthe,
So hit him Palamon ere he were take.
1790 But all for nought: he was brought to the stake.
His hardy herte might him helpe naught;
He most abide whan that he was caught,
By force and eek by composicioun.°
     Who sorrweth now but woeful Palamoun,
1795 That mot namore goon again to fighte?
And whan that Theseus had seen this sighte,
Unto the folk that foughten thus echon
He cride, "Ho, namore, for it is don!

1768 **Galgopheye** Gargaphie, mentioned in Ovid, *Metamorphoses* III,
155   1772 **Belmarye** See General Prologue, line 57   1785 **rescous**
rescue   1793 **By . . . composicioun** out of necessity and also accord-
ing to their agreement

I wol be trewe judge and not partye.°
Arcite of Thebes shall have Emelye,   1800
That by his fortune hath hir fair y-wonne."
Anon there is a noise of peple begunne,
For joy of this, so loud and heigh withalle,
It seemed that the listes sholde falle.
    What can now faire Venus doon above?   1805
What saith she now? What doth this queen of love?—
But weepeth so for wanting of hir wille,
Till that hir teres in the listes fille.
She said, "I am ashamed,° douteless."
Saturnus saide: "Daughter, hold thy pees!   1810
Mars hath his will—his knight hath all his boone.°
And, by mine heed, thou shalt been esed soone."
    The trumpours with the loude minstralcye,
The heraudes that full loude yell and crye,
Been in hir wele for joy of daun Arcite.   1815
But herkneth me, and stinteth noise a lite,°
Which a miracle there befell anon—
    This fierce Arcite hath off his helm y-don,°
And on a courser for to shew his face,
He pricketh endelong the large place,   1820
Looking upward upon this Emelye;
And she again him cast a freendly eye—
For women, as to speken in commune,°
They follwen all the favour of Fortune—
And she was all his cheer as in his herte.°   1825
Out of the ground a Fury infernal° sterte,
From Pluto sent at request of Saturne,
For which his horse for fere gan to turne
And leep aside, and foundred as he leep.
And ere that Arcite may taken keep,   1830

1799 **partye** partisan   1809 **ashamed** shamed   1811 **boone** petition
1816 **But herkneth . . . lite** note how the Knight speaks here as to an
audience   1818 **off . . . y-don** taken off his helmet   1823 **in com-
mune** in general   1825 **she . . . herte** she was all his joy, in his heart
1826 **Fury infernal** the Fury, which Boccaccio took from Statius, was
a hellish monster

He pight him on the pommel of his heed,°
That in the place he lay as he were deed,
His brest to-brosten with his saddle-bowe.°
As black he lay as any cole or crowe,
1835 So was the blood y-runnen in his face.
Anon he was y-born out of the place,
With herte sore, to Theseus' palais.
Tho was he corven° out of his harneis,
And in a bed y-brought full fair and blive,°
1840 For he was yet in memory° and alive,
And alway crying after Emelye.
    Duke Theseus with all his compaignye
Is comen home to Athens his citee
With alle bliss and greet solempnitee.
1845 Al be it that this aventure was falle,
He nolde not discomforten hem alle.
    Men said eek that Arcite shall not die—
"He shall been heeled of his maladye."
And of another thing they were as fain:
1850 That of hem alle was there none y-slain,
Al were they sore y-hurt, and namely oon,
That with a spere was thirled his brest-boon.°
To other woundes and to broken armes
Some hadden salves and some hadden charmes;
1855 Fermacies° of herbes and eek save°
They drunken, for they wold hir limes have.
For which this noble Duke, as he well can,
Comforteth and honoureth every man,
And made revel all the longe night
1860 Unto the straunge° lordes, as was right.
Ne there was holden no disconfitinge,°

1831 **pight . . . heed** pitched him (so that he fell) on the top of his head
1833 **to-brosten . . . bowe** shattered by the front edge of the saddle
1838 **corven** cut   1839 **blive** quickly   1840 **in memory** conscious
1852 **That . . . boon** "that his breastbone was pierced with a spear"—
i.e., "*whose* breastbone was . . ."   1855 **Fermacies** medicines
1855 **save** an herb   1860 **straunge** foreign   1861 **disconfitinge** defeat

But as a joustes or a tourneyinge,
For soothly there was no disconfiture—
For falling nis not but an aventure,
Ne to be lad by force unto the stake,   1865
Unyolden, and with twenty knightes take,
Oo person alone, withouten mo,
And harried° forth by arme, foot, and to,°
And eek his steede driven forth with staves,
With footmen, bothe yeman and eek knaves—   1870
It nas aretted him no villainye;°
There may no man clepe it cowardye.

    For which anon Duke Theseus let crye,°
To stinten° alle rancour and envye,
The gree° as well of oo side as of other,   1875
And either side y-like as other's brother;
And yaf hem yiftes after hir degree,
And fully held a feeste dayes three,
And conveyed the kinges worthily
Out of his town a journee largely.°   1880
And home went every man the righte way—
There was namore but "Farewell, have good day."
Of this battaile I wol namore endite,
But speke of Palamon and of Arcite.

    Swelleth the brest of Arcite, and the sore   1885
Encresseth at his herte more and more;
The clothered° blood, for any leechecraft,°
Corrupteth, and is in his bouk y-laft,°
That neither veine-blood, ne ventusinge,°
Ne drink of herbes may been his helpinge.   1890

1868 **harried** dragged   1868 **to** toe   1871 **It . . . villainye** it was not
put down against him as a disgrace   1873 **let crye** caused to be
announced   1874 **To stinten** in order to stop   1875 **gree** goodwill
1880 **a journee largely** fully a day's journey   1887 **clothered** clotted
1887 **for . . . leechecraft** in spite of any medical skill   1888 **in . . . y-
laft** left in the trunk of his body   1889 **veine . . . ventusinge** drawing
blood from a vein or from the skin (by "cupping," i.e., by a partial
vacuum)

The vertu expulsif or animal
Fro thilke vertu cleped natural
Ne may the venim voiden ne expelle;°
The pipes of his lunges gan to swelle,
1895 And every lacert° in his brest adown
Is shent with venim and corrupcioun.°
Him gaineth neither, for to get his lif,
Vomit upward, ne downward laxatif.°
All is to-brosten thilke regioun;°
1900 Nature hath now no dominacioun;
And certainly, ther Nature wol not werche,°
Farewell, physic—go bere the man to cherche.
This all and sum: that Arcite moot die.
For which he sendeth after Emelye,
1905 And Palamon that was his cosin dere.
Than said he thus, as ye shall after heere:
    "Not may the woeful spirit in mine herte
Declare a point° of all my sorrwes smerte
To you, my lady, that I love most;
1910 But I biquethe the service of my gost°
To you aboven every creature
Sin that my life may no lenger dure.
Alas the woe, alas the paines stronge
That I for you have suffered, and so longe!
1915 Alas the deeth, alas, mine Emelye!
Alas, departing of our compaignye!

1891–93 **The vertu . . . expelle** in medieval medicine there were three
"virtues"—natural, vital, and animal (associated with the liver, heart,
and brain respectively). Here, the animal virtue is unable to expel the
poison from the natural virtue   1895 **lacert** muscle   1896 **shent . . .
corrupcioun** damaged by poison and decomposition; as a result he
cannot cough to expel congestion from his lungs   1897–98 **Him . . .
laxatif** because his expulsive virtue is impaired, emetics and laxatives
given him fail to purge the unnatural humor   1899 **to-brosten . . .
regioun** that region (his breast) is completely afflicted   1901 **ther
Nature . . . werche** where Nature will not work; his natural virture is
poisoned (see lines 1892–93)   1908 **point** even a small detail
1910 **gost** soul, i.e., after death

Alas, mine hertes queen, alas, my wif,
Mine hertes lady, ender of my lif!
What is this world? What asketh men to have?
Now with his love, now in his colde grave—   1920
Alone, withouten any compaignye.
    Farewell, my sweete foe, mine Emelye,
And softe take me in your armes twaye,
For love of God, and herkneth what I saye:
I have here with my cosin Palamon   1925
Had strife and rancour many a day agon
For love of you, and for my jalousye.
And Jupiter so wis my soule gie°
To speken of a servant proprely
With circumstances alle trewely—   1930
That is to sayn, truth, honour, knighthede,
Wisdom, humbless, estate, and heigh kinrede,
Freedom, and all that longeth to that art—
So Jupiter have of my soule part,
As in this world right now ne know I non   1935
So worthy to been loved as Palamon,
That serveth you and wol doon all his lif.
And if that ever ye shall been a wif,
Foryet not Palamon, the gentil man."
And with that word his speeche faile gan;   1940
For from his feet up to his brest was come
The cold of deeth that had him overcome.
And yet more over,° for in his armes two
The vital strength is lost and all ago;
Only, the intellect° withoute more,   1945
That dwelled in his herte sick and sore,
Gan failen whan the herte felte deeth.
Dusked° his eyen two and failed breeth—
But on his lady yet cast he his eye.

1928 **so . . . gie** guide my soul surely   1943 **yet more over** still more
than that   1945 **intellect** the intellect was thought to reside in the
heart; it is the last faculty to go—"the intellect began to fail only
when . . ."   1948 **Dusked** dimmed

1950 His laste word was: *"Mercy, Emelye!"*
      His spirit chaunged house and wente ther
      As *I* came never,° I can not tellen wher;
      Therefore I stint—I nam no divinistre:°
      Of soules find I not in this registre,°
1955 Ne me ne list thilke opinions to telle
      Of hem, though that they writen where they dwelle.
      Arcite is cold, ther Mars his soule gie.°
      Now wol I speken forth of Emelye.
          Shright° Emely and howleth Palamon,
1960 And Theseus his suster took anon
      Swouning, and bare hir fro the corpse away.
      What helpeth it to tarrien forth the day
      To tellen how she weep both eve and morrwe?
      For in swich cas women have swich sorrwe,
1965 Whan that hir husbonds been from hem ago,
      That for the more part they sorrwen so,
      Or elles fallen in swich a maladye,
      That at the laste certainly they die.
          Infinite been the sorrwes and the teres
1970 Of olde folk and folk of tendre yeeres
      In all the town for deeth of this Theban;
      For him there weepeth bothe child and man.
      So greet weeping was there noon, certain,
      Whan Ector was y-brought all fresh y-slain
1975 To Troy. Alas, the pitee that was ther—
      Cratching° of cheekes, renting eek of heer—
      "Why woldestou be deed," thise women crye,
      "And haddest gold enough, and Emelye?'"
          No man mighte gladden Theseus

1951–52 **His . . . never** "His vital spirit changed its abode (i.e., per-
haps from body to immortal soul) and went to a place where *I* never
came . . ." Chaucer breaks the tragic feeling of the passage with a char-
acteristic bit of self-humor   1953 **divinistre** theologian   1954 **Of . . .
registre** I'm not providing anything about souls for this table of
contents   1957 **ther . . . gie** wherefore may Mars guide his soul
1959 **Shright** shrieked   1976 **Cratching** scratching

Saving his olde fader Egeus,   *1980*
That knew this worldes transmutacioun,
As he had seen it chaungen, up and down,
Joy after woe, and woe after gladnesse,
And shewed hem ensample and likenesse:
"Right as there died never man," quod he,   *1985*
"That he ne lived in erth in some degree,
Right so there lived never man," he saide.
"In all this world that some time he ne deide.
This world nis but a thurghfare full of wo,
And we been pilgrims passing to and fro: *1990*
Deeth is an end of every worldly sore."
    And overall this yet said he muchel more
To this effect, full wisely to enhorte°
The peple that they shold hem reconforte.°
    Duke Theseus with all his bisy cure°   *1995*
Caste now where that the sepulture
Of good Arcite may best y-maked be,
And eek most honourable in his degree.
And at the last he took conclusioun
That there as first Arcite and Palamoun   *2000*
Hadden for love the battaile hem betweene,
That in the selve° grove, swoot and greene,
There as he had his amorous desires,
His complaint, and for love his hote fires,
He wolde make a fire in which th'office   *2005*
Funeral he might all accomplice—
And let anon command to hack and hewe
The okes old, and layen hem on a rewe,
In colpons° well arrayed for to brenne.
His officers with swifte feet they renne   *2010*
And ride anon at his commandement,
And after this Thesens hath y-sent
After a beer,° and it all overspradde

1993 **enhorte** exhort   1994 **hem reconforte** console themselves
1995 **cure** care   2002 **selve** self-same   2008–09 **on . . . colpons** in a
row, in pieces   2013 **beer** bier

With cloth of gold, the richest that he hadde.
2015 And of the same suite° he clad Arcite—
Upon his handes two his gloves white,
Eek on his heed a crown of laurer greene,
And in his hand a swerd full bright and keene;
He laid him, bare the visage,° on the beere.
2020 Therewith he weep that pitee was to heere!—
And for the peple sholde seen him alle,
Whan it was day he brought him to the halle,
That roreth of the crying and the soun.
Tho came this woeful Theban Palamoun,
2025 With fluttery beerd and ruggy asky heres,°
In clothes black, y-dropped all with teres;
And passing other of weeping, Emelye,
The rewfullest of all the compaignye.
In as much as the service sholde be
2030 The more noble and rich in his degree,
Duke Theseus let forth three steedes bringe
That trapped were in steel all glitteringe,
And covered with the arms of daun Arcite.
Upon thise steedes fair, so huge and white,
2035 There seten folk of which one bare his sheeld;
Another his spere upon his handes held;
The thridde bare with him his bow Turkeis—
Of brend gold was the case and eek th' harneis—
And riden forth a pas with sorrweful cheere
2040 Toward the grove, as ye shall after heere.
     The noblest of the Greekes that there were
Upon hir shouldres carrieden the beere,
With slacke pas,° and eyen red and wete,
Thurghout the citee by the maister streete,
2045 That sprad was all with black. And wonder hye

2015 **of . . . suite** in the same array; the white gloves in the next line
were traditional mourning for the unmarried   2019 **bare the visage**
his face uncovered   2025 **ruggy . . . heres** unkempt hair covered with
ashes—symbolic of mourning   2043 **slacke pas** slow steps

Right of the same is the street y-wrye.°
Upon the right hand went old Egeus,
And on that other side Duke Theseus,
With vessels in hir hand of gold full fin,
All full of honey, milk, and blood, and win;   2050
Eek Palamon with full greet compaignye;
And after that came woeful Emelye,
With fire in hand, as was that time the guise,
To do the office of funeral servise.
    High labour and full greet apparailinge°   2055
Was at the service and the fire-makinge,
That with his greene top the heven raughte,°
And twenty fadme of brede the armes straughte—
This is to sayn, the boughes were so brode.
Of stree° first there was laid many a lode;   2060
But how the fire was maked upon highte,°
Ne eek the names how the trees highte
(As ook, fir, birch, asp, alder, holm, popler,
Willow, elm, plane, ash, box, chestain, linde, laurer,
Maple, thorn, beech, hasel, ew, whippletree)   2065
How they were feld shall not been told for me;
Ne how the goddes runnen up and down,
Disherited of hir habitacioun
In which they woneden in rest and pees—
Nymphes, faunes, and hamadryades;   2070
Ne how the beestes and the briddes alle
Fledden for fere whan the wood was falle;
Ne how the ground aghast was of the light,
That was not wont to seen the sunne bright;
Ne how the fire was couched first with stree,   2075
And than with drye stickes cloven a-three,
And than with greene wood and spicerye,

2046 **y-wrye** hung   2055 **apparailinge** preparation   2057 **with . . .
raughte** with its green top (i.e., piled with boughs) reached toward
heaven   2060 **stree** straw   2061 **how . . . highte** how high the fire
was made. From here to line 2108 is a protracted *occupatio* in which
Chaucer condenses Boccaccio's elaborate epic funeral rites

And than with cloth of gold and with perrye,°
And garlands hanging with full many a flowr—
2080 The myrrh, th'incense with all so greet odour:
Ne how Arcite lay among all this,
Ne what richess about the body is,
Ne how that Emely, as was the guise,
Put in the fire of funeral servise,
2085 Ne how she swouned whan men made the fir,
Ne what she spak, ne what was hir desir,
Ne what jewels men in the fire caste
Whan that the fire was greet and brente faste;
Ne how some cast hir sheeld and some hir spere,
2090 And of hir vestiments which that they were,
And cuppes full of milk and wine and blood
Into the fire that brent as it were wood;
Ne how the Greekes with an huge route
Thries riden all the fire aboute,
2095 Upon the left hand, with a loud shoutinge,
And thries with his speres clatteringe,
And thries how the ladies gonne crye,
And how that lad was homeward Emelye;
Ne how Arcite is brent to ashen colde;
2100 Ne how that liche-wake° was y-holde
All thilke night; ne how the Greekes playe
The wake-playes,° ne keep° I nought to saye;
Who wrastleth best naked with oil anoint,
Ne who that bare him best in no disjoint.°
2105 I wol not tellen alle how they goon
Home til Athens whan the play° is doon,
But shortly to the point than wol I wende,
And maken of my longe tale an ende.

*   *   *

2078 **perrye** jewels 2100 **liche-wake** wake (a medieval Christian
term) 2102 **wake-playes** funeral games (an epic convention)
2102 **keep** bother 2104 **in no disjoint** in any difficulty 2106 **play**
event

By process° and by length of certain yeeres,
All stinted is the mourning and the teres   *2110*
Of Greekes by one general assent.
Than seemed me there was a parlement
At Athens, upon a certain point and cas;
Among the whiche points y-spoken was
To have with certain contrees alliaunce,   *2115*
And have fully of Thebans obeisaunce;
For which this noble Theseus anon
Let senden after gentil Palamon,
Unwist of him what was the cause and why.
But in his blacke clothes sorrwefully   *2120*
He came at his commandement in hie.°
Tho sente Theseus for Emelye.

    Whan they were set, and hust° was all the place,
And Theseus abiden hath a space
Ere any word came from his wise brest,   *2125*
His eyen set he ther as was his lest,
And with a sad visage he siked stille,°
And after that right thus he said his wille:

    "The Firste Mover of the cause above,
Whan he first made the faire Chain of Love,   *2130*
Greet was th'effect, and high was his entente;
Well wist he why and what thereof he mente.
For with that faire Chain of Love he bond
The fire, the air, the water, and the lond
In certain boundes that they may nat flee.   *2135*
That same Prince and that Mover," quod he,
"Hath stablissed in this wretched world adown
Certaine dayes and duracioun
To all that is engendred in this place,
Over the whiche day they may not pace,   *2140*
Al mow they yet tho dayes well abregge.°
There needeth noon auctoritee to allegge,
For it is proved by experience,

2109 **By process** in due course   2121 **in hie** in a hurry   2123 **hust**
hushed   2127 **siked stille** sighed quietly   2141 **abregge** shorten

But that me list declaren my sentence.
2145 Than may men by this order well discerne
That thilke Mover stable is and eterne.
Well may men knowe, but it be a fool,
That every part deriveth from his hool.
For Nature hath not taken his beginning
2150 Of no party or cantel° of a thing,
But of a thing that parfit is and stable,
Descending so till it be corrumpable.
And therefore for his wise purveyaunce
He hath so well biset his ordinaunce
2155 That speces of thinges and progressiouns
Shullen enduren by successiouns,
And not eterne, withouten any lie.
This maistou understand and seen at eye.°
     Lo, th' ook that hath so long a norishinge
2160 Fro time that it first beginneth springe,
And hath so long a life, as ye may see,
Yet at the laste wasted is the tree.
Considereth eek how that the harde ston
Under our foot on which we tred and gon,
2165 Yet wasteth it as it lith by the waye.
The brode river some time wexeth dreye.
The greete townes see we wane and wende.
     Than ye see that all this thing hath ende.
Of man and woman see we well also
2170 That needes in one of thise termes two—
This is to sayn, in youth or elles age—
He mot be deed, the king as shall a page:
Some in his bed, some in the deepe see,
Some in the large feeld, as ye may see.
2175 There helpeth nought—all goth that ilke waye.

2150 **party or cantel** part or portion   2129–58 **The Firste ... eye**
this passage, based on Boethius, sets forth an idea as old at least as
Plato, that all things in the universe are bound together by love, in a
hierarchy (chain). The idea that all things have a limited time on earth
and must pass away is of course very medieval

Than may I sayn that all this thing mot deye.
What maketh this but Jupiter the king,
That is Prince and cause of alle thing,
Converting all unto his propre welle°
From which it is derived, sooth to telle?   *2180*
And here agains no creature on live,
Of no degree, availeth for to strive.
    Than is it wisdom, as it thinketh me,
To maken vertu of necessitee,
And take it well that we may not eschue—°   *2185*
And namelich that° to us all is due.
And whoso grucheth aught,° he doth follye,
And rebel is to Him that all may gie.°
And certainly a man hath most honour
To dien in his excellence and flower,   *2190*
Whan he is siker° of his goode name.
Than hath he done his freend ne him° no shame;
And gladder ought his freend been of his deeth
Whan with honour up yolden° is his breeth,
Than whan his name appalled° is for age,   *2195*
For all forgetten is his vasselage.°
Than is it best, as for a worthy fame,
To dien whan that he is best of name.
    The contrary of all this is wilfulnesse.
Why gruchen we, why have we hevinesse,   *2200*
That good Arcite, of chivalry the flowr,
Departed is with duetee° and honour
Out of this foule prison of his lif?
Why gruchen here his cosin and his wif
Of his welfare that loveth hem so well?   *2205*

2179 **propre welle** own will   2185 **that ... eschue** what we cannot avoid   2186 **that** what   2187 **grucheth aught** complains at all 2188 **to ... gie** to Him who guides all   2191 **siker** certain. The idea that it is best to die at the height of one's glory is a very chivalric notion of the kind a Knight would have believed; from a Christian viewpoint, one should die in a state of grace   2192 **him** himself 2194 **yolden** yielded   2195 **appalled** faded   2196 **vasselage** knightly prowess   2202 **duetee** dignity

Can he hem thank?—Nay, God wot, neveradeel—
That both his soul and eek himself offende.
And yet they mow hir lustes not amende.°
    What may I conclude of this longe serie,°
2210 But after woe I rede° us to be merrye,
And thanken Jupiter of all his grace;
And, ere we departen from this place,
I rede that we make of sorrwes two
Oo parfit joye, lasting evermo.
2215 And looketh now where most sorrwe is herinne,
There wol I first amenden and beginne.
Suster," quod he, "this is my full assent,
With all th'avis here of my parlement:
That gentil Palamon, your owne knight,
2220 That serveth you with will and hert and might
And ever hath done sin ye first him knewe,
That ye shall of your grace upon him rewe,
And taken him for husbond and for lord.
Lene me your hand, for this is our accord:
2225 Let see now of your womanly pitee.
He is a kinges brother son,° pardee,
And though he were a povre bacheler,
Sin he hath served you so many a yeer
And had for you so greet adversitee,
2230 It moste been considered, leveth° me;
For gentil mercy oughte passen right."°
    Than said he thus to Palamon the knight:
"I trow there needeth litel sermoning
To make you assente to this thing.
2235 Come neer and taketh your lady by the hond."
Bitwixen hem was made anon the bond
That highte matrimoigne or marriage,

2208 **mow . . . amende** cannot improve upon their happiness. The
idea in the passage is that too much mourning is a disservice to the
dead   2209 **serie** argument   2210 **rede** advise   2226 **kinges . . .
son** King's brother's son   2230 **leveth** believe   2231 **passen
right** prevail over justice

By all the conseil and the baronage.
And thus with alle bliss and melodye
Hath Palamon y-wedded Emelye.   2240
And God, that all this wide world hath wrought,
Send him his love that hath it dere abought;
For now is Palamon in alle wele,
Living in bliss, in richess, and in hele,
And Emely him loveth so tenderly,   2245
And he hir serveth also gentilly,
That never was there no word hem betweene
Of jalousy or any other teene.°
   Thus endeth Palamon and Emelye,
And God save all this faire compaignye.   2250
                              Amen

2248 **teene** trouble

THE MILLER'S PROLOGUE

Whan that the Knight had thus his tale y-told,
In all the route nas there yong ne old
That he ne said it was a noble storye
And worthy for to drawen to memorye—
5 And namely° the gentils everichoon.
    Our Hoste lough and swore, "So mote I goon,
This goth aright! Unbuckeled is the male!°
Let see now who shall tell another tale,
For trewely the game is well begunne!
10 Now telleth ye, sir Monk, if that ye conne,
Somewhat to quite with the Knightes tale."°
    The Miller, that for drunken° was all pale
So that unnethe° upon his horse he sat,
He nolde avalen° neither hood ne hat,
15 N'abiden no man for his curteisye,
But in Pilate's voice° he gan to crye,
And swore, "By armes and by blood and bones!°
I kan a noble tale for the nones,
With which I wol now quit the Knightes tale!"
20 Our Host saw that he was drunk of ale,
And said, "Abide, Robin, leve brother,
Some better man shall tell us first another.
Abide, and let us werken thriftily."°

5 **namely** in particular   7 **Unbuckeled ... male** the bag is unfastened
11 **to quite ... tale** to match the Knight's tale with   12 **for drunken**
because of being drunk (and it is still morning!)   13 **unnethe** hardly
14 **avalen** remove (i.e., out of respect)   16 **Pilate's voice** in the mystery plays Pilate ranted and shrieked   17 **armes ... bones** the arms, blood, and bones of Christ; such inventiveness in swearing was not unusual   23 **thriftily** profitably

"By Goddes soul," quod he, "that wol not I!
For I wol speke or elles go my way."   25
　　Our Host answered, "Tell on, a devil way!
Thou art a fool—thy wit is overcome."
　　"Now herkneth," quod the Miller, "all and some . . .
But first I make a protestacioun
That I am drunk. I know it by my soun.°   30
And therefore if that I misspeke or saye,°
Wite it° the ale of Southwerk, I you praye.
For I wol tell a legend and a lif
Both of a carpenter and of his wif,
How that a clerk hath set the wrightes cappe."°   35
　　The Reeve answered and saide, "Stint thy clappe.°
Let be thy lewed drunken harlotrye.°
It is a sin and eek a greet follye
T'apairen° any man, or him defame,
And eek to bringen wives in swich fame.   40
Thou maist enough of other thinges sayn."
　　This drunken Miller spak full soon again,
And saide, "Leve brother Osewold,
Who hath no wife, he is no cockewold°—
But I say not therefore that thou art oon.   45
There been full goode wives many oon,
And ever a thousand good ayains one badde.
That knowestou well thyself, but if thou madde.°
Why artou angry with my tale now?
I have a wife, pardee, as well as thou,   50
Yet nolde I, for the oxen in my plough,

---

30 **soun** sound of my voice　31 **misspeke or saye** misspeak or missay
32 **Wite it** blame it on　35 **set . . . cappe** made a fool of the craftsman
36 **Stint thy clappe** shut your mouth. The Reeve, who is a carpenter,
assumes that the miller is going to satirize him personally. Reeves
(managers of farms) and millers had dealings with each other, of
course, and doubtless tried to cheat each other; hence they are natural
enemies　37 **harlotrye** ribaldry　39 **apairen** injure　44 **cockewold**
cuckold—note the miller's logic here　48 **but . . . madde** unless
you're crazy

Take upon me more than enough
As deemen of myself that I were oon;°
I wol bileve well that I am noon.
55 An husbond shall not been inquisitif
Of Goddes privetee—nor of his wif.
So he may finde Goddes foison there,°
Of the remnant needeth nought enquere."

*   *   *

What shold I more sayn but this Millere
60 He nold his wordes for no man forbere,
But told his cherles tale in his mannere.
M'athinketh° that I shall reherse it here.
And therefore every gentil wight, I praye,
Deemeth not, for God's love, that I saye
65 Of yvel entent, but for I mot reherse
Hir tales alle, be they bet or werse,
Or elles falsen some of my mattere.
And therefore, whoso list it not y-heere
Turn over the leef and chese another tale.
70 For he shall find enoughe, greet and smalle,
Of storial° thing that toucheth gentilesse
And eek moralitee and holinesse.
Blameth not me if that ye chese amiss.
The Miller is a cherl, ye know well this—
75 So was the Reeve eek, and other mo;
And harlotry they tolden bothe two.
Aviseth you, and put me out of blame—
And eek men shall not make ernest of game.°

52–53 **Take . . . oon** go so far beyond evidence as to decide that *I'*m
one (i.e., a cuckold)   57 **so . . . there** So long as he finds God's plenty
there (in his wife)   62 **M'athinketh** I regret to say   71 **storial**
historical   78 **ernest of game** something serious out of a joke

THE MILLER'S TALE°

Whilom there was dwelling at Oxenford
A riche gnof that guestes held to bord,°
And of his craft he was a carpenter.
With him there was dwelling a poor scholer,
Had lerned art;° but all his fantasye°   5
Was turned for to lerne astrologye—
And koud a certain of conclusiouns,
To deemen by interrogaciouns,°
If that men asked him in certain houres
Whan that men shold have drought or elles showres;   10
Or if men asked him what shold befalle
Of everything—I may not recken hem alle.
    This clerk was cleped hende° Nicholas.
Of derne love he koud,° and of solas;
And thereto he was sly and full privee,   15

The Miller's Tale this tale is a "fabliau"—a comic tale reflecting the
life of common people. Such tales were told orally and passed by word
of mouth, but some—a good many all told—were written down. In
writers like Sercambi, Boccaccio, and Chaucer they gain literary sta-
tus. Chaucer's art in the Miller's Tale lies in his combining *two* tales,
that of the "second flood" and that (as it is politely called) of the "mis-
directed kiss." He combines them in such a way that the climax of both
occurs at once—with the cry of "Water!" And he adds to the fun by
making the whole a parody of the Knight's Tale   2 **riche . . . bord** a
rich lout that took in boarders; "gnof" suggests a common fellow and
a cheat   5 **art** i.e., had completed the first part of a liberal arts educa-
tion, the "trivium"   5 **fantasye** fascination, real interest (note that
astrology loomed large in the Knight's Tale)   7–8 **koud . . . interro-
gaciouns** (he) knew a certain number of astrological procedures, to
answer questions (by determining the position of heavenly bodies at
the hour the question was asked)   13 **hende** a fine old word which
combines the meaning of "handy," "clever" with "pleasant," "gentle"
14 **Of . . . koud** he knew all about secret love affairs; but his kind of
love is very different from that depicted in the Knight's Tale. Chaucer
hints at this contrast in line 18 (cf. Knight's Tale, line 1921)

And like a maiden meeke for to see.
A chambre had he in that hostelrye°—
Alone, withouten any compaignye—
Full fetisly y-dight with herbes swoote;°
20 And he himself as sweet as is the roote
Of licoris or any setewale.
His *Almageste*° and bookes greet and smalle,
His astrelaby, longing for his art,°
His augrim stones,° layen fair apart
25 On shelves couched at his beddes heed,
His press y-covered with a falding red;°
And all above there lay a gay sautrye,°
On which he made a-nightes melodye
So sweetely that all the chambre rung—
30 And *Angelus ad Virginem* he sung,
And after that he sung the *Kinges Note*.
Full often blessed was his murry throte!
And thus this sweete clerk his time spente,
After his freendes' finding and his rente.°
35   This carpenter had wedded new a wif
Which that he loved more than his lif.
Of eighteene yeer she was of age.
Jalous he was, and held hir narrwe in cage:
For she was wild and yong, and he was old,
40 And deemed himself been like a cokewold.
He knew not Caton, for his wit was rude,
That bade man shold wed his similitude:

17 **hostelrye** lodging. The fact that he has a private room would have
been very unusual   19 **fetisly . . . swoote** nicely fixed up with sweet-
smelling plants   22 **Almageste** a textbook of astrology   23 **His . . .
art** his astrolabe pertaining to his art (an astronomical instrument, an-
cestor of the sextant; Chaucer himself wrote a treatise on the astrolabe)
24 **augrim stones** instrument for mathematical calculations
26 **press . . . red** his clothes closet (or chest) covered with a red cloth
27 **sautrye** psaltery, a string instrument played by plucking   34 **Af-
ter . . . rente** living on money his friends gave him plus his own in-
come. The whole passage suggests a well-to-do student with a taste for
the good life

"Men sholde wedden after hir estat,
For youth and eld is often at debat."
But sith that he was fallen in the snare,   45
He most endure, as other folk, his care.
    Fair was this yonge wife, and therewithal
As any wesel° hir body gent and small.
A ceint° she wered, barred all of silk,
A barmecloth° as white as morne milk   50
Upon hir lendes,° full of many a gore.°
White was hir smock,° and broiden° all before
And eek behind, on hir coller aboute,
Of col-black silk, within and eek withoute.
The tapes of hir white voluper°   55
Were of the same suite of° hir coller,
Hir fillet° brod of silk and set full hye.
And sikerly she had a likerous° eye.
Full small y-pulled° were hir browes two,
And tho were bent, and black as any slo.   60
She was full more blissful on to see
Than is the newe perejonette tree,
And softer than the wool is of a wether.°
And by hir girdle heng a purse of lether,
Tasseled with silk and perled with latoun.°   65
In all this world, to seeken up and down,
There nis no man so wise that coude thenche
So gay a popelote° or swich a wenche!
Full brighter was the shining of hir hewe
Than in the Tower the noble y-forged newe.°   70
But of hir song, it was as loud and yerne°

48 **wesel** weasel. Notice the large amount of animal imagery in the
description of her   49 **ceint** belt, girdle   50 **barmecloth** apron
51 **lendes** hips   51 **gore** pleat   52 **smock** petticoat   52 **broiden**
embroidered   55 **tapes . . . voluper** ribbons of her white cap
56 **suite of** color (or cloth) as   57 **fillet** hair-band   58 **likerous** frisky
59 **small y-pulled** thinly plucked   63 **wether** sheep   65 **perled with
latoun** beaded with brass beads   67–68 **thenche . . . popelote** imag-
ine such a good-looking doll   70 **in . . . newe** the newly minted gold
coin in the Tower of London   71 **yerne** peppy

As any swallow sitting on a berne;°
Thereto she coude skip and make game
As any kid or calf follwing his dame.
75 Hir mouth was sweet as bragot or the meeth,°
Or hoord of apples laid in hay or heeth.
Winsing° she was as is a jolly colt,
Long as a mast, and upright as a bolt.
A brooch she bare upon hir low coller
80 As brood as is the boss of a buckeler.
Hir shoes were laced on hir legges hye.
She was a primerole, a piggesnye,°
For any lord to leggen° in his bedde,
Or yet for any good yeman to wedde.
85   Now, sir, and eft, sir, so bifell the cas
That on a day this hende Nicholas
Fill with this yonge wife to rage and playe,
While that hir husbond was at Oseneye°
—As clerkes been full subtil and full queinte°—
90 And prively he caught hir by the queinte,°
And said, "Ywis, but if ich° have my wille,
For derne love of thee, lemman,° I spille,"°
And held hir harde by the haunche-bones,
And saide, "Lemman, love me all atones,°
95 Or I wol dien, also God me save."
And she sprong as a colt doth in the trave,°
And with hir heed she wried° fast away.
She said, "I wol not kiss thee, by my fay.
Why, let be!" quod she, "let be, Nicholas,
100 Or I wol cry 'Out! Harrow! And Alas!'

---

72 **berne** barn 75 **bragot . . . meeth** ales made with honey
77 **Winsing** skittish 82 **primerole, piggesnye** names of flowers
83 **leggen** lay 88 **Oseneye** an island in the Thames, just west of
Oxford 89 **queinte** clever 90 **queinte** genitals; the gesture is illus-
trated, from a fourteenth-century book of hours, in Robertson, *Preface
to Chaucer*, plate 5 91 **ich** I 92 **lemman** sweetheart 92 **spille**
perish; waste time; with a possible bawdy sense as well, which would
make it a triple pun 94 **atones** at once 96 **trave** a device for hold-
ing horses still while being shod 97 **wried** turned

Do way your handes—for your curteisye."
    This Nicholas gan "mercy" for to crye,°
And spak so fair, and proffred him so faste,
That she hir love him graunted atte laste;
And swore hir ooth, by Saint Thomas of Kent,   *105*
That she wold been at his commandement,
Whan that she may hir leiser well espye.°
"Mine husbond is so full of jalousye
That but ye waite well and been privee,
I wot right well I nam but deed," quod she—   *110*
"Ye moste been full derne° as in this cas."
    "Nay, thereof care thee nought," quod Nicholas.
"A clerk had litherly biset his while°
But if he coud a carpenter beguile."
And thus they been accorded and y-sworn   *115*
To wait a time, as I have told biforn.
Whan Nicholas had done this everydeel,
And thakked hir about the lendes° well,
He kist hir sweet, and taketh his sautrye,
And playeth fast and maketh melodye.   *120*
    Than fill it thus, that to the parish chirche,
Christes owne werkes for to wirche,°
This goode wife went on an holiday:
Hir foreheed shone as bright as any day,
So was it washen when she let hir werk.   *125*
Now was there of that chirch a parish clerk,°
The which that was y-cleped Absolon.
Crul° was his heer, and as the gold it shoon,
And strouted° as a fanne large and brode:
Full straight and even lay his jolly shode.°   *130*

---

102 **"mercy" . . . crye** compare Arcite's dying words, Knight's Tale,
line 1950   107 **hir leiser . . . espye** find her chance   111 **derne** se-
cret. Secrecy was one of the requirements in courtly love   113 **had . . .
while** would have used his time badly   118 **thakked . . . lendes** pat-
ted her on the behind   122 **wirche** perform   126 **clerk** in Absolon's
case, a clerk in minor orders who is the handyman about the church
and jack-of-all-trades; see lines 140–41.   128 **Crul** curly
129 **strouted** spread out   130 **shode** part in his hair

His rode° was red, his eyen grey as goos.
With Poules window° corven on his shoes,
In hoses red he wente fetisly.
Y-clad he was full small and properly,°
135   All in a kirtel of a light waget°—
Full fair and thicke been the pointes° set—
And thereupon he had a gay surplis,
As white as is the blossme upon the ris.°
A merry child he was, so God me save!
140   Well coud he laten blood, and clip, and shave,
And maken a chartre of land, or acquitaunce.°
In twenty manner coud he trip and daunce
After the scole of Oxenforde tho,°
And with his legges casten to and fro,
145   And playen songes on a small rubible.°
Thereto he song sometime a loud quinible,°
And as well coud he play on a giterne.°
In all the town nas brewhouse ne taverne
That he ne visited with his solas,
150   Ther any gaillard tappestere° was.
But, sooth to sayn, he was somedeel squaimous°
Of farting; and of speeche daungerous.°
      This Absolon, that jolly was and gay,
Goth with a sencer° on the holiday,
155   Sencing the wives of the parish faste,
And many a lovely look on hem he caste,

---

131 **rode** complexion   132 **Poules window** design cut in his shoes
resembling in shape the windows of St. Paul's Cathedral   134 **small
and properly** discreetly and splendidly   135 **kirtel . . . waget** coat of
light blue   136 **pointes** laces   138 **ris** twig   140–41 **laten . . . ac-
quitaunce** let blood, cut hair, shave, write a charter for the sale of land
or a deed of release   143 **scole . . . tho** manner of Oxford then
145 **rubible** the rebeck, a two-stringed instrument played with a bow
146 **quinible** high-pitched voice, perhaps counter tenor or falsetto
147 **giterne** guitar   150 **gaillard tappestere** merry barmaid
151 **squaimous** squeamish   152 **daungerous** delicate   154 **sencer**
censer, incense-burner; he censes the church or their homes, a form of
blessing

And namely on this carpenteres wif.
To look on hir him thought a merry lif!
She was so propre and sweet and likerous,
I dare well sayn, if she had been a mous   *160*
And he a cat—he wold hir hent° anon!
This parish clerk, this jolly Absolon,
Hath in his herte swich a love-longinge
That of no wife took he noon offringe—
For curteisy he said he wolde noon.   *165*
The moon, whan it was night, full brighte shoon,
And Absolon his giterne hath y-take,
For paramours, he thoughte for to wake;°
And forth he goth, jolif and amorous,
Till he came to the carpenteres hous,   *170*
A litel after cockes had y-crowe,
And dressed him up by a shot-windowe°
That was upon the carpenteres wall.
He singeth in his voice gentil and small,
Now, dere lady, if thy wille be,   *175*
I praye you that ye wol rew on me—
Full well accordant to his giterninge.
This carpenter awoke, and herd him singe,
And spak unto his wife and said anon,
"What, Alison, heerestou not Absolon   *180*
That chaunteth thus under our bowre's wall?"
And she answered hir husbond therewithal,
"Yis, God wot, John, I heer it everydeel."
    This passeth forth—what wol ye bet than well?
Fro day to day this jolly Absolon   *185*
So woweth° hir that him is woe-bigon.
He waketh all the night and all the day;
He kembeth his lockes brod and made him gay.
He woweth hir by menes and brocage,°

---

161 **hent** catch   168 **For . . . wake** for the sake of love he planned to
stay up   172 **shot-windowe** casement window   186 **woweth** woos
189 **menes and brocage** go-betweens and agents

190 And swore he wolde been hir owne page.
    He singeth, brokking° as a nightingale.
    He sent hir piment, meeth,° and spiced ale,
    And wafers piping hot out of the gleede,°
    And—for she was of town—he proffred meede:°
195 For some folk wol be wonnen for richesse,
    And some for strokes, and some for gentilesse.
    Sometime to shew his lightness and maistrye,
    He playeth Herodes upon a scaffold hye.°
    But what availeth him, as in this cas?
200 She loveth so this hende Nicholas
    That Absolon may blow the buckes horn;°
    He n'hadde for his labour but a scorn!
    And thus she maketh Absolon hir ape,°
    And all his ernest turneth til a jape.
205 Full sooth is this proverb, it is no lie,
    Men saith right thus: *Alway the nye slye*
    Maketh the ferre leve to be loth.°
    For though that Absolom be wood or wroth,
    By cause that he fer was from hir sighte,
210 This nye Nicholas stood in his lighte.
    Now beer thee well, thou hende Nicholas!
    For Absolon may wail and sing "alas!"

                    *   *   *

    And so befell it on a Saterday
    This carpenter was gone til Oseney,
215 And hende Nicholas and Alisoun
    Accorded been to this conclusioun,
    That Nicholas shall shapen him a wile°

191 **brokking** in a breaking voice   192 **piment, meeth** honeyed
wine, mead   193 **gleede** iron (like a waffle iron)   194 **meede** cash
198 **Herodes . . . hye** i.e., he played Herod in a mystery play; the scaf-
fold would be a temporary stage   201 **blow . . . horn** i.e., he is wast-
ing   his   time   203 **ape** Cf.   General   Prologue,   line   706
206–07 **Alway . . . loth** always the sly fellow nearby causes the loved
one far off to be despised   217 **wile** trick

This sely° jalous husbond to beguile;
And if so be the game went aright,
She sholde sleepen in his arm all night—   220
For this was hir desire, and his also.
And right anon, withouten wordes mo,
This Nicholas no lenger wolde tarrye,
But doth full soft unto his chambre carrye
Both mete and drinke for a day or twaye,   225
And to hir husbond bade hir for to saye—
If that he asked after Nicholas—
She sholde say she niste where he was,
Of all that day she saw him nought with eye;
She trowed that he was in maladye,   230
For, for no cry hir maide coud him calle,
He nold answer for no thing that might falle.

    This passeth forth all thilke Saterday
That Nicholas still in his chambre lay,
And eet, and sleep, or dide what him leste,   235
Till Sunday that the sunne goth to reste.
This sely carpenter hath greet mervaile
Of Nicholas, or what thing might him aile,
And said, "I am adrad, by Saint Thomas,
It stondeth not aright with Nicholas.   240
God shilde° that he deide suddenly!
This world is now full tikel,° sikerly!
I saw today a corpse y-born to chirche
That now on Monday last I saw him wirche.
Go up," quod he unto his knave° anon,   245
"Clepe° at his door or knocke with a ston.
Look how it is and tell me boldely."
    This knave goth him up full sturdily,
And at the chambre door while that he stood
He cried and knocked as that he were wood,   250
"What! How! What do ye, maister Nicholay?
How may ye sleepen all the longe day?"

218 **sely** poor, silly, foolish   241 **shilde** forbid   242 **tikel** unstable
245 **knave** servant   246 **Clepe** call

But all for nought: he herde not a word.
An hole he foond full low upon a boord,
255 Ther as the cat was wont in for to creepe,
And at that hole he looked in full deepe,
And atte last he had of him a sighte:
This Nicholas sat gaping ever uprighte
As he had kiked° on the newe moone.
260   Adown he goth and told his maister soone
In what array he saw this ilke man.
This carpenter to blessen him° began,
And saide, "Help us, Sainte Frideswide!°
A man wot litel what him shall bitide!
265 This man is falle, with his astromye,°
In some woodnesse or in some agonye.°
I thought ay well how that it sholde be°—
Men shold not know of Goddes privetee.
Ye, blessed be alway a lewed° man
270 That nought but only his bileve kan!°
So ferde another clerk with astromye:
He walked in the feeldes for to prye
Upon the sterres, what there shold bifalle,
Till he was in a marle-pit y-falle—
275 He saw not *that!* But yet, by Saint Thomas,
Me reweth sore for hende Nicholas—
He shall be rated of his studying,°
If that I may, by Jesus, heven king.
Get me a staff that I may underspore°
280 While that thou, Robin, hevest up the doore.
He shall out of his studying, as I guesse"—
And to the chambre door he gan him dresse.

---

259 **As . . . kiked** as if he were staring (i.e., as if moon-struck)
262 **blessen him** cross himself   263 **Sainte Frideswide** patron saint
of Oxford   265 **astromye** the carpenter mispronounces "astronomy"
266 **woodnesse . . . agonye** madness or fit   267 **I . . . be** I always
thought it would be this way   269 **lewed** ignorant   270 **That . . .
kan** who knows nothing but his creed   277 **rated . . . studying**
scolded for his musing   279 **underspore** pry

His knave was a strong carl for the nones,
And by the hasp he haf it up° atones—
Into the floor the doore fill anon.   *285*
This Nicholas sat ay as still as ston,
And ever gaped up into the air.
This carpenter wend he were in despair,°
And hent him by the shoulders mightily,
And shook him hard, and cride spitously,°   *290*
"What, Nicholay! what, how! What! Look adown!
Awake, and thenk on Christes passioun!
I crouche thee from elves and fro wightes!"°
Therewith the nightspell said he anonrightes°
On foure halves° of the house aboute,   *295*
And on the threshfold on the door withoute:
"Jesu Christ and Saint Benedict,
Bless this house from every wicked wight!
For nightes verye, the white Pater Noster!
Where wentestou, Saint Petres soster?"°   *300*
And at the last this hende Nicholas
Gan for to sike sore°—and said, "Alas!
Shall all the world be lost eftsoones now?"
    This carpenter answerde, "What saistou?
What! think on God, as *we* doon, men that swinke!"°   *305*
    This Nicholas answerde, "Fetch me drinke!
And after wol I speke in privetee
Of certain thing that toucheth me and thee.
I wol tell it noon other man, certain."
    This carpenter goth down and cometh again,   *310*
And brought of mighty ale a large quart,

---

284 **haf it up** pulled it off   288 **wend . . . despair** supposed he was in
some desperate plight   290 **spitously** harshly   293 **crouche . . .
wightes** defend with the sign of the cross from elves and living
creatures   294 **nightspell . . . anonrightes** he said the night spell
right away (a charm against evil spirits)   295 **halves** sides   299–
300 **For . . . soster** like most charms this is chiefly nonsense. The
white Pater Noster was a prayer against evil spirits in the night; where
St. Peter's sister went remains unanswered   302 **sike sore** sigh deeply
305 **swinke** work

And whan that ech of hem had drunk his part,
This Nicholas his doore faste shette,
And down the carpenter by him he sette,
315 And saide, "John, mine hoste lief and dere,
Thou shalt upon thy trouthe swere me here
That to no wight thou shalt this conseil wraye;°
For it is Christes conseil that I saye,
And if thou tell it man, thou art forlore;°
320 For this vengeance thou shalt have therefore,
That if thou wraye me, thou shalt be wood."°
      "Nay, Christ forbede it, for his holy blood!"
Quod tho this sely man, "I nam no labbe,°
And, though I say,° I nam not lief to gabbe.
325 Say what thou wolt, I shall it never telle
To child ne wife, by Him that harrwed helle."°
      "Now John," quod Nicholas, "I wol not lie:
I have y-found in mine astrologye,
As I have looked in the moone bright,
330 That now a-Monday next, at quarter night,
Shall fall a rain, and that so wild and wood,
That half so greet was never Noeh's flood.
This world," he said, "in lasse than an hour
Shall all be dreint,° so hidous is the shower.
335 Thus shall mankinde drench° and lese hir lif."
      This carpenter answered, "Alas, my wif!
And shall *she* drench? Alas, mine Alisoun!"
For sorrow of this he fill almost adown,
And said, "Is there no remedy in this cas?"
340 "Why, yis,° for God," quod hende Nicholas,
"If thou wolt werken after lore and reed;°
Thou maist not werken after thine own heed.

317 **this ... wraye** betray this secret 319 **forlore** utterly lost
321 **if ... wood** if you betray me you will go mad 323 **labbe**
blabbermouth 324 **though I say** if I do say so myself 326 **Him ...
helle** Christ descended into Hell to save virtuous souls born before the
Incarnation; the incident was depicted in mystery plays 334 **dreint**
drowned 335 **drench** drown 340 **yis** the emphatic form (as opposed
to "ye"): "why, yes—for *sure*" 341 **lore and reed** learning and advice

For thus saith Salomon that was full trewe:
Werk all by conseil and thou shalt nought rewe.°
And if thou werken wolt by good conseil,   345
I undertake, withouten mast or sail,
Yet shall I save hir, and thee, and me.
Hastou not herd how saved was Noeh
Whan that Our Lord had warned him biforn
That all the world with water shold be lorn?"   350
    "Yis," quod this carpenter, "full yore ago."
    "Hastou not herd," quod Nicholas, "also
The sorrow of Noeh with his fellawshipe?°
Ere that he mighte get his wife to shipe,
Him had lever, I dare well undertake,   355
At thilke time than all his wetheres° blacke
That she hadde had a ship hirself alone.
And therefore wostou what is best to doone?
This asketh haste, and of an hastif thing
Men may not preche or maken tarrying.   360
Anon go get us fast into this inn°
A kneeding-trough or elles a kimelin°
For ech of us—but look that they be large—
In which we mowen swim as in a barge,
And han therein vitaille suffisaunt   365
But for a day—fy on the remenaunt!
The water shall aslake and goon away
Aboute prime upon the nexte day.
But Robin may not wite of this, thy knave,
Ne eek thy maide Gille I may not save.   370
Axe not why, for though thou axe me,
I wol not tellen Goddes privetee.
Suffiseth thee, but if thy wittes madde,°

344 **rewe** be sorry   353 **sorrow . . . fellawshipe** in the mystery play
Noah's wife will not get on the boat, scolds him, and so on; the Noah
play was sponsored by the carpenter's guild, and old John, doubtless
having seen it, has a clear idea of Noah's troubles in escaping the flood
356 **wetheres** sheep   361 **inn** house   362 **kimelin** brewing-tub
373 **but . . . madde** unless your wits have gone mad

To han as greet a grace as Noeh hadde.
375 Thy wife shall I well saven, out of doute.
Go now thy way, and speed thee hereaboute.
But whan thou hast for hir and thee and me
Y-geten us thise kneeding-tubbes three,
Than shaltou hang hem in the roof full hye,
380 That no man of our purveyance° espye.
And whan thou thus hast done as I have said,
And hast our vitaille fair in hem y-laid,
And eek an ax to smite the cord atwo
Whan that the water cometh, that we may go,
385 And breke an hole on high upon the gable
Unto the gardenward, over the stable,
That we may freely passen forth our way,
Whan that the greet shower is gone away—
Than shaltou swim as murry, I undertake,
390 As doth the white duck after hir drake!
Than wol I clepe, 'How, Alison? How, John?
Be murry, for the flood wol pass anon!'
And thou wolt sayn, 'Hail, maister Nicholay!
Good morrwe, I see thee well, for it is day!'
395 And than shall we be lordes all our lif
Of all the world, as Noeh and his wif.
But of oo thing I warne thee full right:
Be well avised on that ilke night
That we been entred into shippes boord
400 That none of us ne speke not a word,
Ne clepe, ne cry, but been in his prayere,
For it is Goddes owne heste dere.°
Thy wife and thou mot hange fer atwinne,°
For that bitwixe you shall be no sinne—
405 Namore in looking than there shall in deede.
This ordinance is said. Go, God thee speede.
Tomorrwe at night whan men been all asleepe,
Into our kneeding-tubbes wol we creepe,

---

380 **purveyance** preparation   402 **Goddes . . . dere** God's own dear
command   403 **fer atwinne** far apart

And sitten there, abiding° Goddes grace.
Go now thy way, I have no lenger space   410
To make of this no lenger sermoning.
Men sayn thus, *Send the wise and say no thing.*
Thou art so wise it needeth thee not teche.
Go save our life, and that I thee biseeche."
    This sely carpenter goth forth his way.   415
Full oft he said "Alas!" and "Weilaway!"
And to his wife he told his privetee—
And she was ware, and knew it bet than he,
What all this quainte cast was for to saye.°
But natheless she ferd as she wold deye,°   420
And said, "Alas! go forth thy way anon!
Help us to scape, or we been dede echon!
I am thy trewe veray wedded wif:
Go, dere spouse, and help to save our lif."
—Lo, which a greet thing is affeccioun!°   425
Men may die of imaginacioun,
So deepe may impression be take!
This sely carpenter beginneth quake;
Him thinketh verailich that he may see°
Noeh's flood come wallowing as the see   430
To drenchen Alison, his honey dere.
He weepeth, waileth, maketh sorry cheere;
He siketh with full many a sorry swough,°
And goth and geteth him a kneeding-trough,
And after, a tubbe and a kimelin,   435
And prively he sent hem to his inn,
And heng hem in the roof in privetee.
His owne hand° he made ladders three,
To climben by the runges and the stalkes
Unto the tubbes hanging in the balkes,°   440

---

409 **abiding** waiting for   419 **What . . . saye** what all this weird plan
was about   420 **ferd . . . deye** acted as if she were about to die   425 **af-
feccioun** love—but it also means "state of mind"   429 **Him . . . see** it
really seems to him that he can see   433 **swough** a loud sigh   438 **His
owne hand** with his own hand   440 **balkes** beams between the rafters

And hem vitailled, bothe trough and tubbe,
With breed and cheese and good ale in a jubbe,°
Suffising right enough as for a day.
But ere that he had made all this array,°
445 He sent his knave, and eek his wench also,
Upon his need to London for to go.
     And on the Monday whan it drow to night,
He shet his door withouten candle-light,
And dressed alle thing as it shold be,
450 And shortly up they clomben alle three.
They seten stille well a furlong way.°
"Now, *Pater Noster, clum,*"° said Nicholay,
And *"Clum"* quod John, and *"Clum"* said Alisoun.
This carpenter said his devocioun,
455 And still he sit and biddeth his prayere,
Awaiting on the rain, if he it heere.
     The dede sleep, for wery bisinesse,
Fill on this carpenter right as I guesse
Aboute curfew time, or litel more.
460 For travail of his gost° he groneth sore,
And eft he routeth,° for his heed mislay.
     Down off the ladder stalketh Nicholay,
And Alison full soft adown she spedde:
Withouten wordes mo they goon to bedde
465 Ther as the carpenter is wont to lie.
There was the revel and the melodye,
And thus lith Alison and Nicholas
In bisiness of mirth and in solas,
Till that the bell of laudes° gan to ringe,
470 And freres in the chauncel gonne singe.

                    *   *   *

---

442 **jubbe** jug   444 **array** preparation   451 **furlong way** the time it
takes to walk two hundred twenty yards   452 **Pater Noster, clum**
"say a Pater Noster, and then mum"   460 **travail ... gost** i.e., his
troubled spirit   461 **routeth** snores   469 **laudes** about four-thirty
a.m.

   This parish clerk, this amorous Absolon,
That is for love alway so woe-bigon,
Upon the Monday was at Oseneye,
With compaigny him to disport and playe,
And asked upon a cas° a cloisterer   *475*
Full prively after John the carpenter.
And he drow him apart out of the cherche,
And said, "I noot; I saw him here not werche
Sith Saterday. I trowe that he be went
For timber ther our abbot hath him sent;   *480*
For he is wont for timber for to go,
And dwellen at the grange a day or two;
Or elles he is at his house, certain.
Where that he be I can not soothly sayn."
   This Absolon full jolly was and light,   *485*
And thoughte, "Now is time to wake all night,
For sikerly I saw him not stirringe
About his door sin day began to springe.
So mot I thrive, I shall at cockes crowe
Full prively knocken at his windowe   *490*
That stant full low upon his bowres wall.°
To Alison now wol I tellen all
My love-longing, for yet I shall not misse
That at the leste way I shall hir kisse.
Some manner comfort shall I have, parfay.   *495*
My mouth hath itched all this longe day—
That is a sign of kissing, at the leeste.
All night me mette° eek I was at a feeste.
Therefore I wol go sleep an hour or twaye,
And all the night than wol I wake and playe."   *500*
   Whan that the firste cock hath crow, anon
Up rist this jolly lover Absolon,
And him arrayeth gay at point devis.°

---

475 **upon a cas** by chance   491 **low . . . wall** just how low on the wall
of his house is to be an important detail; cf. line 510   498 **me mette**
I dreamed (*lit*. it dreamed to me)   503 **gay . . . devis** fancily to the last
detail

But first he cheweth grain° and licoris
505 To smellen sweet, ere he had kembd his heer.
Under his tonge a trewe-love° he beer,
For thereby wende he to be gracious.°
He rometh to the carpenteres hous,
And still he stant under the shot-windowe
510 (Unto his brest it raught, it was so lowe)
And soft he cougheth with a semy° soun.
"What do ye, honey-comb, sweet Alisoun,
My faire brid,° my sweete cinnamome?
Awaketh, lemman° mine, and speketh to me.
515 Well litel thinken ye upon my wo
That for your love I swete ther I go.°
No wonder is though that I swelt° and swete:
I morne as doth a lamb after the tete.°
Ywis, lemman, I have swich love-longinge,
520 That like a turtle trew is my morninge;°
I may not ete namore than a maide."
    "Go fro the window, Jacke fool!" she saide.
"As help me God, it wol not be *com-pa-me!*°
I love another, and elles I were to blame,
525 Well bet than thee, by Jesu, Absolon.
Go forth thy way, or I wol cast a ston,
And let me sleep, a twenty devil way!"
    "Alas," quod Absolon, "and weilaway,
That trewe love was ever so yvel biset.
530 Than kiss me, sin that it may be no bet,
For Jesus' love, and for the love of me."
    "Woltou than go thy way therewith?" quod she.
    "Ye, certes, lemman," quod this Absolon.

---

504 **grain** a spice   506 **trewe-love** an herb-leaf, perhaps thought to
give luck—or sweeten the breath   507 **wende ... gracious** he imag-
ined he'd be irresistible   511 **semy** delicate   513 **brid** bird
514 **lemman** sweetheart   516 **swete ... go** sweat wherever I go.
Sweating was hardly conventional for courtly lovers; the whole pas-
sage is in fact a bumpkin's idea of love-longing   517 **swelt** get faint
from the heat   518 **tete** teat   520 **like ... morninge** my suffering is
true as the turtledove's   523 **com-pa-me** come kiss me

"Than make thee redy," quod she. "I come anon."
And unto Nicholas she saide stille,   535
"Now hust, and thou shalt laughen all thy fille."

    This Absolon down set him on his knees
And said, "I am a lord at all degrees!°
For after this I hope there cometh more.
Lemman, thy grace! and sweete brid, thine ore!"°   540

    The window she undoth, and that in haste.
"Have do," quod she, "come off° and speed thee faste,
Lest that our neighebores thee espye."

    This Absolon gan wipe his mouth full drye.
Derk was the night as pitch or as the cole;   545
And at the window out she put hir hole.
And Absolon, him fill no bet ne wers,
But with his mouth he kist hir naked ers—
Full savourly—ere he were ware of this.
Aback he stert, and thought it was amiss,   550
For well he wist a woman hath no beerd.
He felt a thing all rough and long y-herd,°
And saide, "Fy, alas! what have I do?"

    "*Teehee*," quod she, and clapt the window to.
And Absolon goth forth a sorry pas.   555

    "A beerd! a beerd!"° quod hende Nicholas,
"By Goddes corpus, this goth fair and well!"

    This sely Absolon herd everydeel,
And on his lip he gan for anger bite,
And to himself he said—"I shall thee quite."°   560
Who rubbeth now, who froteth° now his lippes
With dust, with sand, with straw, with cloth, with
    chippes,
But Absolon, that saith full oft "alas"?
"My soul bitake I unto Sathanas,

---

538 **at all degrees** in all respects—love has ennobled him already!
540 **ore** grace   542 **Have ... off** "let's get it over with, come on"
552 **y-herd** haired   556 **beerd** beard (the word was also slang for a
trick)   560 **quite** get even with. Note how fast his artificiality
disappears   561 **froteth** scrapes

565 But me were lever than all this town," quod he,
    "Of this despite awroken° for to be.
    Alas," quod he, "Alas I n'had y-bleint!"°
    His hote love was cold and all y-queint,°
    For fro that time that he had kist hir ers
570 Of paramours he sette not a kers°—
    For he was heled° of his maladye.
    Full ofte paramours he gan defye,
    And weep as doth a child that is y-bete.
        A softe pas he went over the streete
575 Until a smith men clepen daun Gervais,
    That in his forge smithed plough-harneis:
    He sharpeth shar and cultour bisily.
    This Absolon knocketh all esily,
    And said, "Undo, Gervais, and that anon!"
580 "What, who artou?" "It am I, Absolon."
    "What, Absolon? What, Christes sweete tree!°
    Why rise ye so rathe?° Ey, *ben'dic'te,*
    What aileth you? Some gay girl, God it wot,
    Hath brought you thus upon the veritoot.°
585 By Sainte Note, ye wot well what I mene."
        This Absolon ne roughte° not a bene
    Of all his play; no word again he yaf.
    He hadde more tow on his distaff
    Than Gervais knew, and saide, "Freend so dere,
590 This hote cultour in the chimnee here,
    As, lene° it me; I have therewith to doone.
    I wol bring it thee again full soone."
        Gervais answerde, "Certes, were it gold,
    Or in a poke nobles all untold,°
595 Thou sholdest have, as I am trewe smith.

---

566 **awroken** avenged 567 **I . . . y-bleint** if only I had held back
568 **y-queint** put out 570 **Of . . . kers** he didn't give a damn about
love affairs 571 **heled** healed. Healing the lover's malady, a tradi-
tional phrase, was usually done by the lady's favor 581 **tree** cross
582 **rathe** early 584 **veritoot** "on the move" 586 **roughte** cared
591 **lene** lend 594 **in . . . untold** countless gold coins in a sack

Ey, Christes foe, what wol ye do therewith?"
    "Thereof," quod Absolon, "be as be may.
I shall well tell it thee tomorrwe day"—
And caught the cultour by the colde steele.
Full soft out at the door he gan to stele,   600
And went unto the carpenteres wall.
He cougheth first, and knocketh therewithal
Upon the window, right as he did er.
    This Alison answerde, "Who is ther
That knocketh so? I warrant it a thief."   605
    "Why, nay!" quod he, "God wot, my sweete lief,
I am thine Absolon, my dereling!°
Of gold," quod he, "I have thee brought a ring;
My moder yaf it me, so God me save.
Full fine it is and thereto well y-grave.   610
This wol I yiven thee, if thou me kisse."
    This Nicholas was risen for to pisse,
And thought he wold amenden all the jape°—
He sholde kiss *his* ers ere that he scape.
And up the window did he hastily,   615
And out his ers he putteth prively,
Over the buttock to the haunche-bon.
And therewith spak this clerk, this Absolon:
"Spek, sweete brid, I noot not where thou art."
This Nicholas anon let flee a fart   620
As greet as it had been a thunder-dent,
That with the stroke he was almost y-blent;°
And he was redy with his iren hot,
And Nicholas amid the ers he smoot.
Off goth the skin an hande-brede aboute;   625
The hote cultour brende so his toute
That for the smert he wende for to die;
As he were wood, for woe he gan to crye,
"Help! Water! *Water!* Help, for Goddes herte!"
    This carpenter out of his slumber sterte,   630

607 **dereling** darling   613 **amenden . . . jape** improve upon the joke
622 **y-blent** blinded

And herd one cryen *"Water!"* as he were wood,
And thought, "Alas, now cometh Noweles flood!"
He set him up withoute wordes mo,
And with his ax he smote the cord atwo,
635 *And down goth all!* He fond neither to selle
Ne breed ne ale till he came to the celle°
Upon the floor—and there aswoun he lay.
   Up stirt hir Alison and Nicholay,
And criden "Out!" and "Harrow!" in the streete.
640 The neighebores, bothe small and greete,
In runnen for to gauren° on this man
That aswoun lay bothe pale and wan—
For with the fall he brosten° had his arm.
But stond he most unto his owne harm,°
645 For whan he spak he was anon bore down
With° hende Nicholas and Alisoun.
They tolden every man that he was wood:
He was so aghast of Noweles flood,
Thurgh fantasy, that of his vanitee°
650 He had y-bought him kneeding-tubbes three
And had hem hanged in the roof above,
And that he prayed hem, for Goddes love,
To sitten in the roof, *par compaignye*.
The folk gan laughen at his fantasye.
655 Into the roof they kiken° and they gape,
And turned all his harm unto a jape;
For what so that this carpenter answerde
It was for nought—no man his reson herde.
With othes greet he was so sworn adown
660 That he was holden wood in all the town,
For every clerk anonright held with other:
They said, "The man was wood, my leve brother,"
And every wight gan laughen at this strif.

635–36 **He fond ... celle** he didn't stop to sell bread or ale till he hit
the floor   641 **gauren** gape   643 **brosten** broken   644 **stond ...
harm** accept the blame   645–46 **anon bore down with** immediately
put down by   649 **vanitee** silliness   655 **kiken** gawk

Thus swived° was the carpenteres wif
For all his keeping and his jalousye;   665
And Absolon hath kist hir nether eye;
And Nicholas is scalded in the toute.
This tale is done and God save all the route!°

664 **swived** layed   669 **route** crowd, bunch

THE REEVE'S PROLOGUE

Whan folk had laughen at this nice cas
Of Absolon and hende Nicholas,
Diverse folk diversely they saide,
But for the more part they laugh and playde;°
5 Ne at this tale I saw no man him greve
But it were only Osewold the Reeve:
Because he was of carpenteres craft
A litel ire is in his hert y-laft°—
He gan to grucche° and blamed it a lite:
10   "So thee'k,"° quod he, "full well coud I thee quite
With blering of a proud milleres eye,°
If that me liste speke of ribaudye.°
But ik° am old; me list not play for age.
Grass time is done, my fodder is now forage;
15 This white top writeth mine olde yeeres.
Mine hert is also mouled° as mine heeres,
But if° ik fare as doth an open-ers°—
That ilke fruit is ever lenger the wers°
Till it be rotten in mullok or in stree.°
20 We olde men, I drede, so fare we—
Till we be rotten can we not be ripe;

4 **playde** joked 8 **y-laft** left 9 **grucche** grumble 10 **So thee'k** (so thee ik) so may I prosper; heaven help me 11 **blering . . . eye** deceiving 12 **ribaudye** ribaldry 13 **ik** I. The Reeve speaks in the dialect of East Anglia, a region influenced by northern speech forms. His dialect falls somewhere between the dialect of the two northern clerks (see line 95) and the London dialect of Chaucer's audience 16 **also mouled** as decayed, aged 17 **But if** unless 17 **open-ers** the fruit of the medlar tree, edible only after it has partially decayed 18 **ever lenger the wers** always worse and worse 19 **in mullok . . . stree** in refuse or in straw

We hoppen ay, while that the world wol pipe,°
For in our will there sticketh ever a nail
To have an hoor hed and a greene tail,
As hath a leek; for though our might be goon,   25
Our will desireth folly ever in oon:°
For whan we may nought doon, than wol we speke.
Yet in our ashen old is fire y-reke.°
Four gleedes° have we which I shall devise:
Avaunting,° lying, anger, coveitise—   30
Thise foure sparkles longen unto elde.°
Our olde limes° mowe well been unwelde,°
But will ne shall not failen, that is sooth.
And yet ik have alway a coltes tooth,°
As many a yeer as it is passed henne°   35
Sin that my tap of life began to renne°—
For sikerly, whan ik was bore, anon
Deeth drow° the tap of life and let it gon,
And ever sith hath so the tap y-ronne
Till that almost all empty is the tonne:°   40
The streem of life now droppeth on the chimbe.°
The sely tonge may well ring and chimbe°
Of wretchedness that passed is full yore—
With olde folk save dotage is namore."°

Whan that our Host had herd this sermoning,   45
He gan to speke as lordly as a king:
He saide, "What amounteth all this wit?
What shall° we speke alday of holy writ?
The devil made a reeve for to preche,
Or of a soutere° a shipman or a leeche!°   50

---

22 **We hoppen . . . pipe** we hop behind always while the world calls
the tune   26 **ever in oon** all the same   28 **y-reke** raked up
29 **gleedes** burning coals   30 **Avaunting** boasting   31 **longen unto
elde** belong to old age   32 **limes** limbs   32 **unwelde** unwieldy, weak
34 **coltes tooth** young lusts, lecherous streak   35 **henne** from now
36 **renne** run   38 **drow** pulled out   40 **tonne** cask, barrel   41 **chimbe**
rim of the barrel   42 **chimbe** chime   44 **save dotage is namore**
there is nothing but dotage   48 **What shall** why must   50 **soutere**
cobbler   50 **leeche** physician

Say forth thy tale, and tarry not the time:
Lo, Depford,° and it is halfway prime!°
Lo, Greenwich, ther many a shrew° is inne!
It were all time thy tale to beginne."
55   "Now, sires," quod this Osewold the Reeve,
"I pray you alle that ye nought you greve
Though I answer and somedeel set his houve,°
For leveful is with force force off-shouve.°
This dronken Miller hath y-told us heer
60   How that beguiled was a carpenter—
Paraventure in scorn, for I am oon;
And by your leve, I shall him quite anoon:
Right in his cherles° termes wol I speke.
I pray to God his necke mot tobreke—
65   He can well in mine eye seen a stalke,
But in his own he can not seen a balke."°

THE REEVE'S TALE

At Trumpington, not fer fro Cantebridge,°
There goth a brook, and over that a bridge,
Upon the whiche brook there stant a melle°—
And this is veray sooth that I you telle.
5   A miller was there dwelling many a day;
As any pecock he was proud and gay;

---

52 **Depford** Deptford, about four miles outside of Southwark
52 **halfway prime** seven-thirty a.m.   53 **shrew** scoundrel   57 **set his houve** arrange his hood, i.e., make him look silly   58 **leveful . . . shouve** it is lawful to repel force with force   63 **cherles** peasant's
66 **balke** beam   1 **Cantebridge** Cambridge   3 **melle** mill

Pipen° he coud, and fish, and nettes beete,°
And turne coppes° and well wrastle and sheete.°
And by his belt he bare a long panade,°
And of a swerd full trenchant° was the blade;   10
A jolly poppere° bare he in his pouche—
There was no man for peril dorst him touche;
A Sheffeld thwitel° bare he in his hose,
Round was his face, and camuse° was his nose;
As piled° as an ape was his skulle.   15
He was a market-beter° atte fulle.
There dorste no wight hand upon him lege°
That he ne swore he shold anon abege.°
A thief he was forsooth of corn and mele,
And that a sly, and usant° for to stele.   20
His name was hoten deinous° Simekin.
    A wife he hadde, comen of noble kin:
The person° of the town hir fader was.
With hir he yaf full many a pan° of brass,
For that Simekin shold in his blood allye;°   25
She was y-fostred in a nonnerye,
For Simekin wolde no wife, as he saide,
But she were well y-norished and a maide,°
To saven his estate of yemanrye.°
And she was proud and pert as is a pie.°   30
A full fair sight was it upon hem two—
On holidays biforn hir wold he go

---

7 **Pipen** play the bagpipe (see General Prologue, lines 565–66)
7 **nettes beete** mend nets   8 **turne coppes** drink heavily   8 **sheete**
shoot   9 **panade** cutlass   10 **trenchant** sharp   11 **poppere** dagger
13 **thwitel** knife   14 **camuse** flat   15 **piled** bald   16 **market-beter**
loafer in a market, bully   17 **lege** lay   18 **abege** be punished   20 **us-
ant** accustomed   21 **hoten deinous** called haughty   23 **person**
parson   24 **pan** penny; or perhaps "pan," i.e., panfuls of money. The
point is that the priest's daughter is illegitimate and the priest has had
to put up a good dowry to marry her off   25 **For . . . allye** to get Sim-
kin to make a blood alliance with her   28 **well y-norished . . . maide**
well brought up and a virgin   29 **saven . . . yemanrye** to preserve his
status as a freeman (which carried with it certain exemptions from
obligations and hence a certain prestige)   30 **pie** magpie

With his tippet° wound about his heed,
And she came after in a gite° of red,
35　And Simekin hadde hosen of the same.
There dorste no wight clepen° hir but "dame."
Was none so hardy that went by the waye
That with hir dorste rage or ones playe,°
But if he wold be slain of Simekin,
40　With panade, or with knife or boidekin;°
For jalous folk been perilous° everemo—
Algate they wold hir wives wenden so.°
And eek, for she was somedeel smoterlich,°
She was as digne as water in a ditch,°
45　And full of hoker and of bisemare.°
Hir thoughte that a lady shold hir spare,°
What for hir kinred, and hir nortelrye°
That she had lerned in the nonnerye.
　　A doughter hadde they bitwix hem two
50　Of twenty yeer, withouten any mo,
Saving a child that was of half yeer age:
In cradle it lay and was a proper page.°
This wenche thick and well y-growen was,
With camuse nose, and eyen grey as glass,
55　With buttocks brod, and brestes round and hye,
But right fair was hir heer, I wol nat lie.
The person of the town, for she was fair,
In purpose was° to maken hir his heir
Both of his catel and his mesuage,°
60　And straunge he made it of° hir marriage.

---

33 **tippet** scarf　34 **gite** gown　36 **clepen** call　38 **dorste . . . playe** dared to fool around or make one joke　40 **boidekin** dagger　41 **perilous** dangerous　42 **Algate . . . so** anyway, they would have their wives think so　43 **smoterlich** sullied, stained because of her illegitimacy　44 **digne . . . ditch** i.e., as unapproachable as stagnant ditch water　45 **hoker . . . bisemare** scorn . . . contempt　46 **hir spare** be aloof, reserved　47 **What . . . nortelrye** what with her background and good breeding　52 **proper page** sturdy lad　58 **In purpose was** intended　59 **catel . . . mesuage** possessions and household　60 **straunge . . . of** was particular about

His purpose was for to bistow hir hye
Into some worthy blood of auncetrye,
For holy chirches good moot been dispended
On holy chirches blood that is descended;°
Therefore he wold his holy blood honoure,   65
Though that he holy chirche shold devoure.
    Greet soken° hath this miller out of doute
With whete and malt of all the land aboute;
And namelich there was a greet college,
Men clepth the Soler Hall° of Cantebrege;   70
There was hir whete and eek hir malt y-grounde.
And on a day it happed in a stounde°
Sick lay the manciple° on a maladye;
Men wenden wisly° that he sholde die,
For which this miller stal° both mele and corn   75
An hundred time more than biforn—
For therebiforn he stal but curteisly,
But now he was a thief outrageously.
For which the wardein chidde and made fare;°
But thereof set the miller not a tare—   80
He cracked boost,° and swore it was not so.
    Than were there yonge povre° scholers two
That dwelten in the hall of which I saye.
Testif° they were and lusty for to playe,
And only for hir mirth and revelrye   85
Upon the wardein bisily they crye
To yive hem leve but a litel stounde
To go to mill and seen hir corn y-grounde,
And hardily they dorste lay hir necke
The miller shold not stele hem° half a pecke   90

63–64 **dispended . . . descended** spent on those who spring from holy
church's blood   67 **soken** power, monopoly   70 **Soler Hall** King's
Hall, Cambridge, for thirty-two scholars   72 **in a stounde** at one time
73 **manciple** steward, purchaser   74 **wisly** surely   75 **stal** stole
79 **made fare** made a to-do   81 **cracked boost** talked loudly, sounded
off   82 **povre** poor   84 **Testif** headstrong   90 **stele hem** steal from
them

Of corn by sleighte, ne by force hem reve;°
And atte last the wardein yaf hem leve.
John hight that one, and Alain hight that other;
Of one town were they born that highte Strother,
95   Fer in the north°—I can not telle where.
This Alain maketh redy all his gere,
And on a horse the sack he cast anon;
Forth goth Alain the clerk and also John,
With good swerd and with buckler by his side.
100 John knew the way—him needede no guide;
And at the mill the sack adown he laith.
    Alain spak first: "All hail, Simond, in faith.
How fares° thy faire doughter and thy wif?"
    "Alain, welcome!" quod Simekin, "by my lif!
105 And John also! How now, what do ye heer?"
    "By God," quod John, "Simond, need has na peer;°
Him boes° serve himself that has na swain,°
Or elles he is a fool, as clerkes sayn.
Our manciple, I hope° he will be deed,
110 Swa werkes ay the wanges° in his heed.
And therefore is° I come, and eek Alain,
To grind our corn and carry it haam° again.

---

91 **hem reve** take away from them   95 **Fer in the north** The East
Anglian Reeve (*Pro.* line 13) identifies Aleyn and John as northerners.
In Chaucer's day the southern universities were invaded from the north
by young clerks interested in university education and university life
in the south. The clerks' speech in the tale contains a number of north-
ern words but no northern forms with which a Londoner would have
been unfamiliar. Chaucer gives to their speech what would have
seemed a rustic peasant sound. The most important dialect form is the
use of ā for Chaucer's usual ō (*na,* no; *banes,* bones; *haam,* hoom;
bathe, bothe). Also note the 3rd sing. pres. ind. -s, -es for -eth (how
fares thy faire doughter); the third plural pres. ind. -s, -es for -en; and
til (to), *I* is (I am), *gif* (if), *sall* (shall), and *swa* (so). Dialect words will
be marked (dial.) in the text   103 **fares** (dial.) Chaucer's dialect
would have had *faren*   106 **need . . . peer** (dial.) necessity has no
equal   107 **Him boes** (dial.) one should   107 **na swain** no servant
109 **hope** fear   110 **Swa . . . wanges** (dial.) so ache always the
molars   111 **is** (dial.) am   112 **haam** (dial.) home

I pray you, speed us heithen° that ye may."
   "It shall be done," quod Simekin, "by my fay.°
What wol ye doon while that it is in hande?"°   *115*
   "By God, right by the hopper will I stande,"
Quod Johan, "and see how the corn gaas° in.
Yet saw I never, by my fader° kin,
How that the hopper wagges til and fra."°
   Alain answered, "Johan, and wiltou swa?°   *120*
Than will I be binethe, by my crown,
And see how that the mele falles down
Into the trough—that sall° be my desport.
For John, in faith, I may been of your sort:
I is as ill a miller as are° ye."   *125*
   This miller smiled of hir nicetee,°
And thought, "All this nis done but for a wile.°
They wene that no man may hem beguile
But by my thrift, yet shall I blere hir eye,°
For all the sleight in hir philosophye.°   *130*
The more quainte crekes° that they make,
The more wol I stele whan I take—
In stede of flour yet wol I yive hem bren.°
The grettest clerks been not the wisest men,
As whilom to the wolf thus spak the mare.   *135*
Of all hir art count I not a tare."°
Out at the door he goth full prively,
Whan that he saw his time softely:
He looketh up and down till he hath founde
The clerkes' horse there as it stood y-bounde   *140*
Behind the mille, under a leefsel,°
And to the horse he goth him fair and well.

---

113 **heithen** (dial.) from here   114 **fay** faith   115 **in hande** in the making   117 **gaas** goes   118 **fader** father's   119 **til and fra** (dial.) to and fro   120 **wiltou swa** (dial.) will you do that   123 **sall** (dial.) shall   125 **are** (dial.) Chaucer's dialect had "ye ben"   126 **nicetee** naïveté   127 **wile** subterfuge   129 **blere hir eye** fool them 130 **sleight ... philosophye** cleverness in their logic-chopping 131 **quainte crekes** clever tricks   133 **bren** bran   136 **tare** weed 141 **leefsel** leafy arbor

He strepeth off the bridel right anoon,
And whan the horse was laus,° he ginneth goon°
145 Toward the fen ther wilde mares renne,°
And forth with "Weehee," thurgh thick and thenne.
The miller goth ayain°—no word he saide—
But doth his note° and with the clerkes playde,
Till that hir corn was fair and well y-grounde.
150 And whan the mele is sacked and y-bounde,
This John goth out and fint° his horse away,
And gan to cry "Harrow and weilaway!
Our horse is lost! Alain, for Goddes banes,°
Step on thy feet! Come off, man, all atanes!°
155 Alas, our wardein has his palfrey° lorn!"
      This Alain all forgat both mele and corn—
All was out of his mind his housbondrye.°
"What, whilk way is he gaan?"° he gan to crye.
      The wife came leping inward with a ren;
160 She said, "Alas, your horse goth to the fen
With wilde mares, as fast as he may go.
Unthank° come on his hand that bond him so,
And he that better shold have knit° the reine!"
      "Alas," quod John, "Alain, for Christes paine,
165 Lay down thy swerd, and I will mine alswa.°
I is full wight, God waat, as is a raa.°
By Goddes herte, he sal nat scape us bathe.°
Why n'had thou pit the capil in the lathe?°
Illhail,° by God, Alain, thou is a fonne."°
170   Thise sely clerkes han full fast y-ronne
Toward the fen, both Alain and eek John;
And whan the miller saw that they were goon,

---

144 **laus** loose 144 **ginneth goon** began to go 145 **renne** run
147 **goth ayain** returns 148 **note** work 151 **fint** finds 153 **banes**
(dial.) bones 154 **atanes** (dial.) at once 155 **palfrey** riding-horse
157 **housbondrye** alert management 158 **whilk . . . gaan** (dial.)
which way is he gone 162 **Unthank** misfortune 163 **knit** tied
165 **alswa** (dial.) also 166 **wight . . . raa** (dial.) fast, God knows, as
a roe 167 **bathe** (dial.) both 168 **pit . . . lathe** (dial.) put the horse
in the barn 169 **Illhail** a curse on you 169 **fonne** fool

He half a bushel of hir flour hath take
And bade his wife go kneed it in a cake.
He said, "I trowe the clerkes were aferd. 175
Yet can a miller make a clerkes beerd°
For all his art. Ye, let hem gon hir waye.
Lo, where he goth! Ye, let the children playe.
They get him not so lightly, by my crown."

Thise sely clerkes rennen up and down 180
With "Keep! Keep! Stand! Stand! Jossa! Warderere!
Gaa° whistle thou, and I sall keep him here."
But shortly, till that it was veray night,
They coude not, though they did all hir might,
Hir capil catch, he ran alway so faste, 185
Till in a ditch they caught him at the laste.

Wery and wet as beest is in the rain,
Comth sely John, and with him comth Alain.
"Alas," quod John, "the day that I was born!
Now are we driven til hething° and til scorn— 190
Our corn is stoln, men will us fooles calle,
Bath the wardein and our fellawes° alle,
And namely the miller, wailaway . . ."
Thus plaineth John as he goth by the way
Toward the mill, and Bayard in his hond. 195
The miller sitting by the fire he foond,
For it was night, and ferther might they nought;
But for the love of God they him bisought
Of herberwe° and of ese, as for hir peny.°

The miller said again, "If there be eny, 200
Swich as it is yet shal ye have your part.
Mine house is strait,° but *ye* han lerned *art°*—
Ye can by argumentes make a place
A mile brood of twenty feet of space!

176 **make ... beerd** get the better of a clerk   182 **Gaa** (dial.) go
190 **til hething** into derision   192 **fellawes** fellow clerks   199 **her-
berwe** lodging   199 **as ... peny** for their money   202 **strait** small
202 **lerned art** learned dialectic; he maliciously taunts the debating
and logic of medieval universities

205   Let see now if this place may suffise,
       Or make it roum° with speech, as is your guise."°
            "Now Simond," said this John, "by Saint Cutberd,
       Ay is thou mirye,° and that is fair answered.
       I have herd say men sal taa of twa thinges,°
210   Swilk° as he findes, or taa swilk as he bringes;
       But specially I pray thee, hoste dere,
       Get us some mete and drink and make us cheere,
       And we wol payen trewely atte fulle—
       With empty hand men may na hawkes tulle.°
215   Lo, here our silver, redy for to spende."
       This miller into town his doughter sende
       For ale and breed, and rosted hem a goos,
       And bond hir horse, it shold namore go loos.
       And in his owen chambre hem made a bed
220   With sheetes and with chalons° fair y-spred,
       Not from his owen bed ten foot or twelve.
       His doughter had a bed all by hirselve
       Right in the same chambre by and by.
       It mighte be no bet, and cause why?—
225   There was no roumer herberwe° in the place.
       They soupen and they speken hem to solace,
       And drinken ever strong ale at the beste.
       Aboute midnight wente they to reste.
            Well hath this miller vernished his heed;°
230   Full pale he was for dronke, and nought red.
       He yexeth° and he speketh thurgh the nose
       As he were on the quake or on the pose.°
            To bed he goth, and with him goth his wif.
       As any jay she light° was and jolif,
235   So was hir jolly whistle well y-wet.

---

206 **roum**   spacious   206 **guise**   custom   208 **mirye**   merry
209 **sal . . . thinges** (dial.) shall get either of two things   210 **Swilk**
(dial.) such   214 **tulle** lure   220 **chalons** blankets   225 **roumer**
herberwe more spacious lodging   229 **vernished his heed** got him-
self thoroughly drunk   231 **yexeth** hiccups   232 **were . . . pose** were
hoarse or had a cold   234 **light** frivolous

The cradle at hir beddes feet is set
To rocken, and to yive the child to souke.°
  And whan that dronken all was in the crouke,°
To bedde went the doughter right anon.
To bedde goth Alain and also John.   240
There nas namore—hem needede no dwale.°
This miller hath so wisly bibbed ale°
That as an horse he fnorteth° in his sleep;
Ne of his tail behind he took no keep.°
His wife bare him a burdon,° a full strong—   245
Men might hir routing° heeren a furlong.
The wenche routeth eek, *par compaignye.*°
  Alain the clerk, that herd this melodye,
He poked John and saide, "Sleepestou?
Herdstou ever slik° a sang ere now?   250
Lo, swilk a coupling is ymel hem alle°—
A wilde fire upon their bodies falle!
Wha herkned ever swilk a ferly thing?°
Ye, they sal have the flower of ill ending!
This lange night there tides me na reste.°   255
But yit, na fors,° all sal be for the beste;
For John," said he, "als ever mote I thrive,
If that I may, you wenche will I swive.°
Some esement° has lawe shapen us;
For John, there is a lawe that says thus,   260
That gif° a man in a point be agreved,
That in another he sal be releved.
Our corn is stolen soothly, it is na nay,
And we han had an ille fit° today,

237 **yive . . . souke** to give suck   238 **crouke** crock   241 **dwale**
sedative   242 **wisly bibbed ale** stoutly drunk ale   243 **fnorteth**
snores   244 **took no keep** paid no attention   245 **burdon**
accompaniment   246 **routing** snoring   247 **par compaignye** to-
gether with them   250 **slik** (dial.) such   251 **swilk . . . alle** (dial.)
such a collaboration is among them   253 **Wha . . . thing** who ever
heard such a weird thing   255 **there . . . reste** no rest is in store for
me   256 **na fors** no matter   258 **swive** lay   259 **esement** recourse,
benefit   261 **gif** (dial.) if   264 **ille fit** (dial.) bad time

265 And sin I sal have naan° amendement
     Again my loss, I will have esement.
     By Goddes saule, it sal naan other be."
         This John answered, "Alain, avise thee!°
     The miller is a perilous man," he saide,
270 "And if that he out of his sleep abraide,°
     He mighte doon us bath a villainye."
     Alain answered, "I count him nought a flye,"
     And up he rist, and by the wench he crepte.
     This wenche lay upright and faste slepte,
275 Till he so neigh was ere she might espye
     That it had been too late for to crye;
     And shortly for to sayn, they were at oon.°
     Now play, Alain, for I wol speke of John.
         This John lith still a furlong way or two,
280 And to himself he maketh routh° and wo.
     "Alas," quod he, "this is a wicked jape.°
     Now may I sayn that I is but an ape.
     Yet has my fellaw somewhat° for his harm—
     He has the miller's doughter in his arm.
285 He auntred him,° and has his needes sped,°
     And I lie as a draf-sack° in my bed.
     And whan this jape is tald another day,
     I sal be halden a daff, a cokenay.°
     I will arise and auntre it, by my faith!
290 Unhardy is unsely,° thus men saith."
     And up he rose, and softely he wente
     Unto the cradle, and in his hand it hente,
     And bare it soft unto his beddes feet.
         Soon after this the wife hir routing leet,°
295 And gan awake, and went hir out to pisse,

---

265 **naan** (dial.) no   268 **avise thee** think it over   270 **abraide**
should   wake   277 **at   oon** together   280 **routh** lamentation
281 **jape** joke   283 **somewhat** something   285 **auntred him** took a
risk   285 **sped** accomplished   286 **draf-sack** junk-sack   288 **daff,
cokenay**, jerk, sissy   290 **Unhardy is unsely** i.e., nothing ventured
nothing gained   294 **leet** stopped

And came again, and gan hir cradle misse,
And groped here and there, but she foond noon.
"Alas," quod she, "I had almost misgoon;
I had almost gone to the clerkes bed—
Ey, *ben'dic'te*, than had I foul y-sped!"   *300*
And forth she goth till she the cradle foond.
She gropeth alway ferther with hir hond,
And foond the bed, and thoughte nought but good,
Bicause that the cradle by it stood;
And niste where she was, for it was derk,   *305*
But fair and well she creep into the clerk,
And lith full still, and wold have caught a sleep.°
    Within a while this John the clerk up leep,
And on this goode wife he laith on sore.°
So murry a fit ne had she not full yore: *310*
He pricketh hard and deep as he were mad.
This jolly life han thise two clerkes lad
Till that the thridde cock began to singe.
    Alain wex° wery in the daweninge,
For he had swonken° all the longe night,   *315*
And saide, "Farewell, Malin, sweete wight.
The day is come, I may no lenger bide.
But everemo, whereso I go or ride,
I is thyn awen° clerk, swa have I seel."°
    "Now dere lemman"° quod she, "go, farewell.   *320*
But ere thou go, oo thing I wol thee telle:
Whan that thou wendest homeward by the melle,
Right at the entree of the door behinde
Thou shalt a cake of half a bushel finde,
That was y-maked of thine owne mele,   *325*
Which that I help my sire for to stele.
And goode lemman, God thee save and keepe."
And with that word almost she gan to weepe.
    Alain up rist and thought, "Ere that it dawe,

---

307 **caught a sleep** gone to sleep   309 **sore** hard   314 **wex** grew
315 **swonken** labored   319 **awen** (dial.) own   319 **swa ... seel** as I
may have bliss   320 **lemman** lover

330 I will go creepen in by my fellawe,"
     And foond the cradle with his hand anon.
     "By God," thought he, "all wrang I have misgon.
     Mine heed is toty° of my swink tonight;
     That maketh me that I go nought aright.
335 I wot well by the cradle I have misgo;
     Here lith the miller and his wife also."
     And forth he goth a twenty devil way°
     Unto the bed ther as the miller lay.
     He wende have cropen by his fellow John,
340 And by the miller in he creep anon,
     And caught him by the neck and soft he spak.
     He said, "Thou John, thou swines-heed, awak,
     For Cristes saul, and heer a noble game:
     For by that lord that called is Saint Jame,
345 As I have thries in this shorte night
     Swived the miller's doughter bolt upright,°
     While thou hast as a coward been aghast."
     "Ye, false harlot," quod the miller, "hast?
     Ah, false traitour, false clerk," quod he,
350 "Thou shalt be deed, by Goddes dignitee—
     Who dorste be so bold to disparage°
     My doughter, that is come of swich linage?"
     And by the throte-boll° he caught Alain,
     And he hent him despitously° again,
355 And on the nose he smote him with his fest—
     Down ran the bloody streem upon his brest.
     And on the floor, with nose and mouth to-broke,
     They walwen° as doon two pigs in a poke,°
     And up they goon and down again anoon,
360 Till that the miller sporned at° a stoon,
     And down he fill backward upon his wif

333 **toty** dizzy   337 **twenty devil way** way of twenty devils, i.e., an
unfortunate path   346 **bolt upright** flat on her back   351 **disparage**
dishonor   353 **throte-boll** Adam's apple   354 **despitously** spitefully
358 **walwen** wallow, grovel   358 **poke** sack   360 **sporned at** tripped
on

That wiste nothing of this nice strif,
For she was fall asleep a lite wight°
With John the clerk that waked had all night—
And with the fall out of hir sleep she braide.° *365*
"Help, holy crois of Bromeholm!" she saide.
"*In manus tuas,*° Lord, to thee I calle!
Awake, Simond, the feend is on me falle!
Mine hert is broken. Help! I nam but deed!
There lith one upon my womb and on mine heed! *370*
Help, Simekin, for the false clerkes fighte!"
This John stert up as fast as ever he mighte,
And graspeth by the walles to and fro
To find a staff; and she stert up also,
And knew the estres° bet than did this John, *375*
And by the wall a staff she foond anoon,
And saw a litel shimmering of a light—
For at an hole in shone the moone bright—
And by that light she saw hem bothe two,
But sikerly she niste who was who, *380*
But as she saw a white thing in her eye,
And whan she gan this white thing espye,
She wende the clerk had wered a voluper,°
And with the staff she drow ay neer and neer,
And wende han hit this Alain atte fulle— *385*
And smote the miller on the piled° skulle
That down he goth and cried, "Harrow, I die!"
Thise clerkes bete him well and let him lie,
And greithen hem,° and took hir horse anon
And eek hir mele, and on hir way they goon, *390*
And at the mille yet they took hir cake,
Of half a bushel flour full well y-bake.
Thus is this proude miller well y-bete,
And hath y-lost the grinding of the whete,
And payed for the supper everydeel *395*

363 **lite wight** short while 365 **braide** woke 367 **In manus tuas**
"Into Thy hands . . ." 375 **estres** layout of the room 383 **voluper**
nightcap 386 **piled** bald 389 **greithen hem** ready themselves

Of Alain and of John, that bete him well;
His wife is swived and his doughter als.
Lo, swich it is a miller° to be fals!
    And therefore this proverb is said full sooth:
400 Him thar nat weene well° that yvele doth;
A gilour° shall himself biguiled be.
And God, that sitteth heigh in majestee,
Save all this compaignye, greet and smalle:
Thus have I quit the Miller in my tale.

---

398 **swich . . . miller** it is that way for a miller   400 **Him . . . well** he
must not expect good   401 **gilour** trickster

THE SHIPMAN'S TALE

A marchant whilom° dwelled at Saint Denis°
That riche was, for which men held him wis.
A wife he had of excellent beautee,
And compaignable and revelous° was she—
Which is a thing that causeth more dispence°   5
Than worth is all the cheer° and reverence
That men hem doon at feestes and at daunces;
Swich salutacions and countenances
Passen as doth a shadwe upon the wall.
But woe is him that payen mot for all: 10
"The sely° husbond algate° he mot paye!
He mot us clothe and he mot us arraye,
All for his owne worship, richely—
In which array we dauncen jollily!
And if that he not may, paraventure,   15
Or elles list no swich dispence endure,
But thinketh it is wasted and y-lost,
Than mot another payen for our cost
Or lene° us gold—and that is perilous!"°
    This noble marchant held a worthy hous,   20
For which he had alday so greet repair°
For his largesse,° and for his wife was fair,

1 **whilom** once upon a time   1 **Saint Denis** near Paris   4 **revelous**
pleasure loving   5 **dispence** spending   6 **cheer** friendly greeting
11 **sely** unfortunate   11 **algate** at any rate. In lines 11–19 the Ship-
man mimics women's attitudes; but perhaps these lines show that
Chaucer originally meant this tale to be told by the Wife of Bath and
forgot to cancel them when he assigned it to the Shipman   19 **lene**
lend   19 **perilous** dangerous   21 **so . . . repair** such frequent
visitation   22 **For . . . largesse** because of his liberality. Largesse was
considered an aristocratic virtue

That wonder is. But herkneth to my tale:
Amonges all his guestes greet and smalle
25 There was a monk, a fair man and a bold—
I trowe° a thrity winter he was old—
That ever in one° was drawing to that place.
This yonge monk, that was so fair of face,
Acquainted was so with the goode man
30 Sith that hir firste knowliche° began
That in his house as familier was he
As it is possible any freend to be.
And for as muchel as this goode man,
And eek this monk of which that I began,
35 Were bothe two y-born in oo village,
The monk him claimeth as for cosinage°—
And he again, he saith not ones nay,
But was as glad thereof as fowl of day,
For to his hert it was a greet plesaunce.
40 Thus been they knit with eterne alliaunce,
And ech of hem gan other for t'assure
Of bretherhede° while that hir life may dure.
    Free was Daun° John—and namely of dispence,
As in that house, and full of diligence
45 To doon plesance and also greet costage.°
He not forgat to yive the leeste page
In all that house; but after hir degree
He yaf the lord and sithen all his meinee,°
Whan that he came, some manner honest thing.°
50 For which they were as glad of his coming
As fowl is fain° whan that the sun up riseth.
Namore of this as now, for it suffiseth.
    But so bifell,° this marchant on a day
Shop him° to make redy his array°

26 **trowe** believe 27 **ever ... one** continually 30 **knowliche**
acquaintance 36 **for cosinage** as a relative 42 **bretherhede** sworn
friendship—a very sacred relationship 43 **Daun** lord, master
45 **costage** spending 48 **meinee** household 49 **some ... thing** i.e.,
something appropriate 51 **fain** glad 53 **so bifell** it so happened
54 **Shop him** prepared 54 **array** gear

Toward the town of Bruges° for to fare   *55*
To byen there a portion of ware;
For which he hath to Paris sent anon
A messager, and prayed hath Daun John
That he shold come to Saint Denis and playe
With him and with his wife a day or twaye,   *60*
Ere he to Bruges went, in alle wise.°
This noble monk of which I you devise
Hath of his abbot as him list licence,°
Because he was a man of high prudence
And eek an officer, out for to ride   *65*
To seen hir granges and hir bernes wide.°
And unto Saint Denis he comth anon.
Who was so welcome as my lord Daun John,
Our dere cosin, full of curteisye?
With him brought he a jubbe of malvesye°   *70*
And eek another, full of fine vernage,°
And volatil,° as ay was his usage.
And thus I let hem ete and drink and playe,
This marchant and this monk, a day or twaye.

   The thridde day this marchant up ariseth,   *75*
And on his needes sadly him aviseth,°
And up into his countour-house° goth he
To recken with himself, as well may be,
Of thilke yeer how that it with him stood,
And how that he dispended had his good,°   *80*
And if that he encresed were° or noon.
His bookes and his bagges many oon
He laith biforn him on his counting-boord:
Full riche was his tresor and his hoord,
For which full fast his countour-door he shette,°   *85*

55 **Bruges** a great Flemish mercantile center   61 **in alle wise** in all
respects   63 **licence** Daun John had permission to travel outside the
boundaries of his abbey in order to inspect the landholdings of his
order   66 **hir ... wide** their farms and barns far off   70 **jubbe ...
malvesye** jug of Malmsey   71 **vernage** Italian sweet wine   72 **vola-
til** game fowls   76 **on ... aviseth** seriously goes over his business
affairs   77 **countour-house** office   80 **good** wealth   81 **encresed
were** had profited   85 **shette** shut

And eek he nold that no man shold him lette
Of his accountes° for the mene time.
And thus he sit° till it was passed prime.°
    Daun John was risen in the morrwe also
90 And in the garden walketh to and fro,
And hath his thinges° said full curteisly.
This goode wife came walking prively°
Into the garden ther he walketh softe
And him salueth, as she hath done ofte.
95 A maide child came in hir compaignye,
Which as hir list she may govern and gie,°
For yet under the yerde° was the maide.
"O dere cosin mine, Daun John," she saide,
"What aileth you so rathe° for to rise?"
100   "Nece," quod he, "it ought enough suffise
Five houres for to sleep upon a night,
But it were for an old appalled wight,°
As been thise wedded men that lie and dare°
As in a fourme° sit a wery hare
105 Were all forstraught° with houndes greet and smalle
But dere nece, why be ye so pale?
I trowe° certes that our goode man
Hath you laboured sith the night began,
That you were need to resten hastily."
110 And with that word he lough full murrily,
And of his owne thought he wex° all red.
    This faire wife gan for to shake hir heed
And saide thus, "Ye, God wot° all," quod she.
"Nay, cosin mine, it stant not so with me.
115 For by that God that yaf me soul and lif,
In all the reaume° of France is there no wif

86–87 **lette . . . accountes** keep from his accounts   88 **sit** sits
88 **prime** nine a.m.   91 **thinges** devotions   92 **prively** alone   96 **gie**
guide   97 **under . . . yerde** under the rod, i.e., subject to discipline
99 **rathe** early   102 **appalled wight** palsied man   103 **dare** wait
motionless   104 **fourme** rabbit mound   105 **Were . . . forstraught**
which was distraught, harried   107 **trowe** think   111 **wex** grew
113 **wot** knows   116 **reaume** realm

That lasse lust hath to that sorry play.
For I may sing 'alas' and 'weilaway
That I was born'—but to no wight," quod she,
"Dare I not tell how that it stant with me;°   120
Wherefore I think out of this land to wende,
Or elles of myself to make an ende,
So full am I of drede and eek of care."

  This monk began upon this wife to stare
And said, "Alas, my nece, God forbede   125
That ye for any sorrwe or any drede
Fordo° yourself! But telleth me your grief.
Paraventure I may in your meschief°
Conseil or help. And therefore telleth me
All your annoy, for it shall been secree.   130
For on my porthors° I make an ooth
That never in my life, for lief ne loth,°
Ne shall I of no conseil you biwraye."°

  "The same again to you," quod she, "I saye.
By God and by this porthors I you swere,   135
Though men me wold all into pieces tere,
Ne shall I never, for to goon° to helle,
Biwray a word of thing that ye me telle—
Not for no cosinage ne alliance,
But verraily for love and affiance."°   140
Thus been they sworn, and hereupon they kiste,
And ech of hem told other what hem liste.

  "Cosin," quod she, "if that I hadde space,
As I have none, and namely in this place,
Than wold I tell a legend° of my lif—   145
What I have suffered sith I was a wif
With mine husbond, al be he° your cosin."

  "Nay," quod this monk, "by God and Saint Martin,

120 **how . . . me** what my situation is   127 **Fordo** destroy   128 **mes-
chief** distress   131 **porthors** breviary, containing the daily canonical
prayers   132 **for . . . loth** i.e., for love or hate   133 **biwraye** give
away, betray   137 **for . . . goon** though I go   140 **affiance** trust
145 **legend** moral story of suffering   147 **al . . . he** even though he is

He is namore cosin unto me
150 Than is the leef that hangeth on the tree!
I clepe him so, by Saint Denis of France,
To han the more cause of acquaintance
Of *you,* which I have loved specially
Aboven alle women, sikerly.
155 This swere I you on my professioun.°
Telleth your grief, lest that he come adown,
And hasteth you,° and goth away anon."
     "My dere love," quod she, "O my Daun John,
Full lief were me this conseil for to hide!°
160 But out it mot°—I may namore abide:
Mine husbond is to me the worste man
That ever was sith that the world began!
But sith I am a wife it sit not me°
To tellen no wight of our privetee—
165 Neither abed ne in noon other place.
God shilde° I shold it tellen, for his grace!
A wife ne shall not sayn of hir husbonde
But all honour, as I can understonde.
Save unto you this much I tellen shall:
170 As help me God, he is not worth at all
In no degree the value of a flye!
But yet me greveth most his niggardye.°
And well ye wot that women naturelly
Desiren thinges six as well as I:
175 They wolde that hir husbonds sholde be
Hardy and wise and rich, and thereto free,
And buxom° unto his wife, and fresh abedde.
And by that ilke Lord that for us bledde,
For his honour myself for to arraye
180 A° Sunday next I moste needes paye

155 **professioun** monastic vow of poverty, chastity, and obedience
157 **hasteth you** be quick about it   159 **Full . . . hide** I would be
much happier to conceal this matter   160 **But . . . mot** but it must be
divulged   163 **it . . . me** it is not my place   166 **shilde** forbid
172 **niggardye** miserliness   177 **buxom** obedient   180 **A** on

An hundred frankes, or elles I am lorn.°
Yet were me lever° that I were unborn
Than me were done a slaundre° or villainye.
And if mine husbond eek might it espye,
I nere but lost. And therefore I you praye   185
Lene me this sum, or elles mot I deye!
Daun John—I say lene me thise hundred frankes!
Pardee,° I wol not faile you my thankes
If that you list to doon that I you praye;
For at a certain day I wol you paye,   190
And doon to you what plesance and servise
That I may doon, right as you list devise.
And but I do,° God take on me vengeance
As foul as ever had Genelon of France."°
    This gentil monk answered in this mannere: 195
"Now trewely, mine owne lady dere,
I have," quod he, "on you so greet a routhe°
That I you swere and plighte you my trouthe
That whan your husbond is to Flandres fare°
I wol deliver you out of this care,°   200
For I wol bringe you an hundred frankes."
And with that word he caught hir by the flankes
And hir embraceth hard, and kist hir ofte.
"Goth now your way," quod he, "all still and softe,
And let us dine as soon as that ye may,   205
For by my chilindre° it is prime of day.
Goth now, and beth as trew as I shall be."
    "Now elles God forbede, sir," quod she—
And forth she goth as jolif as a pie,°
And bade the cookes that they shold hem hie°   210
So that men mighte dine—and that anon.

181 **lorn** undone   182 **were ... lever** I had rather   183 **slaundre**
slander   188 **Pardee** par dieu, by God   193 **but ... do** if I do not
194 **Genelon** Ganelon, Roland's enemy, who was torn apart by wild
horses   197 **so ... routhe** such great pity   199 **fare** gone   200 **care**
trouble   206 **chilindre** portable sundial   209 **jolif ... pie** jolly as a
magpie   210 **hie** hurry

Up to hir husbond is this wife y-gon
And knocketh at his countour boldely.
"Qui la?"° quod he. "Peter!"° it am I,"
215   Quod she. "What, sir! How longe wol ye faste?
How longe time wol ye recken and caste
Your summes° and your bookes and your thinges?
The devil have part on° all swich reckeninges!
Ye have enough, pardee, of Goddes sonde!°
220   Come down today, and let your bagges stonde.
Ne be ye not ashamed that Daun John
Shall fasting all this day alenge° gon!
What, let us heer a mass and go we dine."
       "Wife," quod this man, "litel canstou divine
225   The curious° bisinesse that we have.
For of us chapmen,° also God me save,
And by that lord that cleped is Saint Ive,
Scarsely, amonges twelve, twain° shall thrive
Continuelly, lasting unto our age.
230   We may well make cheer and good visage
And drive forth° the world as it may be
And keepen our estate in privetee°
Till we be deed, or elles that we playe°
A pilgrimage, or goon out of the waye.°
235   And therefore have I greet necessitee
Upon this quainte° world t'avise me,
For evermore we mote stond in drede
Of hap° and Fortune in our chapmanhede.°
To Flandres wol I go tomorrwe at day
240   And come again as soon as ever I may.
For which, my dere wife, I thee biseeke°

---

214 **Qui la** (*qui est la,* Fr.) who's there?   214 **Peter** by St. Peter
216–17 **caste . . . summes** compute your figures   218 **The . . . on** the
devil take   219 **sonde** gift   222 **alenge** miserable   225 **curious** in-
volved, elaborate   226 **chapmen** merchants   228 **twain** two
231 **drive forth** pass through   232 **keepen . . . privetee** go about our
affairs quietly   233 **playe** make   234 **goon . . . waye** run off some-
where (to avoid debts)   236 **quainte** strange   238 **hap** chance
238 **chapmanhede** business   241 **biseeke** beg

As be to every wight buxom and meeke.
And for to keep our good be curious,°
And honestly° governe well our hous.
Thou hast enough in every manner wise°   *245*
That to a thrifty household may suffise—
Thee lacketh noon array ne no vitaille;°
Of silver in thy purse shaltou not faile."
And with that word his countour-door he shette,
And down he goth, no lenger wold he lette;°   *250*
But hastily a masse was there said,
And speedily the tables were y-laid
And to the dinner faste they hem spedde,
And richely this monk the chapman fedde.

    At after-dinner Daun John sobrely°   *255*
This chapman took apart, and prively
He said him thus: "Cosin, it standeth so
That well I see to Bruges wol ye go.
God and Saint Austin° speede you and guide.
I pray you, cosin, wisely that ye ride.   *260*
Governeth you also of your diete
Attemprely,° and namely in this hete.
Bitwix us two needeth no strange fare.°
Farewell, cosin, God shilde you fro care.°
And if that any thing by day or night,   *265*
If it lay in my power and my might,
That ye me wol command in any wise,
It shall be done, right as ye wol devise.
Oo thing ere that ye goon, if it may be:
I wolde pray you for to lene me   *270*
An hundred frankes for a wike or twaye,
For certain beestes that I moste beye
To store with a place° that is oures.

---

243 **curious** careful   244 **honestly** honorably   245 **in ... wise** in every way possible   247 **vitaille** foodstuffs   250 **lette** delay   255 **sobrely** seriously   259 **Saint Austin** St. Augustine   262 **Attemprely** moderately   263 **strange fare** formality   264 **shilde ... care** keep you from harm   273 **To ... place** with which to stock a plot of land

God help me so, I wold it were youres!
275 I shall not faile surely of my day,
Not for a thousand franks, a mile way.°
But let this thing be secree,° I you praye:
For yet tonight thise beestes mot I beye.
And fare now well, mine owne cosin dere;
280 Graunt mercy of your cost° and of your cheere."
     This noble marchant gentilly° anon
Answered and said, "O cosin mine, Daun John,
Now sikerly this is a small requeste.
My gold is youres whan that it you leste—
285 And not only my gold, but my chaffare;°
Take what you list, God shilde that ye spare.°
But oo thing is, ye know it well enow,
Of chapmen°—that hir money is hir plow.
We may creance° while we han a name
290 But goldless for to been, it is no game.
Pay it again whan it lith° in your ese;
After my might full fain wold I you plese."
Thise hundred franks he fette° forth anon,
And prively he took hem to Daun John.
295 No wight in all this world wist of this lone,
Saving this marchant and Daun John alone.
They drink, and speke, and rome a while and playe,
Till that Daun John rideth to his abbeye.
     The morrow came, and forth this marchant rideth
300 To Flandresward; his prentis° well him gideth
Till he came into Bruges murrily.°
Now goth this marchant fast and bisily
About his need, and byeth and creaunceth°—
He neither playeth at the dees,° ne daunceth,

---

276 **a . . . way** by a mile's distance   277 **secree** secret   280 **Graunt . . . cost** thank you for your generosity   281 **gentilly** courteously   285 **chaffare** possessions   286 **spare** refrain   287–88 **But . . . chapmen** but there is one thing . . . about businessmen   289 **creance** borrow on credit   291 **lith** lies   293 **fette** brought   300 **prentis** apprentice   301 **murrily** pleasantly   303 **creaunceth** borrows   304 **dees** dice

But as a marchant, shortly for to telle,   *305*
He let his life.° And there I let him dwelle.

*   *   *

The Sunday next the marchant was agon,
To Saint Denis y-comen is Daun John
With crown and beerd all fresh and new y-shave.
In all the house there nas so litel a knave,   *310*
Ne no wight elles, that he nas full fain°
That my lord Daun John was come again.
And shortly to the point right for to goon,
This faire wife accorded° with Daun John
That for thise hundred franks he shold all night   *315*
Have hire in his armes bolt upright.°
And this accord parfourned° was in deede:
In mirth all night a bisy life they lede
Till it was day, that Daun John went his way,
And bade the meinee° "Farewell, have good day"—   *320*
For none of hem, ne no wight in the town,
Hath of Daun John right no suspicioun.°
And forth he rideth home to his abbeye,
Or where him list. Namore of him I saye.

This marchant whan that ended was the faire   *325*
To Saint Denis he gan for to repaire,
And with his wife he maketh feest and cheere
And telleth hir that chaffare is so dere
That needes most he make a chevissaunce°—
For he was bounden in a reconissaunce°   *330*
To paye twenty thousand sheeld° anon.
For which this marchant is to Paris gon
To borrwe of certain freendes that he hadde

306 **He . . . life** conducted himself   311 **fain** glad   314 **accorded**
agreed   316 **bolt upright** flat on her back   317 **parfourned**
performed   320 **meinee** household, i.e., servants   322 **right . . . sus-**
picioun no suspicions at all   329 **make . . . chevissaunce** get a loan
330 **reconissaunce** promissory note   331 **sheeld** gold coins

A certain franks,° and some with him he ladde.°
335　And whan that he was come into the town,
For greet cheertee° and greet affeccioun
Unto Daun John he first goth, him to playe—
Not for to ask or borrwe of him moneye,
But for to wite° and seen of his welfare,
340　And for to tellen him of his chaffare,
As freendes doon whan they been met yfere.°
Daun John him maketh feest and murry cheere,
And he him told again full specially
How he had well y-bought and graciously,
345　Thanked be God, all whole his marchandise—
Save that he most, in alle manner wise,°
Maken a chevissance as for the beste,°
And than he sholde been in joy and reste.
　　　Daun John answerde, "Certes, I am fain
350　That ye in hele° are comen home again!
And if that I were rich, as have I blisse,°
Of twenty thousand sheeld shold ye not misse,
For ye so kindely this other day
Lente me gold. And as I can and may
355　I thanke you, by God and by Saint Jame!
But natheless, I took unto our dame—
Your wife at home—the same gold again
Upon your bench. She wot it well, certain,
By certain tokens° that I can you telle.
360　Now by your leve, I may no lenger dwelle—
Our abbot wol out of this town anon,
And in his compaignye mot I gon.
Greet well our dame, mine owne nece sweete;
And farewell, dere cosin, till we meete."
365　　　This marchant which that was full ware° and wis

---

334 A . . . franks an amount of francs　334 ladde took along
336 cheertee fondness　339 wite know　341 yfere together
346 in . . . wise in any even　347 as . . . beste in the best manner
350 hele health　351 as . . . blisse as I may have bliss　359 tokens
signs, evidence　365 full ware very prudent

Creanced hath° and paid eek in Paris
To certain Lumbards,° redy in hir hond,
The sum of gold, and gat of hem his bond;
And home he goth, murry as a papinjay.°
For well he knew he stood in swich array°   370
That needes most he win in that viage°
A thousand franks aboven his costage.°

   His wife full redy met him at the gate,
As she was wont of old usage algate.°
And all that night in mirthe they bisette°   375
For he was rich and cleerly out of dette.

   Whan it was day this marchant gan embrace
His wife all new, and kist hir on hir face;
And up he goth and maketh it full tough.°
"Namore," quod she, "by God, ye have enough!"   380
And wantounly again with him she playde
Till at the laste thus this marchant saide,
"By God," quod he, "I am a litel wroth
With you, my wife, although it be me loth.°
And wot ye why? By God, as that I guesse   385
That ye han made a manner straungenesse°
Bitwixen me and my cosin Daun John.
Ye shold han warned me ere I had gon
That he you had an hundred frankes paid
By redy token.° And held him yvel apaid°   390
For that I to him spak of chevissaunce—
Me seemed so as° by his countenaunce.
But natheless, by God our hevene king,
I thoughte not to ask of him no thing.

---

366 **Creanced hath** got credit   367 **Lumbards** Lombards of north-
ern Italy, who were noted bankers and money-lenders   369 **papinjay**
parrot   370 **stood . . . array** was in such a position   371 **viage**
enterprise   372 **costage** expenses   374 **algate** always   375 **bisette**
applied themselves   379 **maketh . . . tough** shows great energy
384 **it . . . loth** I don't like to be   386 **straungenesse** disaffection
390 **By . . . token** in ready money, i.e., in ready exchange (a double
entendre)   390 **held . . . apaid** he took offense   392 **Me . . . as** it
seemed so to me

395   I pray thee, wife, ne do namore so!
    Tell me alway ere that I fro thee go
    If any dettour hath in mine absence
    Y-payed° thee, lest thurgh thy necligence
    I might him ask a thing that he hath paid."

400   This wife was not afered ne afraid,
    But boldely she said, and that anon,
    "Marie!° I defy the false monk Daun John!
    I keep not° of his 'tokens' neveradele!
    He took me certain gold, this wot I well!

405   What, yvel thedam° on his monkes snoute!
    For God it wot, I wend° withouten doute
    That he had yive it me because of you
    To doon therewith mine honour and my prow,
    For cosinage and eek for *belle cheere*°

410   That he hath had full ofte times here.
    But sith I see I stand in this disjoint°
    I wol answer you shortly to the point:
    Ye han mo slacker° dettours than am I!
    For I wol pay you well and redily

415   Fro day to day, and if so be I faile,
    I am your wife—score it upon my taile!°
    And I shall pay as soon as ever I may;
    For by my truth I have on mine array,°
    And not in waste, bistowed every deel.°

420   And for I have bistowed it so well
    For your honour, for Goddes sake, I saye
    As be not wroth, but let us laugh and playe:
    Ye shall my jolly body have to wedde.
    By God, I wol nought pay you but abedde!

425   Forgive it me, mine owne spouse dere—

---

398 **Y-payed** paid. "Pay" has a double meaning   402 **Marie** by St.
Mary   403 **keep not** care not   405 **yvel thedam** misfortune
406 **wend** understood   409 **belle cheere** good times   411 **disjoint**
predicament   413 **mo slacker** more delinquent   416 **score ...
taile** i.e., put it on my bill (with a pun on "tail")   418 **array** clothing
419 **bistowed ... deel** spent everything

Turn hiderward° and maketh better cheere . . ."
   This marchant saw there was no remedye,
And for to chide it nere but follye.
"Sith that the thing may not amended be,
Now wife," he said, "and I foryive it thee.   *430*
But by thy life, ne be namore so large.°
Keep bet my good, this yive I thee in charge."°
Thus endeth now my tale; and God us sende
Tailing enough unto our lives ende!

426 **hiderward** toward me 431 **large** generous 432 **Keep . . .
charge** I charge you to take better care of what belongs to me

THE SHIPMAN-PRIORESS LINK

"Well said, by *corpus dominus*," quod our Host.
"Now longe mote thou saile by the coost,
Sir gentil maister, gentil mariner.
God yive the monk a thousand last quad yeer!°
5 Aha, fellaws! beth ware of swich a jape!
The monk put in the mannes hood an ape,°
And in his wives eek, by Saint Austin!
Draweth no monkes more into your inn!
     But now pass over, and let us seek aboute . . .
10 Who shall now telle first of all this route
Another tale?"—and with that word he saide,
As curteisly as it had been a maide,°
"My Lady Prioresse: by your leve,
So that° I wist I sholde you not greve,
15 I wolde deemen that ye tellen sholde
A tale next, if so were that ye wolde.
Now wol ye vouche sauf, my lady dere?"
"Gladly," quod she, and said as ye shall heere:

---

4 **thousand . . . yeer** a thousand cartloads of bad years   6 **in . . . ape**
i.e., made a monkey out of him (who would then wear his hood)
12 **as . . . maide** as if it were a young girl he was addressing. The
speech that follows is indeed delicately put   14 **So that** so long as

THE PRIORESS' PROLOGUE

Domine Dominus noster . . .°

O Lord, Our Lord, thy name how merveilous
Is in this large world y-sprad (quod she),
For not only thy laude° precious
Performed is by men of dignitee,
But by the mouth of children thy bountee   5
Performed is: for on the brest suckinge
Sometime shewen they thine heryinge.°

Wherefore in laud, as I best can or may,
Of thee and of the white lily-flower°
Which that thee bare, and is a maid alway,   10
To tell a story I wol do my labour;
Not that I may encreesen hir honour,
For she hirself is honour and the roote
Of bountee, next hir son, and soules boote.°

Domine Dominus noster . . . the opening verse of Psalm 8, which oc-
curs in the *Little Office of the Blessed Virgin,* recited in nunneries; the
following lines translate it. The Prioress' Prologue is thus in effect a
hymn to the Blessed Virgin, as her tale is a miracle of the Virgin. Both
are in the seven-line rhyming stanza (later to be called rhyme royal),
which suggests a hymn in the prologue and a ballad in the tale. (See note
on line 197.)   3 **laude** praise   7 **heryinge** praise. The reference is to
St. Nicholas, who in infancy fasted on Wednesdays and Fridays by suck-
ing only once. Cf. lines 27–28 of her tale   9 **white lily-flower** symbol
of the Virgin   14 **boote** salvation

15   O moder maid, O maide moder free!
     O bush unbrent, brenning in Moises' sighte,°
     That ravisedest° down fro the deitee,
     Thurgh thine humbless, the Ghost that in thee alighte,
     Of whose vertu, whan He thine herte lighte,
20   Conceived was the Fadre's Sapience—
     Help me to tell it in thy reverence.

     Lady, thy bountee, thy magnificence,
     Thy vertu and thy greet humilitee
     There may no tonge express in no science.
25   For sometime, lady, ere men pray to thee,
     Thou gost biforn of thy benignitee,
     And gettest us the light, of° thy prayere,
     To guiden us unto thy Son so dere.

     My konning is so waik,° O blissful Queene,
30   For to declare thy grete worthinesse,
     That I ne may the weighte not sustene;
     But as a child of twelfmonth old or lesse,
     That can unnethe° any word expresse,
     Right so fare I. And therefore, I you praye,
35   Guideth my song that I shall of you saye.

16 **bush . . . sighte** the burning bush of *Exodus* 3:2–4 was another
symbol of the Virgin: the bush remained uninjured, as the Mother of
God remained undefiled 17 **ravisedest** drew 27 **of** through
29 **waik** weak 33 **unnethe** hardly

THE PRIORESS' TALE°

There was in Asie° in a greet citee,
Amonges Christen folk, a Jewerye,°
Sustened by a lord of that contree
For foul usure and lucre of villainye°
Hateful to Christ and to his compaignye.   5
And thurgh the streete men might ride and wende,
For it was free and open at either ende.

A litel scole of Christen folk there stood
Down at the ferther end, in which there were
Children an heep, y-comen of Christen blood,   10
That lerned in that scole yeer by yeere
Swich manner doctrine° as men used there;
This is to sayn, to singen and to rede,
As smalle children doon in her childhede.

Among thise children was a widow's sone,   15
A litel clergeon° seven yeer of age,
That day by day to scole was his wone;°
And eek also, where as he saw th'image

<hr>

The Prioress' Tale the tale the Prioress tells is a "miracle of the Virgin," a characteristic kind of story found in Latin as well as in the vernacular languages. This particular tale—of a Christian child murdered by Jews—had a long history before Chaucer's time and accounted for a long and bloody chapter in medieval anti-Semitic persecution. Chaucer seems to present her tale as an example of naïve and thoughtless cruelty submerged under sentimental piety   1 **Asie** Asia Minor. No other version places the incident so far away. Possibly Chaucer's motive was to emphasize at the end (lines 197ff.) the nearness and actuality of similar incidents   2 **Jewerye** colony of Jews, ghetto   4 **foul . . . villainye** wicked usury and evil kinds of money-making. Usury was forbidden by the Church, as was excessive profit   12 **manner doctrine** such kind of subjects   16 **clergeon** schoolboy   17 **to . . . wone** was accustomed to go to school

Of Christes moder, had he in usage,
20 As him was taught, to kneel adown and saye
His *Ave Marie* as he goth by the waye.

Thus hath this widwe hir litel son y-taught
Our blissful Lady, Christes moder dere,
To worship ay; and he forgat it naught,
25 For sely child wol alday soone lere.°
But ay whan I remembre on this mattere,
Saint Nicholas stant ever in my presence,
For he so yong to Christ did reverence.

This litel child his litel book lerninge,
30 As he sat in the scole at his primer,°
He *Alma redemptoris*° herde singe,
As children lerned hir antiphoner;°
And as he dorst, he drow him neer and neer,
And herkned ay the wordes and the note,
35 Till he the firste verse koud all by rote.

Nought wist he what this Latin was to saye,
For he so yong and tender was of age;
But on a day his fellaw° gan he praye
T'expounden him this song in his langage,
40 Or tell him why this song was in usage—
This prayed he him to construen and declare,
Full ofte time upon his knowes° bare.

His fellaw, which that elder was than he,
Answered him thus: "This song, I have herd saye,
45 Was maked of° our blissful Lady free,
Hir to salue,° and eek hir for to praye
To been our help and succour whan we deye.

25 **For . . . lere** for the innocent child will always learn fast
30 **primer** an elementary schoolbook primarily of prayers, the creed,
etc. 31 **Alma redemptoris** a hymn to the Virgin 32 **antiphoner**
hymnbook 38 **fellaw** friend 42 **knowes** knees 45 **of** about
46 **salue** greet, praise

I can namore expound in this mattere.
I lerne song; I kan but small° grammere."

"And is this song maked in reverence   50
Of Christes moder?" said this innocent.
"Now certes I wol do my diligence
To kon it all ere Christemas is went.
Though that I for my primer shall be shent°
And shall be beten thries in an houre,   55
I wol it kon Our Lady for t'honoure."

His fellaw taught him homeward prively,
Fro day to day, till he koud it by rote.
And than he song it well and boldely,
Fro word to word, according with the note.   60
Twies a day it passed thurgh his throte—
To scoleward and homeward whan he wente;
On Christes moder set was his entente.

As I have said, thurghout the Jewerye
This litel child, as he came to and fro,   65
Full murrily wolde he sing and crye
O alma redemptoris evere mo.
The sweetness hath his herte perced so
Of Christes moder, that to hir to praye
He can not stint of singing by the waye.   70

Our firste foe, the serpent Sathanas,
That hath in Jewes' hert his waspes nest,
Up swal,° and said: "O Hebraic peple, alas!
Is this to you a thing that is honest,°
That swich a boy shall walken as him lest   75
In your despite, and sing of swich sentence,
Which is agains our lawes° reverence?"

49 **I ... small** I know but little   54 **for ... shent** shall be punished
for not learning my primer   73 **Up swal** swelled up   74 **honest**
honorable   77 **our lawes** due to our law. Satan identifies himself with
the Jews. But some manuscripts read "your"

Fro thennes forth the Jewes han conspired
This innocent out of the world to chase.
80 An homicide thereto han they hired
That in an alley had a privee place.
And as the child gan forby for to pace,°
This cursed Jew him hent and held him faste,
And kit° his throt, and in a pit him caste.

85 I say that in a wardrobe° they him threwe,
Where as thise Jewes purgen hir entraile.
O cursed folk of Herodes all newe,°
What may your yvel entente you availe?
Murder wol out, certain it wol not faile!
90 And namely ther th'honour of God shall sprede,
The blood out cryeth on your cursed deede!

O martyr souded to° virginitee,
Now maistou singen, follwing ever in oon
The White Lamb celestial (quod she)
95 Of which the greet evangelist Saint John
In Pathmos° wrote—which saith that they that gon
Biforn this Lamb and sing a song all newe,
That never fleshly° women they ne knewe.

This poore widwe awaiteth all that night
100 After hir litel child, but he came nought.
For which, as soon as it was dayes light,
With face pale of drede and bisy thought
She hath at scole and elleswhere him sought;
Till finally she gan so fer espye,°
105 That he last seen was in the Jewerye.

---

82 **forby ... pace** pass by 84 **kit** cut 85 **wardrobe** privy
87 **folk ... newe** people composed of new Herods 92 **souded to** con-
firmed in 96 **Pathmos** Patmos, an island in the Aegean, where St. John
was thought to have written the Apocalypse. The vision of the 144,000 vir-
gins (*Revelations* 14:1–4) was thought to involve "innocents"—baptized
children who died 98 **fleshly** in a carnal way 104 **gan ... espye** found
out this much

With modres pitee in hir brest enclosed
She goth, as she were half out of hir minde,
To every place where she hath supposed
By likliheed hir litel child to finde.
And ever on Christes moder, meek and kinde,   *110*
She cried—and at the laste thus she wroughte:
Among the cursed Jewes she him soughte.

She fraineth° and she prayeth pitously
To every Jew that dwelt in thilke place
To tell hir if hir child went ought forby.   *115*
They saide nay; but Jesu of his grace
Yaf in hir thought, inwith a litel space,°
That in that place after hir son she cride
Where he was casten in a pit beside.

O grete God, that parfourmest thy laude   *120*
By mouth of innocents, lo, here thy might!
This gem of chastitee, this emeraude,°
And eek of martyrdom the ruby° bright,
Ther he with throt y-corven lay upright
He *Alma redemptoris* gan to singe   *125*
So loud that all the place gan to ringe!

The Christen folk that thurgh the streete wente
In comen for to wonder upon this thing,
And hastily they for the Provost° sente.
He came anon, withouten tarrying,   *130*
And herieth° Christ, that is of hevene king,
And eek his moder, honour of mankinde,
And after that the Jewes let he binde.°

---

113 **fraineth** asks   117 **inwith . . . space** in a short time   122 **emer-
aude** symbolic of chastity   123 **ruby** symbolic of martyrdom
129 **Provost** chief magistrate   131 **herieth** praises   133 **the
Jewes . . . binde** he had the Jews bound. Note the abruptness of the
Magistrate's judgment and the lack of an inquiry

This child with pitous lamentacioun
135 Up taken was, singing his song alway;
And with honour of greet processioun
They carryen him unto the next° abbay.
His moder swouning by his beere lay:
Unnethe° might the peple that was there
140 This newe Rachel° bringen fro his beere.

With torment and with shameful deeth echon
The Provost doth thise Jewes for to sterve°
That of this murder wist, and that anon.
He nolde no swich cursedness observe:°
145 "Yvel shall have that yvel wol deserve!"
Therefore with wilde horse he did hem drawe;°
And after that he heng hem by the lawe.

Upon his beer ay lith this innocent
Biforn the chief auter,° while the mass laste;
150 And after that the abbot with his covent
Han sped hem° for to buryen him full faste;
And whan they holy water on him caste
Yet spak this child when spreind° was holy water
And song *O alma redemptoris mater.*

155 This abbot which that was an holy man,
As monkes been—or elles oughten be°—
This yonge child to conjure° he began,
And said, "O dere child, I halse° thee,
In vertu of the Holy Trinitee,
160 Tell me what is thy cause for to singe,
Sith that thy throt is cut, to my seeminge."

137 **next** nearby   139 **Unnethe** hardly   140 **newe Rachel** Rachel
stood for the mothers of the slaughtered Innocents (*Matthew* 2:18)
142 **doth ... sterve** has these Jews killed   144 **observe** put up with
146 **with ... drawe** he had them drawn by wild horses   149 **auter**
altar   150–51 **abbot ... sped hem** the abbot and his convent (of
monks) hastened   153 **spreind** sprinkled   156 **or ... be** the Prioress
is perhaps thinking here of the evil monk in the Shipman's Tale
157 **conjure** entreat   158 **halse** beseech

"My throt is cut unto my necke-bon,"
Saide this child, "and as by way of kinde°
I shold have died, ye, long time agon.
But Jesu Christ, as ye in bookes finde,   165
Will that his glory last and be in minde;
And for the worship of his moder dere
Yet may I° sing *O alma* loud and clere.

This well of mercy, Christes moder sweete,
I loved alway as after my konninge;   170
And whan that I my life sholde forlete°
To me she came, and bade me for to singe
This anthem veraily in my deyinge,
As ye han herd. And whan that I had songe,
Me thought she laid a grain° upon my tonge.   175

Wherefore I sing and singe mot, certain,
In honour of that blissful maiden free,
Till fro my tonge off taken is the grain;
And after that thus saide she to me,
'My litel child, now will I fetche thee   180
Whan that the grain is fro thy tonge y-take.
Be not aghast, I wol thee not forsake.' "

This holy monk, this abbot, him mene I,
His tonge out caught, and took away the grain;
And he yaf up the ghost full softely.   185
And whan this abbot had this wonder seen,
His salte teres trickled down as rain
And gruf he fill all plat° upon the grounde,
And still he lay as he had been y-bounde.

---

163 **as ... kinde** according to nature   168 **Yet may I** I can still
171 **sholde forlete** was about to give up   175 **grain** probably a seed,
the "grain of paradise" (*cardamom*); but in other versions the "grain"
is a precious stone—notably a pearl, which symbolized chastity
188 **gruf ... plat** he fell on his face all flat

190 The covent eek lay on the pavement
      Weeping, and herying° Christes moder dere.
      And after that they rise and forth been went,
      And took away this martyr from his beere.
      And in a tomb of marblestones cleere
195 Enclosen they his litel body sweete,
      Ther he is now—God leve us for to meete!

      O yonge Hugh of Lincoln, slain also
      With cursed Jewes,° as it is notable
      (For it is but a litel while ago)
200 Pray eek for us, we sinful folk unstable,
      That of his mercy God so merciable
      On us his greete mercy multiplye,
      For reverence of his moder Marie. Amen.

---

191 **herying** praising   197–98 **O . . . Jewes** O young Hugh of Lincoln, also slain by cursed Jews . . . The eight-year-old Hugh was supposed to have been murdered by Jews at Lincoln in 1255. The story became the subject of a ballad, "Sir Hugh" or "The Jew's Daughter"—see F. J. Child, *English and Scottish Ballads,* III, 233ff. He is sometimes confused with St. Hugh, Bishop of Lincoln (d. 1200). The Jews were expelled from England in 1290, and the persecution of them for "ritual murders" was not known in England during Chaucer's time; but such legends remained, and such persecutions continued on the continent, for example in the cremation of the Strasburg Jewry in 1349

PROLOGUE TO SIR THOPAS

Whan said was all this miracle, every man
As sober was that wonder was to see;
Till that our Hoste japen he began,
And than at erst he looked upon me,
And saide thus: "What man artou?" quod he.   5
"Thou lookest as thou woldest find an hare,
For ever upon the ground I see thee stare.

Approche neer and look up murrily!
Now, ware you, sirs, and let this man have place.
He in the waast is shape as well as I: 10
This were a puppet in an arm t'enbrace,
For any woman, small and fair of face!
He seemeth elvish° by his contenaunce,
For unto no wight doth he dalliaunce.°

Say now somewhat, sin other folk han said: 15
Tell us a tale of mirth, and that anon."
"Host," quod I, "ne beth not yvel apaid,°
For other tale, certes, kan° I non,
But of a ryme I lerned long agon."
"Ye, that is good," quod he. "Now shull we heere   20
 Some daintee° thing, me thinketh by his cheere."

---

13 **elvish** mysterious, withdrawn   14 **unto ... dalliaunce** is not so-
ciable with anyone   17 **ne ... apaid** don't be displeased   18 **kan**
know   21 **daintee** worthy

THE TALE OF SIR THOPAS°

THE FIRST FIT

Listeth, lords, in good entent,°
And I wol telle verayment°
   Of mirth and of solas;
All of a knight was fair and gent
5 In battail and in tournament—
   His name was Sir Thopas.°

Y-born he was in fer contree,
In Flandres° all beyond the see,
   At Popering in the place;

The Tale of Sir Thopas this tale is a burlesque of the metrical romances.
Romance itself had an aristocratic heritage, and in this Chaucer was well
schooled: the Knight's Tale is a high-minded romance, and *Troilus and
Criseyde* is often called the greatest of romances. By the fourteenth cen-
tury, however, the form and subject of romance had become sadly de-
based. Stories of heroic knights, set in a singsong rhyme scheme, were
recited by minstrels for audiences of middle-class burghers. Hence the
idealism of romance came to be tailored for a middle-class mentality,
and the form itself became tedious and cliché. The best way to see the
humor of *Sir Thopas* is to read one of its prototypes—*Guy of Warwick,*
for example. But it should be understood that there were good metrical
romances as well—*Sir Gawin and the Green Knight* being the greatest.
Chaucer's burlesque takes an effeminate and cowardly hero, attributes
to him decidedly middle-class characteristics, sets him off looking for
an elf-queen (it was supposed to be the other way around, the elf-queen
finding *him*). And he tells the whole in a deadly singsong filled with
clichés. *Sir Thopas* is often compared with *Don Quixote,* but Cer-
vantes' work comments profoundly upon the nature of human life it-
self; Chaucer is content to have his fun briefly at the expense of
middle-class romances and be done—hence the Host's interruption
1 **Listeth ... entent** a characteristic stock opening line   2 **verayment**
truly; used here for a desperate rhyme   6 **Thopas** i.e., topaz. The topaz
was a charm worn by young girls against luxury. It may have been used
as a feminine name as well   8 **Flanders** Flanders was generally thought
a nation of burghers; it was scarcely "in a far country"

His fader was a man full free,   *10*
And lord he was of that contree,
　　As it was Goddes grace.

Sir Thopas wax a doughty swain°—
White was his face as paindemain,°
　　His lippes red as rose;   *15*
His rode is like scarlet in grain,°
And I you tell in good certain
　　He had a seemly nose.

His heer, his beerd, was like saffroun,
That to his girdle raught adown,   *20*
　　His shoon of Cordewane;
Of Brugges were his hosen brown,
His robe was of siklatoun,°
　　That coste many a jane.°

He koude hunt at wilde deer,°   *25*
And ride on-hawking for river,°
　　With grey goshawk° on hande;
Thereto he was a good archer,°
Of wrastling° was there none his peer,
　　Ther any ram shall stande.   *30*

Full many a maide bright in bower
They moorne for him paramour,
　　Whan hem were bet to sleepe;
But he was chaste and no lechour,

---

13 **wax . . . swain** grew into a brave young fellow—a romance tag; but
the description which follows is that of an effeminate burgher
14 **pandemain** fine white bread   16 **rode . . . grain** complexion is
like cloth dyed in grain   23 **siklatoun** costly material   24 **jane** small
silver coin   25 **deer** animals   26 **for river** by the river   27 **gos-
hawk** a hawk used by yeomen, not Knights   28 **archer** archery was
not appropriate to Knights   29 **wrastling** wrestling was low class; on
the ram as a prize in wrestling matches, cf. the description of the miller
in the General Prologue, line 548

35   And sweet as is the bramble flower
        That bereth the rede hepe.°

     And so bifell upon a day,
     Forsooth as I you telle may,
        Sir Thopas wold out ride;
40   He worth° upon his steede grey,
     And in his hand a launcegay,°
        A long swerd by his side.

     He pricketh° thurgh a fair forest,
     Therein is many a wilde beest—
45   Ye, bothe buck and hare;
     And as he pricketh north and est,
     I tell it you, him had almest
        Bitide° a sorry care.

     There springen herbes greet and smalle—
50   The licoris and setewale,
        And many a clowe-gilofre;°
     And nutemeg to put in ale,
     Whether it be moist or stale,
        Or for to lay in coffre.

55   The briddes sing, it is no nay,
     The sparhawk and the popinjay,
        That joy it was to heere;
     The thrustlecock made eek his lay,
     The woodedove upon the spray,
60   She sang full loud and clere.

---

36 **hepe** fruit of wild rose   40 **worth** got up   41 **launcegay** short
lance, not a very serious weapon   43 **pricketh** spurs his horse   47–
48 **him ... Bitide** there almost happened to him. "Almost" is the key
word   51 **clowe-gilofre** clove. Such lists are common in romances.
But spices would be of more interest to a tradesman than a knight-
errant

Sir Thopas fill in love-longinge
All whan he herd the thrustle singe,
   And pricked as he were wood;
His faire steed in his prickinge
So swatte° that men might him wringe—   65
   His sides were all blood.

Sir Thopas eek so wery was
For pricking on the softe grass,°
   So fierce was his corage—
That down he laid him in the plas,   70
To make his steede some solas,
   And yaf him good forage.°

"O Sainte Mary, *ben'dic'te,*
What aileth this love at me
   To binde me so sore?   75
Me dreemed all this night, pardee,
An elf-queen shall my lemman° be
   And sleep under my gore.°

An elf-queen wol I love, ywis,
For in this world no woman is   80
   Worthy to be my make°
      In towne.
All other women I forsake,
And to an elf-queen I me take,
   By dale and eek by downe."   85

Into his saddle he clomb° anon,
And pricketh over stile and ston,°

---

65 **swatte** sweated   68 **grass** he is supposed to be pricking through
wild forest   72 **forage** dry fodder, normally found in a barn   77 **lem-
man** sweetheart   78 **gore** garment   81 **make** mate   86 **clomb** Cf.
line 40. He should leap or vault into the saddle   87 **stile and ston** he
should jump the horse over stone walls rather than walking it over a
stile (a set of steps)

An elf-queen for t'espye;
Till he so long hath riden and goon
90 That he fond in a privee woon°
The contree of Fairye
So wilde:
For in that contree was there noon
That to him dorste ride or goon:
95   Neither wife ne childe.

Till that there came a greet geaunt:
His name was Sir Oliphaunt,°
A perilous man of deede.
He saide, "Child, by Termagaunt,°
100 But if thou prick out of mine haunt,
Anon I slee thy steede
With mace.
Here is the queen of Faïrye,
With harp and pipe and symphonye,
105   Dwelling in this place!"

The child said, "Also mote I thee,°
Tomorrwe will I meete thee,
Whan I have mine armoure.°
And yet I hope, *par ma fay,*
110 That thou shalt with this launcegay
Abyen it full sore.
Thy mawe°
Shall I percen, if I may,
Ere it be fully prime of day—
115   For here thou shalt be slawe!"°

---

90 **woon** dwelling-place 97 **Oliphaunt** Elephant 99 **Termagaunt**
a Mohammedan god, supposedly 106 **Also . . . thee** so may I thrive;
another tag 108 **armoure** of course he is supposed to ride in his
armor 112 **mawe** belly 115 **slawe** slain

—Sir Thopas drow aback full faste.
This geaunt at him stones caste,
  Out of a fell staff-slinge.°
But fair escapeth child° Thopas,
And all it was thurgh Goddes gras,   120
  And thurgh his fair beringe.°

Yet, listeth, lordes, to my tale,
Murrier than the nightingale,
  For now I wol you roune°
How Sir Thopas with sides smalle,°   125
Pricking over hill and dale,
  Is come again to towne.

His murry men commanded he
To make him bothe game and glee,
  For needes most he fighte   130
With a geaunt with hevedes° three,
For paramour and jolitee
  Of one that shone full brighte.

"Do come," he saide, "my minstrales
And gestours° for to tellen tales,   135
  Anon in mine arminge,
Of romances that been royales,
Of popes and of cardinales,
  And eek of love-likinge."

They fette him first the sweete win,   140
And meed eek in a maselin,°
  And royal spicerye,

---

118 **fell staff-slinge** dread slingshot   119 **child** commonly used of
young knights   121 **fair beringe** i.e., he ran fast   124 **roune** whis-
per, tell a secret   125 **sides smalle** a detail normally used of ladies
131 **hevedes** heads   134–35 **Do . . . gestours** have my minstrels and
storytellers come   141 **maselin** wooden bowl

And gingerbreed that was full fin,
And licoris, and eek comin,
145   With sugre that is trye.°

He dide next his white leere,
Of cloth of lake° fine and cleere,
    A breech and eek a sherte:
And next his shert an aketoun,°
150 And over that an haubergeoun
    For° percing of his herte:

And over that a fine hauberk,°
Was all y-wrought of Jewes werk,°
    Full strong it was of plate:
155 And over that his cote-armour,
As white as is a lily-flower,
    In which he wol debate.°

His sheeld was all of gold so red,
And therein was a bores heed,
160   A charbocle° by his side;
And there he swore on ale and breed°
How that the geaunt shall be deed,
    Bitide what betide.

His jambeux were of quirboily,°
165 His swerdes sheeth of ivory,
    His helm of latoun bright;

---

145 **trye** choice   146–47 **dide ... lake** put on next to his white skin
(breech and shirt) of linen   149 **aketoun** padded vest   151 **For** to
prevent   152 **hauberk** plate-armor, worn over the habergeon (mail)
153 **Jewes werk** Jews were famed as metal workers   157 **debate**
fight   160 **charbocle** i.e., his shield has a carbuncle and boar's head
painted on it as an emblem   161 **ale and breed** knights in romances
swore on aristocratic fare like peacocks   164 **jambeux ... quirboily**
shin-guards were of leather (which had been boiled, shaped, and let
dry)

His saddle was of rewel bon,°
His bridle as the sunne shon,
   Or as the moone light.

His spere was of fine cypress,°   *170*
That bodeth wer and nothing pees°—
   The heed full sharp y-grounde.
His steede was all dapple grey:
It goth an amble in the way,
   Full softely and rounde,   *175*
      In londe.
Lo, lordes mine, here is a fit!
If ye wol any more of it,
   To tell it wol I fonde° . . .

THE SECOND FIT

—Now hold your mouth, *par charitee,*   *180*
Bothe knight and lady free,
   And herkneth to my spelle:°
Of battail, and of chivalry,
And of ladies' love-drury,°
   Anon I wol you telle.   *185*

Men speken of romances of pris,°
Of Horn Child and of Ypotis,
   Of Beves and Sir Guy,
Of Sir Libeux and Pleindamour;
But Sir Thopas he bereth the flower   *190*
   Of royal chivalry.

---

167 **rewel bon** whalebone   170 **cypress** unusual for lances, but tradi-
tionally associated with death   171 **bodeth . . . pees** signifies war and
not peace   179 **fonde** attempt; note the desperate appeal for silence in
the next line, which suggests the audience's reaction   182 **spelle** tale
(typical romance usage)   184 **love-drury** love-making   186 **pris**
value

His goode steed all he bistrood,
And forth upon his way he glood,
   As sparkle out of the bronde.°
195 Upon his crest he bare a tower,
And therein sticked a lily-flower—
   God shild his corse fro shonde!°

And for he was a knight auntrous°
He nolde sleepen in noon hous,
200   But liggen in his hoode.°
His brighte helm was his wonger,°
And by him baiteth his destrer,°
   Of herbes fine and goode.

Himself drank water of the well,
205 As did the knight Sir Percivell,
   So worthy under weede;
      Till on a day . . .

"Namore of this, for Goddes dignitee!"
Quod oure Hoste, "for thou makest me
210 So wery of thy veray lewednesse°
That, also wisly God my soule blesse,
Mine eres aken of thy drasty speeche!°
Now swich a ryme the devil I biteche!°
This may well be ryme doggerel," quod he.
215   "Why so?" quod I. "Why wiltou lette° me
More of my tale than another man,
Sin that it is the beste ryme I kan?"

   "By God," quod he, "For plainly at oo word—
Thy drasty ryming is not worth a turd!

193–94 **glood . . . bronde** glided like a spark from a firebrand
197 **shild . . . shonde** keep his body from harm   198 **auntrous**
adventurous   200 **liggen . . . hoode** lie (wrapped in) his hood
201 **wonger** pillow   202 **baiteth . . . destrer** his steed grazes
210 **lewednesse** stupidity   212 **eres . . . drasty speeche** ears ache
with your worthless chatter   213 **biteche** give to   215 **lette** cut short

Thou dost nought elles but dispendest° time: *220*
Sir, at oo word, thou shalt no lenger ryme.
Let see wher° thou canst tellen ought in geste,°
Or tell in prose somewhat, at the leste,
In which there be some mirth or some doctrine."
    "Gladly," quod I. "By Goddes sweete pine,   *225*
I wol you tell a litel thing in prose
That oughte liken you, as I suppose,
Or elles certes ye be too daungerous.°
It is a moral tale vertuous,
Al be it told sometime in sundry wise,   *230*
Of sundry folk, as I shall you devise.
As thus:° Ye wot that every evangelist
That telleth us the pain of Jesu Christ
Ne saith not all thing as his fellaw dooth;
But, natheless, hir sentence° is all sooth,   *235*
And all accorden, as in hir sentence,
Al be there in hir telling difference.
For some of hem sayn more and some sayn lesse
Whan they his pitous passion expresse—
I mene of Mark and Matthew, Luke, and John;   *240*
But douteless hir sentence is all oon.
Therefore, lordinges all, I you biseeche,
If that ye think I vary as in my speeche—
As thus, though that I telle somewhat more
Of proverbes than ye han herd before   *245*
Comprehended in this litel tretise here,°
To enforcen with the effect of my mattere,

---

220 **dispendest** waste   222 **wher** whether   222 **ought in geste** any-
thing in the way of a good story   228 **daungerous** finicky   232 **thus**
what follows is Chaucer's typical self-satire: he has himself speak in a
long-winded, vague, apologetic way, using repetitious and awkward
expressions and bumbling language   235 **hir sentence** their meaning
246 **litel tretise here** he refers to the *Melibee,* a translation of a French
allegorical treatise in prose addressed to aristocrats. This is Chaucer's
other tale, omitted here. It is entirely serious, dealing with such prob-
lems as when to declare war, how to choose advisors, how to use tem-
poral goods, how to do justice

And though I not the same wordes saye
As ye han herd—yet to you all I praye
250 Blameth me not, for as in my sentence
Shull ye nowhere finden difference
Fro the sentence of this tretise lite
After the which this mirye tale I write.
And, therefore, herkneth what that I shall saye,
255 And let me tellen *all* my tale, I praye."

THE MONK'S PROLOGUE

Whan ended was my tale of Melibee
And of Prudence and hir benignitee,
Our Hoste said, "As I am faithful man!
And by that precious corpus Madrian,
I hadde lever than a barrel ale   5
That Goodelief my wife had herd this tale!
For she nis nothing of swich pacience
As was this Melibeus' wife Prudence!
By Goddes bones, whan I bete my knaves,°
She bringeth me the greete clobbed° staves,   10
And cryeth—'Slee the dogges everichon,
And breke hem bothe back and every bon!'
And if that any neighebor of mine
Wol not in chirche to my wife encline,°
Or be so hardy to hir to trespace,   15
Whan see cometh home she rampeth in my face
And cryeth—'False coward, wreek thy wif!
By corpus' bones, I wol have thy knif
And thou shalt have my distaff and go spinne!'
Fro day to night right thus she wol beginne: 20
'Alas,' she saith, 'that ever that I was shape
To wedden a milksop or a coward ape,
That wol been overlad of every wight!
Thou darst not stonden by thy wives right!'
This is my life, but if that I wol fighte.   25
And out at door anon I mot me dighte,
Or elles I am but lost, but if that I

9 **bete my knaves** hit my servants 10 **clobbed** clublike 14 **encline** bow. Cf. General Prologue, lines 449–52

Be like a wilde leon foolhardy.
I wot well she wol do me slee° someday
30 Some neighebor and thanne go my way;°
For I am perilous with knife in hande,
Al be it that I dare not *hir* withstande,
For she is big in armes, by my faith—
That shall he find that hir misdoth or saith.
35 But let us pass away fro this mattere.
—My lord the Monk," quod he, "be merry of cheere,
For ye shall tell a tale trewely.
Lo, Rochester stant here faste by!
Ride forth, mine owne lord, breke not our game!
40 But by my truth, I knowe not your name—
Wher shall I calle you my lord Daun John?°—
Or Daun Thomas or elles Daun Albon?
Of what house° be ye, by your fader kin?
I vow to God, thou hast a full fair skin:
45 It is a gentil pasture ther *thou* goost!
Thou art not like a penant° or a ghost!
Upon my faith, thou art some officer,
Some worthy sextein, or some celerer°—
For by my fader soul, as to my doom,°
50 Thou art a maister whan thou art at hoom,
No poore cloisterer, ne no novis,
But a governour, wiley° and wis,
And therewithal of brawnes and of bones
A well-faring persone for the nones!
55 I praye God yive him confusioun
That first thee brought unto religioun:°
Thou woldest han been a tredefowl° aright.
Haddestou as greet a leve as thou hast might

---

29 **do me slee** make me slay   30 **go my way** i.e., be hanged, or flee
41 **Daun John** the name of the evil monk in the Shipman's Tale
43 **house** monastery   46 **penant** penitent   48 **sextein ... celerer** officers of a monastery, in charge respectively of the buildings, altar, vestments, etc., and of the food and drink   49 **doom** judgment
52 **wiley** clever   56 **unto religioun** into the monastic life   57 **tredefowl** a rooster who keeps his hens satisfied. Cf. lines 66–67

To perform all thy lust in engendrure,
Thou haddest begetten many a creature!   60
Alas, why werestou so wide a cope?°
God yive me sorrwe but, and I were Pope,
Not only thou, but every mighty man,
Though he were shorn full high upon his pan,°
Shold have a wife—for all the world is lorn: 65
Religious hath take up all the corn
Of treding; and we burel men been shrimpes!°
Of fieble trees there comen wretched impes;°
This maketh that our heires been so slendre
And fieble that they may not well engendre;   70
This maketh that our wives wol assaye
Religious folk, for they mowe better paye
Of Venus' payements than may we.
God wot, no Lusheburghes° payen ye!
But be not wroth, my lord, though that I playe: 75
Full oft in game a sooth I have herd saye."

    This worthy Monk took all in pacience,
And said, "I wol doon all my diligence,
As fer as souneth into honestee,°
To telle you a tale or two or three.   80
And if you list to herkne hiderward,
I wol you sayn the life of Saint Edward.
Or elles, first, tragedies wol I telle,
Of which I have an hundred in my celle.

    Tragedy is to sayn a certain storye   85
(As olde bookes maken us memorye)
Of him that stood in greet prosperitee
And is y-fallen out of high degree
Into misery—and endeth wretchedly.
And they been versified communely   90

61 **cope** cloak   64 **shorn ... pan** shaved on the top of his skull (i.e.,
had the monk's tonsure)   66–67 **Religioun ... shrimpes** the monas-
teries have taken off the wheat with respect to sexual relations, and we
laymen are shrimps (i.e., weaklings)   68 **impes** shoots   74 **Lushe-
burghes** the bad coin of Luxembourg   79 **souneth ... honestee** ac-
cords with morality

Of six feet, which men clepe hexametron.
In prose eek been endited many oon,
And eek in metre in many a sundry wise.
Lo, this declaring ought enough suffise.
95   Now herkneth if you liketh for to heere.
But first I you beseek in this mattere,
Though I by ordre telle not thise thinges,
Be it of popes, emperours, or kinges,
After hir ages° as men written finde,
100   But tell hem some before and some behinde,
As it now cometh unto my remembraunce;
Have me excused of mine ignoraunce."

[*The Monk's "tale" which follows, omitted in the pres-
ent edition, is a collection of "tragedies"—stories that
describe the capricious turning of Fortune's wheel in the
lives of various figures, from Satan and Adam to Chau-
cer's contemporary Bernabò Visconti, whom Chaucer
might actually have met on his Italian voyage of 1378.
Why the self-indulgent monk (as he is described in the
General Prologue) begins with such a pedantic pro-
logue, and tells so serious and dull a tale, is somewhat
of a puzzle. It is perhaps an effort to keep up a solemn
facade. At all events, the Knight interrupts him and
saves the pilgrims from further boredom—Ed.*]

99 **After hir ages** chronologically

THE NUN'S PRIEST'S PROLOGUE°

"Ho!" quod the Knight. "Good sir, namore of this!
That ye han said is right enough, ywis,
And muchel more; for litel hevinesse
Is right enough to muche folk, I guesse.
I say for me it is a greet disese,°   5
Where as men han been in greet welth and ese
To heeren of hir suddein fall—alas.
And the contrary is joy and greet solas,
As whan a man hath been in poor estat,
And climbeth up and wexeth fortunat,   10
And there abideth in prosperitee:
Swich thing is gladsome, as it thinketh me,
And of swich thing were goodly for to telle."
    "Ye," quod out Host, "by Sainte Poules belle,
Ye say right sooth—this Monk he clappeth° loude!   15

Prologue to the Nun's Priest's Tale this is a beast fable, embodying
a literary device of which Donald Duck or Snoopy are modern exam-
ples. Chaucer's barnyard animals behave with all kinds of human pre-
tensions—they act like courtly lovers, intellectuals, theologians; hence
they delightfully satirize human follies. Much of the humor depends
on Chaucer's periodically reminding us that they are a rooster and a
hen: just as we get involved with their high seriousness, we hear them
make a barnyard noise or "fly down from the beams." The chase of the
fox was a set scene in medieval literature. And the "morality" drawn
at the end (lines 611–15) is so simple that most readers miss it: keep
your eyes open and your mouth shut.
    Part of the effect relies on the incongruity between a high style and
humdrum events. The widow and her little barnyard are described ac-
cording to the rules of medieval rhetoric, with formal "dilations" or
descriptions, "apostrophes" in which the author nobly comments and
moralizes, and much name-dropping of authoritative writers **5 disese**
displeasure **15 clappeth** chatters

He spak how Fortune 'covered with a cloude'
I noot never what! And als° of a tragedye
Right now ye herd, and pardee, no remedye
It is for to biwaile ne complaine
20 That that is done; and als it is a paine,
As ye han said, to heere of hevinesse.
Sir Monk, namore of this, so God you blesse—
Your tale annoyeth all this compaignye!
Swich talking is not worth a butterflye,
25 For therein is there no disport ne game!
Wherefore, sir Monk—or Daun Piers, by your name—
I pray you hertely tell us somewhat elles.
For sikerly, nere° clinking of your belles,
That on your bridle hang on every side,
30 By hevene King° that for us alle dyde
I shold ere this have fallen down for sleep,
Although the slough° had never been so deep!
Than had your tale all be told in vain—
For certainly, as that thise clerkes sayn,
35 Where as a man may have noon audience
Nought helpeth it to tellen his sentence.
And well I wot the substance° is in me,
If any thing shall well reported be.
Sir, say somewhat of *hunting,* I you praye."
40   "Nay," quod this Monk, "I have no lust to playe.
Now let another tell, as I have told."
    Than spak our Host with rude speech and bold
And said unto the Nonnes Preest anon:
"Come neer, thou Preest! Come hider, thou sir John!
45 Tell us swich thing as may our hertes glade.
Be blithe, though thou ride upon a jade!
What though thine horse be bothe foul and lene?
If he wol serve thee, rekke not a bene.
Look that thine hert be murry evermo."
50   "Yis, sir," quod he, "yis, Host, so mote I go,

17 **als** also 28 **nere** were it not for the 30 **hevene King** Heaven's
King 32 **slough** mire 37 **substance** capacity to understand

But I be murry, ywis, I wol be blamed."
And right anon his tale he hath attamed,"°
And thus he said unto us everichon,
This sweete preest, this goodly man sir John:

THE NUN'S PRIEST'S TALE

A povre° widow, somedeel stape° in age
Was whilom dwelling in a narrwe° cottage,
Beside a grove, standing in a dale.
This widwe, of which I telle you my tale,
Sin thilke day that she was last a wif,   5
In pacience lad a full simple lif;
For litel was hir catel and hir rente:°
By husbondry° of swich as God hir sente
She fond° hirself and eek hir daughtren two.
Three large sowes had she, and namo,   10
Three kin,° and eek a sheep that highte Malle.
Full sooty was hir bower and eek hir halle,°
In which she eet full many a slendre meel:
Of poignant sauce hir needed neveradeel;
No daintee morsel passed thurgh hir throte—   15
Hir diet was accordant to hir cote.°
Repleccioun° ne made hir never sick:
Attempre° diet was all hir physik,

---

52 **attamed** started 1 **povre** poor 1 **stape** advanced 2 **narrwe**
small 7 **catel . . . rente** possessions . . . income 8 **husbondry** thrifty
management 9 **fond** provided for 11 **kin** cows 12 **bower . . . halle**
inner apartment . . . main hall (the words exaggeratedly suggest a
castle; they are likely one room divided by a curtain, and sooty from
the fireplace) 16 **cote** hut 17 **Repleccioun** overindulgence 18 **At-
tempre** temperate

And exercise, and hertes suffisaunce;°
20 The goute let° hir nothing for to daunce,
N'apoplexye shente° not hir heed.
No wine ne drank she, neither white ne red:
Hir boord was served most with white and black—
Milk and brown breed, in which she fond no lack;
25 Seind° bacon, and sometime an ey or twaye,°
For she was as it were a manner daye.°
    A yerd she had, enclosed all aboute
With stickes, and a drye ditch withoute,
In which she had a cock heet° Chauntecleer.
30 In all the land, of crowing nas his peer:°
His voice was murrier than the murrye orgon°
On massedayes that in the chirche gon;
Well sikerer° was his crowing in his lodge
Than is a clock or an abbey orlogge;°
35 By nature he knew ech ascensioun
Of th'equinoxial in thilke town—
For whan degrees fifteene weren ascended,°
Than crew he that it might not been amended.°
His comb was redder than the fine coral,
40 And battailed as it were a castel wall;
His bill was black, and as the jet it shoon;
Like azure were his legges and his toon,°
His nailes whiter than the lily-flower,
And like the burned° gold was his colour.
45   This gentil cock had in his governaunce
Seven hennes for to doon all his plesaunce,
Which were his sustres and his paramours—
And wonder like to him as of colours.

19 **suffisaunce** contentment   20 **let** hindered   21 **shente** injured
25 **Seind** singed, broiled   25 **ey or twaye** egg or two   26 **a manner
daye** a kind of dairy farmer   29 **heet** named   30 **of . . . peer** in crow-
ing there was none his peer   31 **orgon** organ pipes   33 **sikerer** more
accurate   34 **orlogge** chiming steeple clock; very fashionable in
Chaucer's time, they indicated phases of the moon, struck the hours,
etc.   37 **degrees . . . ascended** i.e., one hour   38 **amended** improved
upon   42 **toon** toes   44 **burned** burnished

Of which the fairest hewed on hir throte
Was cleped fair damoiselle° Pertelote: 50
Curteis she was, discreet, and debonaire,
And compaignable, and bare hirself so faire
Sin thilke day that she was seven night old
That trewely she hath the hert in hold
Of Chauntecleer, locken in every lith.°   55
He loved hir so that well was him therewith.
But swich a joy was it to heer hem singe,
Whan that the brighte sunne gan to springe,
In sweet accord—*"My lief is faren in lande . . ."*
For thilke time, as I have understande,   60
Beestes and briddes coude speke and singe.

  And so bifell that in a daweninge,
As Chauntecleer, among his wives alle,
Sat on his perche that was in the halle—
And next him sat this faire Pertelote—   65
This Chauntecleer gan gronen in his throte,
As man that in his dreem is drecched sore.°
And whan that Pertelote thus herd him rore
She was aghast and saide, "Herte dere!°
What aileth you to grone in this mannere?   70
Ye been a veray sleeper°—fy, for shame!"

  And he answered and saide thus: "Madame,
I pray you that ye take it not agrief,
By God, me mette° I was in swich meschief
Right now, that yet mine hert is sore afright.   75
Now God," quod he, "my sweven recche aright°
And keep my body out of foul prisoun!
Me mette how that I romed up and down

---

50 **damoiselle** a very aristocratic word—a noble young lady. The adjectives which follow are similarly aristocratic, up to the reminder "seven night old" 55 **locken . . . lith** locked in every limb 67 **drecched sore** deeply troubled 69 **Herte dere** dear heart—a courtly phrase; but note that, pronounced with the final *e*'s, it sounds exactly like a hen's clucking. Cf. *"Avoi"* (line 88) and *"chuk"* (line 354) 71 **a veray sleeper** a fine sleeper 74 **me mette** i.e., I dreamed 76 **my . . . aright** make my dream turn out favorably

Within our yerd, wher as I saw a beest°
80 Was like an hound, and wold han made arrest
Upon my body, and han had me deed.
His colour was bitwix yellow and red,
And tipped was his tail and both his eres
With black, unlike the remnant of his heres;
85 His snoute small, with glowing eyen twaye.
Yet of his look for fere almost I deye!
This caused me my groning, douteless."
    "*Avoi!*" quod she, "fy on you, herteless!°
Alas," quod she, "for by that God above
90 Now han ye lost mine hert and all my love!
I can not love a coward, by my faith.
For certes, what so any woman saith,
We all desiren, if it mighte be,°
To han husbondes hardy, wise, and free,
95 And secree, and no niggard, ne no fool,
Ne him that is aghast of every tool,°
Ne noon avauntour°—by that God above.
How dorst ye sayn, for shame, unto your love
That any thing might make you aferd!—
100 Have ye no mannes hert, and han a beerd?
Alas! and can ye been aghast of swevenes!°
Nothing, God wot, but vanitee in sweven is!
Swevenes engendren of replexions,
And oft of fume, and of complexions,°
105 Whan humours been too abundant in a wight.
Certes, this dreem which ye han mette tonight
Comth of the grete superfluitee
Of youre rede cholera,° pardee,

79 **beest** he goes on to describe a fox, which in the old idea of "animal magnetism" would have been the natural enemy of all roosters. See lines 459–61   88 **herteless** coward   93 **We ... be** she describes the qualities expected of the ideal courtly lover   96 **tool** weapon   97 **avauntour** boaster   101 **swevenes** dreams   103–04 **engendren ... complexions** come from overeating, and often from vapors rising to the head (after drinking), and from imbalance of bodily humors. She goes on to describe the theory of the physical ("natural") origin of dreams   108 **rede cholera** red choler (bile)

Which causeth folk to dreden in hir dreemes
Of arrwes, and of fire with rede lemes,°   *110*
Of rede beestes that they wol hem bite,
Of contek,° and of whelpes greet and lite;
Right as the humour of malencolye
Causeth full many a man in sleep to crye
For fere of blacke beres, or boles° blacke,   *115*
Or elles blacke devils wol hem take.
Of other humours coud I tell also
That werken many a man in sleep full wo;
But I wol pass as lightly as I can.
Lo, Caton, which that was so wise a man   *120*
Said he not thus: 'Ne do no fors of dreemes'?°
Now, sir," quod she, "whan we flee fro the beemes,
For Goddes love, as take some laxatif.
Up° peril of my soul and of my lif
I conseil you the best, I wol not lie,   *125*
That both of choler and of malencolye
Ye purge you. And for ye shall not tarrye,
Though in this town is noon apothecarye,
I shall myself to herbes techen° you
That shall been for your hele and for your prow;°   *130*
And in our yerd tho herbes shall I finde
The which han of hir propretee by kinde°
To purge you binethe and eek above.
Foryet not this, for Goddes owne love:
Ye been full cholerik of complexioun.   *135*
Ware the sun in his ascencioun
Ne find you not replete of humours hote.
And if it do, I dare well lay a grote°
That ye shull have a fever terciane,°
Or an ague that may be youre bane.°   *140*

110 **lemes** flames   112 **contek** strife   115 **boles** bulls   121 **"Ne . . .
dreemes"** pay no attention to dreams   124 **Up** upon   129 **techen**
direct   130 **hele . . . prow**   health . . . benefit   132 **kinde**   nature
138 **lay a grote** bet a groat (small silver coin)   139 **fever terciane**
fever recurring within three days, i.e., every other day   140 **youre
bane** the death of you

A day or two ye shull have digestives°
Of wormes, ere ye take your laxatives
Of lauriol, centaure, and fumetere,
Or elles of ellebor that groweth there,
145   Of catapuce or of gaitrys berries,
Of herb-ive growing in our yerd, ther merry is.°
Peck hem up right as they grow and ete hem in.
Be merry, husbond, for your fader kin;
Dredeth no dreem! I can say you namore."
150   "Madame," quod he, "graunt mercy of your lore.°
But, natheless, as touching Daun Catoun,
That hath of wisdom swich a greet renown,
Though that he bade no dreemes for to drede,
By God, men may in olde bookes rede
155   Of many a man more of auctoritee
Than ever Caton was—so mote I thee°—
That all the reverse sayn of his sentence—
And han well founden by experience
That dreemes been significaciouns°
160   As well of joy as tribulaciouns
That folk enduren in this life present.
There needeth make of this noon argument—
The veray preve° sheweth it in deede.
        One of the greetest auctour that men rede
165   Saith thus: that whilom two fellawes wente
On pilgrimage, in a full good entente,
And happed so they comen in a town
Where as there was swich congregacioun
Of peple, and eek so strait of herbergage,°

---

141 **digestives** medicines to absorb the humors before purging. Her
remedy is an accurate account of medieval treatment; worms were
actually used for tertian fever, and the medicines which follow were
in fact laxatives or emetics   146 **ther merry is** where it's nice
150 **graunt . . . lore** thank you for your instruction (the French phrase
was very toney)   156 **so . . . thee** so may I prosper   159 **significa-
ciouns** forewarnings. Chauntecleer proceeds to argue the notion that
his dream was a *somnium celeste*, a warning from on high—which
would make him a heroic figure. His citing of authorities and *exempla*
is very learned   163 **veray preve** real occurrence (of such dreams)

That they ne found as much as oo cottage   *170*
In which they bothe might y-lodged be.
Wherefore they mosten of necessitee
As for that night departe compaignye.
And ech of hem goth to his hostelrye
And took his lodging as it wolde falle.   *175*
That one of hem was lodged in a stalle
Fer in a yerd, with oxen of the plow.
That other man was lodged well enow
As was his aventure or his fortune
—That us governeth all as in commune.°   *180*
And so bifell that long ere it were day
This man mette in his bed, ther as he lay,
How that his fellaw gan upon him calle
And said, 'Alas! for in an oxes stalle
This night I shall be murdred ther I lie!   *185*
Now help me, dere brother, or I die!
In alle haste come to me!' he saide.
This man out of his sleep for fere abraide,°
But whan that he was wakened of his sleep
He turned him and took of this no keep—   *190*
Him thought his dreem nas but a vanitee.
Thus twies in his sleeping dreemed he,
And atte thridde time yet his fellawe
Came, as him thought, and said, 'I am now slawe:°
Behold my bloody woundes deep and wide.   *195*
Arise up erly in the morrwe tide
And at the west gate of the town,' quod he,
'A carte full of dung there shaltou see,
In which my body is hid full prively:
Do thilke cart arresten° boldely.   *200*
My gold caused my murdre, sooth to sayn'
—And told him every point how he was slain,

---

169 **so . . . herbergage** such a shortage of lodgings   180 **That . . .
commune** the Nun's Priest throws in a reference to the Monk's Tale
which has preceded, a collection of various men's "falls" on Fortune's
wheel   188 **abraide** started   194 **slawe** slain   200 **Do . . . arresten**
have that cart stopped

With a full pitous face, pale of hewe.
And truste well, his dreem he fond full trewe,
205 For on the morrwe, as soon as it was day,
To his fellawes inn he took the way.
And whan that he came to this oxes stalle,
After his fellaw he began to calle.
The hostiler answerde him anon
210 And saide, 'Sir, your fellaw is agon;
As soon as day he went out of the town.'
This man gan fallen in suspecioun
Remembring on his dreemes that he mette,
And forth he goth, no lenger wold he lette,°
215 Unto the west gate of the town, and fond
A dung-cart, went, as it were, to dunge-lond—
That was arrayed in that same wise
As ye han herd the dede man devise.
And with an hardy hert he gan to crye,
220 'Vengeance and justice of this fellonye!
My fellaw murdred is this same night
And in this cart he lith gaping upright!°
I cry out on the ministres,'° quod he,
'That sholden keep and rulen this citee!
225 Harrow! Alas, here lith my fellaw slain!'
What shold I more unto this tale sayn?
The peple out stert and cast the cart to grounde,
And in the middle of the dung they founde
The dede man that murdred was all newe.
230   O blissful God that art so just and trewe,
Lo, how that thou biwrayest° murdre alway!
Murdre wol out—that see we day by day:
Murdre is so wlatsome° and abhominable
To God, that is so just and resonable,
235 That He ne wol not suffre it heled° be
Though it abide a yeer or two or three.

214 **lette** delay   222 **lith gaping upright** lies with mouth open, face
up   223 **ministres** magistrates   231 **biwrayest** reveal   233 **wlat-
some** loathsome   235 **heled** concealed

Murdre wol out—this my conclusioun.°
And right anon ministres of that town
Han hent the carter, and so sore him pined,°
And eek the hostiler so sore engined,°   *240*
That they biknew hir wickedness anon—
And were anhanged by the necke-bon.
Here may men seen that dreemes been to drede!
  And, certes, in the same book I rede
Right in the next chapitre after this   *245*
(I gabbe° not, so have I joy or bliss)
Two men that wold han passed over see
For certain cause into a fer contree,
If that the wind ne hadde been contrarye,
That made hem in a citee for to tarrye,   *250*
That stood full mirry upon an haven side:
But on a day again the even tide°
The wind gan chaunge, and blew right as hem leste.
Jolif and glad they went unto his reste,
And casten hem° full erly for to saile.   *255*
But to that oo man fill a greet mervaile:
That one of hem, in sleeping as he lay,
Him mette a wonder dreem again the day.°
Him thought a man stood by his beddes side
And him commanded that he shold abide   *260*
And said him thus: 'If thou tomorrwe wende,°
Thou shalt be dreint:° my tale is at an ende.'
He woke and told his fellaw what he mette,
And prayed him his viage to lette°—
As for that day he prayed him to abide.   *265*
His fellaw that lay by his beddes side
Gan for to laugh, and scorned him full faste:
'No dreem,' quod he, 'may so mine hert aghaste°
That I wol lette for to do my thinges.

230–37 **O . . . conclusioun** a rhetorical "apostrophe" in which the narrator
comments emotionally and moralizes   239 **pined** tortured   240 **engined**
put to the rack   246 **gabbe** lie   252 **again . . . tide** toward evening
255 **casten hem** planned   258 **again the day** toward dawn   261 **wende**
leave   262 **dreint** drowned   264 **viage to lette** delay his voyage
268 **aghaste** frighten

270 I sette not a straw by thy dreeminges,
     For swevenes been but vanitees and japes.°
     Men dreem alday of owles and of apes
     And eek of many a maze° therewithal;
     Men dreem of thing that never was, ne shall.

275 But sith I see that thou wolt here abide
     And thus forsleuthen° willfully thy tide,°
     God wot it reweth me,° and have good day.'
     And thus he took his leve and went his way.
     But ere that he had half his course y-sailed—

280 Noot I not why, ne what meschaunce it ailed—
     But, casuelly,° the shippes bottme rente,
     And ship and man under the water wente
     In sight of other shippes it beside°
     That with hem sailed at the same tide.

285 And therefore, faire Pertelote so dere,
     By swich ensaumples olde maistou lere
     That no man sholde been too reccheless°
     Of dreemes. For I say thee douteless
     That many a dreem full sore is for to drede!

290   Lo, in the life of Saint Kenelm I rede
     (That was Kenulphus' son, the noble King
     Of Mercenrike) how Kenelm mette a thing
     A lite ere he was murdred on a day.
     His murdre in his avision he sey.°

295 His norice him expounded everydeel
     His sweven, and bade him for to keep him well
     For° traison. But he nas but seven yeer old,
     And therefore litel tale hath he told
     Of any dreem, so holy was his herte.

300 By God, I hadde lever than my sherte
     That ye had rad his legend, as have I.
         Dame Pertelote, I say you trewely,

---

271 **japes** deceits   273 **maze** fantasy   276 **forsleuthen** idle away
276 **tide** time   277 **God . . . me** God knows I'm sorry   281 **casuelly**
by chance   283 **it beside** near it   287 **reccheless** unheedful
294 **sey** saw   296–97 **keep . . . For** guard himself against

Macrobeus,° that writ th'*Avisioun*
In Afrik of the Worthy Scipioun
Affermeth° dreemes, and saith that they been   305
Warning of thinges that men after seen.
And furthermore I pray you looketh well
In th'Olde Testament of Daniel,
If he held dreemes any vanitee.
Rede eek of Joseph and there shull ye see   310
Where dreemes be sometime (I say not alle)
Warning of thinges that shull after falle.
Look of Egypte the king Daun Pharao,
His baker and his botteler° also,
Wher° they ne felte noon effect in dreemes.   315
Whoso wol seek actes of sundry remes°
May rede of dreemes many a wonder thing!
   Lo Cresus, which that was of Lyde king,
Mette he not that he sat upon a tree,
Which signified he shold anhanged be?   320
Lo here Andromacha, Ectores° wif,
That day that Ector sholde lese his lif,
She dreemed on the same night biforn
How that the life of Ector shold be lorn
If thilke day he went into battaile.   325
She warned him, but it might not availe:
He wente for to fighte natheless,
But he was slain anon of Achilles
—But thilke tale is all too long to telle,
And eek it is nigh day, I may not dwelle.   330
Shorly I say, as for conclusioun,
That I shall han of this avisioun
Adversitee. And I say furthermoor
That I ne tell of laxatives no stoor.

303 **Macrobeus** author of a commentary on Cicero's *Somnium Scipi-onis*; the work was one of the great medieval authorities on dreams 305 **Affermeth** acknowledges 314 **botteler** butler 315 **Wher** whether 316 **actes . . . remes** histories of various realms 321 **Ec-tores** Hector's

335 For they been venimous, I wot it well—
    I hem defy! I love hem neveradeel!
    Now let us speke of mirth and stint all this:
    Madame Pertelote, so have I bliss,
    Of oo thing God hath sent me large grace:
340 For whan I see the beautee of your face—
    Ye been so scarlet red about your eyen—
    It maketh all my drede for to dien.
    For also siker as *in principio,*°
    'Mulier est hominis confusio'°—
345 Madame, the sentence of this Latin is
    'Woman is mannes joy and all his bliss.'
    For whan I feel anight your softe side—
    Al be it that I may not on you ride,
    For that our perch is made so narrwe, alas—
350 I am so full of joy and of solas
    That I defye bothe sweven and dreem."
    And with that word he fley° down fro the beem,
    For it was day, and eek his hennes alle,
    And with a *"chuk"* he gan hem for to calle,
355 For he had found a corn lay in the yerd.
    Real° he was! *He* was namore aferd—
    He fethered° Pertelote twenty time,
    And trad° hir eek as oft ere it was prime.
    He looketh as it were a grim leoun;
360 And on his toes he rometh up and down—
    Him deigned not to set his foot to grounde.
    He *chuk*eth whan he hath a corn y-founde
    And to him rennen than his wives alle.
    Thus royal as a prince is in his halle
365 Leve I this Chauntecleer in his pasture;
    And after wol I tell his aventure.

---

343 **also . . . in principio** as sure as *in principio* (first words of Gospel
according to John, used as a charm; see General Prologue, line 254)
344 **'Mulier . . . confusio'** 'Woman is man's confusion.' Probably in
line 346 Chauntecleer mistranslates it purposely; though he might mis-
understand it himself   352 **fley** flew   356 **Real** regal   357 **fethered**
covered with his wings   358 **trad** laid

*   *   *

Whan that the month in which the world began,
That highte March, whan God first maked man,
Was complet, and passed were also,
Sin March began, thirty days and two,   370
Bifell that Chauntecleer in all his pride,
His seven wives walking him beside,
Cast up his eyen to the brighte sunne
(That in the signe of Taurus had y-runne
Twenty degrees and one, and somewhat more),   375
And knew by kind,° and by noon other lore,
That it was prime;° and crew with blissful stevene.°
"The sun," he said, "is clomben up on hevene
Fourty degrees and one and more, ywis.
Madame Pertelote, my worldes bliss,   380
Herkneth thise blissful briddes how they singe,
And see the freshe flowres how they springe!
Full is mine hert of revel and solas!"
But suddenly him fill a sorrweful cas:°
For ever the latter end of joy is wo—   385
God wot that "worldly joy is soon ago,"°
And if a rethor° coude fair endite
He in a chronicle saufly might it write,
As for a sovereign notabilitee.
Now every wise man, let him herkne me: 390
This story is also trew, I undertake,
As is the book of Launcelot de Lake,°
That women hold in full greet reverence.
Now wol I turn again to my sentence:

---

376 **kind** nature   377 **prime** the astrological references accurately
make it nine a.m. of May 3, the same date as the battle in the Knight's
Tale   377 **stevene** voice   384 **him . . . cas** a sorrowful chance befell
him   386 **ago** gone. The Monk's "tragedies" illustrated this point
387 **rethor** rhetorician   392 **Launcelot de Lake** a romance, scarcely
notable for truthfulness; it was this book which Paolo and Francesca were
reading when they fell in love (Dante, *Inferno* V)

395   A colfox°—full of sly iniquitee—
       That in the grove had woned° yeres three
       By high imaginacion forncast,°
       The same night thurghout the hedges brast
       Into the yerd ther Chauntecleer the faire
400   Was wont, and eek his wives, to repaire.
       And in a bed of wortes° still he lay
       Till it was passed undren of the day,°
       Waiting his time on Chauntecleer to falle
       As gladly doon thise homicides alle
405   That in await liggen° to murdre men.
       O false murdrour, lurking in thy den!
       O newe Scariot! Newe Geniloun!°
       False dissimilour! O Greek Sinoun°—
       That broughtest Troy all outrely° to sorrwe!
410   O, Chauntecleer! Accursed be that morrwe
       That thou into the yerd flaugh fro the beemes!
       Thou were full well y-warned by thy dreemes
       That thilke day was perilous to thee—
       But what that God forwot° mot needes be,
415   After th'opinion of certain clerkes:
       Witness on him that any parfit clerk is
       That in scole° is greet altercacioun
       In this matter, and greet disputisoun,°
       And hath been of an hundred thousand men;
420   But I ne can not bult it to the bren,°

---

395 **colfox** coal-fox, having black feet, ears, and tail. Cf. lines 82–85
396 **woned** lived   397 **By . . . forncast** foreseen by the noble imagina-
tion (i.e., in Chauntecleer's "celestial" dream); the imaginative faculty
of the mind was thought to mediate between the senses and the
intellect, producing pictures, ideas, and dreams   401 **wortes** herbs
402 **undren . . . day** midmorning   405 **liggen** lie   407 **Scariot . . .
Geniloun** Judas Iscariot, betrayer of Jesus, and Genilon, betrayer of
Roland in the *Chanson de Roland*   408 **Sinoun** Sinon, who deceived
the Trojans by the wooden horse   409 **outrely** utterly   414 **forwot** fore-
knows   417 **scole** the universities   418 **disputisoun** the disputation
over predestination and free will was indeed heated in the fourteenth
century, and the three positions outlined below were held by various
parties   420 **bult . . . bren** sift it down to the bran

As can the holy doctour Augustin,
Or Boece,° or the bishop Bradwardin,°
Wheither that Goddes worthy forwiting
Straineth° me needly for to doon a thing
—"Needly" clepe I "simple necessitee";   425
Or elles if free choice be graunted me
To do that same thing, or do it nought
Though God forwot it ere that it was wrought;
Or, if his witing straineth neveradeel
But by "necessitee condicionel"—   430
I wol not han to do of swich mattere:
My tale is of a cock, as ye may heere,
That took his conseil of his wife, with sorrwe,
To walken in the yerd upon that morrwe
That he had mette the dreem that I you tolde.   435
Women's conseils been full ofte colde!°
Woman's conseil brought us first to wo,
And made Adam fro paradise to go,
Ther as he was full mirrye and well at ese!
—But, for I noot to whom it might displese,   440
If I conseil of women wolde blame,
Pass over, for I said it in my game:°
Rede auctours where they trete of swich mattere,
And what they sayn of women ye may heere—
Thise been the cockes wordes and not mine;   445
I can noon harm of no woman divine.°
    Fair in the sond° to bath hir mirrily
Lith Pertelote, and all hir sustres by,
Again the sun; and Chauntecleer so free

---

422 **Boece** Boethius   422 **Bradwardin** Bp. Thomas Bradwardine (d.
1349) had lectured at Oxford against free will. St. Augustine believed
that God granted free will to man. Boethius believed that God knew
what any man would choose but His foreknowledge did not cause
man's choice ("conditional necessity")   424 **Straineth** constrains
436 **colde** fatal. The Nun's Priest launches into a typical expression of
medieval antifeminism; then presumably remembers that the Prioress
is present, backs down, and claims the idea was Chauntecleer's
442 **in my game** for fun   446 **divine** imagine   447 **sond** sand

450 Song mirrier than the mermaid in the see
       —For Physiologus° saith sikerly
     How that they singen well and mirrily.
     And so bifell that as he cast his eye,
     Among the wortes,° on a butterflye,
455 He was ware of this fox that lay full lowe.
     No thing ne list him thanne for to crowe,
     But cried anon *"Cok cok!"* and up he sterte
     As man that was affrayed° in his herte
       —For, naturelly, a beest desireth flee
460 Fro his contrary, if he may it see
     Though he never erst had seen it with his eye.
     This Chauntecleer, whan he gan him espye,
     He wold han fled, but that the fox anon
     Said: "Gentil sir! Alas, where wol ye gon?
465 Be ye afraid of *me*, that am your freend?
     Now, certes, I were worse than a feend
     If I to *you* wold harm or villainye.
     I am not come your conseil for t'espye,°
     But trewely, the cause of my cominge
470 Was only for to herkne how that ye singe.
     For trewely, ye han as mirry a stevene
     As any angel hath that is in hevene.
     Therewith ye han in music more feelinge
     Than had Boece,° or any that can singe.
475 My lord your fader—God his soule blesse!—
     And eek your moder, of hir gentilesse,
     Han in mine house y-been—to my greet ese.°
     And certes, sir, full fain wold I *you* plese.
       But for men speke of singing, I wol saye—
480 So mote I brouke° well mine eyen twaye!—
     Save ye, I herde never man so singe

---

451 **Physiologus** the "naturalist," i.e., the Bestiary, a collection of fan-
ciful facts about different kinds of creatures   454 **wortes** herbs
458 **affrayed** frightened   468 **your ... espye** butt into your private
business   474 **Boece** Boethius had written a treatise on music
477 **ese** pleasure   480 **brouke** use

As did your fader in the morrweninge.
Certes, it was of hert all that he song!
And for to make his voice the more strong
He wold so pain him that with both his eyen   485
He moste *wink*°—so loud he wolde cryen,
And standen on his tiptoon therewithal,
And stretche forth his necke long and small!
And eek he was of swich discrecioun
That there nas no man in no regioun   490
That him in song or wisdom mighte passe.
I have well rad in *Daun Burnel the Asse*
Among his verse how that there was a cock,
For a preestes son yaf him a knock
Upon his leg while he was yong and nice,   495
He made him for to lese his benefice.°
But certain, there nis no comparisoun
Bitwix the wisdom and discrecioun
Of youre fader and of his subtiltee.
Now singeth, sir, for sainte charitee!   500
Let see, can ye your fader countrefete?"°
    This Chauntecleer his winges gan to beete,
As man that coud his traison not espye
So was he ravished° with his flatterye.
—Alas, ye lordes! Many a false flattour°   505
Is in your court, and many a losengeour,°
That plesen you well more, by my faith,
Than he that soothfastness unto you saith!
Redeth Ecclesiaste of flatterye.
Beth ware, ye lordes, of hir trecherye!   510
    This Chauntecleer stood hye upon his tos,
Stretching his neck, and held his eyen clos,
And gan to crowe loude for the nones.

---

486 **wink** close his eyes   496 **lese his benefice** the young man in Nigel Wireker's story did not get to his ordination as priest because the cock did not wake him; so he could not take possession of a priest's benefice   501 **countrefete** imitate   504 **ravished** overcome   505 **flattour** flatterer   506 **losengeour** liar

And Daun Russell the fox stert up atones
515 And by the gargat° hente Chauntecleer
And on his back toward the wood him beer,
For yet ne was there no man that him sued.°
—O Destinee, that maist not been eschued!
Alas that Chauntecleer fleigh fro the beemes!
520 Alas his wife ne roughte not of dreemes!
And on a Friday fill all this meschaunce!°
O Venus, that art goddess of plesaunce,
Sin that thy servant was this Chauntecleer,
And in thy service did all his power—
525 More for delit than world to multiplye—
Why woldestou suffre him on thy day to die?
O Gaufred,° dere maister sovereign,
That whan thy worthy King Richard was slain
With shot, complainedest his deeth so sore,
530 Why n'had I now thy sentence and thy lore,
The Friday for to chide, as diden ye?
For on a Friday soothly slain was he!
Than wold I shew you how that I coud plaine
For Chauntecleeres drede and for his paine!
535   Certes swich cry ne lamentacioun
Was never of ladies made whan Ilioun°
Was won, and Pyrrus with his straite swerd,
Whan he had hent King Priam by the beerd
And slain him (as saith us *Eneidos*),
540 As maden all the hennes in the cloos,
Whan they had seen of Chauntecleer the sighte.
But sovereignly Dame Pertelote shrighte
Full louder than did Hasdrubales wif

---

515 **gargat** throat   517 **sued** pursued   521 **Friday ... meschaunce**
Friday, Venus' day, was also associated with misfortune   527 **Gaufred**
Geoffrey of Vinsauf, author of the standard textbook of rhetoric used
in medieval schools. It gives rules and examples. His example of a
lamentation treats the death of Richard I, slain on a Friday; he was hit
by an arrow ("shot," line 529)—a somewhat unromantic death for a
king. The Nun's Priest's "apostrophe" in the next paragraph follows
Geoffrey's rules   536 **Ilioun** Troy

Whan that hir husbond hadde lost his lif,
And that the Romains hadden brend Cartage   *545*
(She was so full of torment and of rage
That willfully into the fire she sterte,
And brend hirselven with a stedefast herte).
O woeful hennes, right so criden ye
As, whan that Nero brende the citee   *550*
Of Rome, criden senatoures wives
For that hir husbonds losten all hir lives—
Withouten guilt this Nero hath hem slain.
Now wol I turne to my tale again.

   The sely widwe and eek hir daughtres two   *555*
Herden thise hennes cry and maken wo,
And out at doores sterten they anon
And sien° the fox toward the grove gon
And bare upon his back the cock away,
And criden—"Out, harrow, and weilaway!   *560*
Ha, ha—the fox!" and after him they ran,
And eek with staves many another man—
Ran Colle our dog and Talbot and Gerland,°
And Malkin with a distaff in hir hand,
Ran cow and calf and eek the veray hogges,   *565*
So afered for barking of the dogges
And shouting of the men and women eke!
They runne so hem thought hir herte breke!
They yelleden as feendes doon in helle:
The duckes criden as men wold hem quelle,   *570*
The geese for fere flowen over the trees,
Out of the hive came the swarm of bees:
So hidous was the noise, ah, *ben'dic'te,*
Certes, he Jacke Straw and his meinee°
Ne made never shoutes half so shrille   *575*
Whan that they wolden any Fleming kille,

---

558 **sien** saw   563 **Talbot and Gerland** stock names of dogs, like
Fido and Rover   574 **Jacke ... meinee** Jack Straw was one of the
leaders of the Peasant's Revolt (1381). The Flemings were their com-
petition in labor, and the "meinee" killed many of them

As thilke day was made upon the fox.
Of brass they broughten bemes,° and of box,°
Of horn, of bone, in which they blew and pouped,
580 And therewithal they skriked and they houped
—It seemed as that heven sholde falle!
    Now, goode men, I pray you, herkneth alle:
Lo, how Fortune turneth suddeinly
The hope and pride eek of hir enemy.
585   This cock that lay upon the fox's back,
In all his drede unto the fox he spak
And saide, "Sir: if that I were as ye,
Yet shold I sayn, as wise God helpe me,
'Turneth again, ye proude cherles alle!
590 A veray pestilence upon you falle!
Now am I come unto this woodes side,
Maugree° your heed, the cock shall here abide!
I wol him ete, in faith, and that anon!'"
    The fox answered, "In faith, it shall be don!"—
595 And as he spake that word, all suddeinly
The cock brak from his mouth deliverly,°
And hye upon a tree he fley anon!
And whan the fox saw that the cock was gon,
"Alas!" quod he, "O, Chauntecleer! Alas!
600 I have to you," quod he, "y-done trespass—
In as much as I maked you aferd,
Whan I you hent and brought out of the yerd.
But, sir, I did it in no wicke entente.
Come down! and I shall tell you what I mente.
605 I shall say sooth to you, God help me so."
    "Nay than," quod he, "I shrew° us bothe two,
And first I shrew myself both blood and bones,
If thou beguile me ofter than ones!
Thou shalt namore thurgh thy flatterye
610 Do me to sing and winken with mine eye.

---

578 **bemes** trumpets   578 **box** boxwood   592 **Maugree** in spite of
596 **deliverly** nimbly   606 **shrew** beshrew

For he that winketh whan he sholde see,
All willfully, God let him never thee."°
     "Nay," quod the fox, "but, God yive him meschaunce
That is so undiscreet of governaunce
That jangleth° whan he sholde hold his pees."   615
     Lo, swich it is for to be reccheless°
And necligent and trust on flatterye!
But ye that holden this tale a follye
As of a fox, or of a cock and hen,
Taketh the moralitee, good men.   620
For Saint Paul saith that all that written is
To our doctrine° it is y-writ, ywis:
Taketh the fruit and let the chaff be stille.°
Now goode God, if that it be thy wille,
As saith my Lord, so make us all good men,   625
And bring us to His heighe bliss. Amen.

612 **thee** prosper   615 **jangleth** chatters   616 **reccheless** careless
622 **To our doctrine** for our learning   623 **fruit ... stille** the "fruit"
is the grain of wheat extracted from the "chaff"—i.e., the kernel of
moral truth in a story

THE WIFE OF BATH'S PROLOGUE

Experience, though noon auctoritee°
Were in this world, is right enough for me
To speke of woe that is in marriage.
For lordings, sith I twelve yeer was of age,
Thanked be God that is eterne on live,
Husbands at chirche door° I have had five
(If I so ofte might han wedded be).°
And all were worthy men in hir degree.
But me was told, certain, not long agon is,
That sith that Christ ne went never but ones
To wedding in the Cane of Galilee,
That by the same ensample taught he me
That I ne sholde wedded be but ones.
Herk eek, lo, which a sharp word for the nones,
Beside a welle, Jesus, God and man,
Spak in repreve of the Samaritan:°
"Thou hast y-had five husbandes," quod he,

5
10
15

1 **Experience ... auctoritee** the Wife claims to use experience in presenting her views on marriage. She is right that to the Middle Ages experience was not generally viewed as having validity for establishing truth. Truth was usually claimed by citing "authorities"—the Bible, or "authors" generally—a habit of mind satirized in the Nun's Priest's Tale. It will be seen that the Wife herself cites a good many authorities, no doubt picked up from her fifth husband the clerk   6 **at chirche door** Cf. General Prologue, line 460   7 **If ... be** if I may have been validly married that many times. She raises an important point in moral theology. Chasity was considered the highest grade of perfection; monogamous marriage was a lesser grade, but still righteous. Some felt, however, that "monogamy" meant one could not remarry after the death of one's spouse. This opinion is what troubles her   16 **Samaritan** see *John* 4:6–26

218

"And that ilke man that now hath thee
Is not thine husband." Thus he said certain;
What that he *ment* thereby I can not sayn— 20
But that I ask why that the fifthe man
Was noon husband to the Samaritan?
How many might she have in marriage?
Yet herd I never tellen in mine age
Upon this number diffinicioun. 25
Men may divine and glossen° up and down,
But well I wot, express° withouten lie,
God bade us for to wex and multiplye.
That gentil text can I well understande.
Eek well I wot he said that mine husbande 30
Shold lete fader and moder and take to me.
But of no number mencioun made he
Of bigamy, or of octogamye:
Why shold men than speke of it villainye?

    Lo, here the wise king daun Salomon, 35
I trow he hadde wives mo than oon—
As wolde God it leveful were to me
To be refreshed half so oft as he!
Which° yift of God had he for all his wives!
No man hath swich that in this world alive is! 40
God wot this noble king, as to my wit,
The firste night had many a merry fit
With ech of hem, so well was him on live.
Blessed be God that I have wedded five,
Of which I have picked out the beste, 45
Both of hir nether purse and of hir cheste.°
Diverse scoles maken parfit clerkes,
And diverse practik in many sundry werkes
Maken the werkman parfit sikerly:
Of five husbands' scoleying° am I— 50

26 **divine and glossen** conjecture and write commentaries   27 **express** explicitly   39 **Which** what a (he had seven hundred wives and three hundred concubines according to *I Kings* 11)   46 **nether . . . cheste** lower purse and of their coffer (with a pun on each no doubt)   50 **scoleying** studying

Welcome the sixte whan that ever he shall!
For sith I wol not keep me chaste in all,°
Whan mine husband is fro the world y-gon
Some Christen man shall wedde me anon.
55 For than th'apostle saith that I am free
To wed, a Goddes half, where it liketh me—
He saith that to be wedded is no sinne:
"Bet is to be wedded than to brinne."°
What rekketh me though folk say villainye
60 Of shrewed Lameth and his bigamye?
I wot well Abraham was an holy man,
And Jacob eek, as fer as ever I kan,
And ech of hem had wives mo than two,
And many another holy man also.

65   Where can ye say in any manner age
That heighe God defended° marriage
By express word? I pray you telleth me.
Or where commanded he virginitee?
I wot as well as ye, it is no drede,
70 Th'apostle, whan he speketh of maidenhede,°
He said that precept° thereof had he noon:
Men may *conseil* a woman to be oon,°
But conseiling is no commandement.
He put it in our owne judgement.
75 For hadde God commanded maidenhede,
Than had he dampned wedding with the deede;°
And certes, if there were no seed y-sowe,
Virginitee than whereof shold it growe?°
Paul dorste not commanden at the leeste
80 A thing of which his maister yaf noon heeste.°

---

52 **in all** entirely   58 **Bet ... brinne** it is better to be married than to
burn (*I Corinthians* 7:9); but St. Paul meant to imply that it was best
not to burn (with lust). The Wife shifts the emphasis   66 **defended**
forbade   70 **maidenhede** virginity   71 **precept** commandment
72 **oon** single. *Conseil* refers to the "counsels of perfection"—desir-
able rules for a virtuous life but not commandments all must follow
76 **with the deede** in the act (of commanding)   77–78 **And ...
growe** the argument was used by St. Jerome   80 **heeste** command

The dart° is set up for virginitee:
Catch° whoso may, who renneth best let see.
But this word is not take of every wight,°
But there as God list yive it of his might.
I wot well that th'apostle was a maide;   *85*
But natheless, though that he wrote and saide
He wold that every wight were swich as he,
All nis but *conseil* to virginitee:
And for to been a wife he yaf me leve
Of indulgence. So is it no repreve   *90*
To wedde me if that my make° die,
Without excepcioun of bigamye.°
Al were it° good no woman for to touche,
He ment as in *his* bed or in *his* couche:
For peril is both fire and tow t'assemble°—   *95*
Ye know what this ensample may resemble.
This all and some, he held virginitee
More parfit than wedding in freletee°—
Freletee clepe I but if that he and she
Wold leden all hir life in chastitee.   *100*
I graunt it well—I have noon envye
Though maidenhede preferre bigamye:°
It liketh hem to be clene in body and gost.
Of mine estate° ne wol I make no boost;
For well ye know, a lord in his household   *105*
Ne hath not every vessel all of gold—
Some been of tree,° and doon hir lord servise.
God clepeth folk to him in sundry wise,
And everich hath of God a proper yifte.
Some this, some that, as Him liketh shifte.°   *110*

---

81 **dart** prize (in a race)   82 **Catch** win   83 **take ... wight** applicable to everyone   91 **make** mate   92 **Without ... bigamye** without being charged with bigamy   93 **Al were it** although it is   95 **fire ... assemble** to put fire and flax together   98 **freletee** frailty, imperfection   102 **preferre bigamye** is better than remarrying   104 **estate** state   107 **tree** wood   110 **as ... shifte** as it pleases Him to ordain. She is arguing that the state of virginity is one to which some are especially called; a legitimate view

Virginitee is greet perfeccioun,
And continence eek with devocioun;
But Christ, that of perfeccioun is welle,
Bade not every wight he shold go selle
115 All that he had and yive it to the poore,
And in swich wise follwe him and his foore;°
He spak to hem that wold live parfitly—
And lordings, by your leve, that am not I.
I wol bestow the flower of all mine age°
120 In th'actes and in fruit° of marriage.
    Tell me also, to what conclusioun°
Were members made of generacioun
And of so parfit wise a Wright y-wrought?°
Trusteth right well, they were not made for nought!
125 Gloss whoso wol, and say both up and down
That they were made for purgacioun
Of urine, and our both thinges smalle
Was eek to know a female from a male
And for noon other cause—say ye no?
130 Th'experience wot well it is not so!
So that the clerkes be not with me wrothe,
I say this, that they maked been for bothe—
That is to say, for office° and for ese
Of engendrure, there we not God displese.
135 Why shold men elles in hir bookes sette
That man shall yelde to his wife hir dette?°
Now wherewith shold he make his payement
If he ne used his sely instrument?
Than were they made upon a creature

---

116 **foore** footsteps. She refers to *Matthew* 19:21, a text applied to the monastic life   119 **flower . . . age** best years of my life   120 **fruit** i.e., childbearing; but there is no suggestion that she has children   121 **to what conclusioun** for what purpose   123 **And of . . . y-wrought** and made by so perfectly wise a Creator (or, "Wright" may be "wight" and the line may mean "and a creature made in such a perfect way")   133 **office** their obvious function   136 **dette** the "marriage debt" is the necessity incumbent upon both partners to encourage fidelity by satisfying the other sexually. See *I Corinthians* 7:3

To purge urine, and eek for engendrure.   140
    But I say not that *every* wight is holde°
That hath swich harneis° as I to you tolde
To goon and used hem in engendrure;
Than shold men take of chastitee no cure.
Christ was a maid and shapen as a man,   145
And many a saint sith that the world began,
Yet lived they ever in parfit chastitee.
I nil envye no virginitee.
Let hem be breed of pured whete seed,
And let us wives hote° barly breed—   150
And yet with barly breed, Mark telle can,
Our Lord Jesu refreshed many a man.
In swich estate as God hath cleped us
I wol persevere: I nam not precious.°
In wifehood wol I use mine instrument   155
As freely as my Maker hath is sent;
If I be daungerous,° God yeve me sorrwe.
Mine husband shall it have both eve and morrwe,
Whan that him list come forth and pay his dette.
An husband wol I have, I wol not lette,°   160
Which shall be both my dettour and my thrall,
And have his tribulacioun withal
Upon his flesh, while that I am his wif.
I have the power during all my lif
Upon his proper body, and not he.   165
Right thus th'apostle told it unto me,
And bade our husbands for to love us well.
All this sentence me liketh everydeel . . .

                    *   *   *

    Up stirt the Pardoner and that anon:
"Now dame," quod he, "by God and by Saint John,   170
Ye been a noble prechour in this cas.

---

141 **holde** obliged 142 **harneis** equipment 150 **hote** be called
154 **precious** overly particular 157 **daungerous** sparing, unap-
proachable 160 **lette** conceal it; or, hesitate, desist

I was about to wed a wife! alas,
What shold I bye it on my flesh so dere?°
Yet had I levere wed no wife to-yere."°

175   "Abide," quod she, "my tale is not begunne.
Nay, thou shalt drinken of another tonne,°
Ere that I go, shall savour worse than ale.
And whan that I have told thee forth my tale
Of tribulacioun in marriage,

180   Of which I am expert in all mine age—
This is to say, myself hath been the whippe—
Than maistou chese° whether thou wolt sippe
Of thilke tonne that I shall abroche.°
Be ware of it, ere thou too neigh approche,

185   For I shall tell ensamples mo than ten.
'Whoso that nil be ware by other men,
By him shall other men corrected be.'°
Thise same wordes writeth Ptolomee—
Rede in his *Almageste* and take it there."

190   "Dame, I wold pray you if your will it were,"
Saide this Pardoner, "as ye began,
Tell forth your tale. Spareth for no man,
And teeche us yonge men of your practike."°

"Gladly," quod she, "sith it may you like;

195   But that I pray to all this compaignye,
If that I speke after my fantasye,°
As taketh not agrief° of that I saye:
For mine entente nis but for to playe."

*   *   *

Now sire, than wol I tell you forth my tale.
200   As ever mot I drinke wine or ale,

---

173 **What . . . dere?** Why should I pay such a price?   174 **to-yere**
this year   176 **tonne** barrel   182 **chese** decide   183 **abroche** open
186–87 **Whoso . . . be** he who will not take warning from others, by
him others will be reproved   193 **practlike** experience   196 **after
my fantasye** according to my fancy, as I please   197 **As . . . agrief**
don't take offense

I shall say sooth: tho husbands that I hadde,
As, three of hem were good and two were badde.
The three men were good, and rich, and olde:
Unnethe° mighte they the statute holde
In which that they were bounden unto me—   205
Ye wot well what I mene of° this, pardee.
As help me God, I laughe whan I thinke
How pitously anight I made hem swinke!°
And by my fay, I told of it no stoor:°
They had me yeven hir land and hir tresor—   210
Me needed not do lenger diligence
To win hir love or doon hem reverence.
They loved me so well, by God above,
That I ne told no daintee of° hir love.
A wise woman wol bisy hir ever in oon°   215
To get hir love, ye, there as she hath noon.
But sith I had hem holly in mine hand,
And sith that they had yeven me all hir land,
What shold I take keep hem for to plese,
But it were for my profit and mine ese?   220
I set hem so awerke, by my fay,
That many a night they songen "weilaway."
The bacon was not fet for hem, I trowe,
That some men han in Essex at Dunmowe.°
I governed hem so well after my lawe   225
That ech of hem full blissful was and fawe°
To bring me gaye thinges fro the faire.
They were full glad whan I spak to hem faire,
For God it wot, I chid° hem spitously.
   Now herkneth how I bare me properly,°   230
Ye wise wives that can understande:

204 **Unnethe** hardly   206 **of** by   208 **swinke** work   209 **told . . .
stoor** didn't care anything about it   214 **told no daintee of** put any
value on   215 **ever in oon** always   223–24 **bacon . . . Dunmowe** the
bacon was offered as a prize to any married couple who lived a year
without quarreling or regretting their marriage   226 **fawe** willing
229 **chid** chided   230 **properly** well

Thus shold ye speke and bere hem wrong on hande;°
For half so boldely can there no man
Swere and lien as a woman can.

235   I say not this by wives that been wise,
But if it be whan they hem misavise.°
A wise wife, if that she kan hir good,°
Shall beren him on hond the cow is wood,°
And take witness of hir owne maide

240   Of hir assent.° But herkneth how I saide:
    "Sir olde cainard,° is this thine array?°
Why is my neighebores wife so gay?°
She is honoured overal ther she gooth;
I sit at home, I have no thrifty cloth . . .

245   "What dostou at my neighebores hous?
Is she so fair? Artou so amorous? . . .
    "What roune° ye with our maide, *ben'dic'te*?
Sir olde lechour, let thy japes be!
And if I have a gossib° or a freend,

250   Withouten guilt ye chiden as a feend,
If that *I* walk or play unto *his* hous! . . .
    "Thou comest home as dronken as a mous,
And prechest on thy bench, with yvel preef.°
Thou saist° to me, it is a greet meschief

255   To wed a povre woman for costage.°
And if that she be rich, of heigh parage,°
Than saistou that it is a tormentrye
To suffre hir pride and hir malencolye.

---

232 **bere . . . hande** talk them down, accuse them   236 **But . . . misavise** except when they act inadvisedly   237 **can hir good** knows what's good for her   238 **beren . . . wood** deceive him into believing that the chough is crazy: referring to a folk tale in which a bird (a chough) tells a cuckold of his wife's infidelity but the wife convinces him the chough is crazy   239–40 **take . . . assent** call her maid to testify that she agrees   241 **cainard** dotard   241 **thine array** how you are   242 **gay** well-dressed   247 **roune** whisper   249 **gossib** acquaintance   253 **with yvel preef** bad luck to you   254 **Thou saist . . .** there follows a long compendium of antifeminist clichés   255 **for costage** because of the expense   256 **heigh parage** good family

And if that she be fair, thou veray knave,
Thou saist that every holour° wol hir have—   260
She may no while in chastitee abide
That is assailed upon ech a side.

    "Thou saist some folk desire us for richesse,
Some for our shape, and some for our fairnesse,
And some for she can either sing or daunce,   265
And some for gentilesse and daliaunce,
Some for hir handes and hir armes smalle—
Thus goth all to the devil by thy tale!

    "Thou saist men may not keep a castel wall,
It may so long assailed been overal.°   270
And if that she be foul, thou saist that she
Coveiteth every man that she may see;
For as a spaniel she wol on him lepe,
Till that she finde some man hir to chepe.°
Ne none so grey goose goth there in the lake   275
As, saistou, wol be withoute make;
And saist it is an hard thing for to welde
A thing that no man wol, his thankes, helde.°

    "Thus saistou, lorel,° whan thou gost to bedde,
And that no wise man needeth for to wedde,   280
Ne no man that entendeth unto hevene—
With wilde thunder-dint and firy levene
Mote thy welked° necke be to-broke!

    "Thou saist that dropping houses, and eek smoke,
And chiding wives maken men to flee   285
Out of hir owne houses—a, ben'dic'tee,
What aileth swich an old man for to chide?

    "Thou saist we wives will our vices hide
Till we be fast,° and than we wol hem shewe—
Well may that be a proverb of a shrewe!   290

    "Thou saist that oxen, asses, horse, and houndes,

---

260 **holour** lecher   270 **It...overal** if it is attacked a long time
everywhere   274 **chepe** take   277–78 **welde...helde** control a
thing which no one will willingly hold on to   279 **lorel** wretch
283 **welked** wrinkled   289 **fast** safely married

They been assayed° at diverse stoundes;°
Basins, lavours,° ere that men hem bye,
Spoones, stooles, and all swich husbondrye,°
295   And so be pottes, clothes, and array;
But folk of wives maken noon assay
Till they be wedded—olde dotard shrewe—
And than, saistou, we will our vices shewe.
    "Thou saist also that it displeseth me
300   But if that thou wolt praise my beautee,
And but thou pour alway upon my face,
And clepe me 'faire dame' in every place,
And but thou make a feest on thilke day
That I was born, and make me fresh and gay,
305   And but thou do to my norice° honour,
And to my chamberere° within my bower,
And to my fadres folk, and his allies
—Thus saistou, olde barrel-ful of lies!
    "And yet of our apprentice Janekin,
310   For his crisp heer shining as gold so fin,
And for he squiereth me both up and down,
Yet hastou caught a false suspecioun:
I will him not,° though thou were deed tomorrwe.
    "But tell me this, why hidestou with sorrwe
315   The keyes of thy chest away fro me?
It is my good as well as thine, pardee.
What, weenestou make an idiot of our dame?°
Now by that lord that called is Saint Jame,
Thou shalt not bothe, though that thou were wood,
320   Be maister of my body and of my good:
That one thou shalt forgo, maugree thine eyen.
What helpeth it of me enquere and spyen?
I trow thou woldest lock me in thy chiste.
Thou sholdest saye, 'Wife, go where thee liste.

---

292 **assayed** tried out   292 **stoundes** times   293 **lavours** washbasins
294 **husbondrye**   household   equipment   305 **norice**   nurse
306 **chamberere** chambermaid   313 **I will him not** I don't want him
317 **our dame** me—i.e., "the lady of the house"

Take your disport. I nil leve no talis:°   325
I know you for a trewe wife, dame Alis.'
We love no man that taketh keep or charge
Where that we goon—we wol been at our large.°
Of alle men y-blessed mote he be
The wise astrologen daun Ptolomee,   330
That saith this proverb in his *Almageste*:
'Of alle men his wisdom is hyeste
That rekketh not who hath the world in hande.'
By this proverbe thou shalt understande,
Have thou enough, what thar thee rekke° or care   335
How mirrily that other folkes fare?
For certes, olde dotard, by your leve,
Ye shall han queinte° right enough at eve!
He is too greet a niggard that will werne°
A man to light a candle at his lanterne;   340
He shall han never the lasse light, pardee.
Have thou enough, thee thar not plaine thee!°
    "Thou saist also that if we make us gay
With clothing and with precious array,
That it is peril of our chastitee;   345
And yet with sorrwe thou most enforce thee,°
And say thise wordes in th'apostle's name:
'In habit made with chastitee and shame
Ye women shall apparail you,' quod he,
'And not in tressed heer and gay perree,°   350
As perles ne with gold ne clothes riche.'
After thy text, ne after thy rubriche,
I wol not werk as muchel as a gnat.
Thou saidest this, that I was like a cat:
For whoso wolde senge° a cattes skin,   355
Than wold the cat well dwellen in his inn;

---

325 **leve no talis** believe any tales   328 **large** liberty   335 **thar . . .
rekke** do you need to worry   338 **queinte** sex (*lit.* female genitals)
339 **werne** forbid   342 **thar . . . thee** needn't complain   346 **en-
force thee** back yourself up   350 **perree** jewelry   355 **senge** singe
(to make it shine)

And if the cattes skin be slick and gay,
She wol not dwell in house half a day,
But forth she wol, ere any day be dawed,
360 To shew her skin and goon a-caterwawed.°
This is to say, if I be gay, sir shrewe,
I wol ren out, my borel° for to shewe.
Sir olde fool, what helpeth thee t'espyen?
Though thou pray Argus with his hundred eyen
365 To be my wardecorse,° as he can best,
In faith, he shall not keep me but me lest°—
Yet coud I make his berd,° so mote I thee!
     "Thou saidest eek that there been thinges three,
The whiche thinges troublen all this erthe,
370 And that no wight may endure the ferthe.°
O leve sir shrewe, Jesu short thy lif!
Yet prechestou and saist an hateful wif
Y-rekened° is for one of thise mischaunces.
Been there not none other resemblaunces
375 That ye may liken your parables to,
But if a sely wife be one of tho?
     "Thou liknest eek womanes love to helle,
To barren land ther water may not dwelle;
Thou liknest it also to wilde fir—
380 The more it brenneth, the more it hath desir
To consume everything that brent wol be.
Thou saist, right as wormes shend° a tree,
Right so a wife destroyeth hir husbonde—
This knowen they that been to wives bonde . . ."
385   Lordinges, right thus, as ye han understande,
Bare I stiffly mine old husbands on hande°
That thus they saiden in hir dronkenesse—
And all was false; but that I took witnesse
On Janekin and on my nece also.

---

360 **a-caterwawed** prowling about howling for a mate   362 **borel**
clothes   365 **wardecorse** guardian   366 **but me lest** unless I please
367 **make his berd** pull the wool over his eyes   370 **ferthe** fourth
373 **Y-rekened** named   382 **shend** ruin   386 **Bare . . . on hande**
accused

O Lord, the pain I did hem, and the wo!   390
Full guilteless, by Goddes sweete pine!°
For as an horse I coude bite and whine;
I coude plaine°—and I was in the guilt—
Or elles often time I had been spilt.°
Whoso that first to mille comth first grint.   395
I plained first, so was our werre stint.°
They were full glad t'excusen hem full blive°
Of thing of which they never agilt hir live.°
Of wenches wold I beren hem on hande°
Whan that for sick they might unnethe° stande;   400
Yet tickled I his herte for that he
Wende that I had of him so greet cheertee.°
I swore that all my walking out by nighte
Was for t'espye wenches that he dighte.°
Under that colour had I many a mirthe.   405
For all swich wit is yiven us in our birthe:
Deceite, weeping, spinning God hath yive
To women kindely° while they may live.
And thus of oo thing I avaunte me:°
At end I had the bet in ech degree   410
By sleight or force, or by some manner thing,
As by continuel murmur or grucching:°
Namely,° abedde hadden they meschaunce.
There wold I chide and do hem no plesaunce;
I wold no lenger in the bed abide   415
If that I felt his arm over my side,
Till he had made his raunceon° unto me;
Than wold I suffre° him do his nicetee.
And therefore every man this tale I telle:
Win whoso may, for all is for to selle.°   420

---

391 **pine** suffering   393 **plaine** accuse   394 **spilt** ruined   396 **werre
stint** warfare stopped   397 **blive** hastily   398 **agilt hir live** were guilty
in their lives   399 **Of . . . hande** I would accuse them of seducing girls
400 **might unnethe** could hardly   402 **cheertee** affection   404 **dighte**
lay with   408 **kindely** by nature   409 **avaunte me** boast   412 **gruc-
ching** grumbling   413 **Namely** especially   417 **raunceon** penalty,
ransom   418 **suffre** let   420 **all . . . selle** everything has its price

With empty hand men may no hawkes lure.
For winning° wold I all his lust endure
And make me a feined appetit—
And yet in bacoun° had I never delit!

425 That made me that ever I wold hem chide—
For though the pope had seten hem beside,
I wold not spare hem at hir owne boord.°
For by my truth, I quit° hem word for word.
As help me veray God omnipotent,

430 Though I right now shold make my testament,
I n'owe hem not a word that it nis quit!
I brought it so aboute by my wit
That they most yeve it up as for the beste,
Or elles had we never been in reste.

435 For though he looked as a wood leoun,
Yet shold he fail of his conclusioun.
    Than wold I saye, "Goode lief,° take keep
How meekly looketh Wilkin, oure sheep!
Come neer, my spouse, let me ba° thy cheeke—

440 Ye sholden be all pacient and meeke,
And han a sweete-spiced conscience,
Sith ye so prech of Jobes pacience.
Suffreth alway, sin ye so well can preeche;
And but ye do, certain, we shall you teeche

445 That it is fair to han a wife in pees.
One of us two most bowen, douteless,
And sith a man is more resonable
Than woman is, ye mosten been suffrable.°
What aileth you to grucche thus and grone?

450 Is it for ye wold have my queint alone?
Why, take it all—lo, have it everydeel!
Peter, I shrew you but ye love it well!
For if I wolde sell my *belle chose*
I coude walk as fresh as is a rose;

---

422 **winning** my own advantgage   424 **bacoun** i.e., preserved meat,
not fresh   427 **boord** table   428 **quit** got even with   437 **Goode lief**
dearest   439 **ba** kiss   448 **suffrable** patient

But I wol keep it for your owne tooth.   455
Ye be to blame, by God, I say you sooth!"
—Swich manner wordes hadde we on hande.
Now wol I speke of my ferthe husbande.

                    *   *   *

    My ferthe husband was a revelour:
This is to sayn, he had a paramour.°   460
And I was yong and full of ragerye,°
Stibourn° and strong and jolly as a pie!°
How coud I daunce to an harpe smalle,
And sing, ywis, as any nightingale,
Whan I had drunk a draught of sweete win.   465
Metellius, the foule cherl, the swin,
That with a staff biraft his wife hir lif
For she drank wine, though *I* hadde been his wif,
Ne sholde not han daunted *me* fro drinke.
And after wine on Venus most I thinke.   470
For also siker as° cold engendreth hail,
A likerous mouth most han a likerous tail:
In women vinolent is no defence°—
This knowen lechours by experience.
    But Lord Christ, whan that it remembreth me   475
Upon my youth and on my jolitee,
It tickleth me about mine herte roote!
Unto this day it doth mine herte boote°
That I have had my world° as in my time!
But age, alas, that all wol envenime,   480
Hath me biraft my beautee and my pith°—
Let go, farewell, the devil go therewith!
The flower is gone, there is namore to telle;
The bren° as I best can now most I selle.

---

460 **paramour** mistress   461 **ragerye** passion   462 **Stibourn** stub-
born   462 **pie** magpie   471 **also siker as** as sure as   473 **In . . . de-
fence** in women who drink wine, there's no refusing   478 **boote** good
479 **world** fun   481 **pith** vigor   484 **bren** bran

485 But yet to be right murry wol I fonde.°
       Now wol I tellen of my ferth husbonde.
           I say I had in herte greet despit
       That he of any other had delit,
       But he was quit, by God and by Saint Joce:
490 I made him of the same wood a croce°—
       Not of my body in no foul mannere—
       But, certainly, I made folk swich cheere°
       That in his owne grece I made him frye,
       For anger and for veray jalousye.
495 By God, in erth I was his purgatorye—
       For which I hope his soule be in glorye.
       For God it wot, he sat full oft and sung
       Whan that his shoe full bitterly him wrung.°
       There was no wight save God and he that wiste
500 In many wise how sore I him twiste.°
       He deide whan I came fro Jerusalem;
       And lith y-grave under the roode-beem.°
       Al is his tombe not so curious°
       As was the sepulcre of him Darius,
505 Which that Appelles wroughte subtilly.
       It nis but waste to bury him preciously.
       Let him fare well, God give his soule reste;
       He is now in his grave and in his cheste.

                    *   *   *

           Now of my fifthe husband wol I telle—
510 God let his soule never come in helle!
       And yet was he to me the moste shrewe!°
       That feel I on my ribbes all by rewe°
       And ever shall unto mine ending day.

---

485 **fonde** try   490 **croce** cross   492 **made . . . cheere** treated peo-
ple so   498 **shoe . . . wrung** shoe pinched him   500 **twiste** tortured
502 **lith . . . beem** lies buried in the church under the entrance to the
choir   503 **curious** elaborate   511 **moste shrewe** biggest rascal
512 **all by rewe** one after another

But in our bed he was so fresh and gay,
And therewithal so well coud he me glose° 515
Whan that he wolde han my *belle chose*,
That though he had me beet on every bon,
He coude win again my love anon.
I trow I loved him best for that he
Was of his love daungerous° to me. 520
  We women han, if that I shall not lie,
In this matter a quainte fantasye:°
Waite what° thing we may not lightly have,
Thereafter wol we cry all day and crave.
Forbid us thing, and that desiren we; 525
Press on us fast, and thanne wol we flee.
With daunger oute we all chaffare:°
Greet press at market maketh dere ware,°
And too greet chepe° is holden at litel pris.
This knoweth every woman that is wis. 530
  My fifthe husband—God his soule blesse!—
Which that I took for love and no richesse,
He sometime was a clerk of Oxenford,
And had left scole and went at home to bord
With my gossib,° dwelling in our town— 535
God have hir soul!—hir name was Alisoun;
She knew mine hert and eek my privetee°
Bet than our parish preest, so mote I thee.
To hir biwrayed I my conseil all;°
For had mine husband pissed on a wall, 540
Or done a thing that shold have cost his lif,
To hir, and to another worthy wif,
And to my nece which that I loved well,
I wold han told his conseil everydeel—

---

515 **glose** cajole, please 520 **daungerous** sparing 522 **quainte fantasye** curious fancy 523 **Waite what** whatever 527 **With . . . chaffare** sparingly we give out our wares 528 **Greet . . . ware** a big crowd in the market makes the merchandise expensive 529 **too greet chepe** too much of a bargain 535 **gossib** friend 537 **privetee** secrets 539 **biwrayed . . . all** told all my secrets

545 And so I did full often, God it woot,
    That made his face often red and hot
    For veray shame, and blamed himself for he
    Had told to me so greet a privetee.
    And so bifell that ones in a Lente,
550 So often times I to my gossib wente—
    For ever yet I loved to be gay,
    And for to walk in March, April, and May,
    From house to house, to heere sundry tales—
    That Jankin clerk and my gossib dame Alis
555 And I myself into the feeldes wente.
    Mine husband was at London all that Lente.
    I had the better leiser for to playe,
    And for to see, and eek for to be seye°
    Of lusty folk—what wist I where my grace
560 Was shapen° for to be, or in what place?
    Therefore I made my visitacions
    To vigilies and to processions,°
    To preeching eek, and to thise pilgrimages,
    To plays of miracles and to marriages,
565 And wered upon my gaye scarlet gites;°
    Thise wormes ne thise mothes ne thise mites,
    Upon my peril, fret° hem neveradeel—
    And wostou why? For they were used well.
        Now wol I tellen forth what happed me.
570 I say that in the feeldes walked we,
    Till trewely we had swich daliaunce,°
    This clerk and I, that of my purveyaunce°
    I spak to him and said him how that he,
    If I were widow, sholde wedde me.
575 For certainly, I say for no bobaunce,°
    Yet was I never withouten purveyaunce

---

558 **seye** seen   559–60 **what . . . shapen** how did I know where my
good luck was destined   562 **vigilies . . . processions** religious cere-
monies and processions   565 **wered . . . gites** wore my fine red
cloaks   567 **fret** ate   571 **daliaunce** chitchat, flirtation, intimacy
572 **purveyaunce** foresight   575 **bobaunce** pride

Of marriage n'of other thinges eek.
I hold a mouse's hert not worth a leek
That hath but one hole for to sterte to,
And if that faile than is all y-do.   580
I bare him on hand° he had enchaunted me
(My dame° taughte me that subtiltee).
And eek I said I mette° of him all night:
He wold han slain me as I lay upright
And all my bed was full of veray blood—   585
"But yet I hope that ye shall do me good;
For blood bitokeneth gold, as me was taught."
And all was false—I dreemed of it right naught;
But as I followed ay my dames lore
As well of that as other thinges more.   590
    But now sir—let me see, what shall I sayn? . . .
Aha! by God, I have my tale again—
    Whan that my fourthe husband was on beere,°
I weep algate, and made sorry cheere,
As wives moten, for it is usage,   595
And with my coverchief covered my visage:
But for that I was purveyed of a make,°
I wept but small, and that I undertake.
To chirche was mine husband born a-morrwe
With neighebors that for him maden sorrwe,   600
And Jankin oure clerk was one of tho.
As help me God, whan that I saw him go°
After the beer, me thought he had a paire
Of legges and of feet so clene and faire
That all mine hert I yaf unto his hold.   605
    He was, I trowe, twenty winter old,
And I was forty, if I shall say sooth.
But yet I had alway a coltes tooth:°
Gat-toothed° I was, and that became me well;

---

581 **bare . . . hand** made him think   582 **dame** mother   583 **mette**
dreamed   593 **on beere** on his bier   597 **for . . . make** since I was
provided with a mate   602 **go** walk   608 **coltes tooth** youthful
appetite   609 **Gat-toothed** see General Prologue, line 468

610   I had the prent of Sainte Venus seel.°
     As help me God, I was a lusty oon,
     And fair and rich and yong and well-bigon,°
     And trewly, as mine husbands tolde me,
     I had the beste *quoniam*° mighte be.
615   For certes I am all Venerien
     In feeling, and mine hert is Marcien:
     Venus me yaf my lust, my likerousnesse,
     And Mars yaf me my sturdy hardinesse;
     Mine ascendent was Taur and Mars thereinne—
620   Alas, alas, that ever love was sinne!
     I followed ay mine inclinacioun
     By vertu of my constellacioun;
     That made me I coude not withdrawe
     My chambre of Venus from a good fellawe.
625   Yet have I Martes mark upon my face,
     And also in another privee place.
     For God so wis be my savacioun,
     I loved never by no discrecioun,
     But ever followede mine appetit.
630   Al were he short or long or black or whit,
     I took no keep, so that he liked me,
     How poor he was, ne eek of what degree.
       What shold I say but at the monthes ende
     This jolly clerk, Jankin, that was so hende,°
635   Hath wedded me with greet solempnitee.°
     And to him yaf I all the land and fee
     That ever was me yeven therebefore.
     But afterward repented me full sore:
     He nolde suffer no thing of my list.°
640   By God, he smote me ones on the list°

610 **seel** birthmark. Medieval physiognomists believed that everyone had certain marks imparted at birth through the influence of the stars. The Wife goes on to argue that because of these influences she cannot help being as she is   612 **well-bigon** having a good disposition   614 **quoniam** genitalia   634 **hende** pleasant, clever   635 **greet solempnitee** much ceremony   639 **suffer . . . list** permit any of my desire   640 **list** ear

For that I rent out of his book a leef,
That of the stroke mine ere wex all deef.
Stibourn I was as is a leonesse,
And of my tong a veray jangleresse,
And walk I wold, as I had done biforn,   *645*
From house to house, although he had it sworn;°
For which he often times wolde preeche,
And me of the olde Romain gestes° teeche,
How he Simplicius Gallus left his wif,
And hir forsook for term of all his lif,   *650*
Nought but for open-heveded he hir say°
Looking out at his door upon a day.
Another Romain told he me by name
That, for his wife was at a summer's game°
Withouten his witing, he forsook hir eke;   *655*
And than wold he upon his Bible seeke
That ilke proverb of Ecclesiaste
Where he commandeth and forbedeth faste
Man shall not suffre his wife go roule° aboute;
Than wold he say right thus withouten doute: *660*
"Whoso that buildeth his house all of salwes,°
And pricketh his blinde horse over the falwes,°
And suffreth his wife to go seeken halwes,°
Is worthy to be hanged on the galwes."
But all for nought—I sette not an hawe°   *665*
Of his proverbes n'of his olde sawe.°
Ne I wold not of him corrected be;
I hate him that my vices telleth me,
And so do mo, God wot, of us than I.
This made him with me wood all outrely:°   *670*
I nolde not forbere° him in no cas.
   Now wol I say you sooth, by Saint Thomas,

---

646 **sworn** forbidden   648 **gestes** tales   651 **open . . . say** he saw her
bareheaded   654 **game** midsummer revels, which included plays
659 **roule** roam   661 **salwes** willow branches   662 **falwes** fallow
ground, i.e., plowed fields   663 **halwes** shrines, i.e., on pilgrimages
665 **hawe** hawthorn berry   666 **sawe** saws   670 **wood . . . outrely**
utterly furious   671 **forbere** put up with

Why that I rent out of his book a leef,
For which he smote me so that I was deef.
675 He had a book that gladly night and day
For his disport he wolde rede alway.
He cleped it Valerie and Theofraste,°
At whiche book he lough alway full faste.
And eek there was sometime a clerk at Rome,
680 A cardinal, that highte Saint Jerome,
That made a book again Jovinian.
In which book eek there was Tertulan,°
Crysippus, Trotula, and Hélois
(That was abbesse not fer fro Paris),
685 And eek the *Parables of Salomon,*
Ovides *Art,* and bookes many oon—
And alle thise were bounden in oo volume.
And every night and day was his custume
Whan he had leiser and vacacioun
690 From other worldly occupacioun,
To reden in this book of wicked wives.
He knew of hem mo legendes and lives
Than been of goode wives in the Bible!
For trusteth well, it is an impossible
695 That any clerk wol speke good of wives,
But if° it be of holy saintes lives,
N'of noon other woman never the mo.
Who paintede the leon,° tell me who?
By God, if *women* hadde written stories,
700 As clerkes han within hir oratories,
They wold han written of men more wickednesse
Than all the mark of Adam° may redresse.

677 **Valerie and Theofraste** these were the presumed authors of two
widely read treatises urging men not to marry; they often appeared in
manuscripts along with antifeminist treatises, some of which are listed
below   682 **Tertulan** Tertullian (d. 225), a church father who wrote
in favor of chastity   696 **But if** unless   698 **paintede the leon** the
tale referred to is this: a man shows a lion a picture of a man killing a
lion; the lion replies, "If the artist had been a lion, the picture would
be different."   702 **mark of Adam** i.e., men

The children of Mercúrye and Venus
Been in hir werking full contrarious:
Mercúrye loveth wisdom and science,   *705*
And Venus loveth riot and dispence;
And for hir diverse disposicioun
Ech falleth in other's exaltacioun,
And thus, God wot, Mercúrye is desolat
In Pisces where Venus is exaltat,   *710*
And Venus falleth ther Mercúrye is raised:°
Therefore, no woman of no clerk is praised.
The clerk, whan he is old and may not do
Of Venus' werkes worth his olde shoe,
Than sit he down and write in his dotage   *715*
That women can not keep hir marriage!
    But now to purpose why I tolde thee
That I was beten for a book, pardee:
Upon a night Jankin, that was our sire,°
Reed on his book as he sat by the fire   *720*
Of Eva first, that for hir wickednesse,
Was all mankinde brought to wretchednesse,
For which that Jesus Christ himself was slain
That bought us with his herte blood again—
Lo, here express° of women may ye finde   *725*
That woman was the loss of all mankinde!
    Tho reed he me how Samson lost his heres°—
Sleeping, his lemman kit° it with hir sheres,
Thurgh which treson lost he both his eyen.
    Tho reed he me, if that I shall not lien,   *730*
Of Hercules and of his Dianire,
That caused him to set himself afire.
    No thing forgat he the sorrwe and the wo
That Socrates had with his wives two:

703–11 **The children . . . raised** Venus and Mars are opposites, so that
when one is in "exaltation" among planets the other is "desolate," i.e.,
without influence. She is not equating Mars with clerks and Venus with
women; she is saying that as Venus' influence wanes, Mars' increases
719 **our sire** my husband   725 **express** explicitly   727 **heres** hair
728 **lemman kit** lover cut

735 How Xantippa cast piss upon his heed—
   This sely man sat still as he were deed;
   He wiped his heed, namore dorst he sayn
   But "Ere that thonder stint, cometh a rain."
        Of Phasipha° that was the queen of Crete—
740 For shrewedness him thought the tale sweete—
   Fy, speek namore! it is a grisly thing
   Of hir horrible lust and hir liking!
        Of Clytermistra for hir lecherye
   That falsely made hir husband for to die,
745 He reed it with full good devocioun.
        He told me eek for what occasioun
   Amphiorax at Thebes lost his lif:
   Mine husband had a legend of his wif
   Eriphylem, that for an ouche° of gold
750 Hath prively unto the Greekes told
   Where that hir husband hid him in a place,
   For which he had at Thebes sorry grace.
        Of Livia told he me and of Lucie;
   They bothe made hir husbands for to die,
755 That one for love, that other was for hate.
   Livia hir husband on an even late
   Empoisoned hath for that she was his fo.
   Lucia likerous loved hir husband so
   That for he shold alway upon hir thinke,
760 She yaf him such a manner love-drinke
   That he was deed ere it were by the morrwe.
   And thus algates° husbandes han sorrwe.
        Than told he me how one Latumius
   Complained unto his fellaw Arrius
765 That in his garden growed swich a tree,
   On which he said how that his wives three
   Hanged hemself for herte despitous.
   "O leve brother," quod this Arrius,
   "Yif me a plant of thilke blessed tree,

739 **Phasipha** Pasiphaë, who was enamored of a bull   749 **ouche**
ornament   762 **algates** either way

And in my garden planted shall it be." 770
   Of latter date of wives hath he red
That some han slain hir husbands in hir bed
And let hir lechour dight hir all the night,
Whan that the corpse lay in the floor upright.
And some han driven nailes in hir brain 775
While that they sleep, and thus they han hem slain.
Some han hem yeven poison in hir drinke.
He spak more harm than herte may bithinke;
And therewithal he knew of mo proverbes
Than in this world there growen grass or herbes: 780
"Bet is,"° quod he, "thine habitacioun
Be with a leon or a foul dragoun
Than with a woman using for to chide."
"Bet is," quod he, "hye in the roof abide
Than with an angry wife down in the hous; 785
They been so wicked and contrarious,
They haten that hir husbands loven, ay."
He said, "A woman cast hir shame away
Whan she cast off hir smock." And furthermo,
"A fair woman, but she be chaste also, 790
Is like a gold ring in a sowes nose."
   Who wolde ween or who wolde suppose
The woe that in mine herte was and pine?
And whan I saw he wolde never fine°
To reden on this cursed book all night, 795
All suddenly three leves have I plight°
Out of his book right as he red, and eke
I with my fist so took° him on the cheeke
That in our fire he fill backward adown.
And he up stirt as doth a wood leoun 800
And with his fist he smote me on the heed
That in the floor I lay as I were deed!
And whan he saw how stille that I lay,
He was aghast, and wold han fled his way—

781 **Bet is** it is better   794 **fine** cease   796 **plight** torn   798 **took** hit

805 Till atte last out of my swough I braide.°
        "O, hastou slain me, false theef," I saide,
     And for my land thus hastou mordred me?
     Ere I be deed yet wol I . . . kisse thee . . ."
     And neer he came and kneeled fair adown
810 And saide, "Dere suster Alisoun,
     As help me God, I shall thee never smite.
     That I have done, it is thyself to wite.°
     Foryeve it me, and that I thee beseeke."
     And yet, eftsoones, I hit him on the cheeke,
815 And saide: "Theef, thus muchel am I wreke.°
     Now wol I die; I may no lenger speke."
        But at the last with muchel care and wo
     We fill accorded by us selven two.
     He yaf me all the bridel in mine hand,
820 To han the govenaunce of house and land,
     And of his tonge and of his hand also;
     And made him bren his book anonright tho.°
     And whan that I had geten unto me
     By maistry all the sovereignetee,
825 And that he said "Mine owne trewe wif,
        Do as thee lust the term of all thy lif,
     Keep thine honour, and keep eek mine estat"—
     After that day we hadden never debat!
     God help me so, I was to him as kinde
830 As any wife from Denmark unto Inde,
     And also trew, and so was he to me.
     I pray to God that sit in majestee,
     So bless his soule for his mercy dere!
     Now wol I say my tale, if ye wol heere.

                    *   *   *

835 The Frere lough whan he had herd all this.
     "Now dame," quod he, "so have I joy or bliss,

805 **out . . . braide** I came out of my faint   812 **to wite** to blame
815 **wreke** avenged; it is evidently a feeble slap   822 **And . . . tho**
and I made him burn his book right then and there

This is a long preamble of a tale!"
   And whan the Somnour herd the Frere gale,°
"Lo," quod the Somnour, "Goddes armes two!
A frere wol entremette him° evermo!   *840*
Lo, goode men, a fly and eek a frere
Wol fall in every dish and eek mattere.
What spekestou of preambulacioun?
What, amble or trot or pees° or go sit down!
Thou lettest our disport in this mannere."   *845*
   "Ye? woltou so, sir Somnour?" quod the Frere.
"Now by my faith, I shall ere that I go
Tell of a somnour swich a tale or two
That all the folk shall laughen in this place."
   "Now elles, Frere, I wol bishrew thy face,"   *850*
Quod this Somnour, "and I bishrew me,
But if I telle tales two or three
Of freres, ere I come to Sidingborne,
That I shall make thine herte for to moorne.
For well I wot thy pacience is goon."   *855*
   Our Hoste cried, "Pees, and that anoon!"
And saide, "Let the woman tell hir tale.
Ye fare as folk that dronken been of ale!
Do, dame, tell forth your tale, and that is best."
   "All redy, sir," quod she, "right as you lest—   *860*
If I have license of this worthy Frere."
   "Yis, dame," quod he, "tell forth and I wol heere."

---

838 **gale** sing out   840 **entremette him** stick his nose in   844 **pees**
hold your peace; or, perhaps, "pace"

THE WIFE OF BATH'S TALE

In th'olde dayes of the King Arthour
Of which that Britons speken greet honour
All was this land fulfilled of faïrye:
The elf-queen with hir jolly compaignye
5   Daunced full oft in many a greene mede—
This was the old opinioun as I rede°—
I speke of many hundred yeers ago.
But now can no man see none elves mo,
For now the greet charitee and prayeres
10   Of limitours,° and other holy freres,
That serchen every land and every streem,
As thick as motes° in the sunne-beem,
Blessing halles, chambres, kitchens, bowres,
Citees, burghes, castles, hye towres,
15   Thropes, bernes, shipnes,° dayeries—
This maketh that there been no fairies.
For there as wont to walken was an elf
There walketh now the limitour himself,
In undermeles° and in morweninges,
20   And saith his matins and his holy thinges
As he goth in his limitacioun.
Women may go now saufly up and down:
In every bush or under every tree
There is noon other incubus° but he—
25   And he ne wol doon hem but° dishonour.
    And so bifell that this King Arthour
Had in his house a lusty bacheler

---

6 **rede** understand   10 **limitours** see General Prologue, line 209
12 **motes** specks of dust   15 **Thropes … shipnes** villages, barns,
cowsheds   19 **undermeles** late mornings   24 **incubus** an evil spirit
which was supposed to lay with a woman while she slept, making her
pregnant with a demon child   25 **ne … but** won't do anything to
them except

That on a day came riding fro river,
And happed that, alone as he was born,
He saw a maide walking him biforn;   30
Of whiche maid anon, maugree hir heed,
By very force he raft hir maidenheed.°
For which oppressioun was swich clamour,
And swich pursuit° unto the King Arthour,
That dampned was this knight for to be deed   35
By course of law, and shold han lost his heed
(Paraventure swich was the statute tho)
But that the queen and other ladies mo
So longe prayeden the king of grace,
Till he his life him graunted in the place,   40
And yaf him to the queen, all at hir wille,
To chese whether she wold him save or spille.°
    The queen thanked the king with all hir might,
And after this thus spak she to the knight
Whan that she saw hir time upon a day: 45
"Thou standest yet," quod she, "in swich array°
That of thy life yet hastou no suretee.
I graunt thee life if thou canst tellen me
What thing is it that women most desiren.
Be ware and keep thy necke-bone from iren.°   50
And if thou canst not tellen me anon,
Yet wol I yeve thee leve for to gon
A twelfmonth and a day to seech and lere
An answer suffisant in this mattere;
And suretee wol I han ere that thou pace,   55
Thy body for to yeelden in this place."
    Woe was this knight, and sorrwefully he siketh.°
But what!—he may not do all as him liketh;
And atte last he chees him for to wende
And come again right at the yeeres ende,   60
With swich answer as God wold him purveye,

32 **raft hir maidenheed** took her virginity   34 **pursuit** suing for
justice   42 **spille** let die   46 **array** condition   50 **iren** i.e., the ax
57 **siketh** sighs

And taketh his leve and wendeth forth his waye.
   He seeketh every house and every place
Where as he hopeth for to finde grace,
65   To lerne what thing women loven most.
But he ne coud arriven in no cost°
Where as he mighte find in this mattere
Two creatures according in fere.°
Some saiden women loven best richesse;
70   Some said honour, some saide jolinesse,
Some rich array, some saiden lust abedde,
And ofte time to be widow and wedde,
Some saide that our herte is most esed
Whan that we been y-flattered and y-plesed—
75   He goth full neigh the sooth, I wol not lie:
A man shall win us best with flatterye,
And with attendaunce and with bisinesse
Been we y-limed,° bothe more and lesse.
And some sayen that we loven best
80   For to be free, and do right as us lest,
And that no man repreve us of our vice,
But say that we be wise and nothing nice.°
For trewely, there is none of us alle,
If any wight wol claw us on the galle,°
85   That we nil kicke for he saith us sooth:°
Assay and he shall find it that so dooth.
For be we never so vicious withinne,
We wol be holden wise and clene of sinne.
And some sayn that greet delit han we
90   For to be holden stable and eek secree,°
And in oo purpose stedfastly to dwelle,
And not biwraye thing that men us telle—
But *that* tale is not worth a rake-stele.°

---

66 **cost** coast, region   68 **in fere** with each other   78 **y-limed** caught
82 **nice** foolish   84 **claw . . . galle** scratch us on a sore spot
85 **for . . . sooth** because he tells us the truth   90 **holden . . . secree**
considered dependable and able to keep a secret   93 **rake-stele** rake-
handle

Pardee, we women conne no thing hele:°
Witness on Mida.° Wol ye heer the tale?   *95*
　Ovid, amonges other thinges smalle,
Said Mida had under his longe heeres,
Growing upon his heed, two asses eres,
The whiche vice he hid as he best mighte
Full subtilly from every mannes sighte,   *100*
That save his wife there wist of it namo.
He loved hir most and trusted hir also.
He prayed hir that to no creature
She sholde tellen of his disfigure.
She swore him nay, for all this world to winne,   *105*
She nolde do that villainy or sinne
To make hir husband han so foul a name—
She nold not tell it for hir owen shame.
But natheless, hir thoughte that she dyde,
That she so longe shold a conseil hide;   *110*
Hir thought it swal so sore about hir herte
That needely some word hir most asterte,°
And sith she dorst not tell it to no man,
Down to a maris° faste by she ran—
Till she came there hir herte was afire!   *115*
And as a bitore bombleth in the mire,°
She laid hir mouth unto the water down:
"Biwray me not, thou water, with thy soun,"
Quod she. "To thee I tell it and namo:
Mine husband hath long asses eres two!   *120*
Now is mine hert all whole, now is it oute!
I might no lenger keep it, out of doute."
(Here may ye see, though we a time abide,
Yet out it moot—we can no conseil hide.)
The remnant of the tale if ye wol heere,   *125*
Redeth Ovid, and there ye may it lere.

94 **hele** conceal　95 **Mida** Midas　112 **asterte** escape　114 **maris**
marsh　116 **bitore . . . mire** bittern (a heronlike bird) makes booming
noises in the mud (i.e., while sticking his bill in mud). It used to be
thought the bird made its noise thus

This knight of which my tale is specially,
Whan that he saw he might not come thereby—
This is to say what women loven most—
130 Within his brest full sorrweful was the gost.°
But home he goth, he mighte not sojourne;
The day was come that homeward most he turne.
And in his way it happed him to ride,
In all this care, under a forest side,
135 Where as he saw upon a daunce go
Of ladies four and twenty and yet mo;
Toward the whiche daunce he drow full yerne,°
In hope that some wisdom shold he lerne.
But certainly, ere he came fully there,
140 Vanished was this daunce, he niste where!
No creature saw he that bare lif,
Save on the green he saw sitting a wif:
A fouler wight there may no man devise!
Again the knight this olde wife gan rise,
145 And said, "Sir knight, here forth ne lith no way.
Tell me what ye seeken, by your fay.
Paraventure it may the better be:
Thise olde folk kon muchel thing," quod she.
     "My leve moder," quod this knight, "certain,
150 I nam but deed but if that I can sayn
What thing it is that women most desire.
Coud ye me wisse, I wold well quit your hire."°
     "Plight me thy trouth here in mine hand," quod she:
"The nexte thing that I requere thee,
155 Thou shalt it do, if it lie in thy might,
And I wol tell it you ere it be night."
     "Have here my trouthe," quod the knight, "I graunte."
     "Thanne," quod she, "I dare me well avaunte°
Thy life is sauf, for I wol stand thereby.
160 Upon my life the queen wol say as I.
Let see which is the proudest of hem alle

130 **gost** spirit   137 **yerne** eagerly   152 **Coud ... hire** if you could
teach me, I would pay you well   158 **avaunte** boast

That wereth on° a coverchief or a calle°
That dare say nay of that I shall thee teche.
Let us go forth withouten lenger speeche."
Tho rouned she a pistel° in his ere   *165*
And bade him to be glad and have no fere.

     Whan they be comen to the court, this knight
Said he had hold his day as he had hight,°
And redy was his answer, as he saide.
Full many a noble wife, and many a maide,   *170*
And many a widow (for that they been wise),
The queen hirself sitting as justise,
Assembled been his answer for to heere,
And afterward this knight was bode appere.
To every wight commanded was silence,   *175*
And that the knight shold tell in audience
What thing that worldly women loven best.
This knight ne stood not still as doth a beest,
But to his questioun anon answerde
With manly voice that all the court it herde: *180*
"My liege lady, generally," quod he,
"Women desire to have sovereigntee
As well over hir husband as hir love,
And for to been in maistry° him above.
This is your most desire, though ye me kille.   *185*
Doth as you list: I am here at your wille."

     In all the court ne was there wife ne maide
Ne widow that contraried that he saide,
But saiden he was worthy han his lif.

     And with that word up stert that olde wif,   *190*
Which that the knight saw sitting on the greene;
"Mercy," quod she, "my sovereign lady queene!
Ere that your court departe, do me right.
I taughte this answer unto the knight,
For which he plighte me his trouthe there   *195*

---

162 **wereth on** has on   162 **calle** hairnet   165 **rouned . . . pistel** she
whispered a little message   168 **hight** agreed   184 **maistry** mastery,
domination

The firste thing I wolde him requere
He wold it do, if it lay in his might.
Before the court than pray I thee, sir knight,"
Quod she, "that thou me take unto thy wif;
200 For well thou wost that I have kept thy lif.
If I say false, say nay, upon thy fay."
　　This knight answered, "Alas and weilaway!
I wot right well that swich was my biheste.
For Goddes love, as chees a new requeste:
205 Take all my good and let my body go."
　　"Nay than," quod she, "I shrew us bothe two.
For though that I be foul, and old, and poore,
I nold for all the metal ne for ore
That under erth is grave or lith above,
210 But if thy wife I were, and eek thy love."
　　"My *love*!" quod he, "nay my dampnacioun!
Alas, that any of my nacioun
Shold evere so foul disparaged° be."
　　But all for nought, the end is this, that he
215 Constrained was: he needes must hir wedde—
And taketh his olde wife and goth to bedde.
　　Now wolden some men say, paraventure,
That for my negligence I do no cure
To tellen you the joy and all th'array
220 That at the feeste was that ilke day.
To which thing shortly answere I shall:
I say there nas no joy ne feest at all.
There nas but heviness and muche sorrwe.
For prively he wedded hir on morrwe,
225 And all day after hid him as an owle,
So woe was him, his wife looked so foule.
　　Greet was the woe the knight had in his thought.
Whan he was with his wife abedde brought,
He wallweth° and he turneth to and fro.
230 His olde wife lay smiling evermo,
And said, "O dere husband, *ben'dic'te!*

213 **disparaged** disgraced   229 **wallweth** tosses

Fareth every knight thus with his wife as ye?
Is this the law of King Arthoures hous?
Is every knight of his thus dangerous?°
I am your owne love and youre wif.   235
I am she which that saved hath your lif.
And certes yet ne did I you never unright.
Why fare ye thus with me this firste night?
Ye faren like a man had lost his wit.
What is my guilt? For Goddes love, tell it,   240
And it shall been amended if I may."
    "Amended!" quod this knight. "Alas, nay, nay,
It wol not been amended neveremo.
Thou art so lothly and so old also,
And thereto comen of so low a kinde,°   245
That litel wonder is though I wallwe and winde.
So wolde God mine herte wolde breste!"
    "Is this," quod she, "the cause of your unreste?"
    "Ye, certainly," quod he. "No wonder is."
    "Now sir," quod she, "I coud amend all this,   250
If that me list, ere it were dayes three,
So° well ye mighte bere you unto me.
But for ye speken of swich gentilesse
As is descended out of old richesse°—
That therefore sholden ye be gentilmen—   255
Swich arrogance is not worth an hen.
Look who that is most vertuous alway,
Privee and apert, and most entendeth ay
To do the gentil deedes that he can,
Take him for the greetest gentilman.   260
Christ wol we claim of Him our gentilesse,
Not of our elders for hir old richesse.
For though they yeve us all hir heritage,

234 **dangerous** sparing 245 **kinde** class, family 252 **So** so that
253–54 **swich . . . richesse** such refinement and prestige as is derived
from inherited wealth. The hag's harangue which follows is an amal-
gam of medieval commonplaces about true nobility, the false value of
youth, wealth, beauty, etc. The hag, like the Wife herself, harangues
her husband into submission

For which we claim to been of heigh parage,°
265 Yet may they not biquethe for no thing
To none of us hir vertuous living,
That made him gentilmen y-called be,
And bade us follwen hem in swich degree.
Well can the wise poet of Florence,
270 That highte Dant', speken in this sentence—
Lo, in swich manner rym is Dante's tale:
'Full selde up riseth by his braunches smalle
Prowess of man, for God of his prowesse
Wol that of him we claim our gentilesse.'
275 For of our elders may we no thing claime
But temporel thing that man may hurt and maime.
Eek every wight wot this as well as I,
If gentilesse were planted naturelly
Unto a certain linage down the line,
280 Privee and apert, than wold they never fine°
To doon of gentilesse the fair office—
They mighte do no villainy or vice.
Take fire, and beer it in the derkest hous
Bitwix this and the Mount of Caucasous,
285 And let men shet the doores and go thenne,
Yet wol the fire as faire lie and brenne
As twenty thousand men might it biholde:
His office naturel ay wol it holde,
Up peril of my life, till that it die.
290 Here may ye see well how that genterye°
Is not annexed to possessioun,
Sith folk ne doon hir operacioun
Alway, as doth the fire, lo, in his kinde.
For God it wot, men may well often finde
295 A lordes son do shame and villainye;
And he that wol han pris of his gentrye,
For he was boren of a gentil hous
And had his elders noble and vertuous,
And nil himselven do no gentil deedis,

264 **parage** lineage   280 **fine** cease   290 **genterye** gentility

Ne follwen his gentil auncestre that deed is,   *300*
He nis not gentil, be he duc or erl;
For villaines sinful deedes make a cherl.
For gentilesse nis but renomee°
Of thine auncestres for hir heigh bountee,°
Which is a straunge thing for thy persone.°   *305*
Thy gentilesse cometh fro God alone.
Than comth our veray gentilesse of grace:
It was nothing biqueth us with our place.°
Thenketh how noble, as saith Valerius,
Was thilke Tullius Hostilius   *310*
That out of poverte rose to heigh noblesse.
Redeth Senek, and redeth eek Boece:
There shull ye seen express that no drede is°
That he is gentil that doth gentil deedis.
And therefore, leve husband, I thus conclude: *315*
Al were it that mine auncestres were rude,
Yet may the hye God—and so hope I—
Graunte me grace to liven vertuously.
Than am I gentil whan that I beginne
To liven vertuously and waive° sinne.   *320*
    And there as ye of poverte me repreve,
The hye God, on whom that we beleve,
In willful poverte chees to live his lif;
And certes every man, maiden, or wif
May understond that Jesus, hevene King,   *325*
Ne wold not chese a vicious living.
Glad poverte is an honest thing, certain.
This wol Senek and other clerkes sayn.
Whoso that halt him paid of° his poverte,
I hold him rich al had he not a sherte;   *330*
He that coveiteth is a poore wight,
For he wold han that is not in his might.

---

303 **renomee** renown   304 **bountee** goodness   305 **straunge . . .
persone** a thing foreign to your own person   308 **It . . . place** it was
not left to us with our social position   313 **express . . . is** explicitly
stated that there is no doubt   320 **waive** avoid   329 **halt . . . of** con-
siders himself content with

But he that nought hath, ne coveiteth to have,
Is rich, although we hold him but a knave.
335 Veray poverte it singeth properly.°
Juvenal saith of poverte, 'Mirrily
The poore man, whan he goth by the waye,
Biforn the theves he may sing and playe.'
Poverte is hateful good, and as I guesse,
340 A full greet bringer out of bisinesse;
A greet amender eek of sapience
To him that taketh it in pacience.
Poverte is this, although it seem alenge,°
Possessioun that no wight wol challenge.
345 Poverte full often, whan a man is lowe,
Maketh his God and eek himself to knowe.°
Poverte a spectacle° is, as thinketh me,
Thurgh which he may his veray° freendes see.
And therefore, sir, sin that I not you greve,
350 Of my poverte namore ye me repreve.
    Now sir, of elde ye repreve me:
And certes, sir, though noon auctoritee
Were in no book, ye gentils of honour
Sayn that men shold an old wight doon favour,
355 And clepe him fader for your gentilesse—
And auctours shall I finden, as I guesse.
    Now there ye say that I am foul and old:
Than dred you not to been a cokewold,
For filth° and elde, also mote I thee,
360 Been grete wardeins° upon chastitee.
But natheless, sin I know your delit,
I shall fulfill your worldly appetit.
    Chees now," quod she, "one of thise thinges tweye:
To han me foul and old till that I deye
365 And be to you a trewe humble wif

---

335 **Veray . . . properly** true poverty sings naturally   343 **alenge**
miserable   346 **Maketh . . . to knowe** causes him to know
347 **spectacle** eyeglass   348 **veray** true   359 **filth** ugliness
360 **wardeins** guardinas

And never you displese in all my lif;
Or elles ye wol han me yong and fair
And take your aventure of the repair°
That shall be to your house by cause of me—
Or in some other place, may well be.   370
Now chees yourselven wheither that you liketh."

   This knight aviseth him,° and sore siketh;
But atte last he said in this mannere:
"My lady and my love, and wife so dere,
I put me in your wise governaunce: 375
Cheeseth yourself which may be most plesaunce
And most honour to you and me also.
I do no fors° the wheither of the two,
For as you liketh it suffiseth me."

   "Than have I get of you maistry," quod she,   380
"Sin I may chees and govern as me lest?"

   "Ye, certes, wife," quod he, "I hold it best."

   "Kiss me," quod she. "We be no lenger wrothe.
For by my trouth, I wol be to you bothe—
This is to sayn, ye, bothe fair and good.   385
I pray to God that I mote sterven wood,°
But I to you be all so good and trewe
As ever was wife sin that the world was newe.
And but I be tomorn as fair to seene
As any lady, emperice, or queene,   390
That is bitwix the est and eek the west,
Do with my life and deeth right as you lest:
Cast up the curtin, look how that it is."

   And whan the knight saw veraily all this,
That she so fair was and so yong thereto,   395
For joy he hent hir in his armes two,
His herte bathed in a bath of blisse!
A thousand time a-row he gan hir kisse.
And she obeyed him in every thing

---

368 **take . . . repair** take your chance on the visiting   372 **aviseth him** thinks it over   378 **I . . . fors** I don't care   386 **sterven wood** die insane

400 That mighte do him plesance or liking.
        And thus they live unto hir lives ende
     In parfit joy. And Jesu Christ us sende
     Husbandes meeke, yong, and fresh abedde—
     And grace to overbide° hem that we wedde.
405 And eek I praye Jesu shorte hir lives
     That not wol be governed by hir wives.
     And old and angry niggards of dispence°
     —God send hem soon a veray pestilence!

404 **overbide** outlive   407 **of dispence** in spending

THE CLERK'S PROLOGUE

"Sir Clerk of Oxenford," our Hoste saide,
"Ye ride as coy and still as doth a maide
Were newe spoused, sitting at the boord.
This day ne herd I of your tonge a word;
I trow ye study aboute some sophime.°   5
But Salomon saith, 'Every thing hat time.'
For Goddes sake, as beth of better cheere!
It is no time for to studyen here—
Tell us some murry tale, by your fay!
For what man that is entered in a play,°   10
He needes mot unto the play assente;
But precheth not, as freres doon in Lente,
To make us for our olde sinnes weepe—
Ne that thy tale make us not to sleepe.
Tell us some murry thing of aventures.   15
Your termes, your colours, and your figures,°
Keep hem in store till so be ye endite
High style, as whan that men to kinges write.
Speketh so plain at this time, we you praye,
That we may understande what ye saye."   20
   This worthy Clerk benignely answerde:
"Host," quod he, "I am under your yerde.°
Ye han of us as now the governaunce,
And therefore wol I do you obeisaunce
As fer as reson asketh, hardily.   25
I wol you tell a tale which that I

5 **study . . . sophime** muse over some logic-chopping   10 **play** game
16 **termes . . . figures** terminology of rhetoric, your figures of speech,
and your rhetorical devices   22 **yerde** rule

Lerned at Padwe° of a worthy clerk,
As preved by his wordes and his werk.
He is now deed and nailed in his cheste—
30   I pray to God so yive his soule reste:
Frauncis Petrak,° the lauriat poete,
Highte this clerk, whose rhetorike sweete
Enlumined all Itaile of poetrye,
As Linian° dide of philosophye,
35   Or law, or other art particuler.
But deeth, that wol not suffre us dwellen heer
But as it were a twinkling of an eye,
Hem both hath slain; and alle shull we die.
But forth to tellen of this worthy man
40   That taughte me this tale, as I began,
I say that first with high style he enditeth,
Ere he the body of his tale writeth,
A prohemie° in which descriveth he
Pemond, and of Saluces° the contree,
45   And speketh of Appenin, the hilles hye
That been the boundes of West Lumbardye,
And of Mount Vesulus in special,
Wher as the Po, out of a welle small,
Taketh his firste springing and his sours
50   That estward ay encresseth in his cours
To Emeleward, to Ferrare and Venice,
The which a long thing were to devise.
And trewely, as to my judgement,
Me thinketh it a thing impertinent,
55   Save that he wol conveyen his mattere;
But this his tale, which that ye shall heere."

27 **Padwe** Padua   31 **Frauncis Petrak** Petrarch (d. 1374) was the
great humanist scholar and poet. The Clerk's Tale is based on his Latin
translation of a tale by Boccaccio; he translated it because, he said, it
had moved him to tears and he wished to preserve it for posterity. It is
sometimes imagined, on the basis of this line, that Chaucer met Pe-
trarch during his Italian voyage   34 **Linian** Giovanni di Lignano (d.
1383), professor of canon law at Bologna   43 **prohemie** prologue
44 **Pemond, Saluces** Piedmont, Saluzzo

[The Clerk's Tale, omitted here, is a long and idealistic story of the young peasant girl Griselda, whom a young nobleman, Walter, selects for his wife. He chooses her in response to the request of his people that he marry and produce an heir; his choice seems a mockery of their wishes, and he proceeds to abuse Griselda cruelly. He even claims to send their children off to be slain— because the fickle people wish it—and finally pretends to renounce her and take another wife. Griselda bears her fortunes with incredible patience, making Job-like and solemn, though increasingly dogged, avowals of submission. Finally Walter reveals that he has been testing her, and restores their children out of hiding. Griselda swoons with joy and, for the first time, weeps. They live happily after.

The interesting twist is the ending, in which the idealistic young clerk adds—in the true spirit of the university—an ironic admission that such ideals are little followed. He mentions the Wife of Bath with ironic deference, and ends by turning all into high camp with an improbable song (called "L'Envoy de Chaucer" in the manuscripts), using but three rhymes, in praise of female domination. This ending follows—Ed.]

THE CLERK'S EPILOGUE

This story is said not for that wives sholde
Follwen Grisilde as in humilitee—
For it were importable° though they wolde—
But for that every wight in his degree
Shold be constant in adversitee,   5
As was Grisilde. Therefore, Petrak writeth
This story, which with high style he endicteth.

For sith a woman was so pacient
Unto a moral man, well more us oughte

3 **were importable** would be unbearable

10   Receiven all in gree° that God us sent.
      For greet skile is, he preve that he wroughte:°
      But he ne tempteth no man that he boughte,°
      As saith Saint Jame, if ye his pistel° rede—
      He preveth folk alday, it is no drede,

15   And suffreth us, as for our exercise,
      With sharpe scourges of adversitee
      Full ofte to be bete in sundry wise—
      Not for to know our will, for certes he
      Ere we were born knew all our freletee;°
20   And for our best is all his governance.
      Let us than live in vertuous suffrance.°

      But oo word, lordinges, herkneth ere I go:
      It were full hard to finde nowadayes
      In all a town Grisildes three or two,
25   For if that they were put to swiche assayes,°
      The gold of hem hath now so bad allayes
      With brass, that though the coin be fair at eye,
      It wolde rather breste atwo than plye.°

      For which, here for the Wives love of Bathe—
30   Whose life and all hir secte° God maintene
      In high maistry, and elles were it scathe°—
      I wol with lusty herte, fresh and greene,
      Say you a song to glade you, I weene:
      And let us stinte of ernestful mattere.
35   Herkneth my song that saith in this mannere:

---

10 **in gree** in stride, with goodwill   11 **For ... wroughte** for it is most reasonable that He test what He created   12 **boughte** saved   13 **pistel** epistle   19 **freletee** frailty   21 **suffrance** patience. The remainder of the passage is entirely original with Chaucer   25 **assayes** tests   28 **plye** bend. Good coin, containing enough gold, was pliable   30 **secte** sex, or sect   31 **scathe** a pity

"L'ENVOY DE CHAUCER"

Grisilde is deed and eek hir pacience,
And both atones buried in Itaile,
For which I cry in open audience:
No wedded man so hardy be t'assaile°
His wives pacience in trust to finde   40
Grisildis, for in certain he shall faile.

O noble wives, full of high prudence,
Let noon humilitee your tonge naile,
Ne let no clerk have cause or diligence
To write of you a story of swich merveile   45
As of Grisildis, pacient and kinde,
Lest Chichevache you swallwe in hir entraile.°

Follweth Ekko that holdeth no silence,
But ever answereth at the contretaile.°
Beth not bidaffed° for your innocence,   50
But sharply take on you the governaile.
Emprenteth well this lesson in your minde
For commune profit, sith it may availe.

Ye archewives, stondeth at defence,
Sin ye be strong as is a greet camaile.°   55
Ne suffreth not that men you doon offence.
And sclendre wives, fieble as in battaile,
Beth egre° as is a tiger yond in Inde—
Ay clappeth° as a mill, I you conseile.

Ne drede hem not, doth hem no reverence;   60
For though thine husband armed be in maile,

39 **assaile** try   47 **Chichevache . . . entraile** Chichevache, the skinny
cow, feeds only on patient wives   49 **contretaile** counter tally
50 **bidaffed** made a fool of   55 **camaile** camel   58 **egre** fierce
59 **Ay clappeth** always clatter

The arrwes of thy crabbed eloquence
Shall perce his brest and eek his aventaile.°
In jalousy I rede eek thou him binde,
65 And thou shalt make him couche° as doth a quaile.

If thou be fair, ther folk been in presence
Shew thou thy visage and thine apparaile.
If thou be foul, be free of thy dispence;°
To get thee freendes ay do thy travaile.
70 Be ay of cheer as light as leef on linde,°
And let him care, and weep, and wring, and waile . . .

---

63 **aventaile** chain mail attached to helmet covering neck   65 **couche**
cower   68 **dispence** spending   70 **linde** linden tree

THE MERCHANT'S PROLOGUE

"Weeping and wailing, care and other sorrwe
I know enough, on even and amorrwe!"
Quod the Marchant. "And so doon other mo
That wedded been! I trow that it be so,
For well I wot it fareth so with me!   5
I have a wife, the worste that may be:
For though the feend to hir y-coupled were,
She wold him overmatch, I dare well swere.
What shold I you reherce in special
Hir hye malice? She is a shrew at all!°   10
There is a long and large difference
Bitwix Griselde's greete pacience
And of my wife the passing° crueltee.
Were I unbounden,° also mote I thee,
I wolde never eft comen in the snare.   15
We wedded men live in sorrwe and care:
Assaye whoso wol and he shall finde
I saye sooth, by Saint Thomas of Inde,
As for the more part—I ay not alle;
God shilde° that it sholde so bifalle!   20
   A, good sir Host, I have y-wedded be
Thise monthes two, and more not, pardee,
And yet I trowe he that all his live
Wifeless hath been, though that men wold him rive°
Unto the hert, ne coud in no mannere   25
Tellen so muchel sorrwe as I now here
Coud tellen of my wives cursednesse."

---

10 **at all** in every way   13 **passing** surpassing   14 **unbounden** separated, freed   20 **shilde** forbid   24 **rive** stab

"Now," quod our Host, "Marchant, so God you blesse,
Sin ye so muchel knowen of that art,
30 Full hertely I pray you tell us part."
"Gladly," quod he, "but of mine owne sore
For sorry hert I telle may namore."

THE MERCHANT'S TALE

Whilom there was dwelling in Lumbardye
A worthy knight that born was of Pavie,
In which he lived in greet prosperitee;
And sixty yeer a wifeless man was he,
5 And follwed ay his bodily delit
On women, there as was his appetit,
As doon thise fooles that been seculer.°
And whan that he was passed sixty yeer—
Were it for holiness or for dotage
10 I can not say—but swich a greet corage°
Hadde this knight to been a wedded man,
That day and night he doth all that he can
T'espyen where he mighte wedded be,
Praying our Lord to graunten him that he
15 Might ones know of thilke blissful lif
That is bitwix an husband and his wif,
And for to live under that holy bond
With which that first God man and woman bond:
"Noon other life," said he, "is worth a bene!

7 **As . . . seculer** as these fools do who are secular—i.e., who are not
in monasteries but in "the world." Cf. line 78. These two lines suggest
that the tale was originally assigned to the Monk or Friar, although it
is possible that the Merchant is wishing he were in a monastery
10 **corage** desire

For wedlock is so esy and so clene°   20
That in this world it is a paradis."
—Thus said this olde knight that was so wis.°
    And certainly, as sooth as God is king,
To take a wife, it is a glorious thing,
And namely whan a man is old and hoor.   25
Than is a wife the fruit of his tresor:
Than shold he take a yong wife and a fair,
On which he might engendren him an heir,
And lede his life in joy and in solas;
Where as thise bacheleres sing "alas"   30
Whan that they find any adversitee
In love, which nis but childish vanitee.
And trewely, it sit well to be so°
That bachelers have ofte pain and wo:
On brotel ground they build, and brotelnesse   35
They finde whan they wene sikernesse°—
They live but as a brid or as a beest
In libertee and under noon arrest;
There as a wedded man in his estat
Liveth a life blissful and ordinat   40
Under this yoke of marriage y-bounde:
Well may his hert in joy and bliss abounde.
For who can be so buxom° as a wif?

20 **esy . . . clene** enjoyable, righteous   22 **Thus . . . wis** the lines
which follow (23–148) are a bitterly ironic statement of the various
standard arguments in favor of marriage. It is possible that they are
spoken by January (line 22 being then parenthetical) and constitute his
self-deluded reasons for wanting to marry. Otherwise they are spoken
by the Merchant as a summary of January's reasons, or indeed those
of any idealist or naif. Whether January or the Merchant himself is the
speaker, the irony is suddenly dropped in line 148 and the section con-
cluded with the cynical Merchant's true opinion. (It has sometimes
been thought that the lines are not ironical but a serious statement
meant for the Friar or Monk in an earlier version; but it seems to the
present editor impossible to imagine the lines as anything but ironic in
this context.)   33 **it . . . so** it is fitting   35–36 **On . . . sikernesse** on
unsafe ("brittle") ground they build, and they find insecurity when they
expect security   43 **buxom** obedient, humble

Who is so trew and eek so ententif
45   To keep him, sick and whole, as is his make?
For wele or woe she wol him not forsake.
She nis not wery him to love and serve,
Though that he lie bedred till he sterve.°
And yet some clerkes sayn it is not so,
50   Of which he Theofrast is one of tho;
What fors though Theofraste liste lie?°
"Ne take no wife," quod he, "for husbondrye
As for to spare in household thy dispence.
A trewe servant doth more diligence
55   Thy good to keepe than thine owne wif,
For she wol claime half part all hir lif.
And if thou be sick, so God me save,
Thy veray freendes or a trewe knave
Wol keep thee bet than she that waiteth ay
60   After thy good,° and hath done many a day.
And if thou take a wife unto thine hold,
Full lightly maistou been a cockewold."
This sentence and an hundred thinges worse
Writeth this man—ther God his bones curse!
65   But take no keep of all swich vanitee—
Defye Theofrast, and herke me:
   A wife is Goddes yifte veraily.
All other manner yiftes hardily,
As landes, rents, pasture, or commune,°
70   Or moebles,° all been yiftes of Fortune,
That passen as a shadwe upon a wall.
But drede not, if plainly speke I shall,
A wife wol last and in thine house endure
Well lenger than thee list,° paraventure.
75   Marriage is a full greet sacrament.
He which that hath no wife I hold him shent.°

---

48 **sterve** die   51 **What . . . lie?** What does it matter if Theophrastus
wanted to lie?   60 **After thy good** i.e., to inherit your property
69 **commune** the right to use common lands, like pastures   70 **moe-
bles** furnishings and any movable property   74 **lenger . . . list** longer
than you like (note the irony)   76 **shent** ruined

He liveth helpless and all desolat—
I speke of folk in seculer estat.
    And herke why I say not this for nought
That woman is for mannes help y-wrought: 80
The hye God, whan he had Adam maked
And saw him all alone, belly-naked,
God of his greete goodness saide than,
"Let us now make an help unto this man
Like to himself." And than he made him Eve.   85
Here may ye see, and hereby may ye preve
That wife is mannes help and his confort,
His paradise terrestre and his disport.
So buxom and so vertuous is she
They moste needes live in unitee: 90
Oo flesh they been, and oo flesh, as I guesse,
Hath but one hert in wele and in distresse.
    A wife—a, Sainte Mary, *ben'dic'te!*
How might a man han any adversitee
That hath a wife? Certes, I can not saye.   95
The blisse which that is bitwix hem twaye,
There may no tonge tell or herte thinke.
If he be poor, she helpeth him to swinke.°
She keepeth his good and wasteth neveradeel.
All that hir husband lust hir liketh well.   100
She saith not ones "Nay" whan he saith "Ye."
"Do this," saith he. "All redy, sir," saith she.
    O blissful ordre of wedlock precious,
Thou art so murry and eek so vertuous,
And so commended and approved eek,   105
That every man that halt him° worth a leek
Upon his bare knees ought all his lif
Thanken his God that him hath sent a wif,
Or elles pray to God him for to sende
A wife to last unto his lives ende—   110
For than his life is set in sikernesse,
He may not be deceived, as I guesse,

98 **swinke** work   106 **halt him** holds (considers) himself

So that he werk after his wives reed:°
Than may he boldly beren up his heed,
115 They been so trew and therewithal so wise—
For which, if thou wolt werken as the wise,
Do alway so as women wol thee rede.
Lo how that Jacob, as thise clerkes rede,
By good conseil of his moder Rebekke
120 Bond the kides skin about his necke,
For which his fadres benison he wan.
Lo Judith, as the story eek telle can,
By wise conseil she God's peple kepte,
And slow him Olofernes while he slepte.
125 Lo Abigail, by good conseil how she
Saved her husband Nabal whan that he
Shold han been slain. And look Ester also
By good conseil delivered out of wo
The peple of God, and made him Mardochee
130 Of Assuere enhaunced for to be.
      There is nothing in gree superlatif,°
As saith Senek, above an humble wif.
Suffer thy wives tonge, as Caton bit.
She shall command and thou shalt suffren it,
135 And yet she wol obey of curteisye.
      A wife is keeper of thine husbondrye:
Well may the sicke man biwail and weepe
Ther as there is no wife the house to keepe.
I warne thee, if wisely thou wolt wirche,
140 Love well thy wife, as Christ loved his chirche.°
If thou lovest thyself thou lovest thy wif.
No man hateth his flesh, but in his lif
He fostreth it; and therefore bid I thee,
Cherisse thy wife or thou shalt never thee.°
145 Husband and wife, what so men jape or playe,

113 **reed** advice (again, certainly an ironic statement)   131 **in gree superlatif** superior in degree   140 **as ... chirche** the mystical marriage between Christ and the Church, based on an allegorical interpretation of the *Song of Songs,* was a medieval commonplace   144 **thee** prosper

Of worldly folk holden the siker waye.
They been so knit there may noon harm bitide—
And namely° upont he wives side.

                *   *   *

For which this January of whom I tolde
Considered hath inwith his dayes olde   150
The lusty life, the vertuous quiete
That is in marriage honey sweete;
And for his freendes on a day he sente
To tellen hem th'effect of his entente.
With face sad this tale he hath hem told: 155
He saide, "Freendes, I am hoor and old,
And almost, God wot, on my pittes° brinke.
Upon my soule somewhat most I thinke.
I have my body follily dispended—
Blessed be God that it shall been amended!   160
For I wol be, certain, a wedded man,
And that anon, in all the haste I can,
Unto some maide fair and tendre of age.
I pray you shapeth for my marriage
All suddenly, for I wol not abide;°   165
And I wol fond° t'espyen on my side
To whom I may be wedded hastily.
But for as much as ye been mo than I,
Ye shullen rather swich a thing espyen
Than I, and where me best were to allyen.   170
But oo thing warn I you, my freendes dere:
I wol noon old wife han in no mannere.
She shall not passe twenty yeer certain!
Old fish and yong flesh wolde I have full fain.
Bet is," quod he, "a pike than a pickerel,°   175
And bet than old boef is the tender veel.
I wol no woman thrity yeer of age—

---

148 **namely** especially   157 **pittes** graves   165 **abide** wait   166 **fond**
try   175 **pickerel** a young pike

It is but bene-straw and greet forage.°
And eek thise olde widows, God is woot,
180 They kon so muchel craft on Wades boot,°
So muchel broken harm° whan that hem leste,
That with hem shold I never live in reste.
For sundry scoles maketh subtil clerkes:°
Woman of many scoles half a clerk is.
185 But certainly, a yong thing may men gie,°
Right as men may warm wex with handes plye.°
Wherefore I say you plainly in a clause,
I wol noon old wife han right for this cause:
For if so were I hadde swich meschaunce
190 That I in hir ne coud han no plesaunce,
Than shold I lede my life in avoutrye,°
And go straight to the devil whan I die.
Ne children shold I none upon hir geten—
Yet were me lever houndes had me eten
195 Than that mine heritage sholde falle
In straunge hand. And this I tell you alle—
I dote not—I wot the cause why
Men sholde wed, and ferthermore wot I
There speketh many a man of marriage
200 That wot namore of it than wot my page
For whiche causes man shold take a wif:
If he ne may not live chaste his lif,
Take him a wife with greet devocioun,
Because of leveful° procreacioun
205 Of children, to th'honour of God above,
And not only for paramour or love;
And for they sholde lechery eschue,

178 **bene-straw ... forage** refuse of bean plants and coarse dry
fodder   180 **Wades boot** Wade was a hero of Germanic legend, and
traveled by boat, but the reference remains a mystery   181 **broken
harm** to make use of mischief   183 **For ... clerkes** Cf. Wife of
Bath's Prologue, line 47; the Merchant has picked up several echoes
of her discourse   185 **may men gie** men may rule   186 **wex ... plye**
since wax was a traditional figure for fickleness and instability, the line
has a double meaning   191 **avoutrye** adultery   204 **leveful** lawful

And yeeld hir dette whan that it is due;
Or for that ech of hem shold helpen other
In meschief, as a suster shall the brother,   210
And live in chastitee full holily
—But sires, by your leve, that am not I.°
For God be thanked, I dare make avaunt,
I feel my limes stark and suffisaunt
To do all that a man belongeth to.   215
I wot myselven best what I may do.
Though I be hoor, I fare as doth a tree
That blossmeth ere the fruit y-woxen be,
And blossmy tree nis neither dry ne deed:
I feel me nowhere hoor but on mine heed—   220
Mine hert and all my limes been as greene
As laurer thurgh the yeer is for to seene.
And sin that ye han herd all mine entente,
I pray you to my will ye wol assente."

    Diverse men diversely him tolde   225
Of marriage many ensamples olde.
Some blamed it, some praised it, certain.
But at the laste, shortly for to sayn,
As alday falleth° altercacioun
Bitwixe freendes in disputisoun,   230
There fill a strife bitwiz his brethren two,
Of which that one was cleped Placebo,
Justinus° soothly called was that other.
    Placebo said: "O January, brother,
Full litel need had ye, my lord so dere,   235
Conseil to ax of any that is here,
But that ye been so full of sapience
That you ne liketh, for your heigh prudence,
To waiven fro the word of Salomon:
This word said he unto us everichon,   240
'Werk alle thing by conseil,' thus said he,

---

212 **But . . . I** Cf. Wife of Bath's Prologue, line 118   229 **alday fall-eth** continually occurs   232–33 **Placebo, Justinus** Placebo means "I will please"—in short, they are the flatterer and the just man

'And thanne shaltou not repenten thee.'
But though that Salomon spak swich a word,
Mine owne dere brother and my lord,
245 So wisly God my soule bring at reste,
I hold your owne conseil is the beste.
For brother mine, of me take this motif:°
I have now been a court-man all my lif,
And God it wot, though I unworthy be,
250 I have stonden in full greet degree
Abouten lordes in full high estat;
Yet had I never with none of hem debat—
I never hem contraried, trewely.
I wot well that my lord kan° more than I;
255 What that he saith, I hold it ferm and stable—
I say the same, or elles thing semblable.
A full greet fool is any conseillour
That serveth any lord of high honour
That dare presume of elles thenken it
260 That his conseil shold pass his lordes wit.
Nay, lordes be no fooles, by my fay.
Ye han yourselven shewed here today
So high sentence so holily and well,
That I consent and conferm everydeel
265 Your wordes all and your opinioun.
By God, there nis no man in all this town
Ne in Itaile coud bet han y-said.
Christ halt him of this conseil well apaid.°
And trewely it is an high corage
270 Of any man that stapen° is in age
To take a yong wife. By my fader kin
Your herte hangeth on a jolly pin!
Doth now in this matter right as you leste,
For, finally, I hold it for the beste."
275   Justinus that ay stille sat and herde,
Right in this wise he to Placebo answerde:

---

247 **motif** notion   254 **kan** knows   268 **apaid** pleased   270 **stapen**
advanced

"Now, brother mine, be pacient I praye,
Sin ye han said, and herkneth what I saye.
Senek, amonges other wordes wise,
Saith that a man ought him right well avise   280
To whom he yiveth his land or his catel.°
And sin I ought avisen me right well
To whom I yive my good away fro me,
Well muchel more I ought avised be
To whom I yive my body for alway.   285
I warn you well, it is no childes play
To take a wife withouten avisement.
Men most enquere—this is mine assent°—
Wher she be wise, or sobre, or drunkelewe,°
Or proud, or elles otherways a shrewe,   290
A chidestere,° or wastour of thy good,
Or rich, or poor, or elles mannish wood.°
Al be it so that no man finden shall
None in this world that trotteth whole in all,°
Ne man ne beest swich as men coud devise;   295
But natheless, it ought enough suffise
With any wife, if so were that she hadde
Mo goode thewes° than hir vices badde—
And all this axeth leiser for t'enquere.
For God it wot, I have wept many a tere   300
Full prively sin that I had a wif:
Praise whoso wol a wedded mannes lif,
Certain I find in it but cost and care,
And observances of all blisses bare.
And yet, God wot, my neighebors aboute,   305
And namely of women many a route,
Sayn that I have the moste stedfast wif,
And eek the meekest one that bereth lif—
But I wot best where wringeth me my sho.

281 **catel** possessions 288 **assent** opinion 289 **drunkelewe** a
drunkard 291 **chidestere** scold 292 **mannish wood** man-crazy
294 **trotteth . . . all** trots perfectly in every way (choosing a wife is
thus compared to buying a horse) 298 **thewes** virtues

310   Ye mowe for me right as you liketh do.
      Aviseth you—ye been a man of age—
      How that ye entren into marriage,
      And namely with a yong wife and a fair.
      By him that made water, erth, and air,
315   The yongest man that is in all this route
      Is bisy enough to bringen it aboute
      To han his wife alone. Trusteth me,
      Ye shull not plesen hir fully yeeres three—
      This is to sayn, to doon hir full plesance.
320   A wife asketh full many an observance.
      I pray you that ye be not yvel apaid."°
        "Well," quod this January, "and hastou y-said?
      Straw for thy Senek, and for thy proverbes!
      I counte not a panier full of herbes
325   Of schole-termes.° Wiser men than thou,
      As thou hast herd, assenteden right now
      To my purpose. Placebo, what say ye?"
        "I say it is a cursed man," quod he,
      "That letteth° matrimoigne, sikerly."
330   And with that word they risen suddenly,
      And been assented fully that he sholde
      Be wedded whan him list and where he wolde.

                *   *   *

      High fantasy and curious bisinesse
      Fro day to day gan in the soul impresse
335   Of January about his marriage.
      Many fair shape and many a fair visage
      There passeth thurgh his herte night by night:
      As whoso took a mirrour polished bright,
      And set it in a commune market place,
340   Than shold he see full many a figure pace

---

321 **yvel apaid** displeased, offended   324–25 **I . . . schole-termes** I
wouldn't give a basket of herbs for book-learning   329 **letteth** stands
in the way of

By his mirrour; and in the same wise
Gan January inwith his thought devise
Of maidens which that dwelten him biside.°
He wiste not where that he might abide.°
For if that one have beautee in hir face,   345
Another stant so in the peples grace
For hir sadness° and hir benignitee,
That of the peple greetest voice hath she;
And some were rich and hadden badde name.
But natheless, bitwix ernest and game,   350
He atte last appointed him° on oon
And let all other from his herte goon,
And chees hir of his own auctoritee—
For Love is blind alday, and may not see.
And whan that he was in his bed y-brought,   355
He portrayed in his hert and in his thought
Hir freshe beautee and hir age tendre,
Hir middle small, hir armes long and slendre,
Hir wise governance, hir gentilesse,
Hir womanly bering and hir sadnesse.   360
And whan that he on hir was condescended,°
Him thought his choice might not been amended.°
For whan that he himself concluded hadde,
Him thought ech other mannes wit so badde
That impossible it were to replye   365
Again his choice—this was his fantasye.
    His freendes sent he to at his instance,
And prayed hem to doon him that plesance
That hastily they wolden to him come.
He wold abredge° hir labour all and some: 370
Needeth namore for him to go ne ride—
He was appointed ther he wold abide.
    Placebo came and eek his freendes soone,

---

343 **him biside** near him   344 **where ... abide** which one to settle
on   347 **sadness** gravity, earnestness   351 **appointed him** made up
his mind   361 **condescended** decided   362 **amended** improved
upon   370 **abredge** shorten

And alderfirst he bade hem all a boone—
375 That none of hem none argumentes make
Again the purpose which that he hath take,
Which purpose was plesant to God, said he,
And veray ground of his prosperitee.
He said there was a maiden in the town
380 Which that of beautee hadde greet renown.
Al were it so she were of small degree,°
Suffiseth him hir youth and hir beautee.
Which maid he said he wold han to his wif,
To lede in ese and holiness his lif,
385 And thanked God that he might han hir all,
That no wight his blisse parten° shall;
And prayed hem to labouren in this neede,
And shapen° that he faile not to speede—
For than he said his spirit was at ese.
390 "Than is," quod he, "no thing may me displese.
Save oo thing pricketh in my conscience,
The which I wol reherce in your presence:
I have," quod he, "herd said full yore ago
There may no man han parfit blisses two—
395 This is to say, in erth and eek in hevene.
For though he keep him fro the sinnes sevene,°
And eek from every branch of thilke tree,
Yet is there so parfit felicitee
And so greet ese and lust in marriage,
400 That ever I am aghast° now in mine age
That I shall lede now so murry a lif,
So delicate, withouten woe and strif,
That I shall han mine heven in erthe here.
For sith that veray heven is bought so dere
405 With tribulacioun and greet penance,
How shold I than, that live in swich plesance
As alle wedded men doon with hir wives,

381 **small degree** a lower social class   386 **parten** share
388 **shapen** arrange   396 **sinnes sevene** seven deadly sins
400 **aghast** afraid

Come to the bliss ther Christ etern on live is?
This is my drede. And ye, my brethren twaye,
Assoileth me° this question, I praye."   410
    Justinus, which that hated his follye,
Answered anonright in his japerye.°
And for he wold his longe tale abredge,
He wolde noon auctoritee alledge
But saide, "Sir, so there be noon obstacle   415
Other than this, God of his high miracle
And of his mercy may so for you werche
That ere ye have your right of holy cherche,°
Ye may repent of wedded mannes lif
In which ye sayn there is no woe ne strif.   420
And elles God forbede but he sente
A wedded man him grace to repente
Well ofte rather than a single man.
And therefore, sir, the beste reed I kan:
Despair you not, but have in your memorye,   425
Paraunter she may be your purgatorye—
She may be Goddes mene° and Goddes whippe!
Than shall your soule up to heven skippe
Swifter than doth an arrwe out of a bowe!
I hope to God hereafter shull ye knowe   430
That there nis noon so greet felicitee
In marriage, ne never mo shall be,
That you shall let of° your salvacioun—
So that ye use, as skile is and resoun,°
The lustes of your wife attemprely,   435
And that ye plese hir not too amorously,
And that ye keep you eek from other sinne.
My tale is done, for my wit is thinne.

---

410 **Assoileth me** clear up for me   412 **japerye** mockery, irony. Justinus' deft irony reflects the harsher irony of the Merchant himself. In line 441, for example, the Merchant has Justinus cite the Wife of Bath as if she were one of the great "auctoritees" on marriage!   418 **ere … cherche** before you get the last rites of the Church   427 **mene** instrument   433 **you … of** will keep you from   434 **skile … resoun** proper and reasonable

Beth not aghast hereof, my brother dere,
440 But let us waden out of this mattere.
The Wife of Bath, if ye han understande,
Of marriage which we have on hande
Declared hath full well in litel space.
Fareth now well. God have you in his grace."
445   And with that word this Justin and his brother
Han take hir leeve and ech of hem of other.
For whan they saw that it most needes be,
They wroughten so by sly and wise tretee
That she, this maiden—which that Mayus highte—
450 As a hastily as ever that she mighte,
Shall wedded be unto this Januarye.

*   *   *

I trow it were too longe you to tarrye
If I you told of every scrit° and bond
By which that she was feffed in° his lond;
455 Or for to herknen of hir rich array.
    But finally y-comen is the day
That to the chirche bothe be they went
For to receive the holy sacrament.
Forth comth the preest with stole about his necke,
460 And bade hir be like Sarah and Rebekke
In wisdom and in truth of marriage,
And said his orisons as is usage,
And croucheth hem,° and bade God shold hem blesse,
And made all siker enough with holinesse.
465   Thus been they wedded with solempnitee.
And at the feeste sitteth he and she
With other worthy folk upon the dais.
All full of joy and bliss is the palais,
And full of instruments and of vitaille,
470 The moste daintevous° of all Itaile.

---

453 **scrit** deed   454 **feffed in** made heir to   463 **croucheth hem**
made the sign of the Cross over them   470 **daintevous** delicate

Biforn hem stoode instruments of swich soun
That Orpheus, ne of Thebes Amphioun,
Ne maden never swich a melodye.
At every course than came loud minstralcye,
That never trumped Joab for to heere,   475
Ne he Theodamas yet half so clere
At Thebes whan the citee was in doute.
Bacchus the wine hem shenketh° all aboute,
And Venus laugheth upon every wight:
For Januarye was become hir knight,   480
And wolde both assayen his corage°
In liberte° and eek in marriage—
And with hir firebrand in hir hand aboute
Daunceth before the bride and all the route.
And certainly, I dare right well say this: 485
Ymeneus,° that god of wedding is,
Saw never his life so murry a wedded man!
Hold thou thy pees, thou poet Marcian,
That writest us that ilke wedding murrye
Of hir Philology and him Mercurye,   490
And of the songes that the Muses songe:
Too small is both thy pen and eek thy tonge
For to descriven of *this* marriage!
Whan tender youth hath wedded stouping age,
There is swich mirth that it may not be written.   495
Assayeth it yourself, than may ye witen
If that I lie or noon in this mattere.
     Mayus, that sit with so benign a cheere
Hir to behold it seemed faïrye—
Queen Ester looked never with swich an eye   500
On Assuer, so meek a look hath she.
I may you not devise all hir beautee,
But thus much of hir beautee tell I may,
That she was like the brighte morrwe of May,
Fulfill'd of alle beautee and plesaunce!   505

---

478 **shenketh** pours   481 **assayen . . . corage** try out his power
482 **liberte** single life   486 **Ymeneus** Hymen

This January is ravished in a traunce
At every time he looked on hir face!
But in his hert he gan hir to manace°
That he that night in armes wold hir straine
510 Harder than ever Paris did Elaine.
But natheless yet had he greet pitee
That thilke night offenden hir most he,
And thought, "Alas, O tender creature,
Now wolde God ye mighte will endure
515 All my corage, it is so sharp and keene.
I am aghast ye shull it not sustene;
But God forbed that I did all my might!
Now wolde God that it were woxen night,
And that the night wold lasten evermo!
520 I wold that all this peple were ago."
And finally he doth all his labour,
As he best mighte, saving his honour,
To haste hem fro the mete° in subtil wise.
The time came that reson was to rise,
525 And after that men daunce and drinken faste,
And spices all about the house they caste.
And full of joy and bliss is every man.
—All but a squier highte Damian,
Which carf biforn the knight full many a day:
530 He was so ravished on° his lady May
That for the veray pain he was ny wood;°
Almost he swelt and swouned ther he stood,
So sore hath Venus hurt him with hir brond,
As that she bare it dauncing in hir hond.
535 And to his bed he went him hastily.
Namore of him at this time speke I,
But there I let him weep enough and plaine—
Till freshe May wol rewen° on his paine.
    O perilous fire that in the bedstraw breedeth!
540 O familier foe that his service bedeth!°

---

508 **manace** threaten   523 **mete** feast   530 **ravished on** enamored of
531 **ny wood** nearly mad   538 **rewen** have pity   540 **bedeth** offers

O servant traitour, false homely hewe,
Like to the neddre° in bosom, sly, untrewe!
God shild us alle from your acquaintance!
O January, drunken in plesance
In marriage, see how thy Damian,   *545*
Thine owne squier and thy borne man,°
Entendeth for to do thee villainye!
God grante thee thine homely° foe t'espye,
For in this world nis worse pestilence
Than homely foe alday in thy presence!   *550*
   Parfourmed hath the sun his ark diurne—
No lenger may the body of him sojourne
On th'orisont° as in that latitude.
Night with his mantle that is derk and rude
Gan overspred the hemispery aboute,   *555*
For which departed is this lusty route,°
Fro January with thank on every side.
Home to hir houses lustily they ride,
Where as they doon hir thinges as hem leste,
And whan they saw hir time, go to reste.   *560*
Soon after that this hastif Januarye
Wol go to bed—he wol no lenger tarrye.
He drinketh ipocras, claree, and vernage,
Of spices hot t'encreesen his corage,
And many a letuary° had he full fin,   *565*
Swich as the cursed monk Daun Constantin
Hath written in his book *De Coitu*.
To eten hem all he nas no thing eschu.°
And to his privee freendes thus said he:
"For Goddes love, as soon as it may be,   *570*
Let voiden all this house in curteis wise."
And they han done right as he wol devise:
Men drinken, and the travers° draw anon;
The bride was brought abed as still as ston;

542 **neddre** adder   546 **borne man** vassal from birth   548 **homely**
domestic   553 **orisont** horizon   556 **route** company   565 **letuary**
medicinal syrup   568 **eschu** hesitant   573 **travers** curtain around the
bed

575 And whan the bed was with the preest y-blessed,
Out of the chambre hath every wight him dressed.
And January hath fast in armes take
His freshe May, his paradise, his make:°
He lulleth hir, he kisseth hir full ofte—
580 With thicke bristles of his beerd unsofte,
Like to the skin of houndfish, sharp as brere°
(For he was shave all new in his mannere)
He rubbeth hir about hir tender face,
And saide thus, "Alas, I mot trespace
585 To you, my spouse, and you greetly offende
Ere time come that I wol down descende!
But natheless, considereth this," quod he,
"There nis no werkman, whatsoever he be,
That may both werke well and hastily.
590 This wol be done at leiser parfitly.
It is no fors° how longe that we playe:
In trewe wedlock coupled be we twaye,
And blessed be the yoke that we been inne!
For in actes we mow do no sinne:
595 A man may do no sinne with his wif,
Ne hurt himselven with his owen knif,
For we han leve to play us by the lawe."
Thus laboureth he till that the day gan dawe;
And than he taketh a sop in fine claree,°
600 And upright in his bed than sitteth he,
And after that he sung full loud and clere
And kissed his wife and made wanton cheere.
He was all coltish, full of ragerye,°
And full of jargon as a flecked pie:°
605 The slacke skin about his necke shaketh
While that he sung, so chaunteth he and cracketh.
    —But God wot what that May thought in hir herte
Whan she him saw up-sitting in his sherte,

578 **make** mate   581 **brere** briars—being lately shaven, his beard is
bristly   591 **no fors** no matter   599 **sop ... claree** cake soaked in
wine—a usual breakfast of nobles   603 **ragerye** wantonness
604 **jargon ... pie** chitter-chatter as a spotted magpie

In his night-cap and with his necke lene;
She praiseth not his playing worth a bene.   *610*
Than said he thus: "My reste wol I take.
Now day is come. I may no lenger wake,"
And down he laid his heed and sleep till prime.
And afterward, whan that he saw his time,
Up riseth January. But freshe May   *615*
Held hir chambre unto the fourthe day,
As usage is of wives for the beste.
For every labour some time mot han reste,
Or elles longe may he not endure—
This is to sayn, no lives° creature—   *620*
Be it of fish or brid or beest or man.

*   *   *

Now wol I speke of woeful Damian
That languisheth for love, as ye shall heere.
Therefore I speke to him in this mannere:
I say, "O sely Damian, alas,   *625*
Answer to my demand as in this cas:
How shaltou to thy lady freshe May
Telle thy woe? She wol alway say nay.
Eek if thou speke, she wol thy woe biwraye.°
God be thine help, I can no better saye."   *630*
This sicke Damian in Venus' fir
So brenneth that he dieth for desir,
For which he put his life in aventure.
No lenger might he in this wise endure,
But prively a penner° gan he borrwe,   *635*
And in a letter wrote he all his sorrwe,
In manner of a complaint or a lay
Unto his faire freshe lady May.
And in a purse of silk heng on his sherte
He hath it put and laid it at his herte.   *640*
The moone, that at noon was thilke day

620 **lives** living   629 **biwraye** reveal   635 **penner** pen-case

That January hath wedded freshe May
In two° of Taur, was into Cancer gliden—
So long hath Mayus in hir chambre abiden,
645 As custom is unto thise nobles alle:
A bride shall not eten in the halle
Til dayes four, or three days atte leste,
Y-passed been—than let hir go to feeste.
The fourthe day complet fro noon to noon,
650 Whan that the heighe masse was y-doon,
In halle sit this January and May,
As fresh as is the brighte summer's day.
And so bifell how that this goode man
Remembred him upon this Damian,
655 And saide, "Sainte Mary! how may this be
That Damian entendeth not to me?°
Is he ay sick, or how may this betide?"
His squiers which that stooden there beside
Excused him by cause of his sicknesse,
660 Which letted him to doon his bisinesse—
Noon other cause mighte make him tarrye.
"That me forthinketh,"° quod this Januarye.
"He is a gentil squier, by my truthe.
If that he deid, it were harm and ruthe.
665 He is as wise, discreet, and eek secree
As any man I wot of his degree,
And thereto manly and eek servisable,
And for to be a thrifty man right able.
But after mete as soon as ever I may,
670 I wol myself visit him, and eek May,
To do him all the comfort that I can."
And for that word him blessed every man
That of his bountee and his gentilesse
He wolde so comforten in sicknesse
675 His squier, for it was a gentil deede.
    "Dame," quod this January, "take good heede,

---

643 **two** two degrees   656 **entendeth . . . me** does not attend upon
me   663 **me forthinketh** I regret

At after-mete ye with your women alle,
Whan ye han been in chambre out of this halle,
That all ye go to see this Damian.
Doth him disport—he is a gentil man;   680
And telleth him that I wol him visite,
Have I no thing but rested me a lite;
And speed you faste, for I wol abide
Till that ye sleepe faste by my side"—
And, with that word, he gan to him to calle   685
A squier that was marshall of his halle,
And told him certain thinges what he wolde.
   This freshe May hath straight hir way y-holde
With all hir women unto Damian.
Down by his beddes side sit she than,   690
Comforting him as goodly as she may.
This Damian, whan this his time he sey,
In secree wise his purse and eek his bille,°
In which that he y-written had his wille,
Hath put into hir hand withouten more—   695
Save that he siketh wonder deep and sore
And softely to hir right thus said he:
"Mercy! and that ye not discover me;
For I am deed if that this thing be kid."°
This purse hath she inwith hir bosom hid   700
And went hir way—ye get namore of me.
But unto January y-comen is she,
That on his beddes side sit full softe,
And taketh hir, and kisseth hir full ofte—
And laid him down to sleep and that anon.   705
She feined hir as that she moste gon
There as ye wot that every wight mot neede—
And whan she of this bill hath taken heede,
She rent it all to cloutes° at the laste,
And in the privee softely it caste.   710
   Who studieth° now but faire freshe May?

693 **bille** letter   699 **kid** known   709 **cloutes** shreds   711 **studieth**
thinks things over

Adown by olde January she lay,
That sleep—till that the cough hath him awaked;
Anon he prayed hir strepen hir all naked—
715 He wold of hir, he said, han some plesaunce;
He said hir clothes did him encombraunce;
And she obeyeth, be hir lief or loth.
But lest that precious° folk be with me wroth,
How that he wrought I dare not to you telle—
720 Or whether hir thought it paradise or helle.
But here I let hem werken in hir wise
Till evensong rung, and that they most arise.
    Were it by destinee or aventure,
Were it by influence, or by nature,
725 Or constellacion, that in swich estat
The heven stood that time fortunat
As for to put a bill of° Venus' werkes
(For alle thing hath time, as sayn thise clerkes)
To any woman for to get hir love,
730 I can not say. But greete God above,
That knoweth that noon act is causeless,
He deem° of all, for I wol hold my pees.
But sooth is *this*: how that the freshe May
Hath take swich impression that day
735 Of pitee on this sicke Damian
That from hir herte she ne drive can
The remembrance for to doon him ese!
"Certain," thought she, "whom that this thing displese,
I rekke not. For here I him assure
740 To love him best of any creature,
Though he namore hadde than his sherte."
Lo, pitee renneth soon in gentil herte!
—Here may ye see how excellent franchise°
In women is whan they hem narrwe avise.°
745 Some tyrant is, as there be many oon,
That hath an hert as hard as any ston,

718 **precious** prudish   727 **put . . . of** make a plea for   732 **deem** let
Him judge   743 **franchise** liberality   744 **hem . . . avise** think things
over carefully

Which wold han let him sterven° in the place
Well rather than han graunted him hir grace—
And hem rejoisen in hir cruel pride,
And rekke not to been an homicide.   750

    This gentil May, fulfilled of pitee,
Right of hir hand a letter maked she,
In which she graunteth him hir veray grace—
There lacketh nought, only but day and place
Where that she might unto his lust suffise;   755
For it shall be right as he wol devise.
And whan she saw hir time upon a day,
To visite this Damian goth May,
And subtilly this letter down she threste
Under his pillow—rede it if him leste.   760
She taketh him by the hand and hard him twiste,°
So secreely that no wight of it wiste,
And bade him be all hoole and forth she wente
To January, whan that he for hir sente.

    Up riseth Damian the nexte morrwe—   765
All passed was his sickness and his sorrwe.
He cembeth him, he preineth him and picketh,°
And doth all that his lady lust and liketh.
And eek to January he goth as lowe
As ever did a dogge for the bowe.°   770
He is so plesant unto every man
(For craft is all, whoso that do it can)
That every wight is fain to speke him good;
And fully in his lady grace he stood.
Thus let I Damian about his neede,   775
And in my tale forth I wol proceede.

*   *   *

    Some clerkes holden that felicitee
Stant in delit,° and therefore certain, he,

---

747 sterven die   **761 twiste** squeezed   **767 cembeth ... picketh**
combs his hair, tidies himself up, and puts on the finishing touches
769–70 goth ... bowe bows as low as ever a hunting-dog did
778 Stant in delit depends upon pleasure

This noble January, with all his might
780 In honest wise as longeth to a knight,
Shop him to live full deliciously.
His housing, his array as honestly
To his degree was maked as a kinges.
Amonges other of his honest thinges,
785 He made a garden walled all of ston°—
So fair a garden wot I nowhere non.
For out of doute I veraily suppose
That he that wrote *The Romance of the Rose*
Ne coud of it the beautee well devise;
790 Ne Priapus° ne mighte not suffise,
Though he be god of gardens, for to telle
The beautee of the garden, and the welle
That stood under a laurer alway greene.
Full ofte time he Pluto and his queene
795 Proserpina and all hir faïrye
Disporten hem and maken melodye
About that well, and daunced, as men tolde.
This noble knight, this January the olde,
Swich daintee° hath in it to walk and playe
800 That he wol no wight suffer bere the keye,
Save he himself: for of the smalle wicket°
He bare alway of silver a clicket,°
With which, whan that him lest, he it unshette.
And whan he wolde pay his wife hir dette
805 In summer seson, thider wold he go,
And May his wife, and no wight but they two.
And thinges which that were not done abedde,
He in the garden parfourmed hem and spedde.

---

785 **garden . . . ston** the "enclosed garden" described here has a very
ancient tradition, based upon allegorical interpretation of the *Song of
Songs*. It thus suggests the Garden of Eden and the Fall of Man, the
marriage between Christ and His Church, the Virgin, the soul's union
with God; its function here, needless to say, is ironic. On the back-
ground see Stanley N. Stewart, *The Enclosed Garden*. And cf. lines
894–906   790 **Priapus** fertility god   799 **daintee** delight   801 **wicket**
gate   802 **clicket** key

And in this wise many a murry day
Lived this January and freshe May.   810
But worldly joye may not alway dure
To January, ne to no creature.
—O sudden hap! O thou Fortune unstable,
Like to the scorpion so deceivable,°
That flatterest with thine heed whan thou wold stinge,   815
Thy tail is deeth thurgh thine enveniminge!
O brottel joy! O sweete venim quainte!
O monster, that so subtilly canst painte
Thy yiftes under hew of stedfastnesse,
That thou deceivest bothe more and lesse!   820
Why hastou January thus deceived,
That haddest him for thy full freend received?
And now, thou hast biraft him both his eyen;
For sorrwe of which desireth he to dien.
    Alas! this noble January free,   825
Amid his lust and his prosperitee,
Is woxen blind, and that all suddenly.
He weepeth and he waileth pitously—
And therewithal the fire of jalousye,
Lest that his wife shold fall in some follye,   830
So brent his herte that he wolde fain
That some man bothe hir and him had slain.
For neither after his deeth ne in his lif,
Ne wold he that she were love ne wif,
But ever live as widwe in clothes blacke,   835
Sole as the turtle° that hath lost hir make.
But atte last, after a month or twaye,
His sorrow gan assuage, sooth to saye:
For whan he wist it may noon other be,
He paciently took his adversitee,   840
Save, out of doute, he may not forgoon
That he nas jalous evermore in oon.°
Which jalousy it was so outrageous

814 **deceivable** deceitful   836 **Sole ... turtle** solitary as the
turtledove   842 **evermore in oon** constantly

That neither in hall ne in noon other hous,
845 Ne in noon other place neverthemo,
He nolde suffre hir for to ride or go,
But if that he had hand on hir alway.
For which full ofte weepeth freshe May,
That loveth Damian so benignely
850 That she mot outher dien suddenly
Or elles she mot han him as hir leste.
She waiteth whan° hir herte wolde breste.
    Upon that other side Damian
Becomen is the sorrwefulest man
855 That ever was; for neither night ne day
Ne might he speke a word to freshe May,
As to his purpose of no swich mattere,
But if that January most it heere,
That had an hand upon hir evermo.
860 But natheless, by writing to and fro,
And privee signes, wiste he what she mente;
And she knew eek the fine° of his entente.
    —O January! what might it thee availe
Though thou mightest see as fer as shippes saile?
865 For as good is blind deceived be,
As to be deceived whan a man may see.
Lo Argus, which that had an hundred eyen,
For al that ever he coude pour or pryen
Yet was he blent°—and God wot so been mo
870 That weenen wisly° that it be not so.
Pass over is an ese°—I say namore.
    This freshe May that I spak of so yore,
In warm wex hath emprinted the clicket
That January bare of the small wicket,
875 By which into his garden oft he wente.
And Damian that knew all hir entente

---

852 **waiteth whan** expects that   862 **fine** aim   869 **blent** deceived
870 **weenen wisly** imagine for sure   871 **Pass ... ese** closing your
eyes to something is a convenience —i.e., what you don't know won't
hurt you

The clicket countrefeted prively.
There nis namore to say, but hastily
Some wonder by this clicket shall bitide,
Which ye shall heeren if ye wol abide.   880
    O noble Ovid! sooth saistou, God woot,
What sleight it is, though it be long and hot,
That he nil find it out in some mannere!
By Pyramus and Thisbe may men lere:
Though they were kept full longe strait overall,   885
They been accorded rouning° thurgh a wall,
Ther no wight coud han found out swich a sleighte.
    But now to purpose: ere that dayes eighte
Were passed, ere the month of Juil, bifille
That January hath caught so greet a wille,   890
Thurgh egging of his wife, him for to playe
In his garden, and no wight but they twaye,
That in a morrwe unto his May saith he:
"Rise up, my wife, my love, my lady free—
The turtles voice is herd, my dove sweete!   895
The winter is gone with all his raines wete.
Come forth now with thine eyen columbin.
How fairer been thy brestes than is win!
The garden is enclosed all aboute:
Come forth, my white spouse, out of doute,   900
Thou hast me wounded in mine hert! O wif,
No spot of thee ne knew I all my lif!
Come forth and let us taken our disport;
I chees thee for my wife and my comfort."°
—Swich olde lewed wordes used he.   905
    On Damian a signe made she
That he sholde go biforn with his clicket.
This Damian than hath opened the wicket,
And in he stert, and that in swich mannere
That no wight might it see neither y-heere.   910

---

886 **been . . . rouning** came to an agreement by whispering   894–
904 **Rise up . . . comfort** January's words here are made up almost
entirely of quotes from the *Song of Songs*; cf. line 785 and note

And still he sit under a bush anon.
This January, as blind as is a ston,
With Mayus in his hand and no wight mo,
Into his freshe garden is ago,
915   And clapte to° the wicket suddenly.
"Now wife," quod he, "here nis but thou and I,
That art the creature that I best love.
For by that Lord that sit in heven above,
Lever ich° had to dien on a knif
920   Than thee offende, trewe dere wif.
For Goddes sake, thenk how I thee chees,
Not for no coveitise, douteless,
But only for the love I had to thee.
And though that I be old and may not see,
925   Beth to me trew, and I wol tell you why.
Three thinges, certes, shall ye win thereby:
First, love of Christ; and to yourself honour;
And all mine heritage, town and tower,
I yive it you—maketh chartres° as you leste.
930   This shall be done tomorrwe ere sunne reste,
So wisly God my soule bring in blisse.
I pray you first in covenant ye me kisse.
And though that I be jalous, wite° me nought:
Ye been so deep emprinted in my thought,
935   That whan that I consider your beautee,
And therewithal th'unlikely eld of me,
I may not, certes, though I sholde die,
Forbere to been out of your compaignye
For veray love; this is withouten doute.
940   Now kiss me, wife, and let us rome aboute."
This freshe May, whan she thise wordes herde,
Benignely to January answerde—
But first and forward she began to weepe:
"I have," quod she, "a soule for to keepe
945   As well as ye, and also mine honour;

---

915 **clapte to** shut   919 **Lever ich** I'd rather   929 **chartres** deeds
933 **wite** blame

And of my wifehood thilke tender flower
Which that I have assured in your hond
Whan that the preest to you my body bond.
Wherefore I wol answer in this mannere,
By the leve of you,° my lord so dere: 950
I pray to God that never dawe the day
That I ne sterve as foul° as woman may
If ever I do unto my kin that shame,
Or elles I empaire so my name
That I be false. And if I do that lacke,   955
Do strepe me, and put me in a sacke,
And in the nexte river do me drenche.
I am a gentil woman, and no wenche!
Why speke ye thus? But men been ever untrewe,
And women have repreve of you ay newe!°   960
Ye han noon other countenance,° I leve,
But speke to us of untrust and repreve!"
—And with that word she saw where Damian
Sat in the bush, and coughen she began,
And with hir finger signes made she   965
That Damian shold climb upon a tree
That charged was with fruit, and up he wente;
For verraily he knew all hir entente
And every signe that she coude make
Well bet than January, hir owne make;   970
For in a letter she had told him all
Of this mattere, how he werken shall.
And thus I let him sit upon the pirye,°
And January and May rominge mirrye.

Bright was the day and blew the firmament.   975
Phebus hath of gold his streemes down sent
To gladden every flower with his warmnesse.
He was that time in Geminis, as I guesse,
But litel fro his declinacioun

---

950 **By ... you** i.e., "by your leave" 952 **foul** dreadfully 960 **repreve ...
newe** reproof from you over and over 961 **countenance** constant habit
973 **pirye** pear tree

980 Of Cancer, Joves exaltacioun.
     And so befell that brighte morrwetide
     That in that garden, in the ferther side,
     Pluto, that is king of faïrye,
     And many a lady in his compaignye,
985 Following his wife, the queene Proserpina—
     Which that he ravished out of Etna
     While that she gadred flowres in the mede
     (In Claudian ye may the stories rede
     How in his grisly carte he hir fette)
990 This king of fairy than adown him sette
     Upon a bench of turves° fresh and greene,
     And right anon thus said he to his queene:
     "My wife," quod he, "there may no wight say nay:
     Th'experience so preveth every day
995 The treson which that woman doth to man.
     Ten hundred thousand tales tell I can
     Notable of your untruth and brotelnesse.°
     O Salomon, wise and richest of richesse,
     Fulfill'd of sapience and of worldly glorye,
1000 Full worthy been thy wordes to memorye
     To every wight that wit and reson kan:
     Thus praiseth he yet the bountee of man:
     'Amonges a thousand men yet foond I oon,
     But of women alle foond I noon'—
1005 Thus saith the king that knoweth your wickednesse.
     And Jesus *filius Syrak*,° as I guesse,
     Ne speketh of you but selde reverence;
     A wilde fire and corrupt pestilence
     So fall upon your bodies yet tonight!
1010 Ne see ye not this honourable knight?
     By cause, alas, that he is blind and old,
     His owne man shall make him cokewold!
     Lo where he sit, the lechour in the tree!

---

991 **bench of turves** presumably a terrace or mound fashioned in the
turf   997 **brotelnesse** instability   1006 **Jesus filius Syrak** presumed
author of *Ecclesiasticus*

Now wol I graunten of my majestee
Unto this olde, blinde, worthy knight   *1015*
That he shall have ayain his eyen sight,
Whan that his wife wold doon him villainye.
Than shall he knowen all hir harlotrye,
Both in repreve of hir and other mo."
      "Ye shall?" quod Proserpine. "Wol ye so?   *1020*
Now by my modre's sire's soul I swere
That I shall yiven hir suffisant answere!
And alle women after for hir sake,
That though they be in any guilt y-take,
With face bold they shull hemself excuse,   *1025*
And bere hem down that wolde hem accuse—
For lack of answer none of hem shall dien!
All had men seen a thing with both his eyen,
Yet shall we women visage it hardily,°
And weep, and swere, and chide subtilly,   *1030*
So that ye men shull been as lewed° as gees.
What rekketh me of your auctoritees?
I wot well that this Jew, this Salomon,
Found of us women fooles many oon.
But though that he ne found no good woman,   *1035*
Yet hath there founde many another man
Women full trew, full good and vertuous.
Witness on hem that dwell in Christes hous:
With martyrdom they preved hir constaunce.
The Romain geests eek maken remembraunce   *1040*
Of many a veray, trewe wife also.
But sir, ne be not wroth, al be it so,
Though that he said he found no good woman;
I pray you, take the sentence of the man—
He mente thus: that in sovereign bountee   *1045*
Nis none but God, but neither he ne she.°
—Ey, for veray God that nis but oon,
What make ye so much of Salomon?

1029 **visage it hardily** boldly stare it in the face   1031 **lewed** foolish
1046 **he ne she** man nor woman

What though he made a temple, Goddes hous?
1050 What though he were rich and glorious?
So made he eek a temple of false goddes!
How might he do a thing that more forbode° is?
Pardee, as fair as ye his name emplastre,°
He was a lechour and an idolastre,°
1055 And in his eld he veray God forsook.
And if God ne had, as saith the book,
Y-spared him for his fadres sake, he sholde
Have lost his regne rather° than he wolde.
I set right nought, of all the villainye
1060 That ye of women write, a butterflye.
I am a woman: needes mot I speke,
Or elles swelle till mine herte breke.
For sithen he said that we been jangleresses,
As ever hoole I mote brouk my tresses,°
1065 I shall not spare for no curteisye
To speke him harm that wold us villainye."
    "Dame," quod this Pluto, "be no lenger wroth.
I yive it up. But sith I swore mine ooth
That I wold graunten him his sight again,
1070 My word shall stand, I warne you certain.
I am a king; it sit me not to lie."
    "And I," quod she, "a queen of faïrye.
Hir answer shall she have, I undertake.
Let us namore wordes hereof make.
1075 Forsooth, I wol no lenger you contrarye."
    Now let us turn again to Januarye
That in the garden with his faire May
Singeth full murrier than the papejay,
You love I best, and shall, and other noon . . .
1080 So long about the alleys° is he goon

1052 **forbode** forbidden   1053 **emplastre** whitewash   1054 **idolas-
tre** idolater   1058 **rather** sooner   1064 **As . . . tresses** as sure as I
expect to keep my hair (the point being that women do not go bald).
Note that she has herself the skill of giving a sufficient answer, with
which she proposes to endow the female race   1080 **alleys** paths

Til he was come againes thilke pirye,°
Where as this Damian sitteth full mirrye
On high among the freshe leeves greene.
This freshe May, that is so bright and sheene,
Gan for to sike° and said, "Alas, my side!   1085
Now sir," quod she, "for aught that may bitide,
I most han of the peres that I see,
Or I mot die—so sore longeth me
To eten of the smalle peres greene.
Help, for hir love that is of hevene queene!   1090
I tell you well, a woman in my plit°
May han to fruit so greet an appetit
That she may dien but she of it have."

    "Alas!" quod he, "that I ne had here a knave
That coude climb! Alas, alas!" quod he,   1095
"For I am blind!" "Ye, sir, no fors," quod she,
"But wold ye vouche sauf, for Goddes sake,
The pirye inwith your armes for to take—
For well I wot that ye mistruste me;
Than shold I climbe well enough," quod she,   1100
"So I my foot might set upon your back."

    "Certes," quod he, "thereon shall be no lack,
Might I you helpen with mine herte blood."
He stoupeth down, and on his back she stood,
And caught hir by a twist,° and up she goth—   1105
Ladies, I pray you that ye be not wroth;
I can not glose,° I am a rude man—
And suddenly anon this Damian
Gan pullen up the smock—and in he throng.°

    And whan that Pluto saw this greete wrong,   1110
To January he yaf again his sighte,
And made him see as well as ever he mighte.
And whan that he had caught his sight again,
Ne was there never man of thing so fain:

1081 **pirye** pear tree   1085 **sike** sigh   1091 **plit** condition, i.e., preg-
nant   1105 **And . . . twist** pulled herself on a branch   1107 **glose** talk
around it, be euphemistic   1109 **throng** shoved

1115 But on his wife his thought was evermo.
Up to the tree he cast his eyen two,
And saw that Damian his wife had dressed
In swich manner it may not been expressed,
But if I wolde speke uncurteisly;
1120 And up he yaf a roring and a cry
As doth the moder whan the child shall die—
"Out! Help! Alas! Harrow!" he gan to crye,
"O stronge lady store!° what dostou!"
      And she answerde, "Sir, what aileth you?
1125 Have pacience and reson in your minde.
I have you holp on both your eyen blinde.
Up peril of my soul, I shall not lien,
As me was taught, to hele with your eyen°
Was no thing bet to make you to see
1130 Than struggle with a man upon a tree.
God wot I did it in full good entente."
      "Struggle!" quod he. "Ye! algate in° it wente!
God yive you both on shames deeth to dien!
He swived° thee! I saw it with mine eyen,
1135 And elles be I hanged by the hals."°
      "Than is," quod she, "my medicine fals!
For certainly, if that ye mighte see,
Ye wold not sayn thise wordes unto me.
Ye han some glimsing,° and no parfit sighte."
1140   "I see," quod he, "as well as ever I mighte,
Thanked be God, with both mine eyen two;
And by my truth, me *thought*° he did thee so."
      "Ye maze,° maze, goode sir," quod she.
"This thank have I for I have made you see!
1145 Alas!" quod she, "that ever I was so kinde!"

1123 **O . . . store** Oh, shameless, shocking lady!   1128 **hele . . . eyen**
heal your eyes with   1132 **algate in** right in   1134 **swived** was
laying   1135 **hals** neck   1139 **glimsing** glimpsing, partial vision
1142 **me thought** it seemed to me. Compare this assertion with "I saw
it" (line 1134) and "I wende" (imagined, supposed, line 1149). The
progression comes to rest at line 1152   1143 **Ye maze** you're
confused

"Now dame," quod he, "let all pass out of minde.
Come down, my lief; and if I have missaid,
God help me so as I am yvel apaid.°
But by my fader soul, I *wende* have seen
How that this Damian had by thee lain   *1150*
And that thy smock had lain upon his brest."
    "Ye, sir," quod she, "ye may *ween* as you lest!
But sir, a man that waketh out of his sleep
He may not suddenly well taken keep
Upon a thing, ne seen it parfitly   *1155*
Till that he be adawed° veraily.
Right so a man that long hath blind y-be
Ne may not suddenly so well y-see,
First whan his sight is newe come again,
As he that hath a day or two y-seen.   *1160*
Till that your sight y-sattled° be a while,
There may full many a sighte you beguile.
Beth ware, I pray you! For, by hevene king,
Full many a man weeneth to see a thing
And it is all another than it seemeth.   *1165*
He that misconceiveth, he misdeemeth"°—
And with that word she leep down fro the tree.
    This January, who is glad but he?
He kisseth hir and clippeth hir full ofte,
And on hir womb he stroketh hir full softe,   *1170*
And to his palais home he hath hir lad.
Now, goode men, I pray you to be glad.
Thus endeth here my tale of Januarye.
God bless us and his moder, Sainte Marye.

1148 **yvel apaid** sorry   1156 **adawed** conscious   1161 **y-sattled**
settled   1166 **misdeemeth** misjudges

THE FRANKLIN ADDRESSES
THE SQUIRE

"In faith, Squier, thou hast thee well y-quit°
And gentilly: I praise well thy wit,"
Quod the Franklain. "Considering thy youthe,
So feelingly thou spekest, sir, I allow° thee.
5   As to my doom,° there is none that is heer
Of eloquence that shall be thy peer,
If that thou live—God yeve thee good chaunce!°
And in vertu send thee continuance,
For of thy speech I have greet daintee.°
10 I have a son; and by the Trinitee
I had lever° than twenty pound worth land,°
Though it right now were fallen in mine hand,
He were a man of swich discrecioun°
As that *ye* been. Fy on possessioun
15 But if° a man be vertuous withall!
I have my sone snibbed,° and yet shall,
For he to vertu listeth not entende;°
But for to play at dees° and to dispende°
And lese° all that he hath is his usage.°
20 And he hath lever talken with a page
Than to commune with any gentil wight,

1 **thee ... y-quit** acquitted yourself well   4 **allow** commend
5 **As ... doom** in my judgment   7 **chaunce** fortune   9 **daintee**
pleasure   11 **I ... lever** I would rather have   11 **twenty ... land**
land which produces £20 per annum income   13 **discrecioun** good
judgment   15 **But if** unless   16 **snibbed** chided, scolded
17 **listeth ... entende** chooses to pay no attention   18 **dees** dice
18 **dispende** squander   19 **lese** lose   19 **usage** practice

Where he might lerne gentilesse aright."
    "Straw for thy gentilesse!" quod our Host.
"What, Frankelain, pardee sir, well thou woost
That ech of you mot tellen atte leeste   25
A tale or two, or breken his biheste."°
    "That know I well, sir," quod the Frankelain.
"I pray you, haveth me not in disdain,°
Though to this man I speke a word or two."
    "Tell on thy tale withouten wordes mo."   30
    "Gladly, sir Host," quod he, "I wol obeye
Unto your will. Now herkneth what I saye.
I wol you not contrarien° in no wise,
As fer as that my wittes wol suffise.
I pray to God that it may plesen you.   35
Than wot I well that it is good enow."

THE FRANKLIN'S PROLOGUE

Thise olde gentil Britons° in hir dayes
Of diverse aventures maden layes,°
Rymeyed° in hir firste Briton tonge;°
Which layes with hir instruments they songe,
Or elles redden hem for hir plesaunce.   5
And one of hem have I in remembraunce,
Which I shall sayn with good will, as I can.
    But, sirs, by cause I am a burel° man,

26 **biheste** promise   28 **haveth . . . disdain** do not be offended with
me   33 **contrarien** go against   1 **Britons** Bretons, people of Brit-
tany in northern France   2 **layes** the Breton lays: short narrative po-
ems sung by minstrels, such as those composed by Marie de France
3 **Rymeyed** rhymed   3 **firste . . . tonge** original Breton, a Celtic
language   8 **burel** plain

At my beginning first I you beseeche
10 Have me excused of my rude° speeche.
I lerned never rhetoric, certain;
Thing that I speke it mot be bare and plain.
I sleep° never on the Mount of Parnaso°,
Ne lerned Marcus Tullius Scithero.°
15 Colours° ne know I none, withouten drede,
But swich colours as growen in the mede,°
Or elles swiche as men dye or painte;
Colours of rhetorike been too quainte.°
My spirit feeleth not of swich mattere:
20 But if you list, my tale shull ye heere.

THE FRANKLIN'S TALE

In Armorik,° that called is Britaine,
There was a knight that loved and did his paine°
To serve a lady in his beste wise.
And many a labour, many a greet emprise°
25 He for his lady wrought, ere she were wonne;
For she was one the fairest° under sunne,
And eek thereto come of so heigh kinrede°
That well unnethes° dorst this knight for drede°
Tell hir his woe, his pain, and his distresse.
30 But atte last she for his worthinesse,

10 **rude** humble, rough   13 **sleep** slept   13 **Mount ... Parnaso**
Mount Parnassus, home of the Muses   14 **Marcus ... Scithero**
Cicero   15 **Colours** rhetorical devices   16 **mede** meadow
18 **quainte** strange   21 **Armorik** Armorica (*ar* on + *mor* sea),
Brittany   22 **did ... paine** troubled himself   24 **emprise** enterprise
26 **one ... fairest** one of the most beautiful   27 **kinrede** family
28 **well unnethes** with great difficulty   28 **for drede** for fear

And namely° for his meek obeisaunce,°
Hath swich a pitee caught of his penaunce°
That prively° she fill of his accord°
To take him for hir husband and hir lord,
Of swich lordship as men han over hir wives.   35
And for to lede the more in bliss hir lives°
Of his free will he swore hir as a knight
That never in all his life he day ne night
Ne shold upon him take no maistrye°
Again hir will, ne kith° hir jalousye,   40
But hir obey and follow hir will in all,
As any lover to his lady shall—
Save that the name of sovereignetee,°
That wold *he* have, for shame of his degree.°
    She thanked him, and with full greet humblesse   45
She saide, "Sir, sith of your gentilesse
Ye proffre° me to have so large° a reine,
Ne wolde never God bitwix us twaine,
As in my guilt, were outher wer or strif.°
Sir, I wol be your humble, trewe wif—   50
Have here my trouth—till that mine herte breste."°
Thus been they both in quiet and in reste.
    For oo thing, sires, saufly dare I saye:
That freendes everich other° mot obeye°
If they wol longe holden compaignye.   55
Love wol not be constrained by maistrye.
Whan maistry cometh, the God of Love anon

31 **namely** particularly   31 **meek obeisaunce** humble submission,
attention   32 **penaunce** suffering   33 **prively** inwardly   33 **fill . . .
accord** came to an understanding with him   36 **for . . . lives** in order
to pass their lives in more happiness   39 **maistrye** control   40 **kith**
show   43 **sovereignetee** sovereignty. The Franklin echoes the words
of the Wife of Bath in her tale (cf. lines 182–84), thus continuing the
debate on marriage   44 **for . . . degree** out of respect for his rank
47 **proffre** offer   47 **large** free   48–49 **Ne . . . strif** would to God
that there should never, because of my fault, be war or strife between
us   51 **breste** should burst. The vow of humility here would satisfy
the Clerk's ideas on marriage   54 **everich other** each other   54 **obeye**
i.e., make compromise with

Beteth his wings and farewell—he is gone!
Love is a thing as any spirit free:
60 Women of kind° desiren libertee,
And not to been constrained as a thrall°—
And so doon men, if I sooth sayen shall.
Look who that° is most pacient in love:
He is at his avantage all above.
65 Pacience is an high vertu, certain,
For it venquisheth° (as thise clerkes sayn)
Things that rigour° sholde never attaine.
For every word men may not chide or plaine.
Lerneth to suffre, or elles, so mote I goon,°
70 Ye shull it lerne whereso° ye wol or non.
For in this world, certain, there no wight is
That he ne doth or saith sometime amiss.
Ire, sickness, or constellacioun,°
Wine, woe, or chaunging of complexioun°
75 Causeth full oft° to doon amiss or speken.
On every wrong a man may not be wreken.°
After the time must be temperaunce
To every wight that kan on governaunce.°
And therefore hath this wise worthy knight
80 To live in ese suffrance hir bihight,°
And she to him full wisly° gan to swere
That never shold there be defaute in here.°
—Here may men seen an humble wise accord:
Thus hath she take hir servant and hir lord—
85 Servant in love and lord in marriage.
Than was he both in lordship and servage.

60 **of kind** by nature   61 **thrall** slave   63 **Look who that** whoever
66 **venquisheth** outlasts, overcomes   67 **rigour** force   69 **so . . .
goon** i.e., or I am mistaken   70 **whereso** whether   73 **constellacioun**
fate   74 **complexioun** the balance of humors (hot, cold, moist, dry)
which constitutes one's temperament   75 **full oft** frequently ("many
a man" understood)   76 **wreken** avenged   77–78 **After . . . gover-
naunce** according to the situation there must be moderation on the part
of every man who knows how to control himself   80 **suffrance . . .
bihight** promised patience to her   81 **wisly** certainly   82 **defaute . . .
here** the lack in her, i.e., she promised to do the same

Servage? Nay, but in lordship above,
Sith he hath both his lady and his love—
His lady, certes, and his wife also,
The which that law of love accordeth to.° 90
And whan he was in this prosperitee,
Home with his wife he goth to his contree
Not fer fro Pedmark,° ther his dwelling was
Where as he liveth in bliss and in solas.°

Who coude tell, but he had wedded be, 95
The joy, the ese, and the prosperitee
That is bitwix an husband and his wif?
A yeer and more lasted this blissful lif,
Till that the knight of which I speke of thus—
That of Kairrud° was cleped Arveragus— 100
Shop him° to goon and dwell a yeer or twaine
In Engelond, that cleped was eek Britaine,
To seek in armes worship° and honour
(For all his lust he set in swich labour)
And dwelled there two yeer—the book saith thus. 105

*   *   *

Now wol I stint° of this Arveragus
And speke I wol of Dorigen his wif,
That loveth hir husband as hir hertes lif.
For his absence weepeth she and siketh,°
As doon thise noble wives whan hem liketh.° 110
She mourneth, waketh, waileth, fasteth, plaineth;
Desire of his presence hir so distraineth°
That all this wide world she set at nought.
Hir freendes, which that knew hir hevy thought,

---

90 **accordeth to** agrees to. The Franklin's elaborate compromise encompasses courtly love   93 **Pedmark**, the western extremity of Brittany, which has a rocky coastline   94 **solas** comfort   100 **Kairrud** a village   101 **Shop him** prepared   103 **worship** renown   106 **stint** stop   109 **siketh** sighs   110 **whan ... liketh** when they please (the construction is impersonal)   112 **distraineth** oppresses

115   Comforten hir in all that ever they may.
     They preechen hir, they tell hir night and day
     That causeless she sleeth hirself, alas—
     And every comfort possible in this cas°
     They doon to hir with all hir bisinesse°—
120   All for to make hir leeve hir hevinesse.°
       By process,° as ye knowen everichon,
     Men may so longe graven° in a ston
     Till some figure therein emprinted be.
     So long han they conforted hir, till she
125   Received hath, by hope and by resoun,
     Th'emprinting of hir° consolacioun,
     Thurgh which hir greete sorrwe gan assuage—
     She may not alway duren in swich rage.°
       And eek Arveragus in all this care
130   Hath sent hir letters home of his welfare
     And that he wol come hastily again,
     Or elles had this sorrwe hir herte slain.
     Hir freendes saw hir sorrwe gan to slacke,
     And prayed hir on knees, for Goddes sake,
135   To come and romen hir° in compaignye
     Away to drive hir derke fantasye;°
     And finally she graunted that requeste,
     For well she saw that it was for the beste.
       Now stood hir castel faste° by the see,
140   And often with hir freendes walketh she
     Hir to disport° upon the bank on heigh
     Where as she many a ship and barge seigh°
     Sailing hir course where as hem liste go.
     But than was that a parcel° of hir woe,
145   For to hirself full oft, "Alas!" saith she,
     "Is there no ship of so many as I see

---

118 **cas** situation   119 **bisinesse** anxious attention   120 **hevinesse**
sadness   121 **By process** in due course   122 **graven** engrave, scratch
126 **hir** their   128 **duren . . . rage** remain in such a passion   135 **ro-
men hir** take a walk   136 **derke fantasye** gloomy imaginings
139 **faste** close   141 **Hir . . . disport** to amuse herself   142 **seigh**
saw   144 **parcel** portion

Wol bringen home my lord? Than were mine herte
All warished of his° bitter paines smerte."
Another time there wold she sit and thinke
And cast hir eyen downward fro the brinke—   *150*
But whan she seigh the grisly rockes blacke
For veray fere so wold hir herte quake
That on hir feet she might hir not sustene.
Than wold she sit adown upon the greene
And pitously into the see biholde,   *155*
And sayn right thus, with sorrweful sikes colde:°
"Eterne God, that thurgh thy purveyance°
Ledest the world by certain governance,
In idle,° as men sayn, ye nothing make.
But Lord, thise grisly feendly rockes blacke,   *160*
That seemen rather a foul confusioun
Of werk, than any fair creacioun
Of swich a parfit wise God and a stable,
Why han ye wrought this werk unresonable?
For by this werk south, north, ne west ne est   *165*
There nis y-fostred° man ne brid° ne beest:
It doth no good, to my wit, but annoyeth.
See ye not, Lord, how mankind it destroyeth?
An hundred thousand bodies of mankinde
Han rockes slain, al be they not in minde,   *170*
Which mankind is so fair part of thy werk
That thou it madest like to thine own merk.°
Than seemed it ye had a greet chiertee°
Toward mankind. But how than may it be
That ye swich meenes make it to destroyen,   *175*
Which meenes do no good but ever annoyen?
I wot well clerkes wol sayn as hem leste
By arguments that all is for the beste,
Though I ne can the causes not y-knowe.
But thilke° God that made wind to blowe,   *180*

148 **warished . . . his** relieved on its   156 **sikes colde** unhappy sighs
157 **purveyance** providence   159 **In idle** in vain   166 **y-fostred**
nourished   166 **brid** bird   172 **merk** image   173 **chiertee** fondness
180 **thilke** the same

As keep° my lord! This my conclusioun.
To clerkes let I all disputisoun°—
But wolde God that all thise rockes blacke
Were sunken into helle for his sake!
185   Thise rockes slain mine herte for the feere!"
    Thus wold she sayn with many a pitous teere.
Hir freendes saw that it was no disport
To romen by the see, but discomfort,
And shopen for° to playen somewhere elles.
190   They leden hir by rivers and by welles
And eek in other places delitables;°
They dauncen and they playen at chess and tables.°
So on a day, right in the morrwetide,°
Unto a garden that was there beside
195   In which that they had made hir ordinaunce
Of vitaille,° and of other purveyaunce,°
They goon and play hem all the longe day.
And this was on the sixte morrwe of May,
Which May had painted with his softe showres
200   This garden full of leves and of flowres;
And craft of mannes hand so curiously°
Arrayed had this garden trewely
That never was there garden of swich pris°
But if it were the veray paradis.°
205   The odour of flowers and the freshe sighte
Wold han maked any herte lighte
That ever was born, but if° too greet sicknesse
Or too greet sorrwe held it in distresse,
So full it was of beautee with plesaunce.
210   At after-dinner gonne they to daunce
And singe also, save Dorigen alone,
Which made alway hir complaint and hir mone,

181 **As keep** protect 182 **let . . . disputisoun** I leave all debate
189 **shopen for** determined 191 **delitables** delightful 192 **tables**
backgammon 193 **morrwetide** morning 195–96 **ordinaunce . . .
vitaille** arrangement of foods 196 **purveyaunce** provisions
201 **curiously** carefully 203 **pris** excellence 204 **veray paradis**
Paradise itself 207 **but if** unless

For she ne saw him on the daunce go
That was hir husband and hir love also.
But natheless she most a time abide,   215
And with good hope let hir sorrow slide.
    Upon this daunce, amonges other men,
Daunced a squier before Dorigen
That fresher was and jollier of array,°
As to my doom,° than is the month of May.   220
He singeth, daunceth, passing° any man
That is or was sith that the world began.
Therewith he was, if men him shold descrive,
One of the beste faring man on live.°
Yong, strong, right vertuous, and rich, and wis,   225
And well-beloved, and holden in greet pris.°
And shortly, if the sooth I tellen shall,
Unwitting of this Dorigen at all,
This lusty squier, servant to Venus—
Which that y-cleped was Aurelius—   230
Had loved hir best of any creature
Two yeer and more, as was his aventure;°
But never dorst he tellen hir his grevaunce.
Withouten cup he drank all his penance.°
He was despaired—no thing dorst he saye,   235
Save in his songes somewhat wold he wraye°
His woe, as in a general complaining.°
He said he loved, and was beloved no thing,
Of which mattere made he many layes,
Songes, complaintes, roundels, virelayes,°   240
How that he dorste not his sorrow telle,
But languisheth as a fury° doth in helle.
And die he most, he said, as did Echo°

219 **jollier ... array** livelier in dress   220 **As ... doom** to my way
of thinking   221 **passing** surpassing   224 **beste ... live** handsomest
men alive   226 **pris** esteem   232 **as ... aventure** as it so happened
234 **Withouten ... penance** i.e., he experienced his suffering straight
from the source   236 **wraye** betray   237 **complaining** lament
240 **complaintes ... virelayes** love songs addressed to a lady based
on courtly French models   242 **fury** an avenging spirit   243 **Echo**
Echo could not tell Narcissus of her love for him and died in despair

For Narcissus that dorst not tell hir woe.
245   In other manner than ye heer me saye
Ne dorst he not to hir his woe biwraye,°
Save that paraventure some time at daunces
Ther yonge folk keepen hir observaunces,°
It may well be he looked on hir face
250   In swich a wise as man that asketh grace—
But no thing wiste she of his entente.
Natheless, it happed ere they thennes wente,
By cause that he was hire neighebour
And was a man of worship and honour,
255   And had y-knowen him of time yore,°
They fill in speeche,° and forth more and more
Unto his purpose drow Aurelius,
And whan he saw his time he saide thus:
   "Madame," quod he, "by God that this world made,
260   So that I wist it might your herte glade,
I wold that day that your Arveragus
Went over the see that I, Aurelius,
Had went ther never I shold have come again!
For well I wot my service is in vain—
265   My guerdon is but bresting° of mine herte.
Madame, reweth° upon my paines smerte,
For with a word ye may me sleen or save!
Here at your feet God wold that I were grave!
I ne have as now no leiser more to saye—
270   Have mercy, sweet, or ye wol do me deye!"°
   She gan to look upon Aurelius:
"Is this your will?" quod she, "and say ye thus?
Never erst,"° quod she, "ne wist I° what ye mente.
But now, Aurelie, I know your entente,
275   By thilke God that yaf° me soul and lif,
Ne shall I never been untrewe wif

---

246 **biwraye** disclose 248 **keepen ... observaunces** hold their ceremonies 255 **of ... yore** for a long time 256 **fill ... speeche** got into a conversation 265 **guerdon ... bresting** reward is only the bursting 266 **reweth** take pity 270 **do ... deye** cause me to die 273 **erst** before 273 **ne wist I** did I know 275 **yaf** gave

In word ne werk as far as I have wit.
I wol be his to whom that I am knit°—
Take this for final answer as of° me."
But after that in play thus saide she: 280
"Aurelie," quod she, "by heighe God above,
Yet wold I graunte you to been your love,
Sin I you see so pitously complaine:
Look what° day that endelong Britaine°
Ye remove all the rockes, stone by stoon,   285
That they ne lette° ship ne boot° to goon.
I say, whan ye han made the coost so cleene
Of rockes that there nis no stone y-seene,
Than wol I love you best of any man—
Have here my trouth—in all that ever I can."   290

     "Is there noon other grace in you?" quod he.
     "No, by that Lord," quod she, "that maked me.
For well I wot that it shall never bitide.°
Let swich follies out of your herte slide!
What daintee° shold a man han in his lif   295
For to go love another mannes wif
That hath hir body whan so that him liketh!"
     Aurelius full ofte sore siketh;
Woe was Aurelie whan that he this herde,
And with a sorrweful hert he thus answerde: 300
"Madame," quod he, "this were an impossible!
Than mot I die of sudden deeth horrible!"
And with that word he turned him anon.
     Tho come hir other freendes many oon,
And in the alleys° romeden up and down,   305
And nothing wist of this conclusioun.
But suddenly begonne revel newe
Till that the brighte sunne lost his hewe,
For th'orisont hath reft° the sun his light—
This is as much to say as, it was night—   310

278 **knit** married   279 **as of** from   284 **Look what** whatever
284 **endelong Britaine** all along the coast of Brittany   286 **lette**
prevent   286 **boot** boat   293 **bitide** happen   295 **daintee** pleasure
305 **alleys** walkways   309 **orisont . . . reft** horizon has taken away

And home they goon in joy and in solas.
    Save only wretched Aurelius, alas—
He to his house is gone with sorrweful herte.
He seeth he may not from his deeth asterte:°
315 Him seemed that he felt his herte colde.°
Up to the heven his handes he gan holde,
And on his knowes° bare he set him down
And in his raving said his orisoun.°
For veray woe out of his wit he braide.°
320 He niste what he spake, but thus he saide—
With pitous hert his plaint hath he begonne
Unto the goddes, and first unto the sunne:
He said, "Apollo,° god and governour
Of every plaunte, herbe, tree, and flower,
325 That yevest after thy declinacioun°
To ech of hem his time and his sesoun,
As thine herberwe° chaungeth, low or heighe:
Lord Phebus, cast thy merciable eighe°
On wretch Aurelie which that am but lorn!
330 Lo, Lord, my lady hath my deeth y-sworn
Withouten guilt, but thy benignitee
Upon my deedly hert have some pitee.
For well I wot, Lord Phebus, if you lest,
Ye may me helpen, save my lady, best.
335 Now voucheth sauf that I may you devise°
How that I may been holpen, and in what wise:
Your blissful suster, Lucina the sheene,°
That of the see is chief goddess and queene
(Though Neptunus° have deitee in the see,
340 Yet emperess aboven him is she)
Ye knowen well, Lord, that—right as hir desir

---

314 **asterte** escape 315 **colde** grow cold 317 **knowes** knees
318 **orisoun** prayer 319 **braide** fled 323 **Apollo** Phoebus Apollo,
god of the sun 325 **That ... declinacioun** who bestow (thy rays)
according to thy distance from the celestial equator 327 **herberwe**
residence 328 **eighe** eye 335 **devise** explain 337 **Lucina the
sheene** Diana, goddess of the moon, who is called the "chaste goddess"
339 **Neptunus** Neptune, chief god of the sea

Is to be quicked and lighted of° your fir,
For which she followeth you full bisily°—
Right so the see desireth naturelly
To followen hir, as she that is goddesse   345
Both in the see and rivers more and lesse.
Wherefore, Lord Phebus, this is my requeste:
Do this miracle—or do mine herte breste—
That now next at this opposicioun,°
Which in the sign shall be of the Leoun,   350
As prayeth° hir so greet a flood to bringe
That five fadme at the lest it overspringe°
The hyest rock in Armorik Britaine;
And let this flood endure yeeres twaine.
Than certes to my lady may I saye,   355
'Holdeth your hest,° the rockes been awaye!'
Lord Phebus, doth this miracle for me!
Pray hir she go no faster course than ye—
I say this, prayeth your suster that she go
No faster course than ye thise yeeres two.   360
Than shall she been even at the full° alway,
And spring-flood lasten bothe night and day.
And but she vouche sauf° in swich mannere
To graunte me my sovereign lady dere,
Pray hir to sinken every rock adown   365
Into hir owne derke regioun°
Under the ground ther Pluto dwelleth inne—
Or never mo shall I my lady winne!
Thy temple in Delphos° wol I barefoot seeke.
Lord Phebus, see the terres on my cheeke,   370
And of my pain have some compassioun!"

---

342 **quicked . . . of** stimulated and lighted by   343 **bisily** constantly
349 **now . . . opposicioun** the next time the moon and sun are in op-
position, i.e., when the sun is in the sign of Leo and the moon is in the
sign of Aquarius—in about three months   351 **As prayeth** pray
352 **five . . . overspringe** that (the sea) overrun by at least five fathoms
356 **Holdeth . . . hest** keep your promise   361 **at . . . full** in a full
moon   363 **vouche sauf** sees fit   366 **derke regioun** Lucina in her
manifestation as Proserpina, queen of hell   369 **Delphos** Delphi

And with that word in swoun he fill adown,
And longe time he lay forth in a traunce.
    His brother, which that knew of his penaunce,°
375 Up caught him, and to bed he hath him brought.
Despaired in this torment and this thought
Let I this woeful creature lie—
Chese he for me wher° he wol live or die.

*   *   *

    Arveragus with hele° and greet honour,
380 As he that was of chivalry the flower,
Is comen home, and other worthy men.
O, blissful artou now, thou Dorigen,
That hast thy lusty° husband in thine armes,
The freshe knight, the worthy man of armes,
385 That loveth thee as his own hertes lif!
No thing list him to been imaginatif°
If any wight had spoke while he was oute
To hir of love; he had of it no doute.
He not entendeth° to no swich mattere
390 But daunceth, jousteth, maketh hir good cheere.
    And thus in joy and bliss I let hem dwelle,
And of the sick Aurelius wol I telle.
In langour and in torment furious
Two yeer and more lay wretch Aurelius,
395 Ere any foot he might on erthe gon,
Ne comfort in this time had he non—
Save of his brother, which that was a clerk:
He knew of all this woe and all this werk,
For to noon other creature, certain,
400 Of this matter he dorste no word sayn.
Under his brest he bare it more secree
Than ever did Pamphilus for Galathee.°

374 **penaunce** suffering 378 **wher** whether 379 **hele** health
383 **lusty** joyous 386 **No . . . imaginatif** he is not at all the imaginative
(i.e., suspicious) sort 389 **not entendeth** pays no attention 402 **Pam-
philus . . . Galathee** the two lovers in a twelfth-century Latin dialogue

His breast was whole withoute for to seene,°
But in his hert ay was the arrow keene:
And well ye know that of a sursanure°
In surgery is perilous the cure,   405
But men might touch the arrwe or come thereby.
His brother weep and wailed prively,
Till at the last him fill in remembrance
That whiles he was at Orliens° in France—
As yonge clerkes that been likerous°   410
To reden artes that been curious,°
Seeken in every halk and every herne°
Particuler° sciences for to lerne—
He him remembered that, upon a day,
At Orliens in study a book he sey   415
Of magic naturel,° which his fellawe,
That was that time a bacheler of lawe
(Al were he there to lerne another craft)
Had prively upon his desk y-laft;°
Which book spak muchel of the operacioun   420
Touching the eight and twenty mansiouns°
That longen to the moon—and swich follye
As in our dayes is not worth a flye
(For holy chirches faith in our bileve
Ne suffreth° noon illusion *us* to greve).   425
And whan this book was in his remembraunce,
Anon for joy his herte gan to daunce,
And to himself he saide prively,
"My brother shall be warished° hastily!
For I am siker that there be sciences   430
By whiche men make diverse apparences,°

---

403 **withoute . . . seene** to look at from the outside   405 **sursanure** a
wound healed only on the surface   410 **Orliens** Orleans, site of an old
university   411 **likerous** zealous   412 **curious** occult, out of the
ordinary   413 **every . . . herne** every nook and cranny   414 **Parti-
culer** unusual   417 **magic naturel** i.e., magic opposed to "black"
magic and necromancy   420 **y-laft** left   422 **eight . . . mansiouns**
the positions of the moon in relation to stars   426 **Ne suffreth** does
not permit   430 **warished** cured   432 **apparences** apparitions

Swich as thise subtile tregetoures° playe.
For oft at feestes have I well herd saye
435 That tregetoures within an halle large
Have made come in a water° and a barge,
And in the halle rowen up and down;
Some time hath seemed come a grim leoun,
Some time flowers spring as in a mede,
440 Some time a vine and grapes white and rede,
Some time a castel all of lime and ston,
And whan hem liked voided it° anon—
Thus *seemed* it to every mannes sighte!
Now than conclude I thus, that if I mighte
445 At Orliens some old fellaw y-finde
That had thise moones mansions in minde,
Or other magic naturel above,
He shold well make my brother han his love.
For with an apparence a clerk may make
450 To mannes sight that all the rockes blacke
Of Britaine were y-voided everichon,
And shippes by the brink comen and gon,
And in swich form enduren a day or two.
Than were my brother warished of his woe!
455 Than must she needes holden hir biheste,°
Or elles he shall shame hir at the leeste!"
    What shold I make a lenger tale of this?
Unto his brother's bed he comen is,
And swich comfort he yaf him for to gon
460 To Orliens, that up he stert anon
And on his way forthward than is he fare,
In hope for to been lissed° of his care.
    Whan they were come almost to that citee,
But if it were a two furlong or three,
465 A yong clerk roming by himself they mette,
Which that in Latin thriftily hem grette,°

---

433 **tregetoures** magicians   436 **Have . . . water** have made water
come in   442 **voided it** made it disappear   455 **biheste** promise
462 **lissed** relieved   466 **thriftily . . . grette** formally greeted them

And after that he said a wonder° thing:
"I know," quod he, "the cause of your coming."
And ere they ferther any foote wente,
He told hem all that was in hir entente.   470
This Briton clerk him asked of fellawes,
The which that he had know in olde dawes,°
And he answered him that they dede were—
For which he weep full ofte many a tere.
Down off his horse Aurelius light anon,   475
And with this magicien forth is he gon
Home to his house, and maden him well at ese.
Hem lacked no vitaille° that might hem plese—
So well arrayed house as there was oon
Aurelius in his life saw never noon.   480
    He shewed him ere he went to supper
Forestes, parkes full of wilde deer—
There saw he hertes with hir hornes hye,
The greetest that ever were seen with eye;
He saw of hem an hundred slain wit houndes,   485
And some with arrows bled of bitter woundes.
He saw, when voided were° thise wilde deer,
Thise fauconers° upon a fair river,
That with hir hawkes han the heron slain.
Tho saw he knightes jousting in a plain.   490
And after this he did him this plesaunce,
That he him shewed his lady on a daunce,
On which himself he daunced—as him thoughte.
And whan this maister that this magic wroughte
Saw it was time, he clapt his handes two,   495
And farewell—all our revel was ago!°
And yet removed they never out of the hous
While they saw all this sighte merveillous,
But in his study, ther as his bookes be,
They setten still, and no wight but they three!   500

---

467 **wonder** wondrous   472 **dawes** days   478 **vitaille** foodstuff
487 **voided were** had disappeared   488 **fauconers** falconers
496 **ago** gone

    To him this maister called his squier
And said him thus, "Is redy our supper?
Almost an hour it is, I undertake,
Sith I you bade our supper for to make,
505 Whan that thise worthy men wenten with me
Into my study ther as my bookes be."
"Sir," quod this squier, "whan it liketh you,°
It is all redy, though ye wol right now."
"Go we than soup,"° quod he, "as for the beste:
510 This amorous folk some time mot han hir reste."
    At after-supper fill they in tretee°
What summe shold this maistres guerdon° be
To removen all the rockes of Britaine,
And eek from Gerounde° to the mouth of Seine.
515 He made it straunge,° and swore, so God him save,
Less than a thousand pound he wold not have,
Ne gladly for that sum he wold not gon.
    Aurelius with blissful hert anon
Answered thus: "Fy on a thousand pound!
520 This wide world, which that men say is round,
I wold it yive, if I were lord of it.
This bargain is full drive,° for we been knit!°
Ye shall be payed trewely, by my trouthe!
But looketh now, for no negligence or slouthe,
525 Ye tarry us here no lenger than tomorrwe."
    "Nay," quod this clerk, "have here my faith to
        borrowe."°
To bed is gone Aurelius whan him leste,
And well neigh all that night he had his reste—
What for his labour and his hope of blisse,
530 His woeful hert of penaunce had a lisse.°
    Upon the morrwe, whan that it was day
To Britain tooke they the righte° way,

507 **it . . . you** you like   509 **Go . . . soup** let's go to supper
511 **tretee** negotiaiton   512 **guerdon** reward   514 **Gerounde** the
river Geraunde   515 **made . . . straunge** made it difficult   522 **full
drive** fully made   522 **knit** agreed   526 **to borrwe** as a pledge
530 **lisse** relief   532 **righte** direct

Aurelius and this magicien beside,
And been descended ther they wold abide.
And this was, as thise bookes me remembre,   535
The colde frosty seson of Decembre.
Phebus wax old,° and hewed like latoun,°
That in his hote declinacioun°
Shone as the burned gold with stremes brighte.
But now in Capricorn° adown he lighte,   540
Where as he shone full pale, I dare well sayn:
The bitter frostes with the sleet and rain
Destroyed hath the green in every yerd.
Janus° sit by the fire with double beerd
And drinketh of his bugle horn° the win,   545
Biforn him stant brawen° of the tusked swin,°
And "Nowel!" crieth every lusty man.
Aurelius in all that ever he can
Doth to this maister cheer and reverence,
And prayeth him to doon his diligence   550
To bringen him out of his paines smerte,
Or with a swerd that he wold slit his herte.

    This subtil clerk swich ruth had of° this man
That night and day he sped him that he can°
To waiten a time of his conclusioun°—   555
This is to sayn, to make illusioun
By swich an apparence of juggelrye°
(I ne kan no termes of astrologye)
That she and every wight shold ween° and saye
That of Britain the rockes were awaye,   560
Or elles they were sunken under grounde.
So at the last he hath his time y-founde

537 **Phebus . . . old** i.e., the sun was near setting   537 **latoun** brass
538 **hote declinacioun** i.e., in Cancer, at the zenith north of the
Equator   540 **in Capricorn** i.e., in opposition, or near the Equator
544 **Janus** Janus, the two-faced god ("with double beerd"), i.e.,
January   545 **bugle horn** horn of a wild ox used for drinking
546 **brawen** meat   546 **tusked swin** boar, wild pig   553 **ruth . . . of**
had pity on   554 **sped . . . can** went as quickly as he could
555 **waiten . . . conclusioun** watch for a time to perform his operation
557 **juggelrye** magic   559 **ween** believe

To maken his japes° and his wretchednesse
Of swich a supersticious cursednesse.
565 His tables Tolletanes° forth he brought,
Full well corrected.° Ne there lacked nought,
Neither his collect ne his expanse yeeres,°
Ne his rootes,° ne his other geres°—
As been his centres° and his arguments,°
570 And his proporcionels convenients,°
For his equacions in every thing.
And by his eighte spere° in his werking
He knew full well how fer Alnath was shove°
Fro the heed of thilke fix Aries° above
575 That in the ninthe spere considered is—
Full subtilly he calculed all this.
Whan he had found his firste mansioun,°
He knew the remnant° by proporcioun,
And knew the arising of his moone well,
580 And in whose face and term, and every deel,°
And knew full well the moones mansioun
Accordant to° his operacioun,
And knew also his other observaunces°
For swich illusiouns and swich meschaunces°

563 **japes** tricks   565 **tables Tolletanes** Toledan astronomical tables
566 **corrected** astronomical tables were frequently revised in the late
Middle Ages   567 **collect . . . yeeres** i.e., "collect years" and "expanse
years"—two ways of computing planetary movement based upon lon-
ger and shorter periods respectively   568 **rootes** tables for making
other mathematical computations   568 **geres** equipment   569 **cen-
tres** mechanism on an astrolabe   569 **arguments** measurements from
which other quantities may be derived   570 **proporcionels conve-
nients** tables of proportions   572 **eighte spere** medieval astronomical
theory conceived of nine spheres, or transparent shells, in concentric
and eccentric motion around the earth. The fixed stars reside in the
eighth sphere   573 **Alnath . . . shove** the star Arietes had moved
574 **fix Aries** i.e., the fixed star Aries, which was thought to reside in
the ninth sphere and which served as a basis of other astronomical
computations   577 **firste mansioun** the moon's first position, Alnath
578 **remnant** rest   580 **in . . . deel** in whose zodiacal sign and planet
and every part   582 **Accordant to** having to do with   583 **obser-
vaunces** practices   584 **meschaunces** misguided occupations

As hethen folk useden in thilke dayes.   585
For which no lenger maked he delayes,
But, thurgh his magic, for a week or twaye
It seemed that all the rockes were awaye!

*   *   *

  Aurelius, which that yet despaired is
Wher° he shall han his love or fare amiss,°   590
Awaiteth night and day on this miracle.
And whan he knew that there was noon obstacle,
That voided were thise rockes everichon,
Down to his maistres feet he fill anon
And said, "I, woeful wretch Aurelius,   595
Thank you, lord, and lady mine Venus,
That me han holpen fro my cares colde!"
And to the temple his way forth hath he holde,°
Where as he knew he shold his lady see.
And whan he saw his time, anon-right° he   600
With dredful hert and with full humble cheere
Salued° hath his sovereign lady dere:
  "My righte lady," quod this woeful man,
"Whom I most drede and love as best I can,
And lothest were of all this world displese,   605
Nere it° that I for you have swich disese
That I most dien here at your foot anon,
Nought wold I tell how me is woe-bigon.
But certes outher must I die or plaine!
Ye sleen me guilteless for veray paine!   610
But of my deeth thought that ye have no routhe,
Aviseth you° ere that ye breke your trouthe.
Repenteth you, for thilke God above,
Ere ye me sleen by cause that I you love.
For, Madame, well ye wot what ye han hight°   615

590 **Wher** whether 590 **fare amiss** fail 598 **holde** gone
600 **anon-right** straightaway 602 **Salued** greeted 606 **Nere it** were
it not 612 **Aviseth you** think it over 615 **hight** promised

(Not that I challenge any thing of right
Of you, my sovereign lady, but your grace)—
But in a garden yond at swich a place,
Ye wot right well what ye bihighten me,
620   And in mine hand your trouthe plighten ye
To love me best. God wot ye saide so,
Al be that I unworthy am thereto.
Madame, I speke it for the honour of you
More than to save mine hertes life right now:
625   I have do so as ye commanded me,
And if ye vouche sauf,° ye may go see.
Doth as you list, have your bihest in minde,
For quick or deed right there ye shall me finde.
In you lith all to do me live or deye:
630   But well I wot the rockes been awaye."
        He taketh his leeve and she astoned° stood—
In all hir face nas a drop of blood.
She wende never have come° in swich a trappe.
"Alas," quod she, "that ever this shold happe!
635   For wende I never by possibilitee
That swich a monstre° or merveil mighte be!
It is agains the process of nature."
And home she goth a sorrweful creature;
For veray fere unnethe° may she go.
640   She weepeth, waileth all a day or two,
And swouneth that it routhe was to see.
But why it was, to no wight tolde she,
For out of town was gone Arveragus.
But to hirself she spak and saide thus,
645   With face pale and with full sorrweful cheere
In hir complaint, as ye shall after heere:
        "Alas," quod she, "on thee, Fortune, I plaine,
That unware wrapped hast me in thy chaine,
For which t'escape woot I no succour
650   Save only deeth or elles dishonour—

626 **vouche sauf** see fit   631 **astoned** astonished   633 **She . . . come**
she never thought she would fall   636 **monstre** wondrous thing
639 **unnethe** scarcely

One of thise two bihoveth me° to chese.
But natheless yet have I lever to lese
My life than of my body to have a shame,
Or know myselven false, or lese my name;
And with my deeth I may be quit,° ywis.   655
Hath there not many a noble wife ere this,
And many a maid y-slain hirself, alas,
Rather than with hir body doon trespass?
Yis, certes, lo, thise stories° beren witnesse:
    Whan thritty tyrants full of cursednesse   660
Had slain Phidon in Athens atte feeste,
They commanded his daughtren for t'arreste,°
And bringen hem beforn hem in despit°
All naked, to fulfill hir foul delit;
And in hir fadres blood they made hem daunce   665
Upon the pavement—God yive him mischaunce!°
For which thise woeful maidens, full of drede,
Rather than they wold lese hir maidenhede,
They prively been stirt° into a welle
And dreint° hemselven, as the bookes telle.   670
    They of Messene let enquere and seeke
Of Lacedomye° fifty maidens eke,
On which they wolden doon hir lecherye.
But there was none of all that compaignye
That she nas slain, and with a good entente   675
Chees° rather for to die than assente
To been oppressed° of hir maidenhede.
Why shold I than to die been in drede?
    Lo, eek, the tyrant Aristoclides
That loved a maiden hight Stymphalides,°   680
Whan that hir fader slain was on a night,

651 **bihoveth me** I must   655 **quit** released   659 **thise stories** taken
from Jerome's *Against Jovinian*   662 **They . . . t'arreste** they com-
manded his daughters to be arrested   663 **in despit** in scorn
666 **God . . . mischaunce** God give them misfortune   669 **been stirt**
have jumped   670 **dreint** drowned   672 **Lacedomye** Lacedaemonia
676 **Chees** chose   677 **oppressed** ravished   680 **hight Stymphali-
des** named Stymphalis

Unto Dianes temple goth she aright
And hente° the image in hir handes two,
Fro which image wold she never go.
685 No wight ne might hir hands of it arace,°
Till she was slain right in the selve° place.
Now sith that maidens hadden swich despit°
To been defouled with man's foul delit,
Well ought a wife rather hirselven slee
690 Than be defouled, as it thinketh me.
    What shall I sayn of Hasdrubales wif
That at Cartage biraft hirself hir lif?
For whan she saw that Romains won the town,
She took hir children all and skipt° adown
695 Into the fire, and chees rather to die
Than any Romain did hir villainye.
    Hath not Lucrece y-slain hirself, alas,
At Rome whan that she oppressed was
Of Tarquin, for hir thought it was a shame
700 To liven whan that she had lost hir name?
    The seven maidens of Milesie° also
Han slain hemself for veray drede and woe
Rather than folk of Gaul hem should oppresse.
    Mo than a thousand stories, as I guesse,
705 Coud I now tell as touching° this mattere.
Whan Habradate was slain, his wife so dere
Hirselven slow, and let hir blood to glide
In Habradates woundes deep and wide,
And said, 'My body at the leste way
710 There shall no wight defoulen, if I may!'°
What shold I mo ensamples° hereof sayn?
Sith that so many han hemselven slain
Well rather than they wold defouled be,
I wol conclude that it is bet° for me

---

683 **hente** seized   685 **arace** separate   686 **selve** same   687 **hadden ... despit** had such indignation 694 **skipt** threw herself
701 **Milesie** Miletus, which was sacked by the Galatians in 276 B.C.
705 **as touching** concerning   710 **if ... may** i.e., if I may (prevent it)
711 **ensamples** examples   714 **bet** better

To sleen myself than been defouled thus.   *715*
I wol be trew unto Arveragus,
Or rather slee myself in some mannere—
As did Demociones daughter dere,
By cause that she wold not defouled be.
O Cedasus,° it is full greet pitee   *720*
To reden how *thy* daughtren deid, alas,
That slow hemselven for swich manner cas!°
As greet a pitee was it, or well more,
The Theban maiden° that for° Nichanore
Hirselven slow right for swich manner woe.   *725*
Another Theban maiden° did right so—
For one of Macedonie had hir oppressed,
She with hir deeth hir maidenheed redressed.
    What shall I sayn of Nicerates wif°
That for swich cas biraft hirself hir lif?   *730*
How trew eek was to Alcebiades
His love,° that rather for to dien chees
Than for to suffre his body unburied be?
Lo, which a wife was Alceste?"° quod she.
"What saith Omer° of good Penelopee?°   *735*
All Greece knoweth of hir chastitee.
Pardee, of Laodomia is written thus,
That whan at Troy was slain Protheselaus,
No lenger wold she live after his day.

720 **Cedasus** Scedasus of Boeotia, whose two daughters killed each
other after being violated   722 **swich . . . cas** such an occurrence
724 **Theban maiden** Nicanor captured Thebes and fell in love with a
virgin of the city   724 **for** in fear of   726 **Another . . . maiden** this
maiden killed the Macedonian first and herself afterward   729 **Nicer-
ates wif** when the Athenian leader Niceratus surrendered his power to
the Thirty Tyrants in Athens, his wife killed herself rather than submit
to the Tyrants   731–32 **Alcebiades . . . love** Timandra, Alcibiades'
concubine, buried the dead body of her lover   734 **Alceste** Alcestis,
who died in place of her husband   735 **Omer** Homer   735 **Penelo-
pee** Penelope was to choose a suitor on the completion of an intricate
tapestry, but to remain faithful to her husband Odysseus, she unraveled
the work at night

740 The same of noble Porcia° tell I may:
Withoute Brutus coude she not live,
To whom she had all whole hir herte yive.
The parfit wifehood of Arthemesie°
Honoured is thurgh all the Barbarye.

745 O Teuta° queen, thy wifely chastitee
To alle wives may a mirrour° be!
The same thing I say of Biliea,°
Of Rodogone,° and eek Valeria."°

    Thus plained Dorigen a day or twaye,
750 Purposing° ever that she wolde deye.

    But natheless upon the thridde night
Home came Arveragus, this worthy knight,
And asked hir why that she weep so sore.
And she gan weepen ever lenger the more°—

755 "Alas," quod she, "that ever I was born!
Thus have I said," quod she, "thus have I sworn . . ."
And told him all as ye han herd before;
It needeth not reherce it you namore.

    This husband with glad cheer in freendly wise
760 Answered and said as I shall you devise:
    "Is there ought° elles, Dorigen, but this?"
    "Nay, nay," quod she, "God help me so as wis,°
This is too much, and it were Goddes wille."
    "Ye, wife," quod he, "let sleepen that is stille.°
765 It may be well paraunter° yet today.
Ye shull your trouthe holden, by my fay,°

---

740 **Porcia** Portia is said to have choked on burning coals while being guarded after her husband's death at Philippi   743 **Arthemesie** Artemesia, wife to King Mausolus, built the "mausoleum" in his honor at his death   745 **Teuta** Illyrian queen, whose success was in proportion to her chastity   746 **mirrour** exemplar   747 **Biliea** Bilia, who defeated the Carthaginians in a naval battle   748 **Rodogone** Rhodogune, the daughter of King Darius, who killed her nurse for urging her to remarry   748 **Valeria** suffered martyrdom for her fidelity   750 **Purposing** intending   754 **ever . . . more** always more and more   761 **ought** nothing   762 **God . . . wis** as surely as God help me   764 **let . . . stille** i.e., leave alone what cannot be helped   765 **paraunter** perhaps   766 **by my fay** by my faith

For God so wisly have mercy upon me,
I had well lever y-sticked° for to be,
For veray love which that I to you have,
But if ye shold° your trouthe keep and save. 770
Trouth is the highest thing that man may keepe."
But with that word he brast anon to weepe,°
And said, "I you forbed, up pain of deeth,
That never while thee lasteth life ne breeth,
To no wight tell thou of this aventure. 775
As I may best I wol my woe endure,
Ne make no countenance of hevinesse,
That folk of you may deemen harm or guesse."°
And forth he cleped a squier and a maide:
"Goth forth anon with Dorigen," he saide, 780
"And bringeth hir to swich a place anon."
They took hir leeve and on hir way they gon,
But they ne wiste why she thider wente:
He nolde no wight tellen his entente.

Paraventure an heep° of you, ywis, 785
Wol holden him a lewed° man in this,
That he wol put his wife in jupartye.°
Herkneth the tale ere ye upon hir crye!
She may have better fortune than you seemeth,°
And whan that ye han herd the tale, deemeth.° 790

*   *   *

This squier which that hight Aurelius,
On Dorigen that was so amorous,
Of aventure happed hir to meete
Amid the town, right in the quickest° streete,
As she was bown° to goon the way forth right° 795

768 **y-sticked** stabbed   770 **But . . . shold** rather than you should not
772 **brast . . . weepe** burst into tears   778 **deemen . . . guesse** think
or guess evil   785 **an heep** a number   786 **lewed** foolish   787 **ju-
partye** jeopardy   789 **you seemeth** it seems to you   790 **deemeth**
then judge   794 **quickest** most active   795 **bown** ready   795 **forth
right** directly

Toward the garden ther as she had hight.°
And he was to the gardenward also,
For well he spied whan she wolde go
Out of hir house to any manner place.
800 But thus they met of° aventure or grace,
And he salueth hir with glad entente,°
And asked of hir whiderward she wente.
And she answered half as she were mad,
"Unto the garden as mine husband bad,°
805 My trouthe for to hold—alas! alas!"
    Aurelius gan wondren on this cas,°
And in his hert had greet compassioun
Of hir and of hir lamentacioun,
And of Arveragus, the worthy knight,
810 That bade hir holden all that she had hight,°
So loth him was° his wife shold breke hir trouthe.
And in his hert he caught of° this greet routhe,
Considering the best on every side
That fro his lust yet were him lever abide°
815 Than doon so high a cherlish° wretchednesse
Agains franchise° and alle gentilesse.
For which in fewe wordes said he thus:
"Madame, sayeth to your lord Arveragus
That sith I see his greet gentilesse
820 To you, and eek I see well your distresse
That him were lever han shame—and that were routhe—
Than ye to me shold breke thus your trouthe,
I have well lever° ever to suffer woe
Than I depart° the love bitwix you two.
825 I you releese, Madame, into your hond.°
Quit every serement° and every bond

796 **hight** promised 800 **of** by 801 **with ... entente** cheerfully
804 **bad** requested 806 **cas** situation 810 **holden ... hight** stick to
everything she promised 811 **So ... was** so unwilling was he
812 **caught of** had on 814 **were ... abide** he would rather leave off
815 **so ... cherlish** such an ignoble 816 **franchise** generosity
823 **have ... lever** would much rather 824 **depart** divide
825 **into ... hond** i.e., to yourself 826 **serement** oath

That ye han made to me as herebiforn,
Sith thilke° time which that ye were born.
My trouth I plight,° I shall you never repreve°
Of no bihest. And here I take my leeve,   830
As of the trewest and the beste wif
That ever yet I knew in all my lif.
But every wife be ware of hir biheste:
On Dorigen remembreth at the leste.
Thus can a squier doon a gentil deede   835
As well as can a knight, withouten drede."
She thanketh him upon hir knees all bare
And home unto hir husband is she fare,°
And told him all as ye han herd me said.
And be ye siker, he was so well apaid   840
That it were impossible me to write.
What shold I lenger of this cas endite?°
      Arveragus and Dorigen his wif
In sovereign blisse leden forth° hir lif—
Never eft° ne was there anger hem betweene.   845
He cherisheth hir as though she were a queene,
And she was to him trew for evermore.
Of thise two folk ye get of me namore.
      Aurelius, that his cost hath all forlorn,°
Curseth the time that ever he was born.   850
"Alas!" quod he, "alas that I bihighte
Of pured° gold a thousand pound of wighte°
Unto this philosophre! How° shall I do?
I see namore but that I am fordo.°
Mine heritage° mot I needes selle   855
And been a begger. Here may I not dwelle
And shamen all my kinred° in this place,
But° I of him° may gete better grace.

828 **thilke** that very   829 **trouth . . . plight** give you my word
829 **repreve** blame   838 **fare** gone   842 **endite** relate   844 **leden
forth** pass   845 **eft** again   849 **cost . . . forlorn** has lost all his
investment   852 **pured** refined   852 **wighte** weight   853 **How** what
854 **fordo** undone, lost   855 **heritage** inheritance   857 **kinred**
relatives   858 **But** unless   858 **him** i.e., the magician

But, natheless, I wol of him assaye°
860   At certain dayes yeer by yeer to paye,
And thank him of his greete curteisye.
My trouthe wol I keep, I wol not lie."
      With herte sore he goth unto his coffre
And broughte gold unto this philosophre
865   The value of five hundred pound, I guesse,
And him biseecheth of his gentilesse
To graunten him days of the remenaunt;°
And said, "Maister, I dare well make avaunt°
I failed never of my trouth as yit.
870   For sikerly my dette shall be quit°
Towardes you, how ever that I fare—
To goon abegged in my kirtel bare.°
But wold ye vouche sauf upon suretee°
Two yeer or three for to respiten° me,
875   Than were I well—for elles mot I selle
Mine heritage; there is namore to telle."
      This philosophre soberly answerde
And saide thus, whan he thise wordes herde,
"Have I not holden covenant unto thee?"
880   "Yis, certes, well and trewely," quod he.
      "Hastou not had thy lady as thee liketh?"
      "No, no," quod he—and sorrwefully he siketh.°
      "What was the cause? Tell me if thou can."
      Aurelius his tale anon bigan
885   And told him all as ye han herd before—
It needeth not to you reherce it more.
He said, "Arveragus, of gentilesse,
Had lever die in sorrwe and in distresse
Than that his wife were of hir trouthe fals."
890   The sorrwe of Dorigen he told him als,
How loth hir was to been a wicked wif,
And that she lever had lost that day hir lif,

859 **I . . . assaye** I will try to arrange   867 **of . . . remenaunt** in which
to pay the rest   868 **avaunt** boast   870 **quit** paid back   872 **To . . .
bare** to go begging in my undershirt   873 **suretee** security   874 **re-
spiten** give me an extension   882 **siketh** sighs

And that hir trouth she swore thurgh innocence—
She never erst had herd speke of "apparence."°
—"That made me han of hir so greet pitee.   895
And right as freely as he sent hir me,
As freely sent I hir to him again.
This all and some, there is namore to sayn."
    This philosophre answered, "Leve brother,
Everich° of you did gentilly til other.   900
Thou art a squier, and he is a knight;
But God forbede, for His blissful might,
But if a clerk coud° doon a gentil deede
As well as any of you, it is no drede.
Sir, I relese thee thy thousand pound,   905
As thou right now were croppen° out of the ground
Ne never ere now ne haddest knowen me.
For sir, I wol not take a penny of thee,
For all my craft ne nought for my travaille.°
Thou hast y-payed well for my vitaille;°   910
It is enough. And farewell, have good day"—
And took his horse and forth he goth his way.
—Lordings,° this question wol I aske now:
Which was the moste free,° as thinketh you?
Now telleth me, ere that ye ferther wende.°   915
I kan namore, my tale is at an ende.

894 **apparence** illusion   900 **Everich** each   903 **But . . . coud** if a
clerk could not (cf. line 770)   906 **were croppen** had crept   909 **tra-
vaille** labor   910 **vitaille** food   913 **Lordings** gentlemen. The
Franklin ends in a courtly fashion by posing a question for discussion
914 **free** generous   915 **wende** travel

THE HOST ADDRESSES
THE PARDONER

"Thou *bel ami*,° thou Pardoner," he saide
"Tell us some mirth or japes° right anon."
   "It shall be done," quod he, "by Saint Ronion;
But first," quod he, "here at this ale-stake°
5   I wol both drink and eten of a cake."
—And right anon thise gentils gan to crye,
"Nay, let him tell us of no ribaudye!°
Tell us some *moral* thing, that we may lere
Some wit, and thanne wol we gladly heere."
10   "I graunt, ywis," quod he. "But I mot thinke
Upon some honest° thing while that I drinke."

THE PARDONER'S PROLOGUE

Radix malorum est cupiditas. 1 Timothy 6:10

Lordings (quod he), in chirches when I preeche,
I paine me to han an hautein° speeche
And ring it out as round as goth a belle—
For I kan all by rote° that I telle.

1 **bel ami** pretty friend   2 **japes** jokes   4 **ale-stake** sign for a tavern
hung on a pole 7 **ribaudye** ribaldry 11 **honest** profitable
2 **hautein** lofty   4 **kan . . . rote** know all by heart

334

My theme is alway one,° and ever was: 5
Radix malorum est cupiditas.°
First I pronounce whennes that I come,
And than my bulles° shew I all and some—
Our liege lordes seel on my patente,°
That shew I first, my body to warrente,° 10
That no man be so bold, ne preest ne clerk,°
Me to destourb of° Christes holy werk.
And after that than tell I forth my tales:
Bulles of popes and of cardinales,
Of patriarks and bishopes I shewe, 15
And in Latin I speke a wordes fewe
To saffron with my predicacioun,°
And for to stir hem to devocioun.
Than shew I forth my longe crystal stones,°
Y-crammed full of cloutes° and of bones— 20
Relics been they, as weenen *they* echon!
Than have I in latoun° a shulder-bon
Which that was of an holy Jewes sheep:
    "Good men," I say, "take of my wordes keep!
If that this bone be wash° in any welle, 25
If cow, or calf, or sheep, or oxe swelle,
That any worm hath ete or worm y-stonge,°
Take water of that well and wash his tonge,
And it is whole anon! And furthermor,

---

5 **theme . . . one** text is always the same   6 **Radix . . . cupiditas** ava-
rice is the root of evil. The Pardoner's theme is covetousness, or greed,
one of the Seven Deadly Sins. The other Sins are lust (lechery), envy,
anger (wrath), gluttony, sloth, and pride. The greatest of the Deadly
Sins was thought to be pride, but the Pardoner cites *1 Timothy* 6:10
(*Radix omnium malorum est cupiditas*) in favor of greed, since it
serves his purposes better   8 **bulles** certificates   9 **liege . . . patente**
i.e., a bishop signed the papal decree   10 **warrente** protect   11 **ne**
preest . . . clerk there was general enmity among parish clerks and
pardoners   12 **destourb of** keep from   17 **To . . . predicacioun** to
spice my preaching   19 **crystal stones** glass cases for displaying
relics   20 **cloutes** rags   22 **in latoun** i.e., encased in brass   25 **wash**
washed   27 **That . . . y-stonge** that has been eaten or been stung by
any snake

30   Of pokkes° and of scab and every sor
       Shall every sheep be whole that of this welle
       Drinketh a draught. Take keep eek what I telle:
       If that the good man that the beestes oweth°
       Wol every wike, ere that the cock him croweth,
35   Fasting, drinken of this well a draughte—
       As thilke holy Jew our elders taughte—
       His beestes and his store° shall multiplye.
          And sirs, also it heeleth jalousye:
       For though a man be fall in jalous rage,
40   Let maken with this water his potage,
       And never shall he more his wife mistriste,°
       Though he the sooth of hir defaute wiste
       —Al had she taken preestes two or three.
          Here is a mittein° eek that ye may see:
45   He that his hand wol put in this mittein
       He shall have multiplying of his grain,
       Whan he hath sowen, be it whete or otes—
       So that he offer pence or elles grotes.°
          Good men and women, oo thing warn I you:
50   If any wight be in this chirche now
       That hath done sinne horrible, that he
       Dare not for shame of it y-shriven° be;
       Or any woman, be she yong or old,
       That hath y-maked hir husband cokewold—
55   Swich folk shall have no power ne no grace
       To offren to my relics in this place.
       And whoso findeth him out of swich blame,
       They wol come up and offre in Goddes name,
       And I assoile° him by th'auctoritee
60   Which that by bull y-graunted was to me."
       —By this gaude° have I wonne, yeer by yeer,
       And hundred mark° sith I was pardoner.

---

30 **pokkes** pustules   33 **oweth** owns   37 **store** stock   41 **mistriste** mistrust   44 **mittein** mitten   48 **grotes** a groat was an English silver coin, worth fourpence   52 **y-shriven** absolved, confessed   59 **assoile** absolve   61 **gaude** trick   62 **hundred mark** hundred marks, a large sum (mark = ⅔ of a pound)

I stande like a clerk in my pulpet,
And whan the lewed peple is down y-set
I preeche so as ye han herd before,   65
And tell an hundred false japes more.
Then pain I me to stretche forth the necke,
And est and west upon the peple I becke°
As doth a dove, sitting on a berne:°
Mine handes and my tonge goon so yerne°   70
That it is joy to see my bisinesse!
Of avarice and of swich cursednesse
Is all my preeching, for to make hem free
To yiven hir pence—and namely, unto me.
For mine entent is not but for to winne,°   75
And nothing for correccion of sinne—
I rekke° never, whan that they been beried,°
Though that hir soules goon a-blackeberried!°
For certes, many a predicacioun°
Cometh ofte time of yvel entencioun: 80
Some for plesance of° folk and flatterye,
To been avanced° by hypocrisye;
And some for vaine glory; and some for hate.
For whan I dare noon otherways debate,
Than wol I sting him with my tonge smerte   85
In preeching, so that he shall not asterte
To been defamed falsely—if that he
Hath trespassed to my bretheren° or to me;
For though I telle not his proper name,
Men shall well knowe that it is the same   90
By signes, and by other circumstaunces.
—Thus quit° I folk that doon us displesaunces;
Thus spit I out my venim under hewe

68 **becke** nod 69 **berne** barn 70 **yerne** vigorously 75 **not . . . winne** only to gain profit 77 **rekke** care 77 **beried** buried 78 **a-blackeberried** wandering on a wild-goose chase, i.e., to damnation 79 **predicacioun** sermon 81 **for . . . of** to please 82 **avanced** benefited 88 **to . . . bretheren** against my fellow pardoners 92 **quit** pay back

Of holiness, to *seem* holy and trewe.
95   But shortly mine entent I wol devise.°
I preech of nothing but for coveitise:°
Therefore my theme is yet and ever was
Radix malorum est cupiditas.
Thus can I preech again that same vice
100 Which that I use—and that is avarice.
But though myself be guilty in that sinne
Yet can I maken other folk to twinne°
From avarice, and sore to repente
—But that is not my principal entente:
105 I preeche nothing but for coveitise.
Of this matter it ought enough suffise.
    Then tell I hem ensamples° many on
Of olde stories longe time agon.
For lewed° peple loven tales olde—
110 Swich thinges can they well report and holde.
What, trowe ye that whiles I may preeche
And winne gold and silver for I teeche,°
That I wol live in poverte *will*fully?
Nay, nay, I thought it never, trewely!
115 For I wol preech and beg in sundry landes:
I wol not do no labour with mine handes,
Ne make baskettes and live thereby—
Because I wol not beggen idelly.°
I wol none of the apostles countrefete;°
120 I wol have money, woole, cheese, and whete,
Al were it yiven of° the povrest page
Or of the povrest widwe in a village—
Al shold hir children sterve for famine!
Nay, I wol drinke licour of the vine
125 And have a jolly wench in every town!
    But herkneth, lordings, in conclusioun:

95 **devise** explain   96 **coveitise** covetousness   102 **twinne** turn
107 **ensamples** examples (*exempla*) of moral behavior   109 **lewed**
ignorant   112 **for ... teeche** for what I teach (namely, poverty)
118 **idelly** in vain   119 **countrefete** imitate   121 **of** by

Your liking is that I shall tell a tale?—
Now have I drunk a draught of corny ale,
By God, I hope I shall you tell a thing
That shall by reson° been at your liking!   *130*
For though myself be a full vicious° man,
A moral tale yet I you telle can,
Which I am wont to preeche for to winne.°
Now hold your pees, my tale I wol beginne.

THE PARDONER'S TALE

In Flanders, whilom,° was a compaignye   *135*
Of yonge folk that haunteden° follye—
As riot, hasard, stewes,° and tavernes
Whereas with harpes, lutes, and giternes°
They daunce and playen at dees° both day and night,
And ete also, and drink over hir might°—   *140*
Thurgh which they doon° the Devil sacrifise
Within that Devil's temple in cursed wise
By superfluitee° abhominable!
Hir othes° been so greet and so dampnable
That it is grisly for to heer hem swere: *145*
Our blessed Lordes body they to-tere°—
Hem thought that Jewes rent Him not enough!

---

130 **by reson** for (good) reasons   131 **vicious** wicked, given to vice
133 **to winne** profit   135 **whilom** once upon a time   136 **haunteden**
practiced   137 **riot . . . stewes** revelry, gambling, whorehouses
138 **giternes** guitars   139 **dees** dice   140 **over . . . might** more than
their capacity   141 **doon** make to   143 **superfluitee** overindulgence
144 **othes** oaths   146 **to-tere** tear apart. The Pardoner is concerned
with the habitual swearing of gamblers and hedonists. Cf. Shake-
speare's *'sblood! 'steeth!* (God's blood, God's teeth)

And ech of hem at other's sinne lough!°
And right anon than comen tombesteres,°
150 Fetis° and small, and yonge frutesteres,°
Singers with harpes, bawdes,° wafereres°—
Which been the veray devil's officeres
To kindle and blow the fire of lecherye
That is annexed unto° gluttonye.
155   The Holy Writ take I to my witnesse
That luxury° is in wine and drunkenesse:
Lo, how that drunken Lot unkindely°
Lay by his daughters two unwittingly—
So drunk he was he niste what he wroughte.
160 Herodes,° who so well the stories soughte,
Whan he of wine was replete° at his feste,
Right at his owne table he yaf his heste°
To sleen the Baptist John, full guilteless.
    Senec saith a good word, douteless:
165 He saith he can no difference finde
Bitwix a man that is out of his minde
And a man which that is drunkelewe°—
But that woodness,° y-fallen in a shrewe,°
Persevereth lenger than doth drunkenesse.
170 —O gluttonye, full of cursednesse!
O cause first of our confusioun!
O original° of our dampnacioun,
Till Christ had bought us with his blood again!
Lo, how dere, shortly for to sayn,
175 Abought was thilke cursed villainye:
Corrupt was all this world for gluttonye!—
Adam our fader and his wife also
Fro paradise to labour and to woe

---

148 **lough** laughed   149 **tombesteres** dancing girls   150 **Fetis**
pretty, neat   150 **frutesteres** fruit-sellers   151 **bawdes** prostitutes
151 **wafereres** wafer and cake vendors   154 **annexed unto** allied
with   156 **luxury** (Lat. *luxuria*) lechery   157 **unkindely** unnaturally
160 **Herodes** Herod   161 **replete** full   162 **yaf...heste** gave his
order   167 **drunkelewe** falling-down drunk   168 **woodness** madness
168 **shrewe** scoundrel   172 **original** origin

Were driven for that vice, it is no drede:°
For while that Adam fasted, as I rede,   *180*
He was in paradise, and whan that he
Eet of the fruit defended° on a tree
Anon he was out cast to woe and paine.
O gluttony, on thee well ought us plaine!°
O, wist a man how many maladies   *185*
Follwen of excess and of gluttonies,
He wolde been the more mesurable°
Of his diete, sitting at his table.
Alas, the shorte throt, the tender mouth,
Maketh that est and west and north and south,   *190*
In erth, in air, in water, men to swinke,°
To get a glutton daintee° mete and drinke!
   Of this matter, O Paul, well canstou trete:
"Mete unto womb, and womb eek unto mete,
Shall God destroyen both," as Paulus saith.   *195*
Alas, a foul thing is it, by my faith,
To say this word, and fouler is the deede
Whan man so drinketh of the white and rede°
That of his throt he maketh his privee°
Thurgh thilke cursed superfluitee!   *200*
The apostle weeping saith full pitously,
"There walken many of which you told have I—
I say it now weeping with pitous vois—
That they been enemies of Christes crois,°
Of which the end is deeth: womb° is hir god!"   *205*
—O womb, O belly, O stinking cod,°
Fulfilled of dung and of corrupcioun!
At either end of thee foul is the soun.°
How greet labour and cost is thee to finde!°
Thise cookes, how they stamp, and strain, and grinde,   *210*

179 **it ... drede** there is no doubt   182 **fruit defended** forbidden
fruit (hanging)   184 **well ... plaine** we should complain
187 **mesurable** careful, restrained   191 **swinke** work   192 **daintee**
choice   198 **white ... rede** i.e., wine   199 **privee** toilet   204 **crois**
cross   205 **womb** stomach   206 **cod** bag, stomach   208 **soun** sound
209 **finde** satisfy

And turnen substance into accident°
To fulfillen all thy likerous talent!°
Out of the harde bones knocke they
The marry,° for they caste nought away
215   That° may go thurgh the gullet soft and soote.°
Of spicery° of leef and bark and roote
Shall been his sauce y-maked by delit,°
To make him yet a newer appetit.
But certes he that haunteth swich delices°
220   Is deed while that he liveth in tho vices.
     A lecherous thing is wine, and drunkenesse
Is full of striving° and of wretchednesse.
O drunke man, disfigured is thy face!
Sour is thy breeth, foul artou to embrace!
225   And thurgh thy drunke nose seemeth the soun
As though thou saidest ay "Sampsoun! Sampsoun!"—
And yet, God wot, Sampsoun drank never no win.
Thou fallest as it were a sticked swin;°
Thy tonge is lost, and all thine honest cure,°
230   For drunkeness is veray sepulture°
Of mannes wit and his discrecioun.
In whom that drink hath dominacioun
He can no conseil keep, it is no drede.
Now, keep you fro the white and fro the rede—
235   And namely, fro the white wine of Lepe
That is to sell in Fishstreet, or in Chepe:°
This wine of Spaine creepeth subtilly
In other wines growing faste by,
Of which there riseth swich fumositee°

211 **turnen ... accident** the terms are from scholastic theology and refer to the arguments concerning forms of things: essence (substance) versus appearance (accident) 212 **likerous talent** lecherous needs 214 **marry** marrow 215 **That** (rel. pron.) what 215 **soote** sweetly 216 **spicery** spices 217 **by delit** for delectation 219 **delices** delights 222 **striving** strife 228 **sticked swin** stuck pig 229 **honest cure** care for respectability 230 **veray sepulture** burial itself 236 **Fishstreet ... Chepe** sections of London; note the Pardoner's knowledge of such things 239 **fumositee** wine vapor

That whan a man hath drunken draughtes three   240
And weeneth that he be at home in Chepe,
He is in Spain, right at the town of Lepe—
Not at the Rochelle, ne at Burdeux town°—
And thanne wol he sayn, "Sampsoun! Sampsoun!"
    But herkneth, lordings, oo word I you praye—   245
That all the sovereign actes,° dare I saye,
Of victories in the Olde Testament,
Thurgh veray God that is omnipotent,
Were done in abstinence and in prayere:
Looketh the Bible and there ye may it lere.°   250
Look Atilla, the greete conquerour,
Deid in his sleep with shame and dishonour,
Bleeding at his nose in drunkenesse:
A capitain shold live in sobernesse!
And overall this, aviseth you° right well   255
What was commanded unto Lamuel°
(Not Samuel, but Lamuel, say I)—
Redeth the Bible and find it expressly,
Of wine-yiving to hem that han justise.°
Namore of this, for it may well suffise.   260
    And now that I have spoken of gluttonye,
Now wol I you defenden hasardrye:°
    Hasard is very moder of lesinges°
And of deceit and cursed foresweringes,°
Blaspheme of Christ, manslaughtre, and waste also   265
Of catel° and of time. And furthermo,
It is repreve° and contrary of honour
For to been hold a commune hasardour.
And ever the hyer he is of estat

---

243 **Not ... town** i.e., the drinker of French wines (Rochelle, Bordeaux) may find that Lepe, a more potent Spanish wine, has been mixed in   246 **sovereign actes** important acts   250 **lere** learn 255 **aviseth you** consider   256 **Lamuel** a ruler told not to drink wine as an example to his subjects   259 **justise** judicial power   262 **defenden hasardrye** discourage gambling   263 **moder ... lesinges** mother of lies   264 **foresweringes** falsehoods   266 **catel** possessions 267 **repreve** a shame, reproach

270 The more is he holden desolat:°
     If that a prince useth hasardrye,
     In alle governance and policye
     He is, as by commun opinioun,
     Y-hold the less in reputacioun.
275 Stilboun, that was a wise embassadour,
     Was sent to Corinth in full greet honour
     Fro Lacedomye to make hir alliaunce,
     And whan he came him happede° parchaunce
     That all the greetest that were of that lond
280 Playing at the hasard he hem foond;
     For which as soone as it mighte be
     He stal him home again to his contree,
     And saide, "There wol I not lese my name,
     N'I wol not take on me so greet defame°
285 You to ally unto none hasardours.
     Sendeth othere wise embassadours,
     For by my trouthe, me were lever° die
     Than I you shold to hasadours allye.
     For ye that been so glorious in honours
290 Shall not allye you with hasadours
     As by my will, ne as by my tretee."
     This wise philosophre, thus said he.
        Look eek that to the king Demetrius
     The King of Parthes, as the book saith us,
295 Sent him a pair of dees of gold in scorn,
     For he had used hasard therebiforn;
     For which he held his glory or his renown
     At no value or reputacioun.
     Lordes may finden other manner play
300 Honest° enough to drive the day away.
        Now wol I speke of othes false and greete
     A word or two, as olde bookes treete:
        Greet swering is a thing abhominable,
     And false swering is yet more repervable.

271 **holden desolat** considered decadent   278 **him happede** it
happened   284 **defame** dishonor   287 **me . . . lever** I would rather
300 **Honest** worthwhile

The heighe God forbade swering at all—   305
Witness on Matthew. But in special
Of swering saith the holy Jeremie,°
"Thou shalt swere sooth thine othes and not lie,
And swere in doom° and eek in rightwisnesse;°
But idle swering is a cursednesse."°   310
Behold and see that in the firste table°
Of heighe Goddes hestes honorable
How that the second heste of him is this:
"Take not my name in idle or amiss."
Lo, rather° he forbedeth swich swering   315
Than homicide, or may a cursed thing.
I say that, as by order, thus it standeth:
This knoweth, that° his hestes understandeth,
How that the second heste of God is that.
And ferther over, I wol thee tell all plat°   320
That vengeance shall not parten from his hous
That° of his othes is too outrageous:
"By Goddes precious hert!" and "By His nailes!"
And, "By the blood of Christ that is in Hailes,°
Seven is my chaunce, and thine is cink and traye!"°   325
"By Goddes armes, if thou falsely playe
This dagger shall thurghout thine herte go!"
—This fruit cometh of the bitched bones two:°
Forswering, ire, falseness, homicide.
Now for the love of Christ that for us dyde,   330
Let° your othes, bothe greet and smalle.
   But sires, now wol I telle forth my tale.
Thise riotoures three of which I tell,
Long erst ere prime° rung of any belle,

307 **Jeremie** Jeremiah   309 **doom** considered judgment   309 **right-
wisnesse** righteousness   310 **cursednesse** wickedness   311 **firste
table** of the Ten Commandments, i.e., the first five commandments
315 **rather** sooner   318 **that** he who   320 **all plat** flatly   322 **That**
who   324 **Hailes** there was a tradition that some of Christ's blood was
kept at Hayles abbey, Gloucestershire   325 **cink . . . traye** five and
three (in craps)   328 **bitched . . . two** i.e., dice   331 **Let** leave off
334 **prime** six a.m.

335   Were set hem in a taverne to drinke.
      And as they sat they herd a belle clinke
      Biforn a corse° was carried to his grave.
      That one of hem gan callen to his knave—
      "Go bet,"° quod he, "and axe redily
340   What corse is this that passeth here forby,
      And look that thou report his name well."
         "Sir," quod this boy, "it needeth neveradeel;
      It was me told ere ye came here two houres.
      He was, pardee, an old fellaw° of youres.
345   And suddenly he was y-slain tonight,
      Fordrunk,° as he sat on his bench upright:
      There came a privee° thief men clepeth Deeth,
      That in this contree all the peple sleeth,
      And with his spere he smote his hert atwo,
350   And went his way withouten wordes mo.
      He hath a thousand slain this pestilence.°
      And maister, ere ye come in his presence,
      Me thinketh that it were necessarye
      For to be ware of swich an Adversarye:
355   *Beth redy for to meet him evermore . . .*
      —Thus taughte me my dame; I say namore."
         "By Sainte Mary!" said this taverner,
      "The child saith sooth. For he hath slain this yeer,
      Henne over a mile,° within a greet village,
360   Both man and womán, child and hine° and page.
      I trow his habitacioun be there.
      To been avised greet wisdom it were,
      Ere that he did a man a dishonour."
         "Ye, Goddes armes!" quod this riotour,
365   "Is it swich peril with him for to meete?
      I shall him seek by way and eek by streete,
      I make avow to Goddes digne bones!
      Herkneth, fellows—we three been all ones:

337 **corse** corpse 339 **Go bet** go quickly 344 **fellaw** friend
346 **Fordrunk** thoroughly drunk 347 **privee** clandestine 351 **this pestilence** during this plague 359 **Henne . . . mile** over a mile from here 360 **hine** worker

Let ech of us hold up his hand til other,
And ech of us become other's brother: 370
And we wol sleen this false traitour Deeth.
He shall be slain, he that so many sleeth,
By Goddes dignitee, ere it be night."
—Togidres han thise three hir trouthes plight
To live and dien ech of hem for other,   375
As though he were his own y-bore brother.°
And up they stirt,° all drunken in this rage,°
And forth they goon towardes that village
Of which the taverner had spoke biforn.
And many a grisly ooth than han they sworn,   380
And Christes blessed body they to-rente:°
Deeth shall be deed, if that they may him hente!°
    Whan they han gone not fully half a mile,
Right as they wold han treden over a stile,
An old man and a povre with hem mette.   385
This olde man full meekely hem grette°
And saide thus: "Now, lordes . . . God you see! . . ."°
    The proudest of thise riotoures three
Answered again, "What, carl!° with sorry grace!
Why artou all forwrapped° save thy face?   390
Why livestou so long in so greet age?"
    This olde man gan look in his visage
And saide thus: "For I ne can not finde
A man, though that I walked into Inde°—
Neither in citee, ne in no village—   395
That wolde chaunge his youthe for mine age.
And, therefore, mot I han mine age stille,
As longe time as it is Goddes wille;
Ne Deeth, alas, ne wol not han my lif.
Thus walk I like a resteless caitiff,°   400
And on the ground, which is my modres° gate

376 **own . . . brother** natural-born brothers   377 **stirt** leapt   377 **rage**
fit   381 **to-rente** tore apart with swearing   382 **hente** catch
386 **grette** greeted   387 **God . . . see** God look (with favor) upon you
389 **carl** man, lout   390 **forwrapped** wrapped up   394 **Inde** India
400 **caitiff** wretch   401 **modres** mother's

I knocke with my staff, both erly and late,
And saye, 'Leve moder, let me in!
Lo, how I vanish—flesh, and blood, and skin . . .
405 Alas, whan shall my bones been at reste?
Moder, with you wold I chaunge my cheste°
That in my chambre longe time hath be,
Ye, for an haire-clout to wrap in me.'°
But yet to me she wol not do that grace;
410 For which full pale and welked° is my face.
    But sires, to you it is no curteisye
To speken to an old man villainye,
But he trespass in word or else in deede.
In Holy Writ ye may yourself well rede:
415 *Agains an old man, hoor° upon his heed,*
Ye shold arise . . . Wherefore I yive you reed,°
Ne doth unto an old man noon harm now,
Namore than that *ye* wolde men did to *you*
In age, if that ye so long abide—
420 And God be with you wher ye go° or ride;
I mot go thider as I have to go . . ."
    "Nay, olde cherl!° By God thou shalt *not* so,"
Said this other hasardour anon,
"Thou partest not so lightly, by Saint John!
425 Thou spak right now of thilke traitour, Deeth,
That in this contree all our freendes sleeth.
Have here my trouth, as thou art his espye,°
Tell where he is, or thou shalt it abye,°
By God and by the Holy Sacrament!
430 For soothly thou are one of his assent°
To sleen us yonge folk, thou false theef!"
    "Now, sires—" quod he, "if that ye be so leef°
To finde Deeth—turn up this crooked way.

---

406 **cheste** clothes-chest   408 **haire-clout . . . me** haircloth (for a shroud) to wrap me up in   410 **welked** withered   415 **hoor** white, old age   416 **reed** advice. Note how his advice echoes the golden rule   420 **wher . . . go** whether you walk   422 **cherl** rogue   427 **espye** spy   428 **abye** pay for   430 **assent** party, faction   432 **leef** eager

For in that grove I left him, by my fay,
Under a tree—and there he wol abide . . .   435
Not for *your* boost he wol him no thing hide.
See ye that ook? Right there ye shall him finde!
God save you, that bought again mankinde,
And you amend . . ." Thus said this olde man;
And everich of thise riotoures ran   440
Till they came to that tree, and there they founde
Of florins° fine of gold y-coined rounde
Well ny an eighte bushels as hem thoughte—
No lenger thanne after Deeth they soughte,
But of hem so glad was of the sighte   445
For that the florins been so fair and brighte
That down they set hem by this precious hoord.
The worst of hem he spak the firste word,
"Bretheren," quod he, "take keep what that I saye;
My wit° is greet, though that I bourde° and playe.   450
This tresor hath Fortune unto us yiven
In mirth and jolitee our life to liven—
And lightly as it cometh so wol we spende.
Ey! Goddes precious dignitee! who wende°
Today that we shold han so fair a grace?   455
But might this gold be carried fro this place
Home to mine house—or elles unto youres—
For well ye wot that all this gold is oures—
Than were we in heigh felicitee.°
But trewely, by day it may not be—   460
Men wolde sayn that we were theeves stronge
And for our own tresor doon us honge;°
This tresor most y-carried be by nighte,
As wisly and as slyly as it mighte.
Therefore I rede that cut° among us alle   465
Be draw, and let see where the cut wol falle;
And he that hath the cut with herte blithe

442 **florins** gold coins, originally Florentine   450 **wit** understanding
450 **bourde** play tricks   454 **wende** would have thought   459 **heigh
felicitee** great happiness   462 **doon . . . honge** have us hanged
465 **cut** lots

Shall renne to the town, and that full swithe,°
And bring us breed and wine full prively;
470 And two of us shall keepen subtilly
This tresor well, and if he wol not tarrye,
Whan it is night we wol this tresor carrye
By one assent° where as us thinketh best."
     That one° of hem the cut brought in his fest°
475 And bade hem draw and look where it wol falle;
And it fill on the yongest of hem alle,
And forth toward the town he went anon.
And also soon as that he was agon
That one of hem spak thus unto that other:
480 "Thou knowest well thou art my sworen brother;
Thy profit wol I telle thee anon.
Thou wost well that our fellaw is agon;
And here is gold, and that full greet plentee,
That shall departed° been among us three.
485 But natheless, if I can shape° it so
That it departed were among us two,
Had I not done a freendes turn to thee?"
     That other answered, "I noot how *that* may be.
He wot that the gold is with us twaye.
490 What shall we doon? What shall we to him saye?"
     "Shall it be conseil?"° said the firste shrewe.
"And I shall tellen in a wordes fewe
What we shull doon, and bring it well aboute."
     "I graunte," quod that other, "out of doute,
495 That by my truth I wol thee not biwraye."°
     "Now," quod the first, "thou wost well we be twaye,
And two of us shall strenger° be than oon:
Look whan that he is set, that right anon
Arise as though thou woldest with him playe;
500 And I shall rive° him thurgh the sides twaye,
While that thou strugglest with him as in game;

468 **swithe**   quickly   473 **By . . . assent**   by   common   assent
474 **That one** one   474 **fest** fist   484 **departed** divided   485 **shape**
fix   491 **conseil** a secret   495 **biwraye** give away   497 **strenger**
stronger   500 **rive** stick

And with thy dagger look thou do the same.
And than shall all this gold departed be,
My dere freend, bitwixe me and thee!
Than may we both our lustes° all fulfille   505
And play at dees right at our owne wille!"
And thus accorded° been thise shrewes twaye
To sleen the thrid, as ye han herd me saye.

 This yongest, which that wente to the town,
Full oft in hert he rolleth up and down   510
The beautee of thise florins new and brighte.
"O Lord!" quod he, "if so were that I mighte
Have all this tresor to myself alone,
There is no man that liveth under the trone°
Of God that sholde live so murry as I!"   515
And atte last the Feend, our enemy,
Put in his thought that he shold poison beye°
With which he mighte sleen his fellows twaye;
Forwhy° the Feend found him in swich livinge
That he had leve° him to sorrow bringe.   520
For this was outrely° his full entente:
To sleen hem both and never to repente.
And forth he goth, no lenger wold he tarrye,
Into the town unto a 'pothecarye,
And prayed him that he him wolde selle   525
Some poison, that he might his rattes quelle,°
And eek there was a polecat in his hawe°
That (as he said) his capons had y-slawe,°
And fain he wolde wreke him° if he mighte
On vermin that destroyed him by nighte.   530

 The 'pothecary answered, "And thou shalt have
A thing that, also° God my soule save,

---

505 **lustes** desires, ambitions 507 **accorded** agreed 514 **trone**
throne 517 **beye** buy 519 **Forwhy** because 520 **leve** permission.
The rioter, though young, has forfeited his portion of grace
521 **outrely** utterly, completely. "Outrely his full entente" is a pleo-
nasm suggesting the extent of his wicked purpose 526 **quelle** kill,
control 527 **hawe** yard 528 **his . . . y-slawe** had slain his capons
529 **fain . . . him** he would gladly avenge himself 532 **also** as

In all this world there is no creature
That ete or drunk hath of this confiture,°
535 Not but the montance° of a corn of whete,
That he ne shall his life anon forlete.°
Ye, sterve he shall, and that in lesse while
Than thou wolt goon a pas not but a mile,
The poison is so strong and violent."
540   This cursed man hath in his hand y-hent°
This poison in a box, and sith he ran
Into the nexte street unto a man
And borrwed of him large bottles three.
And in the two his poison poured he—
545 The thrid he kepte clene for *his* drinke;
For all the night he shop him for to swinke°
In carrying of the gold out of that place.
And whan this riotour, with sorry grace,°
Had filled with wine his greete bottles three
550 To his fellaws again repaireth° he.
—What needeth it to sermon of it more?
For right as they had cast his deeth before,
Right so they han him slain, and that anon.
And whan that this was done, thus spak that oon:
555 "Now let us sit and drink and make us merrye,
And afterward we wol his body berye."
And with that word it happed him, *par cas,*°
To take the bottle ther° the poison was
And drank, and yaf his fellaw drink also:
560 For which anon they storven° bothe two!
    But certes I suppose that Avicen°
Wrote never in no canon ne in no *fen*°
Mo wonder signes° of empoisoning

---

534 **confiture** potion   535 **montance** amount, measure   536 **forlete**
give up   540 **y-hent** clutched   546 **shop . . . swinke** proposed to
work   548 **with . . . grace** let bad fortune be with him   550 **re-
paireth** returns   557 **par cas** by chance   558 **ther** in which
560 **storven** died   561 **Avicen** Avicenna, Arabic physician   562 **fen**
chapter   563 **signes** symptoms

Than had thise wretches two ere hir ending.
Thus ended been thise homicides two,   565
And eek the false empoisoner also.
    O cursed sin of alle cursednesse!
O traitours homicide, O wickednesse,
O gluttony, luxury, and hasardrye!
Thou basphemour of Christ with villainye   570
And othes greete of usage and of pride!
Alas, mankinde, how may it bitide
That to thy Creatour which that thee wroughte,
And with his precious herte blood thee boughte,°
Thou art so false and so unkind, alas?   575
—Now, good men, God foryive you your trespass
And ware you fro the sin of *avarice*!
Mine holy pardon may you all warice,°
So that ye offer nobles° or sterlinges—
Or elles silver brooches, spoones, ringes;   580
Boweth your heed under this holy bulle!
Cometh up, ye wives, offreth of your woole!
Your name I enter here in my roll anon;
Into the bliss of Heven shull ye gon.
I you assoile, by mine heigh power—   585
Ye that wol offre—as cleene and eek as cleer°
As ye were born!—And lo, sirs, thus I preeche.
And Jesu Christ, that is our soules leeche,°
So graunte you *His* pardon to receive;
For that is best, I wol you not deceive.   590
    But sirs! oo word forgat I in my tale!
I have relics and pardon in my male°
As fair as any man in Engeland,
Which were me yiven by the Popes hand!
If any of you wol, of devocioun,   595
Offren and han mine absolucioun,
Come forth anon, and kneeleth here adown,
And meekely receiveth my pardoun;

---

574 **boughte** redeemed   578 **warice** heal, absolve   579 **nobles** thin
gold coins   586 **cleer** pure   588 **leeche** physician   592 **male** bag

Or elles taketh pardon as ye wende,°
600 All new and fresh at every miles ende—
So that ye offren alway new and newe°
Nobles or pence which that been good and trewe.
It is an honour to everich that is heer
That ye mow have a suffisant° pardoner
605 T'assoile you in contree as ye ride,
For aventures which that may bitide:
Paraventure there may fall one or two
Down off his horse and breke his neck atwo.
Look which a suretee° is it to you alle
610 That I am in your fellowship y-falle
That may assoile you, both more and lasse,
Whan that the soul shall fro the body passe!
I rede that our Host here shall beginne,
For he is most envoluped° in sinne.
615 Come forth, sir Host, and offer first anon,
And thou shalt kiss the relics everichon,
Ye, for a grote—unbuckle anon thy purs."
    "Nay, nay!" quod he, "than have I Christes curs!
Let be," quod he, "it shall not be, so th'eech!
620 Thou woldest make me kiss thine olde breech°
And swere it were a relic of a Saint—
Though it were with thy fundament depeint.°
But, by the crois which that Saint Elaine fond,
I wold I had thy coilons° in mind hond,
625 Insted of relics or of saintuarye:°
Let cut hem off—I wol thee help hem carrye!
They shall be shrined in an hogges turd!"
    This Pardoner answered not a word.
So wroth he was, no word ne wold he saye.
630   "Now," quod our Host, "I wol no lenger playe
With thee, ne with noon other angry man . . ."

599 **wende** go along   601 **alway . . . newe** always again and again
604 **suffisant** competent   609 **which . . . suretee** what a protection
614 **envoluped** bound up, implicated   620 **breech** underclothes
622 **with . . . depeint** stained by your anus   624 **coilons** testicles
625 **saintuarye** box of relics

But right anon the worthy Knight began,
Whan that he saw that all the peple lough:
"Namore of this, for it is right enough!
Sir Pardoner, be glad and mirrye of cheere.   *635*
And ye, sir Host, that been to me so dere,
I pray you that ye kiss the Pardoner;
And Pardoner, I pray thee, draw thee neer,
And as we diden let us laugh and playe."
Anon they kist, and riden forth hir waye.   *640*

THE PARSON'S PROLOGUE

By that° the Manciple had his tale all ended,
The sunne fro the south line° was descended
So lowe that he nas not to my sighte
Degrees nine and twenty as in highte.
5   Four of the clock it was, so as I guesse—
For eleven foot, or litel more or lesse,
My shadow was at thilke time as there,
Of swich feet° as my lengthe parted were
In six feet equal of proporcioun.
10 Therewith the moones exaltacioun°—
I mene Libra—alway gan ascende,°
As we were entering at a thropes ende.°
    For which our Host, as he was wont to gie°
As in this cas our jolly compaignye,
15 Said in this wise: "Lordings, everichon,
Now lacketh us no tales mo than on!
Fulfilled is my sentence and my decree.
I trow that we han herd of ech degree°—
Almost fulfilled is all mine ordinaunce.
20 I pray to God, so yive him right good chaunce°
That telleth this tale to us lustily.°
Sir Preest," quod he, "artou a vicary,°

1 **By that** by the time that   2 **south line** meridian. Chaucer describes
the relation of the sun to its position at noon and also to his shadow
(lines 6–9)   8 **Of . . . feet** i.e., the ratio of Chaucer's height to the cast
of his shadow is 6:11   10 **exaltacioun** a planet's position in the zo-
diac where the planet has greatest influence   11 **alway . . . ascende**
continued to ascend (above the horizon)   12 **a . . . ende** the outskirts
of a village   13 **gie** conduct, guide   18 **of . . . degree** from each rank
20 **chaunce** fortune   21 **lustily** pleasantly   22 **vicary** vicar

Or art a person?° Say sooth, by thy fay!
Be what thou be, ne breek thou not our play,
For every man save thou hath told his tale.   25
Unbuckle and shew us what is in thy male!°
For trewely, me thinketh by thy cheere
Thou sholdest knit up° well a greet mattere.
Tell us a fable anon, for cockes bones!"

    This Person answerede all atones,   30
"Thou gettest fable none y-told for me;
For Paul, that writeth unto Timothee,
Repreveth hem that waiven soothfastnesse°
And tellen fables and swich wretchednesse.
Why shold I sowen draff out of my fest°   35
Whan I may sowen whete,° if that me lest?
For which I say if that you list to heere
Moralitee and vertuous mattere,
And than that ye wol yive me audience,
I wol full fain,° at Christes reverence,   40
Do you plesance leveful,° as I can.
But trusteth well, I am a southren man—
I can not geste *Rum-Ram-Ruf,* by lettre;°
Ne, God wot, ryme hold I° but litel bettre.
And therefore, if you list, I wol not glose,°   45
I wol you tell a mirrye tale in prose
To knit up all this feest° and make an ende:
—And Jesu for his grace wit° me sende
To shewe you the way, in this viage,
Of thilke parfit glorious pilgrimage   50

---

23 **person** parson   26 **male** bag   28 **knit up** bring together, wrap up
33 **waiven soothfastnesse** neglect truthfulness (by concocting
fictions)   35 **draff . . . fest** chaff out of my fist   36 **whete** wheat
40 **full fain** very gladly   41 **plesance leveful** lawful pleasure   42–
43 **southren . . . lettre** the Parson disclaims any inclination or ability
for romance (*geste*) or alliteration (*Rum-Ram-Ruff, by lettre*), such as
was popular in the North and West of England   44 **hold I** can I keep
up   45 **glose** hedge   47 **feest** feast (of stories)   48 **wit** understand-
ing, inspiration

That highte Jerusalem Celestial.°
   And if ye vouche sauf, anon I shall
Begin upon my tale, for which I praye
Tell your avis:° I can no better saye.
55 But natheless, this meditacioun
I put it ay under correccioun
Of clerkes, for I am not textuel°—
I take but the sentence,° trusteth well;
Therefore I make protestacioun
60 That I wol stande to correccioun."
   Upon this word we han assented soone,
For, as it seemed, it was for to doone°
To enden in some vertuous sentence
And for to yive him space and audience;
65 And bade° our Host he sholde to him saye
That alle we to tell his tale him praye.
   Our Host hadde the wordes for us alle:
   "Sir Preest," quod he, "now faire you bifalle!
Telleth," quod he, "your meditacioun—
70 But hasteth you—the sunne wol adown!
Beth *fructuous*,° and that in litel space
And to do well God sende you his grace.
Say what you list, and we wol gladly heere."

49–51 **this viage ... Celestial** the Parson compares the Canterbury pilgrimage to the large pilgrimage toward the New Jerusalem, or Heaven 54 **avis** consent 57 **textuel** learned in texts 58 **sentence** the essential meaning 62 **for ... doone** proper, fitting 65 **bade** we bade 71 **fructuous** fruitful

"RETRACTION"

Here taketh the maker of this book his leve:

Now pray I to hem all that herken this litel tretise
or rede, that if there be anything in it that liketh hem,
that thereof they thanken our Lord Jesu Christ, of
whom proceedeth all wit° and all goodness. And if
there be anything that desplese hem, I pray hem also   *5*
that they arrette° it to the defaut of mine unkonning,°
and not to my will, that wolde full fain have said better
if I had the konning. For our Book saith,° "All that
is written is written for our doctrine"—and that is
mine intent. Wherefore I beseek you meekly, for the   *10*
mercy of God, that ye pray for me that Christ have
mercy on me and foryive me my guilts, and namely of
my translacions and enditings of worldly vanitees, the
which I revoke in my retraccions: as is the book of
Troilus, the book also of Fame,° the book of the   *15*
five and twenty Ladies,° the book of the Duchess, the
book of Saint Valentines Day of the Parlement of
Briddes, the tales of Canterbury (thilke that sounen
into° sin), the book of the Leon°—and many another
book, if they were in my remembrance, and many a   *20*
song and many a lecherous lay; that Christ for his
greet mercy foryive me the sin.

---

4 **wit** knowledge, wisdom   6 **arrette** attribute   6 **defaut ... unkon-
ning** my ignorance   8 **our ... saith** the Bible says (*II Timothy* 3:16)
15 **book ... Fame** Chaucer's *The House of Fame*   15–16 **book ...
Ladies** Chaucer's *Legend of Good Women*   18–19 **sounen into** tend
toward   19 **Leon** Lion. The work is not known

But of the translacion of Boece *De Consolatione*,° and other books of legends of saints, and omelies,° and
25 moralitee, and devocion, that thank I our Lord Jesu Christ and his blissful Moder and all the saints of heven, beseeking hem that they from henceforth unto my lives end send me grace to bewail my guilts and to study° to the salvacion of my soul, and graunt me
30 grace of veray° penitence, confession, and satisfaccion to doon in this present life, thurgh the benign grace of Him that is King of kings and Preest over all preestes, that bought us with the precious blood of His hert, so that I may been one of hem at the day of doom° that
35 shall be saved; *Qui cum patre et Spiritu Sancto vivit et regnat Deus per omnia saecula. Amen.*

---

23 **Boece . . . Consolatione** Boethius' *De Consolatione Philosophie* (*The Consolation of Philosophy*)   24 **omelies** homilies   29 **study** give attention   30 **veray** true   34 **doom** judgment

GLOSSARY OF BASIC WORDS

Accorden *v* agree; allow.

Al *conj* although.

Algate(s) *adv* at least; at any rate.

Als *adv* also.

Also . . . as as . . . as.

Anon *adv* immediately; right away.

Apaid *pp* pleased; satisfied; *yvele apaid* displeased; offended.

Avisen *v* consider; ponder.

Axen *v* to ask; ask for.

Ay *adv* ever; always.

Been *v* to be; *sg* am, art, is; *pl* are, been; *pt* was, were(n); *imp sg* be; *imp pl* beth; *pp* been y-be(en); *neg* nis; *pt neg* nas, nere.

Bet *adj & adv* better.

Blyve *adv* quickly; *as blyve* as soon as possible.

Brennen *v* to burn; *pp* brend, brent.

But *adv & conj* only; *but as* except that; *but if* unless.

Buxom *adj* obedient, gracious.

Cas *subst* event, happening; circumstance, situation; accident; *par cas* by chance, as it happened.

Certes *adv* certainly.

Clepen *v* to call, name; *pp* cleped, clept, y-cleped.

Devise(n) *v* to decide, determine; relate, explain.

Digne *adj* worthy; proud, haughty.

Doom *subst* judgment, opinion.

Doon *v* to do; cause, bring about; *pt* did; *pp* (y)-doon; *doon + inf* cause to + inf.

Dorst, durst *pt subj & cond* dared, would dare.

Drede *subst* fear, anxiety; *withouten drede* without doubt.

Duren *v* to last, endure.

Eek *adv* also.

Eft *adv* again; *eftsoones* soon; again.

Eld *subst* age, old age.

Elles *adv* else, otherwise.

Erst *adv* before; for the first time.

Everich, everichon *adj & pron* each, each one, every one.

Fain *adj & adv* glad, willing; gladly, willingly.

Fele *adj* many.

Fere *subst* companion; fellow.

Fetis *adj* pretty, neat, elegant; dainty, small.

For- *intensive*, completely; *fordrunke* = very drunk; *forstraught* = distraught.

Forsooth *adv* indeed.

Forthy *adv* therefore.

Fowel *subst* bird; *pl* foweles.

Full *adv* very, entirely.

Gay *adj* gay, carefree; bright, lively; well dressed.

Ginnen *v* to begin; used as auxiliary verb in past tense, like "did"; *pt* gan, gonnen; did.

Gentil *adj* noble, well-bred; courteous; **Gentilesse** *subst* nobility.

Guise *subst* manner, custom, habit.

He *pron* his, him; *pl* they; *gen* hire; *dat* hem, his; its.

Henten *v* to seize, gain; *pt* hente, henten: *pp* hent, (y)-hent.

Heigh, hye *adj* high.

Herken, herknen *v* listen to; *imp* herkneth.

Highte, hoten *v* to be called, named; command, bid; *pt* hatte, highte; *pp* hight, hoten.

Honest *adj* respectable, proper; virtuous.

Ilke, thilke *adj* same; the same.

Kan *v* to know, to know how (to): *pp* koud.

Keep, keepen *v* to take care, take heed, guard; *pp* kept, taken keep = take heed.

Kinde *subst* birth; inclination, instinct; type; *by kinde* by nature.

Lemman *subst* lover.

Lesen *v* to lose; *pp* lorn, y-lornen, y-lost.

Leten *v* to let, permit; *let* + *inf* = cause to + inf.

Leten *v* to hinder, prevent; shut off; delay; cause, desist; *pt* lette, letted; *pp* let.

Leve, lief *adj* dear, beloved.

Lever *adj* rather, more willing, more agreeable; *me were lever* I would rather.

Lewed *adj* ignorant; rude, coarse.

List, lest *3 sg imp v* it pleases; *pt* liste, leste.

Lite, litel *adj* little, small.

Lorn *pp* of lesen = to lose; *I nam but lorn* I am lost for sure.

Lust *subst* pleasure, desire.

Meten *v* to dream; *me mette (impersonal)* = I dreamed.

Mo *adj & pron* more, others.

Moot, mot *v* must, should, may; *pt* most(e), must(e).

Morrwe *subst* morning; next morning; *a-morrwe* next morning, in the early morning.

Muchel, mickel *adj* much.

Murry(e), mirry, merry *adj* merry.

Namo, namore *adj & pron* no more, no other.

Nas *neg* (he) was not.

Natheless *adv* nonetheless.

Nere *pl neg* (we, they) were not.

Nice *adj* foolish.

Nis *neg* (he) is not.

Niste [from *witen* = *ne wiste*] (he) did not know; *he niste what he wroughte* he didn't know what he did.

Nolde [from *will, woll* = *ne wolde*] *pt neg* (he) would not.

Nones for the nonce, for the occasion.

Noot [from *witen* = *ne wot*] (I) do not know; *I noot not where thou art* I don't know where you are.

Nought *subst* nothing; **Not** [unstressed form of *nought*] *adv* not.

Oo *adj* one.

Or *adv* ere, before.

Outher *adj & conj* either.

Over all *adv* everywhere.

Parde *excl* par Dieu, by God.

Pas *subst* pace, step; distance.

Propre, proper *adj* own, one's own; special; good-looking, well-grown.

Quaint *adj* curious, strange; skillful, crafty.

Quod [from *quethen*] *pt* said, quoth.

Rathe *adv* soon; early.

Reden *v* to counsel, advise; study; *pp* red, rad.

Reed, rede *subst* advice, plan.

Rennen *v* to run.

Repairen *v* to return, go.

Save *prep* except.

Sely *adj* 1. happy, good; poor 2. wretched, unfortunate.

Shrew *subst* scoundrel, bum.

Siken *v* to sigh.

Siker, sikerly *adv* surely, certainly.

Sin *conj* since.

Sithen *conj & adv* afterward; since.

Somedeel *adj* somewhat.

Sooth *subst* truth; *adj* true.

Sterven *v* to die; *pt 3 sg* starf; *pp* storven, y-storve.

Stinten, stenten *v* to stop, restrain.

Sufferen *v* to endure, suffer; permit, allow.

Sweven *subst* dream.

Swich *adj & pron* such; such a (one).

Swinken *v* to work, labor; *pp* swonken, y-swonke.

Swithe *adv* quickly.

That *rel pron* that, that which.

Ther *rel adv & conj* where; *theras* = whereas, where.

Thilke *adj* the same, that.

Thinken *impers v* it seems to me (her, him); *sg* me (hir, him) thinketh; *pt* thoughte.

Thise *pron* = the general sense of "those" or "your," as "these pilgrimages."

Tho *pron* those.

Tho *adv* then.

Thries *adv* three times, thrice.

Till *prep* until.

Til *prep* to.

To- *intensive* completely =, entirely =, "to pieces"; *to-hewen*, cut to pieces; *to-shred* all shredded up.

Trowen *v* to believe, think.

Twaye *adj* two; *tweyne* twaine.

Unnethe(s) *adv* scarcely.

Wenden *v* to wend, go; *pt* wente; *pp* (y)-went.

Wenen *v* to think, suppose, imagine; *pt* wende, wenden; *pp* wend, y-went.

Wher *conj* whether.

Whilom *adv* once upon a time.

Wight *subst* man, person; creature; *adj* strong; *a lite wight* a short time.

Will, woll *v* to will, wish; intend (to); would like (to); *pl* wollen; *pt* wolde.

Wis, wisly *adv* certainly, surely.

Witen *v* to know; *sg* wost, woot; *pl* witen; *pt* wiste, wisten; *pp* wist; *neg* noot, nist, etc.

Wood *adj* crazy, insane.

Y- *prefix* [sign of past participle].

Yeven, yiven *v* to give; *pt* yaf; *pp* yeven, yiven.

Yfere *adv* together.

Ywis *adv* certainly.

AFTERWORD
THE PILGRIM SOCIETY

The pilgrims in Chaucer's *The Canterbury Tales* begin their journey as a collection of scattered individuals, randomly gathered in a tavern on the outskirts of London. They consist, as Chaucer says, of sundry or various folk, fallen together by chance: "by aventure y-falle/ In fellawship" ("General Prologue," ll. 25–26, p. 2). They have a common destination, Canterbury, but twenty-nine different reasons for undertaking the journey. Because they are so porous a group anyway, Chaucer, as the self-nominated thirtieth pilgrim, gains easy acceptance.

This pilgrim Chaucer pretends to a certain artlessness, but the shrewd artistic choices of the poet Chaucer are always on display. This is evident in the brilliant descriptions of the varied pilgrim band, minimizing tedium by seizing on sharply characterizing details: the Knight's honorably stained tunic, the Prioress's pampered lapdogs, the Wife's gapped teeth, the Summoner's bad breath, the Pardoner's stringy hair. He asks to be excused for any informality in his approach, for not quite setting them in their "degree" or social rank. Actually, though, a rather formal pattern does underpin his description, for Chaucer details the pilgrims in descending order, based on their place in medieval society. (The exceptions to this general rule involve travel companions, as when he pauses to say that the Knight is accompanied by his son the Squire and his man-at-arms the Yeoman.) He begins with those he calls the *gentils* of the pilgrimage, its gentlefolk or most refined members, and he ends with the *cherles* or churls, those closest to uneducated, or rural, lowlifes. In be-

tween, he pays unprecedented attention to what I have else-
where called the "middle strata" of his society. First to be
described is the Knight, who (despite his travel-stained mili-
tary attire) is the socially superior member of the pilgrimage.
Then, pausing for a glance at his companions, Chaucer re-
sumes with the Prioress (head of her own abbey), the Monk
(worthy to be an abbot), and on into that large middle group-
ing of educated professionals and bureaucrats, the Merchant,
the Physician, the Sergeant at Law, and the rest. He pauses
for the Parson—a person hard to classify because he is ma-
terially poor and spiritually rich—and concludes with a be-
mused and slightly lurid dive into the pilgrimage's lowlife
fringe: the bagpiping Miller, the sexually harassing Sum-
moner, the ethically and physiologically problematic Par-
doner.

Compared with medieval social theory—which normally
recognized only three social "estates" of priests, knights, and
peasants—Chaucer expands his depiction broadly and gen-
erously to include seldom-portrayed ranks in the middle of
the social spectrum. Indeed, he somewhat scants his social
hierarchy at both its ends: His pilgrim band contains no great
aristocrat at the "high" end and only one peasant at the "low"
end. And even his peasant is a self-employed Plowman, an
independent labor contractor who owns his equipment and
hires out services for a decent wage, rather than a bound
worker or serf. If Chaucer were aiming at social accuracy, he
would have not just one peasant (who is barely a peasant at
all), but rather twenty-five or twenty-six, since rural workers
would by any reckoning have composed more than ninety
percent of later medieval society.

But of course photorealism is hardly his game. He is inter-
ested in giving us a body of pilgrims with sufficient internal
variety to justify the highly contrasting and stylistically dif-
fering tales he will assign to them. One shrewd scholar, Da-
vid Benson, has observed that Chaucer probably wrote most
of his tales first, and afterward invented pilgrims to tell them
(*Chaucer's Drama of Style* [North Carolina, 1988]). In any
case, Chaucer has accomplished something truly remarkable

here. Despite a few tactical adjustments, he has given us a depiction of English society as a varied whole, a contentious but nevertheless intimately interrelated body of people who don't necessarily even like one another, and who pursue radically different goals, but who nevertheless find themselves in a common situation and cope with it according to mutually agreed-upon procedures.

In the course of their three-day journey, these thirty disparate people become a society, a collectivity who seek, for better or worse, to regulate their own affairs. This process is inaugurated at the outset by their officious but good-spirited host, Harry Bailly, who arranges a kind of mini constitutional convention, in which they organize themselves as a body. They even undergo a founding ceremony, a swearing in, in which they raise their hands in agreement to abide by common rules. Their purpose will not, of course, be self-governance as an end in itself, but rather a kind of moving literary festival in which they share tales for the improvement and amusement (*sentence* and *solas*) of all. Even the most reluctant—of whom Chaucer presents himself as an example, with his jokingly crude "ryme" of "Sir Thopas"—must contribute for the enjoyment of the whole. This will, in a phrase I've used in my book *Social Chaucer* (Harvard University Press, 1994), be a "commonwealth of discourse," one that experiences many of the problems of any social organization, but with tale telling (rather than domestic improvements or public health or warfare) as its occasion and objective.

Part of the literary novelty of Chaucer's collection rests in the variety of subjects, styles, and genres that his diverse tellers allow him to include, ranging through romances, bawdy tales, works of religious instruction, and more. His is not the first medieval tale collection: There are those of saints' lives, miracles of the Virgin, deeds of princes, and many others, each built around a single subject or literary form. But *The Canterbury Tales* is the first to range so widely, to bring together so many different kinds and styles of stories within a single frame. Chaucer's closest competitor, Boccaccio, beat him to the mark by several decades with his *Decameron*, in which a group of gently born young Florentines traverse the countryside and entertain themselves with tales. Even in *The Decameron*, though, a kind of willed uniformity prevails as Boccaccio strives for a middle style in which he relates his *novelle*, a style that minimizes tonal differences among the many kinds of tales his travelers tell. Chaucer, by contrast, exaggerates stylistic difference, ranging from the decidedly down-to-earth tones of the Miller's and Shipman's tales to the more elevated language of passages in the Knight's and Franklin's tales—as well as several of his more devout tales unrepresented in this collection.

Alongside his primary interest in the varied character of the tales his pilgrims tell, Chaucer pays continual attention to the dynamics of his pilgrim band. As a by-product of their diversity, these pilgrims interact in strenuous and sometimes highly argumentative ways; they are anything but placid and their affairs will not always flow smoothly. Competition is present from the outset, built into the very definition of the tale-telling contest. Part of the competition is aesthetic and abstract, revolving around the elusive question of who will tell the best tale, and this question never really goes away. But competition reverberates through the pilgrimage in other, less idealized ways. Harry Bailly rigs the initial drawing of straws so that—no surprise—the socially superior Knight gets to tell the first tale, and he offers a philosophical narrative of considerable dignity, including weighty reflections on loyalty, love, mortality, and other elevated themes. Yet, even in the course of a narration that some readers (not I!) have found overlong, a revolt has been brewing. Harry's plan is to turn next to the Monk, another man of substance, in his order of intended tellers, but the raucous, head-butting, trash-talking Miller, who has been sousing himself with drink, cannot contain himself. He bursts into the order of tellers with a flagrant oath on Christ's arms, blood, and bones, and declares "I kan [know] a noble tale . . . / With which I wol now quit the Knightes tale!" ("The Miller's Prologue," ll. 19–20, p. 110). To "quit" something is to "requite" it, to pay it back, and also to shut the door on it, to be rid of it. The Miller's class-based scorn for the Knight is evident in his plan to tell his own "noble" tale, noble not in the sense of the Knight's privileged discourse, but in the inherent worth of its own raucous accomplishment.

This clash—between the Knight's philosophical romance and the Miller's comic yarn—is one of the more pronounced on the pilgrimage, but it strikes a competitive note that will resound in various forms as the pilgrimage proceeds in its halting but determined way. Some of the quarrels will be vocational. The next tale comes from the Reeve, a carpenter, who feels his trade has been insulted by the Miller. Other conflicts spring up: The loquacious and protofeminist Wife of Bath, the acerbic Clerk, the disillusioned Merchant, and the sentimental Franklin will disagree about the nature of marriage. In tales not present in this collection, the Friar and the Summoner—two minor ecclesiasts—will deride each other's professional ethics. And, of course, tensions arise within the bounds of individual tales. The self-consciously genteel Prioress tells a tale that erupts with rancorous and violent anti-Semitism. The Pardoner indulges in a boastful rant about his prowess in selling false relics and other items of faith with a shocking disrespect for the devotional premise of the pilgrimage itself. (He makes the mistake of additionally baiting Harry Bailly, who turns on him with an obscene castration threat that viciously assails his ill-concealed sexual secret.) Later, in an exchange not present in this collection, the Manciple cruelly mocks the drunken Cook by forcing more drink upon him and holding him up to ridicule. An electrical field of barely controlled annoyance and anger plays within and around these tales.

Due to the tensions that beset the pilgrims' tales, questions of fair hearing regularly arise. Interruption is a constant possibility. To interrupt a tale is a grave matter, in Chaucer's own culture and in the particular literary culture of the pilgrimage. "Audience" is, originally, a medieval word, and it refers to "those within hearing," those who can and will listen to what a speaker has to say. Chaucer, who presented most of his own poems aloud to live audiences, cared a good deal about matters of telling and listening and what is owed to a speaker. These issues are frequent in *The Canterbury Tales* as a whole, including, ironically, the tale that Chaucer, as a pilgrim, first sets out to tell.

The pilgrim Chaucer is portrayed as a shy nonparticipant who has been observing much but saying little. Harry Bailly, as master of ceremonies, settles his gaze on Chaucer, whom he has evidently not previously noticed and finds him an enigma. "What man artou?" ("Prologue to Sir Thopas," l. 5, p. 179) he asks—What man are thou, with the familiar "thou" (rather than the more formal "you") already expressive of a slight disdain. He goes on to suggest that Chaucer gazes at the ground as if he is looking for rabbits, that he is plump about the middle and as huggable as a little doll, but at least has an "elvish" ("Prologue to Sir Thopas," l. 13, p. 179) look, and in his apartness conveys a slightly mysterious reserve. All this might seem to presage a clever and well-crafted tale, but what Chaucer gives his fellow pilgrims instead is a "ryme" ("Prologue to Sir Thopas," l. 19, p. 179) or rhyme he learned (that is, memorized) a long time ago. And the "ryme" turns out to be the parodic "Sir Thopas," a sendup of wooden and formulaic romances, written in tediously resolute metrical patterns, for recitation to aesthetically uncultivated audiences. His tale can, of course, be enjoyed at the level of literary parody, but for an audience that doesn't get the joke (and Harry certainly doesn't), it becomes unbearable. After 227 grueling lines, Harry interrupts:

"Namore [no more] of this, for Goddes dignitee,"
Quod oure Hooste, "for thou makest me
So wery [weary] of thy verray lewednesse [igno-
    rance] . . .
Mine eres [ears] aken of thy drasty [worthless]
    speeche."
    ("The Tale of Sir Thopas," ll. 208–10, 211, p. 188)

And, lest his point be missed, he adds, "Thy drasty ry-myng is not worth a turd!" ("The Tale of Sir Thopas," l. 219,

p. 188). Chaucer, for his part, feigns ignorance of the short-comings of the tale he has just told and, in persona, responds as anybody else would respond in the same situation, with hurt feelings:

> "Why so?" quod I. "Why wiltou lette [hinder] me
> More of my tale than another man,
> Sin that it is the beste rym I kan [know, am capable of]?"
>   ("The Tale of Sir Thopas," ll. 215–17, p. 188)

Well, sure: Nobody likes to be interrupted or to be cut off in full flow. Chaucer, as a pilgrim, then goes on to tell another tale, omitted in this Signet Classics collection, in which one of the characters suffers a humiliating loss of "audience."

This is Chaucer's "Tale of Melibee," printed in *The Riverside Chaucer*, ed. Larry D. Benson (Boston, 1987). A home invasion has occurred and the householder, Melibee by name, is taking consultation among his friends and neighbors about what kind of revenge he should seek. Among his advisers are young hotheads who recommend war, and then an older, wiser man, who raises his hand to request audience. His cautionary remarks involve the uncertainties of war, and he seeks to underscore his words—"to enforcen his tale"—through examples (*Riverside Chaucer*, p. 219). At this point, the hotheads interrupt: "wel ny alle atones bigonne [began] they to rise for to breken his tale, and beden [bade] hym ful ofte his wordes for to abregge [abridge or cut short]." Chaucer as narrator concedes that nobody enjoys unsolicited advice, saying that when anybody preaches to those who would prefer not to hear his words, his sermon is likely to annoy them ("For soothly, he that precheth to hem that listen nat heeren his wordes, his sermon hem anoieth.") But he then sympathizes with this old wise man in his loss of audience:

> And whan this wise man saugh that hym wanted audi-
> ence, al shamefast he sette hym doun agayn. For Salo-
> mon seith [says]: "There as thou ne mayst have noon
> audience, enforce thee nat to speke."

Having no audience, no immediate listening public, is emotionally distressing, whether for an aged counselor or a not quite so aged poet.

But, however irascible, quarrelsome, and interruptive these pilgrims might be, the tale telling stumbles on. The point here is that a society need not be placid or calm in order to be a society. It can be fissured in every way, riddled with disputes both resolved and unresolved, and still be a society of persons bound by common agreements. A certain amount of conflict may even be a way a society can know itself *as* a society, can feel its tensions and bounds and test the conditions of its own continuance. One of the things Chaucer portrays for us is the survival of a self-regulating society in the face of everything that threatens its existence: the fact that, against all odds, it perseveres, and keeps on stumbling toward its elusive goal. (The pilgrims never quite enter Canterbury— or, as the Parson puts it—this figurative heavenly Jerusalem or "Jerusalem Celestial." But Chaucer's collection, in the partially completed form in which he left it at the time of his death, takes us to its gates.)

I emphasize this matter of pilgrim society, since "society" has itself become a conflicted term in the past few decades. A position initially articulated only in such fringe discourses as Ayn Rand novels, but that has now become virtually mainstream, is that there is no such thing as "society," that we stand or fall based only on our choices and exertions as isolated individuals. This view gained currency in celebrated remarks by Prime Minister Margaret Thatcher back in the eighties, when she said, complaining of those who blame the state of society for their problems, "Who is society? There is no such thing. There are individual men and women. . . ." (interview, *Women's Own*, 23 September 1987). The contrary position of traditional social theory is that a society can be regarded as an intelligible whole, as a "totality," for purposes of analysis, and that collective problems can best be addressed by modeling them as shared social predicaments. A valuable—in my view indispensable— vantage is lost when issues are treated as wholly individual, rather than collective, in their origins and implications.

Great works of literature are marked by the generosity with which they make themselves available to successive generations of readers. One enters into the experience of Chaucer's Canterbury pilgrimage through a variety of portals, and discovers a wealth of divergent possibilities there: amusement and instruction, high style and low style, philosophy and bawdy humor, devotion and profanation. One of the things I discover there, and enter into this great poem to reclaim, is a sense of *society*, its limitations and its possibilities. Chaucer discourages any daydreams of social perfection; strife is the condition of existence in his world. But he proposes that people of different taste, ambition, and inclination can join together in common enterprise, as a provisional and conflicting but still meaningful social whole. Perfection, if attained, is to be sought at that Canterbury Cathedral shrine, and within the precincts of the heavenly Jerusalem itself. But meanwhile he presents an extraordinarily rich depiction of life as it is lived in this aspirational but imperfect world, in quarrelsome but inescapable interdependence.

—Paul Strohm

P.O. 0003681291